# ELECTRICITY

Connor cupped her cheek with his hand and leaned toward her in a fluid movement that caught her off guard.

When his lips touched hers his fingers eased around her ear and jaw, holding her mouth to his, his strange energy buzzing through her at every contact point. For a moment, Jade closed her eyes and surrendered to the kiss and to the humming field of electricity surrounding her.

Something inside her burst to life at his touch, but she wasn't ready for full body contact yet—especially with a man she'd literally raised from the dead. Jade stopped him with a palm on his bare chest, and pushed away from him, her hands and lips tingling and her heart thumping. A peculiar sensation of elation and well-being surged through her.

"Connor!" she gasped.

"Why do ye fight it so, Jade?" His gaze bore into hers. "Canna ye just let it go—see what happens?"

Books by Patricia Simpson

*Whisper of Midnight*
*The Legacy*
*Raven in Amber*
*The Night Orchid*
*The Lost Goddess*
*Lord of Forever*
*Mystic Moon*
*Just Before Midnight*
*Jade*

By Debbie Macomber, Linda Lael Miller,
and Patricia Simpson

*Purrfect Love*

Published by HarperPaperbacks

# JADE

## Patricia Simpson

**HarperPaperbacks**
*A Division of HarperCollinsPublishers*

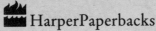HarperPaperbacks
*A Division of* HarperCollins*Publishers*
10 East 53rd Street, New York, N.Y. 10022-5299

This is a work of fiction. The characters, incidents, and
dialogues are products of the author's imagination and are not to
be construed as real. Any resemblance to actual events or
persons, living or dead, is entirely coincidental.

ISBN: 0-06-108495-6

HarperCollins®, 📖®, HarperPaperbacks™, and
HarperMonogram® are trademarks of HarperCollins*Publishers* Inc.

Cover illustration by Jon Paul

First printing: July 1997

Printed in the United States of America

Visit HarperPaperbacks on the World Wide Web at
http://www.harpercollins.com

❖ 10 9 8 7 6 5 4 3 2 1

*'Tis a misty old world*
*and we're only in it*
*for a short sharp while.*

—Gaelic proverb


*To Ken Sharp*
*who saw beauty and potential*
*in Stadium High School.*

# JADE

# 1

*Jade Brennan tucked* her auburn hair behind her ear and bent down to put the key in the lock of her apartment door. She hummed a scale under her breath, concentrating on each note, in an effort to retrain her injured brain—the same way she'd taught herself to speak and write again. One of these days her perseverance would pay off. One of these days she'd sit down at a keyboard and discover her songwriting ability had returned. Then and only then would she be truly recovered. And only then would the others consider her capable of raising her two-year-old daughter, Sabrina.

Jade pushed open the door of her "borrowed" condominium, stepped into the living room, and was startled to see the silhouette of a man standing in front of the large bay window. She flushed with fright. Her brother's butler had warned her that these rooms were haunted, but in the two days she'd stayed in the apartment, she hadn't seen anything unusual. Until now.

"You there!" Jade exclaimed. She backed into the doorway behind her, prepared to run to the elevator down the hall. "What are you doing here?"

The figure turned at the sound of her voice. Her initial fright gave way to a sneaking suspicion that she was seeing not a ghost, but a reporter who had managed to break into her apartment—perhaps one of the troupe that had accosted her the day before in the parking garage.

After a moment, she realized the figure wasn't that of a reporter, either. Watching her from his stance at the window was an old Chinese man with a receding hairline like a silver arch above his high rounded forehead and black eyebrows like moth wings hovering above his dark, glowing eyes. He wore black pants and a blue quilted jacket over a white shirt, and a pair of navy blue canvas tennis shoes.

"What are you doing in my apartment?" Jade demanded again.

He bowed at the waist and rose up, his hands clasped neatly in front of him. "Miss Brennan," he greeted her. "Allow me to introduce myself. I am Herman Fong." He bowed again and then straightened, smiling. At his grin, two round cheeks, like ripe crab apples, rose up on either side of his nose. His teeth were crooked and mismatched.

"How'd you get in?" she demanded, ignoring his courtly manners.

"I am so happy you have returned," he said, ignoring her remarks as thoroughly as she had discounted his. "I must speak with you."

"Sorry. I don't grant interviews to people who break into my house."

He bowed a third time. "My apologies."

When he bowed, his jacket stretched over his shoulders, and she saw that he was frail beneath his clothes and that his neck was baby-bird thin. How old was he? She couldn't call the police and have such an ancient man thrown in jail.

She held open the door. "Leave right now and I'll forget you broke and entered."

"But I very much need to speak to you."

"Why? We don't know each other." She motioned toward the hall. "If you don't leave, I'll call the police."

He paused and then took a step toward her. "But you have the necklace."

Without thinking, she glanced down at the broken jade piece hanging from the chain around her neck. Oddly enough, she'd found the necklace in a bunch of celery the day before, after having fallen through a rotted floor in the basement of the condominium. She had spilled her groceries and in the darkness of the cellar had unknowingly snagged the necklace in the feathery tops of the celery. She had recognized the value of the necklace at once. This was not some cheap bauble purchased at a carnival or dimestore. This was an old, finely wrought piece, probably Chinese by the looks of the characters on the medallion. An image of a ferocious lion had been carved into the glowing, translucent green stone, but since the disk had been cut into two parts and she had possession of the top half, she could make out only the head and shoulders of the beast. "This necklace?" she repeated.

"Yes, that one." The old man motioned toward her, his hand palm up, reminding her of some of the sculptures of Buddha she'd seen in the Far East. "That necklace is why I have come."

"What are you talking about?" She glared at him, hoping he'd go away and leave the necklace with her, even though she had known from the very first that it must belong to someone. "And how did you get in here?"

"How I came here is not important. Why I came is another matter altogether." The Chinese man slipped his hand into the pocket of his jacket and pulled out a folded piece of newsprint. He opened it and held it up for her to see, but his hands trembled so much that she could make out only a large, colored photograph. The subhead and text were too small to read from a distance.

"I saw the necklace in this photograph of you and came immediately."

Jade eased closer, recognizing the green silk outfit she'd worn the day before, when reporters had surprised her as she got out of her rental car. One of the local papers must have printed a story about her return to Seattle and her brother Thomas's bid for the mayor's office. She shrugged. "So?"

"The necklace—it is very important."

"It might be. But you're not getting it. Not unless you can prove it's yours."

"Alas . . ." Painfully he refolded the paper with his shaking hands and returned it to his pocket. "That I cannot do."

"Then why are you here, if it isn't yours?"

"I know the power of the necklace, and what it signifies. It is quite possible that I might be the only one who knows."

"What are you talking about?"

"I come from an old family, Miss Brennan. Very ancient."

"And this necklace has some connection with your family?"

"Oh, yes." He clasped his hands together again in front of his spare frame. "And I must know where you found it."

"Why?"

"Someone's life might be in jeopardy."

"Because of a piece of jewelry?"

"It is not just a piece of jewelry." His smile faded as his eyes devoured the broken jade. "It is more of a key. When the seal is broken and the pieces remain separate, it is very bad, very dangerous."

"Why?"

"Because it means that somewhere two people may be lying half-alive and half-dead, Miss Brennan, floating in a netherworld the likes of which we cannot possibly imagine."

Jade made no reply, as memories of the time she'd spent in the coma washed over her. Mr. Fong was wrong. She'd experienced such a world—a place of endless dreams, of timeless journeying into the dark corners of her mind, a place where human interaction had no rules, no logic, and no boundaries—as close to insanity as she ever wanted to venture. Some people claimed that victims of comas didn't remember their unconscious time, but she had. And traveling through such a world had changed her forever. She no longer craved the fast-paced life, the rush of jumping into the unknown or delving into dark corners for quick thrills. During her coma, she had experienced enough twisted darkness to last a lifetime. All she wanted now was a family, a safe life with Sabrina, and a home full of love and light.

She looked up to find his dark eyes studying her, and she worried that he was seeing more of her than she normally permitted—the softer, more accessible side she shielded from the world. Jade swallowed, and when she spoke, her voice came out in a hoarse rasp. "You're talking non . . ." She struggled for the right word, another residual effect of her brain injury. "Non-nonsense, Mr. Fong."

"I assure you that I am not."

"Well, I don't believe you!" She clutched the handle of the door. "You're going to have to leave now."

"Please. Allow me to show you that I speak the truth, Miss Brennan."

"And how will you do that?"

"Take me to the place where you found the necklace, and perhaps I will find the other half of the seal as well."

"And then what?"

"Should I find the remaining half, Miss Brennan, all will become clear."

She tilted her head and regarded him, narrowing her eyes, struggling to decide what to believe of his entirely unbelievable story.

"That is all I ask," he added.

"I don't know," she mused. "Sounds fishy to me, Mr. Fong."

"It is not." He held his arms out at his sides. "I am an old man, Miss Brennan. I pose no threat to you."

She studied him, unconvinced.

"Please consider the plight of a human being caught between one world and another." He slowly walked toward the door and then stopped before her. "Do you want that person's soul on your conscience, Miss Brennan?"

She held herself stiff. "Spreading it on a bit thick, aren't you?"

He shrugged sheepishly. "Whatever it takes."

She studied him again, trying to discern the barest

hint of deception, and found only an honest glow of sincerity in his face.

"If I show you, you'll leave quietly?" she asked.

"Oh, yes!" He bobbed his head up and down.

"You won't come back here again?"

"Not ever. Assuredly not ever."

"Okay." She scowled, certain she was going to regret granting his request, and closed the door behind her. "But if I see anything suspicious, I'm turning right around and coming back."

"I understand, Miss Brennan."

"All right." She heaved a sigh and adjusted the strap of her purse on her shoulder. "We have to go to the basement. That's where I found the necklace."

He nodded.

Jade set off for the main elevators, but when Mr. Fong realized what direction they were taking, he paused.

"What?" Jade asked, slightly annoyed.

"I know of a better way," he suggested.

"To the cellar?"

He nodded and motioned at her with a frail hand. They backtracked, took a door at the end of the hall, passed through a wide corridor with no doorways opening onto it, and then stopped in front of a set of locked panels. Mr. Fong fumbled in a pocket of his trousers and brought out a small tool with which he picked the lock, his hands trembling.

"Mr. Fong!" Jade admonished him.

He shrugged and smiled at her, and she was begrudgingly won over by his curious mix of old age and devilry. Carefully he slid open the doors to reveal an ancient elevator, the kind with sliding metal grates in the shape of diamonds.

"How do you know about this?" she asked.

"I have many friends," he explained. "In many places." He motioned toward the elevator car. "After you."

She didn't trust him. "No, after you, I insist."

"Very well." Herman Fong shuffled into the ancient car and looked at her expectantly.

"But it can't possibly work!"

"It does. I used this elevator to come up to your floor."

"Unbelievable!" She stepped onto the wooden floor of the car and gingerly touched one of the ornate brass railings, dull with dust and corrosion. The walls were upholstered in dark green velvet, faded with age and moth-eaten.

"Some of the old hotel did not burn," he explained.

"Maybe this entire wing?" she ventured as he shut the grating.

"Entirely possible."

He turned a lever, and with a lurch, the elevator motor chugged into gear, lowering the car downward into the bowels of the hotel and plunging them into utter darkness. As the wheels screeched above her head, Jade clutched her purse strap and chided herself for following this stranger and placing herself in jeopardy. She hadn't done such a stupid thing for years. What had come over her? One little story about a person in a coma and she'd fallen for his tale—hook, line, and sinker. Her two years in the hospital must have taken their toll on her good sense, more than she realized. In the old days she would have slammed the door in Herman Fong's grinning old face, too busy with her work to take the time for anything that put her off schedule.

After a few long moments spent politely ignoring one

another, Jade felt the elevator bump to a stop. She peered through the grating into the dank gloom of the cellar.

Herman Fong jiggled open the grating.

"I have no idea where we are," she said.

"We shall search, then. There is only so much floor space." He motioned her out of the car.

"But the building is huge! We're talking half a city block here."

"I am sure you will recognize something."

"I was down here in the dark, Mr. Fong. I couldn't see a thing."

"You might be surprised what you remember, Miss Brennan, if you really try. Sight is but one of the five senses."

Gingerly Jade advanced, somewhat glad to be concealed by darkness, for already her leg had begun to ache. She hobbled forward, hands in front of her. Suddenly a faint light switched on behind her. Startled, she turned to see that Herman held a small flashlight in his left hand. She wondered what else the man could have hidden in his pockets. And so much for taking it easy on her leg.

"What do you remember?" Herman asked behind her.

"Stairs. I came down stairs."

"From the stairs near your elevator?"

"No, from the parking garage."

"Ah." He paused, and without looking back at him, she could imagine he was bobbing his silver head, probably wondering why she would venture into the dark bowels of the cellar. She had no intention of revealing the reason—that she had become disoriented and suffered a memory lapse that threw her into such a panic, she'd run out of the parking garage and down two flights of stairs into the old part of the hotel. There, lost and frantic, she'd run through the dark halls, until she'd plunged through a rotted floor, landed on a long dusty crate in a forgotten storeroom, and spilled her groceries.

"That would be at the southern part of the building," Herman mused, "in the middle."

He must have studied a floor plan of the old hotel.

"What else do you remember?" he urged.

"Well . . ." She thought back to her ordeal. "I remember smelling something burned. It was real faint, though."

"Ah, then you must have been near the burned section. That means we should head for the southeast portion near the stairs. Very good, Miss Brennan. This way." He shuffled off to the left.

She followed him, not nearly as optimistic, especially since her leg had begun to throb. Fifteen minutes elapsed as they trudged though shadowed corridors, past rooms full of old furniture stacked on top of each other, and boxes and crates shoved against shelves festooned in cobwebs. The farther they walked, the more Jade cursed herself for embarking on this journey. She could practically feel spiders and bugs crawling in her hair and over her arms and wanted more than anything to rush upstairs to fresh air and sunlight.

Then, as they turned another corner, Jade saw a door ahead of them. "Wait a minute," she declared. "This is starting to feel familiar." She sniffed and smelled the same faint burnt odor lingering in the mustiness. She opened the door and saw stairs leading upward. "This is it, Mr. Fong."

He nodded and smiled. "Now, which way did you go?"

"There, to the right." She pointed to the narrow corridor lined in stone, and the old man led the way down it, wiping webs out of his path.

"I think I was in that room," she said, motioning to the right.

"This one?" Herman Fong glanced back at her, his dark, triangular eyebrows raised high over his eyes.

"Yes."

She peered over his shoulder as he carefully unlatched the door and pushed it open, slanting the flashlight downward to flood the floor with light. Like a target, the circle of light centered on the end of a long wooden box, the one that had broken her fall.

"Ah!" he cried, hovering in the doorway.

"What?"

"We have found it!"

"What have we found?"

"The box! The Box of the Deepest Sleep."

"What are you talking about?"

"Here." He thrust the flashlight into her hands. "Hold this."

Then, more nimble than she would have thought for a man of his age, Herman Fong knelt in front of the box and wiped away the dust with a swipe of his sleeve. Even in the dim light, Jade could see the black box was decorated in an intricate pattern of mother-of-pearl, gold leaf, and inlaid wood, depicting a temple scene with clouds and mountains, still intact and glowing beneath countless layers of lacquer.

"Nice little jewelry box," she commented wryly.

"And most valuable," he added. "I did not think any such boxes had survived." He caressed the top of the box with loving, appreciative hands. "Truly a work of art, Miss Brennan. Do you see? Smooth as silk."

"Very nice." She watched him impatiently. A hundred

questions swirled in her mind, but she didn't ask them, too curious to discover what mystery lay inside the beautiful box to discuss her concerns. "What are you waiting for?" she exclaimed. "Open it."

"Are you prepared for what you might see?"

"Of course!" In the world of entertainment, dealing with singers and musicians, she'd seen just about everything—good and bad. Nothing much surprised her anymore. "Go ahead. Open it up."

Herman Fong's hands shook as he explored the side of the box, searching for the lid release. A moment later Jade heard a soft *ping* and the lid cracked open. Herman rose, and she could see the color draining from his face.

What had he expected to find in the box? Jade shifted her weight and trained the light a bit lower, suspecting the most they'd find was a bunch of faded clothing and maybe some baubles from a bygone era. Why else would the box be down here, forgotten in a storage room of a hundred-year-old hotel?

Carefully Herman raised the lid. The hinges creaked. Jade moved closer, craning her neck to see around his arm.

"Well?" she asked. "Looks like a bunch of fabric."

"Silk," he replied, reaching in for it. Cautiously he lifted the folded length and set it aside. Beneath the gold silk was a long, narrow, sandalwood tray, almost as large as a door, with Chinese characters written down its length. Jade could smell a trace of the wood's fragrance, mingled with a richer, sweeter scent.

Herman hovered over the tray. "Keep safe the spirit of this being," he read, tracing the characters with his fingertip. "Until it joins once more with the living flesh." He glanced up at her, his expression dark and unreadable.

"What's that supposed to mean?" Jade edged closer. "What spirit, what living flesh?"

"The flesh of the one who lies here."

"There's someone in this box?"

Herman nodded. "But in what condition? That's the real question. The cycle should never have been interrupted."

"You mean there's a body in that box?"

"Yes."

"There's a dead person in that box—a corpse?"

"Not yet a corpse, Miss Brennan. At least I hope not."

"Look, either it's alive or dead—"

"Or something in between. A state we can change."

"What kind of state?"

"Floating in time, you might say."

"Like suspended animation or something?"

Herman shrugged and glanced down at the box. "In a manner of speaking."

"Why would someone be in this box?"

"To be restored soon after he or she had died, or was so near to death as to be considered gone. The restoration ceremony was the last recourse, costly both to purse and priest, and reserved only for certain people. Emperors, mostly."

"So we might be bringing a Chinese emperor back to life?" Jade rolled her eyes. "You expect me to believe that?"

Herman Fong glared at her. "If you find this a waste of your time, Miss Brennan, give me the necklace and go back upstairs."

"Oh, no!" She held up her free hand. "No, you don't!"

"Then kindly keep your doubts to yourself. An insensitive attitude can cause great damage during the ceremony."

His quiet reprimand bothered her more than she let on. Jade blushed, for the first time in a long while, and stared down at the box, chastened into silence.

"Another concern," he continued, never taking his gaze off the box, "is the amount of time that has elapsed. The restoration ceremony was never meant to be interrupted."

"You mean it's done right after death?"

"Yes. And I have never heard of the ceremony being put off for a hundred years."

"How do you know it's been that long?"

"Because." He nodded at her necklace. "That necklace you are wearing belonged to a young Chinese woman named Qi An, who disappeared in 1886."

"Maybe she got held up, changed her mind." Jade shrugged. "Ran off to the circus."

Herman shook his head. "No. She would never have let the seal remain broken—unless something happened that was beyond her control. Our family assumed she had met her death in the hotel fire, but we could never find her body. We did not know she had begun a restoration ceremony—not until I saw the necklace in the newspaper this morning. That is why I have come. I must see this through. It is a very dangerous thing, Miss Brennan, to leave the ceremony half-completed."

"But if so much time has gone by, wouldn't whoever is in the box be dead for sure?"

"That I do not know."

"Do you think it's safe to be messing with this?"

"Of that I am not certain either." He patted his quilted jacket. "But I am armed, if the need arises." He clasped his hands together. "Let us begin."

After a respectful pause, Herman began to murmur a long prayer, none of which was in English. Then he slowly removed the sandalwood tray. Beneath the tray was a layer of green jade squares held together by threads of gold and floating on a dark, viscous material that looked like sparkling molasses. In the center of the pieces of jade was a golden stele, holding the matching half of the jade amulet the woman Qi An had once worn at her throat.

At the sight, a strange chill shimmered through Jade, and she felt the weight of the medallion upon her breast.

"Gold for immortality," Herman commented in a reverent voice. "Jade for everlasting life."

He turned to her and held out a hand. "The talisman, please."

Without protesting, she unclasped the necklace, slid the sculpted jade off the chain, and placed it upon Herman's palm. He nodded in quiet thanks and held it above the placard, once again lapsing into an extended prayer. As he chanted, Jade studied the contents of the box, trying to see into the dark brown liquid below the jade shroud, wondering if a Chinese emperor lay beneath it, entombed for centuries. She couldn't swallow the idea of resurrecting an unknown being, but she also couldn't bear the thought of a person lying in this box for who knew how long, trapped inside his or her own mind, just as she had been. No one deserved such a fate.

Suddenly Herman's prayer ended and he slowly lowered the broken jade to the golden stele. As carefully as his tremor allowed, he nestled the coin against its matching portion. The instant the pieces aligned, they seemed to merge together, giving off a strange glow in the process. Jade blinked as the glow burst out radially, flowing along the golden threads to each square of jade. The green stone glowed until it flamed blue and green, until the entire box was suffused in light.

Herman staggered backward, his lips slightly open. Jade stood beside him, her heart pounding furiously as she watched the dark, viscous material slowly transform to a translucent, glowing mixture. Jade thought she saw a movement inside it, a stirring, like the first signs of a butterfly awakening in a chrysalis. Then the liquid turned from milky green to a clear gold color, much like fine ale. Just below the jade grating, she thought she saw a human face, the glint of an opening eye.

Jade's hand began to shake, and the puny column of light from the flashlight danced upon the far wall. She clenched her teeth, trapping the scream of terror that burst from somewhere deep inside her. But she could neither scream nor move. Like Herman Fong beside her, she was rooted to the floor, caught up by the sight before her—the awakening of a hundred-year-old human being.

As she watched, she saw a large masculine hand reach up for the jade covering and drag it aside.

# 2

*Jade held her breath* as the shroud was drawn to one side, like a jeweled quilt being folded back from a bed. The heavy mesh slid over the edge of the box and clattered to a heap at their feet, its planes still wet and warm from the chemical reaction. Though a corner of the shroud fell upon her shoe, Jade didn't move, for she was too engrossed in what was happening in the box to bother about her foot.

Beneath the surface of the golden liquid, she could make out the long limbs of a male figure, but nothing in detail, since the liquid had a metallic sheen that produced a reflection and tricked the eye. The limbs stirred, the liquid churned, and then very suddenly the creature sat up, blinking and choking, his long hair and pale skin streaming with gold-colored rivulets, which ran into his eyes and around the corners of his mouth. He took one incredulous blue-eyed stare at Jade and Herman and then hunched over to cough into his hand.

His wide, bare shoulders shook, and the hairs on his powerful forearms glistened in the dim light as he coughed and sputtered.

"He's choking!" Jade exclaimed. "Do something!"

Herman leaned over and slapped the man on the back, trying to dislodge whatever was stuck in his throat. Jade watched him gasp for breath as if he'd just been pulled drowning from a golden river, and she wondered what kind of man they'd revived. He certainly didn't look like any Chinese emperor she'd ever come across in history books or paintings, and she doubted he was from Asia at all—unless there was a race of six-foot, brown-haired, blue-eyed Chinese emperors hiding in the hills somewhere, yet to be discovered.

After a few moments the man stopped coughing, but he remained hunched over the side of the box, his forearms supporting his torso while he tried to catch his breath.

"Faith!" he panted, the word laced with an accent she couldn't identify.

Jade stood quite near him, looking down at the top of his head. She followed the strands of his long hair as they fanned out over his damp shoulders and couldn't help but survey the rippling muscles of his back and his lean, well-developed physique. Many men worked out far too much for her taste, building layer upon layer of muscle until they seemed distorted to her. She was more accustomed to the hard slenderness of male dancers—having met many of them during the filming of videos when her songs were performed by well-known top-forty artists. Jade was partial to the disciplined grace of the dancers. This man, sitting in his peculiar bath of gold, had the type of body any one of those dancers would have envied.

"We must get you out of there," Herman Fong said, reaching down for his arm. "Can you stand?"

Slowly the man's wet head came up, and he stared at Herman, then Jade, and then back at Herman. His face was haggard, and his prominent cheekbones stretched his taut skin into lines that crinkled at the corners of his eyes and disappeared into his reddish beard. He had a wide, square forehead with a strong nose to balance it, a face more broad than long. In his condition, it was difficult to judge whether he was an attractive man or not, or what his age might be, but he was certainly of Caucasian extraction, somewhere short of middle age.

"Where am I?" His baritone voice sounded raspy in the silence of the cellar. "And who are ye?"

"So it's you!" Herman gasped, his mouth agape.

"Of course 'tis me," the man retorted. "But who in blazes are you?"

"We're . . . um . . . friends," Jade explained, glancing at Herman Fong and wondering why the old man seemed to have lost his senses.

"Friends, ye say?" The stranger's gaze raked over her, and she realized that in the space of the past few moments his navy blue eyes had gained considerable clarity and glinted now with sharp intelligence. "I've never seen ye before."

Then a coughing fit overtook him, and he bent down again, hacking and covering his mouth with the barrel of his fist.

"Sir, it isn't good to linger in the box any longer than necessary now." Herman stepped closer. "You should get out."

"Aye." The stranger glanced down at himself. "Strange, but I canna recall gettin' in."

"Let me help you," Herman put in.

"Wait." The stranger glanced at Jade. "The lass'll see me naked."

"Don't worry about it," she countered, crossing her arms. "I've seen naked men before."

"But ye haven't seen me, lass. I might surprise ye." He winked at her, and his wide mouth parted at the left side in a quick smile that showed a row of white, even teeth.

A strange, warm sensation diffused across the surface of Jade's skin. Normally, when a man winked at her, she counted it as an unwelcome flirtation, a come-on by an insincere jerk. But this man's good-natured wink brimmed with humor, not insincerity, and the effect of it surprised her. Jade flushed.

To conceal her blush from him more than to allow him privacy, Jade tossed her hair and turned her back. Out of the corner of her eye, she saw Herman reach for the folded silk and hold it out to the man to use as a wrap.

She heard splashing behind her, a grunt, and then an oath.

"'Tis weak as a bairn, I am!" the man exclaimed.

"It's not surprising." Herman slung the fabric over his shoulder and reached for the strange man again. "Here, take my hand."

The liquid in the box sloshed onto the floor as the tall man heaved himself up, swayed unsteadily, and then staggered out of the box, knocking Herman against a wall of crates.

"Oof!" Herman exclaimed, throwing his arms out wide to catch his balance. The tall man grabbed for a handhold on a crate in an effort to keep to his feet, while the muscles in his thighs and buttocks flexed spasmodically. He had beautiful long legs, lean and strong, and a small round ass that Jade could hardly keep from staring at. She blinked, knowing she should avert her gaze; but she kept right on admiring his body anyway.

"St. Andrew!" he gasped, hanging his head between his upraised arms. "I've stars dancin' in my eyes!"

Jade realized she was the only one in any condition to make a move. Blushing furiously, she grabbed the silk from Herman, who was still sprawled on the floor, and tossed the cloth over the tall man's back. "There. Cover yourself!"

Then she reached down for her ancient Chinese companion. "Are you all right, Mr. Fong?" she inquired, holding out a hand to him.

He nodded and grasped her hand tightly. She pulled him to his feet and bent down to look closely at his face. "You're sure?"

"The wind got knocked out of me, that is all." He brushed himself off. "Thank you, Miss Brennan."

The tall man turned. "Brennan?" His voice rose in tone.

Jade faced him. He had wrapped himself in the gold cloth and looked like a long-haired Roman orator. Most men would have appeared silly in such a costume, but on this particular male, the silk drapery only accentuated the width of his shoulders and confident splay of his feet.

"You're a Brennan?" he added in disgust.

"Yes." She forced her gaze to his face. "I'm Janine Brennan. People call me Jade."

"Dinna recognize you." He cocked his head slightly and studied her, all traces of amusement gone from his face, his expression chilled. "You must be from the East. I know all the Brennans 'round here."

"Maybe not. You'll find things have changed."

"Not th' Brennans. And I willna have one o' their scurvy lot in my hotel."

"*Your* hotel!"

"Aye. And ye have a nerve callin' yourself a friend o' mine—ye Brennan swine."

"Brennan what?" Jade retorted.

"Ye heard me! Swine! Hie out o' here now!"

Jade drew herself up to her full height, which was still a good foot shorter than his, and planted her hands on her hips. "And just who do you think you are?" she demanded, her eyes hot and blazing.

"Dinna fool wi' me!" He set his jaw and returned her glare. "After what your family did to my place, I should wring your scrawny neck!"

"You wouldn't dare!"

He took a step toward her, but Herman Fong grabbed his arm. "Sir!" he cried.

The tall man checked himself and ran a hand through his hair, frustrated.

Jade thrust the flashlight into Herman's other hand. "I want him out of here, now."

"He's too weak."

"I don't care. I want him out of here!"

"You want *me* out o' here?" the tall man put in. "That's a fresh one!" He glared down at Herman. "Where's Chin? Did he send ye?"

"Chin?" Herman's moth wing eyebrows raised.

"Sam Lo Chin, my right-hand man!"

Herman shook his head. "Unfortunately he is not available."

"Qi An, then?"

Herman shook his head.

"St. Andrew!"

"Mr. Fong," Jade interjected, yanking open the door and pointing at the strange man wrapped in gold silk. "Just get him out of here. I don't care how. Just do it!"

She turned and hurried down the hall, fuming and perplexed and stumbling in the darkness. They'd raised a man from the dead, but one who had a grating personality and a maddening effect on her. His hotel! He was crazy—delusional! The hotel had been in the Brennan family since 1900, when her great-grandfather had purchased the gutted shell for thirty thousand dollars, a fraction of what it had been worth a dozen or so years before, when Connor MacKenzie had built it.

Wait a minute! Jade paused at the door to the stairs and looked back over her shoulder toward the storeroom. Connor MacKenzie—the Scot? Connor MacKenzie of her grandfather's stories? Exploiter of the Chinese, womanizer, drunkard—the lying, cheating bastard who'd always done the Brennans wrong? Jade's flush turned cold, and she shuddered involuntarily.

Just whom had she and Herman Fong resurrected?

Determined to get an answer before she went upstairs, she hobbled back to the storeroom and found the tall man sitting on the floor and Herman loading the jade shroud back into the box.

"Excuse me," she called, gaining their attention. "I just want to get something straight here."

Herman paused, holding a corner of the heavy jade covering. "Yes, Miss Brennan?"

"I want to know who he is," Jade retorted, pointing at the Scot. "You seem to know my family, sir," she said, glaring at the stranger. "But you never introduced yourself."

"Dinna play games with me," the man growled tiredly. "Ye know who I am."

"You're that MacKenzie character, aren't you?" she asked. "Connor MacKenzie."

He looked up at her, his blue eyes unwavering,

measuring her, judging her, apparently in no hurry to respond. It had been years since anyone had looked at her like that—directly, honestly—without an ulterior motive, a favor to ask, or a problem to be solved. "The same," he finally declared.

"I thought so." She stood there, hearing her own words and thinking her response was pretty lame, seeing how she was talking with a hundred-year-old man and notorious crook. If she hadn't seen his recovery with her own eyes, she would not have believed it possible. She threw back her shoulders. "Regardless, I want you out of here."

"Oh, aye," he drawled. "I've had enough smoke an' bletherin' for one day myself."

She glared at him and then turned on her heel, wondering as she went up the stairs if he had just referred to the fire that had consumed the hotel a hundred years ago or to her harsh words spoken moments before.

Jade hurried upstairs, took the modern elevator, and glanced at her watch, shocked to discover it was almost two o'clock, the time for her appointment with the child psychologist. She must have wasted more than an hour with Herman Fong and his Chinese hocus-pocus. Ordinarily Jade would have made sure that every hair was in place and her lines rehearsed before granting an important interview. But because of being waylaid downstairs, she didn't even have time to change her shoes.

"Damn," she muttered, yanking at the hem of her short silk skirt and checking to see the zipper was centered in the back. A better choice would have been her navy pantsuit with the nautical motif, the most conservative piece of apparel in her limited wardrobe. But she had no time to change now. While the elevator zipped to the top of the condominium building, she thought of her visit to her brother's penthouse the day before, when her dream of seeing Sabrina had first begun to crack. . . .

Jade's leg had hurt like hell, but she ignored her throbbing knee, grabbed the bag of gifts for Sabrina, and stepped out of the elevator. The door to her brother's penthouse loomed on the left, and as she approached it, she practiced her nearly perfect stroll up to the double paneled doors, achieving a casual albeit painful gait. But even more painful than her knee was the uneven hammering of her heart. No single incident of stage fright had ever affected her heart as thoroughly as this upcoming meeting. But then it wasn't every day a person was introduced to her daughter for the very first time.

She thought of the cards attached to the gifts in the bag she carried and how she had longed to write, "To my darling daughter, Sabrina. Happy Birthday!" Or "Happy Birthday, Sabrina! With all my love, Mom." Instead she had penned a simple, "Happy Birthday, Sabrina!" When it came to Sabrina, she had decided to be cautious. She didn't want to shock her daughter and wasn't sure how the child would react to the sudden appearance of her mother—especially a mother who hadn't even been able to write her name a year ago.

Jade gripped the handles of the bag more tightly, hoping to squeeze out the ache in her chest. Because of the auto accident, she had missed the first two years of Sabrina's life. She hadn't been around for her daughter's first birthday, her first word, or her first Christmas. She had missed so much—so many precious moments. But not any longer. Jade choked back a thick feeling in her throat and rang the bell of the penthouse.

The door slowly swung open to reveal the immaculately dressed bald-headed butler, Phillip Lake. Phillip hadn't changed a bit since she'd last seen him three years ago. In fact, he hadn't changed for the last twenty. Age was something that slipped up unaware on most people, wrinkling them in the night and silvering their hair while they were away from the bathroom mirror. But nothing slipped past the dour regard of Phillip's blue eyes, not even Father Time.

"Miss Brennan," he said, his familiar reserve betraying nothing of the surprise he must have felt at finding her on the Brennan doorstep.

For a moment, Jade's mind went blank and she couldn't recall the simplest response to his greeting. She concealed her awkward hesitation with a nervous smile and prayed she wouldn't blurt out an unintentional swear word or string of gibberish instead of a normal reply. Small talk had never been one of her strong suits, but since her head injury it had become an agony of uncertainty.

"Hi, Phil," she managed to respond. Then, relieved, she grinned. She hadn't said, "Fie hill," or forgotten his name completely. Success was measured through small victories these days, and she was grateful for every tiny step toward complete recovery. "How are you?"

"Fine, thank you, Miss Brennan." He stepped back to allow her entrance. "Do come in."

"Surprised, aren't you, Phil?"

"Well, we weren't expecting you until tomorrow."

"I know I'm a day early." She passed over the threshold.

As usual, Phillip ran an appraising glance down her face and figure, taking in the sight of her sand-colored

linen dress and flats, a far cry from the leather jacket
and pointed black boots she had worn the last time she'd
visited. In two years she'd gone through drastic changes,
and not just in her choice of attire.

Jade swept into the foyer of the penthouse.

"I didn't expect you to be walking, either," Phillip
commented as he surveyed her legs.

"I thought I'd surprise everyone."

"Indeed you have. The last reports from the Swiss
clinic were not encouraging, if I recall Mr. Brennan's
comments correctly."

"Some doctors don't realize the power of determination—especially mine."

"Indeed." He glanced down at her, his eyes lighting
with puzzled interest at her changed personality, but he
caught his lapse before it had a chance to bloom into the
full flower of curiosity. He raised one eyebrow. "Shall I
send for your bags?"

"There's no hurry. I left them in my rental car." She
glanced around at Gail's latest decorating fiasco. This
time her sister-in-law had done the place entirely in a
Southwest motif, with muted terra-cottas and greens on
the walls and furniture and vast seas of potted cacti and
palms rising up from the floor. The decor would have
been fine had the penthouse been located in a New
Mexican hacienda instead of a refurbished Seattle hotel.
The Southwest motif seemed woefully out of place and
made the room look like a modern Mexican restaurant
in the middle of a historic gaslight district.

Shaking her head, Jade looked around at the walls,
hoping to glimpse a photograph of the children, but as
usual Gail kept the public areas of her home free of personal memorabilia.

"So where is everybody?" Jade glanced at Phillip

over her shoulder. Her initial anxiety had eased, and words came more freely now, much to her relief. "Seems kind of quiet. Are they having the party somewhere?"

"Party?" Phillip's eyebrows raised toward the clean dome of his scalp.

"Phil . . ." Jade tilted her head. "Don't play dumb with me."

"Oh, you mean the *birthday* party!"

"Two points, Phil. It's Sabrina's birthday."

She saw him swallow and look skyward.

"Where are they? On the roof?" Jade headed for the door that led up to the rooftop garden.

"I wouldn't if I were you," Phillip warned.

"Why?" She paused, her hand on the doorknob.

"They don't expect you. You know what will happen. You'll upset them."

"So?" Jade rolled her eyes. "Don't I always?"

"But it's different this time, Miss Brennan. There's Miss Sabrina—"

"Yes. And I've never seen her, Phil. I've never seen my own child." Jade pulled open the door. "I'm telling you—wild horses couldn't stop me!"

She hurried up the stairs, trying to ignore the fact that her body still wouldn't respond as it once did. After nearly two years of physical therapy, she still couldn't dance or run, and often swore at her sluggish right leg for dragging her down, as if it were an entity separate from the rest of her being.

Music drifted toward her as she opened the door to the rooftop garden. Ahead of her stretched an imported army of potted and flawlessly sculpted shrubs, among which were twenty or so round tables garlanded in crisp white spreads and pink crepe streamers. Knowing Gail,

Jade guessed that Sabrina was attired in a fluffy pink dress with ruffled tights and bows in her hair.

At the thought of her daughter, Jade felt her heart rise in her throat again. For the past two years she'd lived for this day, this moment. What would it be like to look into Sabrina's blue eyes? Would she see any similarity to herself? Jade stepped forward, her hands shaking.

She scanned the crowd, searching for the tiny figure of a two-year-old girl, hoping to get a glimpse of her daughter. But the children must have been seated beyond the adults, out of view. Disappointed, Jade walked through the late spring sunshine toward the crowd of partygoers, trying her best not to limp and keeping all traces of pain from her expression. She'd lost everything since the accident—her best friend and lyricist, her physical mobility, a house in Connecticut, a soaring career as a songwriter, most of her friends, and nearly all of her savings. But she still had her pride. And she still had Sabrina.

Gail saw her approach. Her perfectly painted lips parted in shock as the color drained from her heart-shaped face and then suddenly reappeared, a deeper pink than before. Without looking at her husband, Thomas, she grabbed his arm and shook his sleeve, nodding toward Jade. As usual, Thomas did his wife's bidding without question. He glanced up and met Jade's steady gaze as she marched toward the party. Then he neatly sliced himself from the crowd and strode toward her, raising his hands in a familiar gesture that infuriated Jade. She knew the gesture well. *Stay out of our life. You don't belong.* The hands spoke many phrases, but they all meant the same thing. *Don't intrude on our perfect little life.*

She clenched her teeth, ignored his sign language, and pressed forward.

"Janine!" Thomas exclaimed in a terse whisper that was more warning than greeting, even though he hadn't seen her for two years. He stood directly in front of her, purposely blocking her from view. "What are you doing here?"

"I'm here to surprise Sabrina." Jade held up the shopping bag stuffed with presents. "I brought a ton of things for her."

Thomas barely glanced at the gifts. "Fine. You can give them to her later."

"Why later? It's her birthday party, isn't it?"

"Yes, but we weren't expecting you until tomorrow."

"Plans changed. Where *is* the birthday girl?" Jade asked, looking around his shoulder as if nothing were amiss.

He adjusted his position to block her view. "She's having fun with her little friends." Thomas reached for her arm. "Let's talk downstairs, shall we?"

Jade shot him a dark glance, hardly believing he meant to waylay her. "I want to see Sabrina."

"Come on, Janine." He tugged her toward the door. "Don't make a scene."

"I will if you don't get your hands off me." Jade glared at him and tried to wrench out of his grip, but he was adamant about detaining her and clutched her tightly—almost painfully.

"Be sensible, Janine. Now is not the time to meet Sabrina." He urged her toward the door, more insistently this time, as if he truly meant to keep her from the celebration.

"Wait a minute," she sputtered. "You can't do this! Get your hands off me!"

"Janine, for God's sake!" Thomas pinched his lips together and glared down at her. There was no mistaking the family resemblance that marked them as siblings. He had the reddish brown hair of the Brennans, the green eyes, and the smattering of freckles across the nose and cheeks. But his coloring was less vibrant than that of his younger sister. He had begun to go gray at the temples and wore copper-colored wire-framed glasses that made him appear even older than his forty-three years. Jade, at thirty-eight, knew she looked much younger than her brother, simply because of her youthful attitude and more contemporary wardrobe. She wouldn't be caught dead in the country-club look both Gail and Thomas sported. "Gail's gone to a lot of trouble," Thomas added. "Don't ruin it for her."

"And how would I ruin it?"

"These are all Gail's and my friends—"

"Meaning?" She arched a brow, refusing to make it easy for him by showing him she understood his judgmental innuendo. She straightened her shoulders, refusing as well to give in to the crumbling sensation she felt inside at the realization she might not see her daughter after all. Not one little peek—after two long years of waiting and dreaming. "Meaning what, Thomas?"

"That you can't just barge in like this—"

"The hell I can't. I want to see my kid!"

"It's a private party—"

"I'm family! You can't get more private than that!"

Suddenly a blur of noise and color streaked by, and the handles of the bag ripped out of Jade's hand.

"Toys!" a child screeched in delight as the bag tore, spilling the boxes onto the rooftop. "Toys, toys, toys!"

Her reactions weren't as immediate as they used to be, and for a moment Jade gaped in frozen alarm as she recognized her five-year-old nephew but couldn't remember his name.

"Whoa there, Robbie!" his father exclaimed, swooping the boy into his arms. "Settle down, cowboy!"

"Toys!" Robbie screeched again, wriggling in his father's grasp and twisting his tailored suit into a riot of wrinkles. "Me want toys!"

"It's not your birthday yet," Jade declared, surprised that the boy still spoke baby talk at five years of age. "It's Sabrina's." She knelt to pick up the spilled gifts.

"Me want toys!" Robbie scowled and stuck out his wet lower lip while his dark blue eyes regarded her without a hint of friendliness.

"We'll get you toys," his father promised. "When it's your birthday. Okay, scout?"

"I want 'em now!" Robbie wiggled free and dropped to his feet. He glared at Jade again and then very deliberately kicked the nearest gift, sending it sliding across the roof until it hit a potted plant. Jade heard the tinkle of broken porcelain and knew he'd destroyed the delicate music box she'd selected for Sabrina.

"Robbie!" she admonished, reaching for his arm. But the boy was too quick for her and ran off laughing. Jade rose and turned to her brother, expecting him to do something to reprimand his child. But Thomas just shook his head.

"Boys will be boys," he stated.

"He just broke one of Sabrina's presents!"

"Don't worry about it." Thomas waved her off. "She's got so many, she'll never miss it."

"Robbie can break a gift and you don't do anything?" Jade retorted, her voice rising.

A few of the partygoers must have heard her, for a couple of heads turned her way, eyes widening. To distract them, Gail clapped her hands and suddenly announced that cake was being served.

Thomas turned back to Jade. "I'll reimburse you, Janine," he said, his voice full of impatience.

"That wasn't my point."

"Regardless," Thomas yanked open the door that led back downstairs, "it's time we had a talk."

Jade glanced over her shoulder and saw Gail watching them anxiously, rubbing her forehead with the tips of her fingers in the telltale sign of the onset of one of her notorious migraines. Once again Jade scanned the crowd for her daughter, hungry for a single glance of her little girl. But Thomas ushered her into the stairwell and nearly dragged her down to his study.

By that time, Jade's anxious but happy mood had plummeted. She dropped the bag of toys to the carpet.

"Thanks a lot!" Her voice rang with bitterness. "And thanks for the usual warm welcome."

Thomas ignored her outburst, turned to his liquor cabinet, and selected a single-malt Scotch. "I need a drink. You want one?"

"No."

He poured the amber liquor into a glass, added soda and ice, and then slowly faced her, the glass half raised to his mouth. "You should have called first, Janine."

"Why?"

"You know how Gail is." He tipped the drink to his lips, and the ice cubes clinked against the glass.

"Yeah. A cross between a pit bull and a feather duster."

Thomas's nostrils flared. "I'll forget you just said that."

"Why? It's true. And I meant it."

"She's my wife."

"And that gives her the right to be cruel and stupid?" Jade crossed her arms. "Then again, maybe that's what it takes to live with a guy like you."

"Very funny," Thomas growled. "You're just a bundle of laughs, as usual."

Jade sighed, exasperated. "Thomas, you don't have to pretend to like me. Just hand over Sabrina and I'll get out of your hair."

He frowned and swirled the ice in the glass, and his silence was more maddening than his words.

Jade shifted her weight and put a fist on her trim hip. "Look, I appreciate all you've done for her, and when I'm back on my feet financially, I'll pay you for all expenses incurred in caring for her. Just give me the bill and a little time."

"Why? Out of funds, Janine?" He regarded her over the rim of his glass in the silent judgmental way he'd learned from their father.

"The medical bills ruined me."

"Or perhaps you can't handle your finances. And maybe other responsibilities as well."

Jade felt her stomach start to burn. Talking to Thomas was exactly like the times she'd tried to speak to her father years ago. He'd never understood her, had never even tried to understand her, and the inability to accept her unconventional lifestyle had been handed down from father to son. "What are you getting at, Thomas?"

"I'm getting at the fact that this isn't going to be simple. You can't just barge into our lives—or into Sabrina's, either."

"I'm not 'just barging in.'" Jade paused and leveled her gaze on him as a new realization struck her. "Wait a second. She *does* know I'm her mother, doesn't she?"

"We have to come to an understanding about that—"

"You *have* told her about me, haven't you?" A surge of outrage flared in her chest.

He raised a hand, and his expensive watch glinted on his wrist. "Now, Janine, don't go getting all fired up. . . ."

"Fired up?" She took a menacing step toward him, disregarding the fact that he stood a head taller. "You haven't told her?"

"We didn't think it was a good idea."

"Why in the hell not?"

"At first we didn't think you'd come out of the coma. Then with all the medical complications, the brain damage—"

"Head injury," she corrected.

"Whatever." He rolled his eyes.

"You've never told Sabrina that I was her mother? Never told her where I was?"

"We were advised that it wouldn't be wise." Thomas took an agitated drink. "No one thought you were going to make it."

"You mean to tell me that all the letters I sent her, all the little gifts, weren't ever given to her?"

Thomas stared down at the desk.

Jade stared at *him*, flabbergasted, her silence demanding an answer.

He shot a glance her way. "Janine, by the time you were medically out of the woods, Sabrina thought of us as her parents. The psychologist advised us to withhold the truth for the time being, to give her a stable base until she was older—when she could grasp the situation."

"Situation?" Jade seethed. "*Situation?*"

"Yes. She's our little girl, Janine. In every sense of the word. She's known only Gail and me, and Robbie. We've been there for her and intend to remain her family."

"Over my dead body!"

"What do you mean? You signed the papers."

"I did *what?*"

"Signed the papers." Thomas took another drink. "The adoption papers."

"What adoption papers?"

"You don't remember, do you?" He crossed his arms. "See? Brain damage. You're not up to snuff, Janine. And you never will be."

Quickly, Jade replayed the last months of her life after the accident and came up with nothing in the way of a memory. Most of the time right before and just after the accident was still a big blur, due to her head injury and the drugs given to her to ease her pain. She might have signed away the rights to all her songs and wouldn't have remembered. But she couldn't have signed away permanent custody of the only child she'd ever have and not have retained a recollection of the incident.

"It can't be true," she murmured. "I don't remember signing any papers."

"I can produce the documents if necessary."

"But she's my d-daughter!" Jade thumped her chest with the flat of her hand. "Sabrina's my daughter!"

"Maybe in a biological sense." He put his glass on the blotter of the desk. "But physically and emotionally she's ours now. And frankly, Janine, we think it's for the best."

Jade could hardly contain her anger or the burgeoning swell of disappointment that nearly swamped her. Thomas meant to keep her from Sabrina. Perhaps forever. "Implying?" Her voice shook.

"That Gail and I can provide a more stable environment for her. More advantages."

"That's nonsense!"

"Oh?" Thomas's cheeks burned crimson. "You don't have a dime, Janine. You just got out of the hospital. You don't have a home. In fact, the last I heard, you couldn't even read or write."

"Maybe you need a little—" She paused, struggling to recall the right word. It was on the tip of her tongue. It started with a "u." Upstart? Upbeat? Upland? Sometimes when she got emotionally agitated, she suffered memory lapses, maddening blanks that undermined her self-confidence when she needed it the most. "Need a little—"

"Cat got your tongue, Janine?" he taunted over the rim of his glass.

Thomas had never been close to her in many ways, stemming from an innate difference in their characters. But not until this moment had she realized the depth of his unkindness.

"That must be it," she answered, frustrated. "The cat got my tongue. Meow. Meow."

"Look at you. You're not capable of raising Sabrina. You can't even speak decently!"

Janine didn't answer, just leveled her gaze upon the glass of alcohol in his hand.

"I need it to put up with you!" He waved her off. "You come in here unexpectedly, crash our party, and have the gall to say you're mother material? That you're here to take Sabrina away? Well, over *my* dead body, Jade." He spat out her famous pseudonym and poked a finger to his breastbone. "*My* dead body!"

Jade studied him, suddenly quiet. She crossed her arms again. "She's my child, Thomas."

"Not legally. And if we have to, we'll take you to court."

"But you've got a child already. You don't need mine."

"That's not the point. We don't think you're capable of raising her."

"Bastard!"

"We're doing this for Sabrina."

"Bastard!" She stomped to the door of the study, biting her lip to keep from crying out in pain. Furious, she flung open the door and nearly collided with Phillip, who must have been hovering on the other side, listening.

"Out of my way, Phil," she barked.

"Miss Brennan!" He pivoted on the soles of his wingtips as she hurried by him. "Will you be staying for dinner?"

"I'd rather eat dirt and die!"

"Don't attempt to see Sabrina," Thomas called after her. "We have a restraining order on you, until you've been evaluated."

Jade turned, livid. "Evaluated by whom?"

"A psychologist. She's coming tomorrow. Be here at two in the afternoon."

"You bastard! You didn't mention this before!"

"Gail thought it might upset you."

"Upset, hell," she retorted. "Why should I have to be evaluated? Gail didn't have to take an IQ test before she had Robbie!"

"I'll forget you said that," Thomas growled again.

Jade narrowed her eyes and glared at him, not accustomed to being ordered around or judged by anyone but herself. She put her hand on the doorknob, taking a moment to consider what torrent of words she could fling at him, but only swear words leapt to mind. Swearing wouldn't get her anywhere with Thomas.

He straightened his tie. "If you don't cooperate this time, you'll never see Sabrina. I'm serious."

"I get it, Thomas."

He gave her one last glare and then strode down the hall toward the stairway to the garden.

Jade stood near the double entry doors, fuming, tight-lipped, and exhausted. She'd come all the way from the clinic in Switzerland, driving herself far past any sensible levels of endurance, just so she could make it to Seattle on Sabrina's birthday. And she'd never even caught a glimpse of her child. Disappointment dragged down her usual straight shoulders, as if there were weights hanging off her arms.

She also had no idea what to do next. She had counted on staying with Thomas and Gail and had imagined all of them as one big happy family, with Sabrina giggling on her lap, and Thomas and Gail looking on and smiling, with their own five-year-old son playing at their feet. What was she—insane?—to have dreamed of such an impossibility? What madness could have sustained such a fantasy? Certainly not previous experience. She'd never gotten along with Thomas, and the situation had grown even worse when he had married Gail ten years ago.

"Shall you be staying the night, Miss Brennan?" Phillip asked behind her.

Slowly Jade turned to respond, struggling to maintain a brusque manner while her world fell apart. She thought of Gail upstairs with her snooty friends and Thomas with his smooth talk and political ambitions. What kind of parents would they be to Sabrina? Their own son was a high-strung tyrant whom she had never liked.

They thought they could keep her away from Sabrina? Well, they didn't know Jade Brennan.

"Yes, I'll be staying, Phil. But not at the penthouse."

"Very good, Miss Brennan. Where, then?"

"There must be an empty unit." She raised her chin, hating the fact that she couldn't demand the very best these days, couldn't expect to go first class, couldn't even afford a nice hotel for any length of time.

"Well, there is one, but . . ." Phillip's voice trailed off in doubt.

Jade glanced at him sharply. "But what?"

# 3

Phillip fiddled with a vase of coral-colored tulips, arranging a stray blossom with a master hand. "I know of a unit in this building that Mr. Brennan has been unable to sell."

"Oh?"

"It's in perfectly good shape."

"Then why hasn't anyone bought it?"

"To be frank, Miss Brennan," Phillip replied, turning back to face her, "there have been some incidences in the unit—but not enough to bother a person like you, I should think."

"What kind of incidents?"

"Inexplicable noises, that sort of thing."

"You mean it's haunted?"

Phillip fussed with the cuffs of his starched shirt. "So one might suppose, should they be the impressionable type. Between you and me, however, I suspect it's more a combination of old pipes and overworked imaginations."

"This I have to see."

"Then if you will excuse me, I will retrieve the key."

Jade waited for him, relieved not to have to find a hotel, even if it meant staying in a "problem unit." This way she would be close to Sabrina and would try to sneak into the penthouse and have a look at her. Surely Phillip would aid her in such an undertaking.

Phillip returned a minute later and led her down the hall to the elevator, which they took to the third floor. From there they walked southward down the hall and passed through a wide doorway that opened into a different section of the refurbished hotel, where the ceilings dipped lower and the molding along the walls was much less ornate.

"I've heard," Phillip explained, motioning around the vestibule they'd stepped into, "that this wing was reserved for employees of the original owner."

"You mean that MacKenzie character?"

"Yes. How do you know of him?"

"Stories handed down in the family. My great-grandfather knew him."

"Ah, yes." Phillip nodded. He walked beside her as they turned right and entered a smaller hallway flanked by four doors.

"From what I've been told, MacKenzie was a real pain in the neck to deal with," Jade said, remembering the tales her grandfather had relayed at the dinner table when she was very young—during the good old days, before her beautiful, flame-haired mother had died. "He cheated and lied his way to the top. Gambled and womanized. Not the most sterling citizen."

Phillip's thin lips twitched with a smile. "I'm amazed that a man with a reputation for dissipation would construct a building fine enough to withstand a terrible fire and still be habitable a century later."

"He built this place out of Chinese sandstone and Italian marble, plus a slate roof. None of those things burn too well, Phil. Just the stuff on the inside went up in smoke."

"You know a surprising amount about this place," Phillip observed, slipping the key into the locked door. "I wasn't aware that you were the history buff type."

"People often misjudge me."

"And you let them?" He held open the door for her.

"Why not?" She shrugged and walked past him into the stuffy apartment. "It's their problem if they do."

Phillip made no further comment as Jade walked boldly into the living room, planted her fists on her hips, and looked around. The unit had a spacious living area with more generous ceilings than in newer buildings and a bank of multipaned windows arranged on a curve that afforded a stunning view of Elliott Bay. She strolled toward them, realizing the unit must be located in the southwest tower of the building, which had been styled after a French château. How quaint to live in a tower. Jade looked down at the historic section of the city known as Pioneer Square three stories below and the blue green water of Elliott Bay beyond it, and she marveled that no one had purchased the condo, haunted or not. What a view!

"It's furnished?" Jade asked, turning back to face the room. She glanced at the mauve-colored chairs and floral couch of the supposedly vacant apartment.

"They put the model unit furnishings in here to store them years ago and never removed them."

"How about the bedrooms?"

"I believe there is furniture in them as well. Enough to get by."

She poked her head around the corner of the dining area and ambled into the kitchen, which was decorated in cream with mauve accents. "It doesn't look haunted at all."

"I don't believe it is. But state law requires a seller to mention hauntings, suicides, and the like. It's been enough to turn buyers away."

"So what makes you think it's haunted?"

"Sometimes the water turns on."

"All by itself?"

"So I've been informed." Phillip tested the level of dust on the windowsill and frowned in dismay as he inspected the resulting smudge on his index finger. "I've never had the occasion to witness it myself."

"Doesn't sound that threatening."

"Some people find the unexplained very unsettling."

"Makes life interesting, though." Jade breezed back into the living room and glanced around again, quickly making up her mind, as was her habit. When upset or blocked in one area, she usually plowed forward in another, as fast and as furious as possible, especially when she felt as brittle as she did now. "Mauve isn't exactly my color, but—what the heck."

"Very good. I'll have the place cleaned and furnished with linens, if you would like to step out for, say, an hour, Miss Brennan."

"All right." Jade nodded, wanting more than anything to collapse in the overstuffed chair, take the weight off her right leg, and have a good cry. She didn't normally let herself break down—sobbing and whining never solved any problems—but not seeing Sabrina had been almost more than she could bear. Tears puddled dangerously close to the surface, and her throat felt hot and raw. But she wouldn't allow herself to collapse. Instead she returned to the doorway, where Phillip waited for her, his hand on the doorknob.

"Here's the key." Phillip gave it to her. "If you need anything, just call. Do you have a cellular phone?"

"Of course." Jade slipped the key into a side pocket of her purse. She looked up at him. "And thanks, Phil. You're a lifesaver. I mean it."

He inclined his head in a slight bow. "I promised your dear mother to look after you—a vow I strive to keep whenever you're in my territory."

"Then move back east with me and be my butler. It would be fun."

Phillip suppressed another smile. "Indubitably."

Jade was still thinking about her first visit to the penthouse when the elevator whisked to a stop. She stepped out of the car and for the second time walked up to the penthouse door, favoring her right leg and worrying about the interview to come.

Phillip opened the door.

"Afternoon, Phil," she chirped, covering up a sudden attack of nerves with her usual bravado. "How's the household slave business?"

"Lucrative," he answered wryly. "They're waiting for you in the library."

Jade nodded and glanced down the hall toward the small stuffy room that Thomas never let Gail redecorate, a room rarely ever used.

"How's it look for me?" she inquired. "Is the doc a male or female?"

"Female. Of the battle-ax variety. Don't be fooled by the floral print."

"Oh, great." So much for her hope of using her womanly wiles on an unsuspecting male.

Phillip's gaze swept over her black silk skirt and cream-colored mohair top, accented by a black vest, her opaque black nylons and black ankle-high boots. From his expression, Jade knew she should have taken time to change, regardless of whether she would have been late for the appointment.

"Should have worn my shirtwaist and pearls, eh?" she remarked, screwing up her features.

"And arrived with freshly baked bread." Phillip closed the door behind her.

"Great. I'm two points behind already." She straightened her shoulders. "Well, here goes nothing. Let's do it, Phil."

"May I offer you the best of luck, Miss Brennan." His good wishes sounded more like condolences.

"Thanks."

He inclined his head briefly. "Follow me and I shall announce you."

Jade trailed behind Phillip's perfectly square shoulders and measured tread, wishing she had a cigarette in her hand—and she didn't even smoke. She'd never felt more ill at ease, more rattled, because so much was at stake with this interview and everyone knew it.

Phillip rapped lightly and then opened the door.

"Madame," he stated. "Miss Brennan has arrived."

"Show her in, Phillip," Gail's voice instructed from the room behind him.

He motioned Jade inside. She took a deep breath and marched into the center of the room, ignoring the cry of protest in her leg. Once in the library, she sized up her opponents: her sister-in-law, Gail, attired in a matronly but chic-looking jersey dress and pumps; and the child psychologist hired to evaluate Jade's fitness as a parent. The psychologist was a big-featured woman with a huge head of auburn hair and a blouse with a border print in primary colors on the collar and cuffs, probably a style attractive to children, but not to Jade, who preferred dark, solid fabrics.

Gail rose. "This is Dr. Sonja Nilsen," she remarked, motioning toward the sturdy woman. "Dr. Nilsen, this is my sister-in-law, Janine Brennan."

"Hi, Sonja," Jade greeted, holding out her hand. "Nice to meet you."

"How do you do," the woman replied in a professionally modulated voice. She had a wide mouth full of wide teeth, framed by bright red lipstick. "And it's Dr. Nilsen, if you please."

"Sorry," Jade declared, shaking her hand. "I like keeping things casual."

"In my profession," Dr. Nilsen replied, "I find it best to observe certain formalities."

"Oh." Jade shifted nervously. This hadn't gotten off to a good start and was going downhill fast.

"Now then, if you will have a seat, we can begin."

Jade glanced at her sister-in-law. "I would prefer that the interview be confidential."

The psychologist glanced up from the papers spread on the desk before her. "Mrs. Brennan has been kind enough to offer to remain, should you find yourself unable to answer my questions. I've been informed that you've suffered some memory loss since the accident."

"Not that much."

"But enough in my estimation to warrant Mrs. Brennan's presence."

"All right. Fine." Jade lowered herself into the

straight-backed chair that had been pulled in front of the desk and waited for the doctor to continue.

"First off, Miss Brennan, we need to fill out some paperwork. Your full name?"

"Janine Katherine Brennan."

She waited, trying not to fidget, as the psychologist carefully printed in her name, age, Social Security number, and date of birth.

"Now then, where are you residing?"

"Right now? Here in the complex."

Jade heard Gail suck in her breath. Little did Gail know that everything in Jade's apartment had come from the Brennans' abundant stockpile of furnishings, except for the purple roses, which Phillip had bought to match the mauve chairs and floral couch in the living room of the condominium.

"Gail and Thomas have graciously allowed me to stay in one of the units," Jade explained, "so I can be close to Sabrina."

Out of the corner of her eye, Jade watched Gail fight to retain her composure and conceal her shock at hearing Jade had moved in without her permission. But she couldn't say anything now without appearing stingy and mean in front of the child advocate. Jade smiled at her and Gail returned the smile, but her eyes were flat with unkindness.

Jade leaned forward in her chair. "After all, I did lend Thomas and Gail a hefty sum of money to remodel this building. I consider it partially mine, in a way."

Dr. Nilsen didn't seem impressed by the information. "I understand you have no current permanent place of residence?"

Jade crossed her legs. "Well, as of this moment—"

"Just answer the question, please, Miss Brennan. I

have a court hearing in an hour, and we have a lot of ground to cover."

"I don't have a permanent address yet. I just got released from the clinic in Europe."

"So it's true you do not own your own home."

"I did, but the medical expenses—"

"Without a permanent residence, Miss Brennan," the doctor commented, looking out from under bangs that were fussy and perfectly curled over her penciled brows, "I have to tell you that your chances of regaining custody are not good. The court does not look favorably on a person who cannot offer a stable environment to a child."

"But she's my daughter!"

"Miss Brennan, there is more to parenting than giving birth."

Jade sat back, deflated, and could almost feel Gail's smirk behind her.

"Now then," Dr. Nilsen continued, getting back to the form she held in her left hand. "What kind of work do you do?"

"I'm a songwriter." Jade looked toward the ceiling, impatient. "Or didn't Thomas and Gail tell you that? Many of my songs have been at the top of the charts."

The doctor narrowed her eyes. "It might surprise you to learn, Miss Brennan, that not all of America watches MTV. In fact, I like to call it Moron TV." She gave a dry little smile and looked back down at the paperwork.

Jade wanted to squeeze the smugness out of the psychologist but had enough sense to conceal all outward signs of her mounting anger.

"Moving on now, Miss Brennan, what is your current monthly income?"

"It's hard to say. It varies."

"Are you saying that you are unemployed?"

Jade flushed. "I've been in a Swiss clinic for the past two years, Dr. Nilsen. I haven't had time to do any writing."

"Would you say you're between jobs, then?"

"Not exactly. I'm self-employed. I have a project in the works, as a matter of fact—a sound track for a movie."

"But you have no steady income at this time?"

"Some royalties. And I do have some savings."

"The amounts?"

"What does that have to do with anything?" Jade jumped to her feet. "I just spent two years fighting back from death's door so I could be a mother to my little girl. That's what kept me going—the thought of being with Sabrina at last. And now you people are making me jump through hoops before I can even see her. She's my child, Dr. Nilsen! Why should there be any question about that? I carried her in my body, dreamed of her, talked to her, gave birth to her. I can support a child. I've always supported myself. We'll do fine!"

Dr. Nilsen heaved an exasperated sigh, laid one hand over the other, and leveled her bright but unsympathetic eyes upon Jade. "A nice speech, Miss Brennan, but it will have no bearing on the decision of the court. A judge wants facts, not emotional outbursts."

Jade glared at her, her stomach burning and her fingernails digging into her palms. She felt belittled by this interview, insulted and discounted. Only for Sabrina would she continue to endure the dispassionate probing of Dr. Nilsen, who had probably been hand-selected by her brother's lawyers and had no sympathy whatsoever for her plight.

"Fine." Jade sank back to her seat, frustrated.

"Very well." Dr. Nilsen scratched something in a comment section and then went on to ask dozens of questions about the nature of Jade's career, her reasons for having herself artificially inseminated at the age of thirty-five when she had no husband, her family history, and her plans for the future, none of which Jade wished to share with Gail. By the time the interview concluded, she was emotionally exhausted and woefully disheartened, because none of her responses seemed to be satisfactory.

"That will be all for today," Dr. Nilsen stated, closing the file and slipping it into a huge briefcase. "I would like to make a home study on Monday at ten A.M., a walk-through to evaluate your living arrangements, if that time is convenient for you."

"All right." Jade stood up. The interview had gone badly, and she realized she would have to make up for it the next time or chance losing Sabrina altogether. "But surely it's possible to see my little girl before that."

"Not really. I believe your brother and sister-in-law have sent the child off to Disneyland."

Jade turned toward Gail. "You mean she isn't even here?"

"My mother offered to take the children." Gail smiled. "Surely you wouldn't begrudge Sabrina the chance to see Disneyland. It's her birthday, after all."

"Such perfect timing." Jade could barely keep her tone civil. "How nice for all of us. When will she be back?"

"Thursday," Gail replied. "It's not that long."

"You wouldn't be allowed visitation anyway," Dr. Nilsen put in. "Not until the evaluation is completed." The doctor slid her briefcase off the desk. "And frankly, Miss Brennan, I'm not sure it would be good for the child to see you in such a, how should I say it, unstable condition."

"Unstable!" Jade retorted. "Haven't you ever heard of extenuating circumstances, Doctor?"

"In my business, everyone's circumstances are extenuating, Miss Brennan." She brushed past Jade and headed for the door. "Good day."

Jade turned, and Gail immediately focused her attention on the doctor, whom she accompanied to the front door, talking in an undertone. Jade remained in the library, stunned that her present situation seemed likely to prevent her from ever seeing Sabrina. She sank against the edge of the desk, fighting back tears, too upset to face anyone.

Then she heard steps approaching, and she dashed away the dampness around her eyes with the heels of her hands. Quickly, she stood up and pivoted toward the window, so whoever came into the room couldn't see her red eyes.

"Thomas is going to be very upset that you're staying in the condo," Gail declared behind her.

"So," Jade retorted, crossing her arms. She clenched her teeth. Gail and Thomas often got hung up on things that Jade found unworthy of much concern. Were they so small-minded they would begrudge her the use of an apartment they couldn't even sell? She'd never asked them to repay the money they'd borrowed ten years ago, when Thomas was nothing but a penniless land developer. Had they no sense of fair play?

"I don't wish to be inhospitable, Janine, but under the circumstances maybe you should go to a hotel."

Jade shot a quick glare over her shoulder. "And maybe you should just leave me the hell alone, Gail."

"Oh!" Gail cried, as if no one ever dared say anything

harsh to her. For a moment she gaped at Jade, arms stiff
with indignation, her fists at her sides; then she turned
on her heel and minced out of the library.

Jade rolled her eyes in disgust and let her arms fall
free. With a sigh, she trudged toward the library door.
What could she do to jump-start her career, get a
spouse, and find a permanent place to live—all in the
space of two days?

Jade returned to her condo and collapsed in one of the
overstuffed mauve chairs in the living room, cursing herself for going into the interview blind. She should have
realized how strict the courts would be about the welfare
of her child. She should have researched the subject,
armed herself with knowledge, and prepared herself for
the worst. But in her wildest dreams she had never imagined Thomas and Gail would contest her right to Sabrina.
She should have known better. Thomas had never
approved of anything she did, and Gail was his unwavering
second-in-command, willing to carry out all of his self-
serving edicts.

"You blew it, sister," Jade said to herself, rolling her
head along the top of the chair. "You blew it big time."

For a moment she closed her eyes and drummed her
fingertips on the plush arm of the chair. Then she
reached for the phone and dialed the number of her
attorney and longtime friend, Laura Wettig. When
Laura found out what had transpired with the psychologist, she insisted upon flying out to help.

Jade hung up, feeling much better about her chances
with Laura on her side. Then she dialed information.

"The number for American Music?" she asked.

She memorized the digits and then punched them in,

ordered the rental and delivery of a keyboard, amp, and headphones, put it on her credit card, and then punched off the phone just as someone rang her doorbell.

Jade rose and hobbled to the door to peek through the peephole. She could see Herman Fong's small figure distorted by the fish-eye lens.

"Great," she mumbled. "Just what I need."

She pulled open the door.

"Miss Brennan!" Herman grinned.

"What do you want?" she barked, out of sorts with him and the rest of the world.

"A pair of scissors?"

"What for?"

"To cut his hair."

"Whose hair?"

"Mr. MacKenzie's." He pointed downward, indicating the strange man who probably remained in the cellar.

"Mr. Fong, I told you I wanted that guy out of here."

"I'm trying my best, Miss Brennan. But he will be a spectacle unless his hair is cut and that beard is shaved off."

"I don't care if he stops traffic for two days, Mr. Fong. I just want him out of the Elliott."

She moved to close the door, but Herman put his foot in its path.

"If he stops traffic, Miss Brennan, he may have to tell people how he returned to this world, and who helped him."

Jade's eyes narrowed. "Are you blackmailing me, mister?"

Herman shrugged.

She glared at him. "Listen, I did you a favor. I showed you where that special box was. Now leave me alone!"

"All I'm asking for is a pair of scissors." He tilted his head and gave her an imploring look. "And maybe a razor."

"Oh, for goodness' sake!" She scowled. "Wait here."

She walked to the bathroom, rummaged through her makeup kit, and found a pair of sharp scissors she used for trimming her bangs. Then she located a disposable razor and some shaving cream.

Herman smiled, delighted with her tools.

"I want them back," she warned.

"Of course, of course!" He bobbed his head. "Thank you."

His hands trembled so much that he almost dropped the can of shaving cream. Jade watched him, trying to visualize what it would be like to have such hands wielding a pair of scissors near her head. The man downstairs could easily lose an eye or part of an ear, not to mention the likelihood of getting a really bad haircut. She couldn't wish that on anyone, not even Connor MacKenzie.

"Wait a minute," she said. "Who's going to cut MacKenzie's hair?"

"I am."

"You?" She shook her head. "Don't you think you'll be a bit dangerous with a pair of scissors? Your hands aren't that steady."

"Yes, but who else is there?" He gazed at her innocently. "Somebody has to do it."

"Don't look at me," she warned. "I don't know the first thing about cutting hair."

"Better your hands than mine."

"Why don't you just take him to a barber?"

"He is not ready for the modern world yet. I cannot tell what he might do. There might be complications as time passes."

"What do you mean, complications?"

"During the ceremony, the soul of the priest or priestess

is linked with the dying person. It is the strength of their soul that heals the spirit of the afflicted one, the soul that urges the dying spirit to remain in the world. In Qi An's case, however, she was interrupted during the healing process. Perhaps violently. There is no telling what has happened to Mr. MacKenzie's soul in the interim. His spirit may have suffered damage."

"Like what?"

"I am not sure. He may be incomplete. Scarred. Perhaps not altogether right."

"Oh, great!"

"Or he may be perfectly normal. Only time will tell."

"And meanwhile?"

"I will not let him out of my sight."

Jade glanced over Herman's shoulder. "Where is he now, then?"

"Sleeping. It is safe. He will be very tired for a few days." Herman held out the scissors. "I ask you for help, Miss Brennan. This one last time."

Jade scowled, realizing he'd sucked her into his affairs once again.

"I don't have time for this, you know," she complained, grabbing her keys. "And I'm warning you— after I cut his hair, I'm not having anything more to do with him—or you."

"Understood, Miss Brennan. Perfectly understood."

Jade took one step into the hall and paused. "Just a second. I'm not going to be able to see what I'm doing down in that dungeon."

Herman crossed his arms and nodded sagely. "That is a consideration."

"And what about his hair? It must be filthy!"

"Most likely."

Jade sighed. "Oh, bring him up here so he can take a

shower. And while I cut his hair, you can get him some clothes. There has to be a store around here where you can buy a pair of jeans and a shirt—as long as you leave the gun with me."

"You are most kind, Miss Brennan."

"I'm not kind, Mr. Fong. I'm efficient. The sooner he's dressed and shaved, the sooner he's gone."

"I shall return quickly." Herman gave a shallow bow and shuffled off, toward the old elevator.

Jade returned to her apartment and called Phillip to bring down extra towels, then worried that she was getting into a situation far better left alone.

# 4

*Connor MacKenzie awoke* with a start when someone shook his shoulder. He'd been inordinately tired, and as soon as the Brennan woman had left, he had leaned against a trunk and promptly fallen asleep.

"Wake up," Herman Fong said, shaking him again.

Connor squinted up at the small, slight man, who couldn't have been much over five feet tall. He had no idea how long he had slept.

"I must take you upstairs now."

"Good. I could use a hot meal an' a warm bed." Slowly Connor struggled to his feet, fighting a dizzy sensation and black blobs that swirled through his field of vision.

"I've arranged for a hot bath and a shave. It will wake you up."

"Then you'll tell me what's goin' on, and where in the name o' Hades Chin is?"

"I'm the next best thing to Chin, Mr. MacKenzie. You will have to make do with me."

"That's th' part I don't understand. What *are* you doin' here, fussin' over me?"

"You are responsible for my being here, Mr. MacKenzie."

"Oh? How—when I don't know ye from Adam?"

"You saved the life of a relative of mine—Lui Fong. You carried him from the burning hotel. Had he not lived, I would not have been born. So in a sense, you were responsible for my birth."

"Sounds like a stretch t' me," Connor replied, pulling at the aching muscles in his shoulders. "How is Lui, anyway?"

"Unfortunately, he is no longer with us."

"Sorry t' hear it. It must've been from inhalin' all that smoke."

Connor frowned and pulled the length of silk more tightly around his body. He couldn't remember anything past the moment he'd staggered out of the burning Elliott Hotel, carrying the kitchen boy, Lui Fong, in his arms. Still more confusing was the fact that a grown man—and an old one at that—was now attributing his existence to a boy too young to have had children. Something was wrong with Fong's logic, but Connor ignored his puzzling explanation as the memory of the hotel fire roared into his thoughts.

The evening had been a nightmare, beginning the moment his business meeting had been interrupted by a clerk rushing in, shouting that the Elliott Hotel was on fire. . . .

Connor ran home to find his grand four-hundred-room hotel, fashioned after a French château—and his hopes and dreams—going up in smoke. Flames from the burning hotel licked the night sky, and all around him people were running and shouting, jostling him as they staggered from the burning building or loped toward it, holding wet blankets over their heads. He could hear the clattering hooves of horses on Yesler Way as the fire engines barreled up the hill toward him, alarm bells clanging. But in a few more minutes the firemen would be too late and all would be lost.

Already fire and smoke billowed out of the third-story windows. One of the elegant turrets was engulfed in flames and had become a giant torch illuminating Elliott Bay beyond. He wondered if the firemen had been instructed to hang back at the station house until his place of business was sure to be destroyed.

Connor had no illusions about his fall from grace with the city fathers. He'd been one of the few whites to stand up to the businessmen who blamed the economic depression on what they termed the "yellow peril." Many Chinese immigrants, desperate to escape famine in their own country, came to America, which they called the Gold Mountain. There they took the most menial jobs—cleaning houses, laundering, hauling refuse, laying track for the railroad, and mining the left-overs once the white men had panned and sluiced all the streams and rivers in Washington Territory. They worked for less money than their Caucasian counter-parts and still sent most of their pay home to China to help their suffering families.

The Chinese put many others out of work, men who couldn't find employment elsewhere during the eco-nomic depression that had descended upon the Northwest. Newly forming labor unions lost what little power they had when their demands and strikes were undermined by the cheap labor pool of immigrant

Chinese. Something had to be done. The Knights of Labor saw the solution in forcing the Chinese out of town. In the past few years, many of the Chinese families Connor had known personally had fled to Portland and San Francisco to escape persecution and violence. But the Chins remained behind, working at the newly opened Elliott Hotel, as loyal to Connor as he was to them.

This fire had broken out—suspiciously close to the time of Connor's last run-in with the Knights of Labor two days ago—when he'd refused to fire his Chinese employees.

As Connor ran toward the burning building, he dropped his suit coat onto the ground and dashed into the hotel. There he found Lui in the kitchen, unconscious. After carrying the boy through smoke and flames, Connor stumbled out to the side yard and collapsed at the feet of Sam Lo's beautiful daughter, Qi An. Everything after that was a stretch of blankness, including his entry into the ornate box that now sat on the floor near his feet. Had Sam Lo Chin put him in the box? Qi An? If so, why? He had a score of questions to pose as soon as he managed to find Chin.

One thing he knew for certain: he'd never felt so weak in his life. He wasn't sure just how far he could walk without his legs buckling beneath him. Each time he rose to his feet, a peculiar light-headed feeling beset him, causing him to sway and nearly swoon. Until he had more control of his faculties, he'd have to trust this stranger and hope Fong wasn't working for the Brennans.

"What about my clothes?" Connor inquired. "Where'd they go?"

"I do not know. But I will procure some for you while you bathe. Come, Mr. MacKenzie."

"I'm not walkin' 'round in this drape, man!"

"No one will see you, I assure you."

"'Twas bad enough when that Brennan lass saw me naked."

"I assure you, there is no one around."

"'Tis bloody embarrassin'!"

"Only for a few minutes more. Come."

Herman Fong led the way toward the elevator, holding a cylinder in his hand that shone a beam of light. Reluctantly, Connor followed him.

"What's that gadget you're carryin'?" Connor asked, pointing to the cylinder.

"This?" Fong held it up. "This is a flashlight."

"'Tis tiny." Connor studied it. "What's it burn for fuel?"

"Nothing. It works on a battery."

"Battery? I've never heard o' such."

Herman opened a door for Connor and held it as he passed through. "I imagine you are in for many such surprises."

Connor let the man's enigmatic comment pass. He was too dizzy and weak to manage more than putting one foot in front of the other. When they arrived at the elevator, Connor stepped into the car and glanced in surprise at the shabby interior, the faded velvet and tarnished brass. Gone were the ornate gas lamps by the door, replaced by strange frosted globes that glowed like the flashlight in Herman Fong's hand.

"What happened t' th' elevator?" He motioned toward one wall. "Fire damage?"

Herman pursed his lips. "Time, more likely."

"What d'ye mean? 'Tis practically brand-new!"

Herman turned the lever to start the elevator on its jerky upward path. Connor glanced up at the ceiling.

Even the sound of the contraption seemed different, and he wondered if the steam-powered mechanism had been changed as well as the light fixtures. He was still staring upward when Herman turned to face him.

"Mr. MacKenzie, I have something to tell you that you might find hard to believe."

"Such as?" Connor adjusted his silk wrap, suddenly suspicious of the small man in front of him and increasingly uncertain of the world around him.

"Well, to begin with—what year would you guess it is?"

"D'ye think I had a blow to th' head, man? I know what year 'tis!"

"Then tell me."

"'Tis eighty-seven."

"Of what century?"

"Century?" Connor scowled and shifted uncomfortably. What was the man getting at? Connor waved him off with an exasperated gesture. "Don't go pullin' my leg, Fong. I'm not in th' mood for jests."

"It is no joke, believe me."

"Then what're ye gettin' at? Speak plainly, man."

"Well—it's *nineteen* ninety-seven, Mr. MacKenzie, not eighteen eighty-seven."

"What?" Connor stared at him, not believing what he'd just heard.

"Nineteen ninety-seven. The twentieth century."

"All my eye and Betty Martin!" Connor retorted. "Asahel Brennan has put you up t' this!"

Herman slowly shook his head in reply and regarded Connor with a compassionate expression, seemingly sensitive to the effect such startling news would have on him.

"But—" Connor glanced around, searching for a single

clue to prove this was all a hoax, but he found no such evidence. "'Tis impossible!"

"You've been lying in a special box for over a hundred years, Mr. MacKenzie, waiting to be revived by an ancient ceremony."

Connor had never heard such nonsense. "Ye expect me t' believe such a tale?"

Herman shrugged, and his silence spoke more convincingly than any words.

Connor stood in absolute silence as the truth sank in. He'd been lying about for more than a hundred years? Impossible! No man could live for one hundred and forty-five years. Then the elevator lurched to a stop, interrupting his thoughts, and Herman opened the metal grating.

"I dinna believe ye," Connor declared, glaring down at him.

"You soon will. You'll see for yourself."

Eyeing the Chinese man with a good deal of suspicion, Connor passed into the hall and then stopped in his tracks, looking around.

"Ha!" he exclaimed. "Look a' this! No fire damage whatever!"

"It's been repaired and remodeled."

"There you're wrong," Connor replied. "Looks th' same t' me."

Herman shook his head and closed the panels to conceal the old elevator. Then he nodded toward a window at the end of the corridor.

"Look outside, Mr. MacKenzie. That is all it will take for you to accept the truth."

"Not bloody likely." Connor strode down the wide hallway, happy to discover that at least part of his building was still intact. There would be a good chance he could have the hotel up and running in a few weeks and work at getting the mess cleaned up where the fire had caused the greatest damage. Better yet, by the looks of things, his fortune in gold hadn't gone up in smoke, either. All he had to do was slip into his old room, lift the floorboard under his bed, recover his chest of gold, and he'd be in business. The Brennans hadn't seen the last of him—and he'd make them wish they had done the job right the first time, by completely burning his hotel and him with it.

The trouble with the Brennans was they'd never been a thorough lot, never wanted to do their own dirty work, never wanted to get caught with their finger in the pie. Well, he'd make sure they were shown for the hoodlums they really were, once he was back in business.

Connor stepped up to the window and had a look outside. "Bloody hell!" he declared, blinking in disbelief. He stared down again, squinting in the bright light, trying to locate familiar landmarks in a disturbingly alien terrain. "Where's th' Pioneer Building?" he asked, thinking he saw the familiar stone pillars, but not recognizing the rest of the structure. "What happened t' th' Occidental Hotel? What's tha' strange round building down there with all th' ramps?"

Herman ambled up behind him. "That's the Kingdome. It's a stadium for football and baseball, and other sports."

"But what happened to the waterfront? Where's th' sawmill?"

"Seattle had a bad fire around the turn of the century. Eighteen eighty-nine, I believe. Somebody's glue pot caught on fire, and the blaze ended up burning most of downtown."

"I'll be damned!" Connor couldn't move, so great was

his shock. Until this moment, he hadn't realized what a strange set of circumstances he'd fallen into. "I dinna even recognize th' place!"

"That's because soon after the fire, the city regraded the hills and filled in the tide flats."

"Always was a foul-smellin' place, the flats." Connor shook his head. "But I still canna believe . . ." His voice trailed off as he lapsed into incredulity.

"Part of the old city is underground now. People take tours to see it."

"Christ in heaven," Connor muttered. "Ye weren't lyin' after all."

"No, I wasn't, Mr. MacKenzie."

"Ye say it's nineteen hundred and ninety-seven, do ye?"

"Yes. May third, to be exact."

"I've been stowed in th' cellar for a hundred and ten years?"

"So it seems."

"I never would ha' believed it, had it happened t' anyone else."

"I'm not sure if it has happened to anyone else," Herman put in. "It isn't generally done, leaving someone in the box for that long a time."

At the thought of lying in a crate for a century, unmoving and unseeing, Connor felt a chilling shaft of dread pass through him. He'd been as good as dead for a hundred years. Maybe he *had* been dead. Immediately he turned his mind away from such an idea. "Will it have harmed me in some way, d'ye think?"

"I'm not certain, Mr. MacKenzie."

"A hundred years." Connor regarded Herman Fong's silver hair and round, open face. "'Tis true, then. Chin and his family are gone. All o' my friends—"

"Unfortunately, yes."

Connor was quiet for a long moment, struggling with the impact of being thrust completely alone and unprepared into another and—from what it appeared—more advanced century. He wouldn't know a soul in this time period. The life he'd built and the "family" he'd gathered around him were all gone, long since dead and forgotten. Sam Lo; his wife, Mi; their daughter, Qi An; and a score of others. Connor's throat constricted with grief, and he decided to change the subject immediately.

He turned back to the window. "Look at th' vehicles down there." His voice was gruff with suppressed emotion and sounded oddly compressed by the nearness of the glass. "So many o' them."

"They're called cars."

"No horses pullin' 'em?"

"No. They're powered by gasoline engines."

"And th' crowds o' people."

"Seattle's become one of the largest cities in the United States."

"Ye don't say." He tried to smile at the obvious prosperity of his adopted city. But a great sadness welled up inside him, smothering his usual good humor. He pushed away from the window and its all-too-disturbing vision of a new and modern world. "Well, Fong, I'll have that bath now, if ye don't mind. And I could use a stiff drink, too, while you're at it. I've got a lot t' think about."

"Of course, Mr. MacKenzie." Herman motioned for him to follow. "Come. It's not far."

Herman took him down a hallway and around a corner, then stopped at the third door on the right.

To Connor's surprise, Jade Brennan answered the door.

"Gentlemen," she greeted crisply, her voice bereft of warmth. "Do come in."

"Ye must be daft," Connor exclaimed, glancing down at Herman in alarm. "Not the Brennan woman!"

Jade returned his scowl. "I'm all you have, mister," she retorted. "Take it or leave it."

"She is right," Herman urged. "Miss Brennan has agreed to cut your hair and allow you to use her bath."

"*Allow* me?" Connor thundered. "*Her* bath?"

Suddenly a door opened down the hall and a woman and man stepped out, laughing together.

"Quickly, Mr. MacKenzie," Herman said, taking his arm. "Someone is coming."

Jade regarded his bearded face more closely. Would it be prudent to allow the scoundrel into her living quarters? From the information her grandfather had relayed, Connor MacKenzie was not to be trusted.

Connor let himself be propelled into the apartment, but as soon as the door closed behind him, he turned to Jade, and his blue eyes flashed over her in an unfriendly manner, justifying her misgivings. "Dinna tell me ye *live* here!"

"My brother owns this building," Jade retorted, frosty.

"A Brennan?" Connor whirled back to face Herman. "Is it true, man?"

Herman nodded.

"Ach!" Connor ran a hand through his wild hair. "'Tis a nightmare I'm in! Ye woke me from that sleep t' find this out? That th' Brennans have overrun the Elliott?"

"I did not know who you were, Mr. MacKenzie, when the ceremony was performed. Would you have preferred to remain in the box?"

"I dinna know what I prefer!" Connor scowled and threw a dark glance around the room, taking in the blocky shapes of the modern furniture, which Jade knew were very different from the elegant turned wood-and-velvet pieces of the fin de siècle. He strode toward the kitchen. "Where's the whiskey? In here?"

"I don't have any liquor," Jade called after him, annoyed by the way he behaved as if he owned the place. Obviously he was the type of man who walked roughshod over others, without a care to their feelings or wishes. She marched after him. "And I would appreciate it if you'd confine yourself to the bathroom."

"Confine myself?" He pivoted and raked her with another of his intense glances. "And why? 'Tis my hotel!"

"Not any longer."

"The hell ye say! No one bought it from me."

"My great-grandfather Asahel paid good money for it years ago."

"Oh? An' where's the gold for it, then, lass? Not in my pocket!"

"You were presumed dead, Mr. MacKenzie. Perhaps your heirs—"

"I had none. I wasna dead, either, and I expect reparations t' be made." His beard twitched, and she assumed he was sneering at her. "But then again, I'm dealin' with th' Brennans, and one canna depend upon fair play wi' your particular bunch."

"What are you saying?"

"I'm sayin' th' Brennans would steal a dead fly from a blind spider, that's what!"

"Really?" Jade put her fists on her hips. "That's exactly what I've heard about the MacKenzies."

"Then ye must've heard wrong, lass. Because there's only one MacKenzie hereabouts, an' that's me." He poked a finger to his broad chest. "And I'm not a lyin' cheat who burns down another man's business!"

"My family didn't burn the Elliott Hotel."

Connor threw back his head and laughed bitterly. "What pony ride did ye fall off, Miss Brennan? Ye must be too dizzy t' think, or you're more a fool than ye look!"

Jade shifted her weight and glared at him. "Listen, buddy, I don't have to take this. In fact, why don't you just clear out, right now!"

"My pleasure!" He broke for the door, but Herman stepped in his path.

"Mr. MacKenzie!" He held up his hands in protest. "You can't leave yet, not until you get something to wear and get your hair cut."

"I'll not be takin' any favors from th' likes o' her!" He jerked his head toward Jade, who stood near the kitchen doorway, still flushed with anger.

"Please, both of you . . ." Herman glanced from Jade to Connor. "Forget the old feud for a moment, just until I return with some clothing."

"I'd rather rot in hell," Connor declared.

"You do not have many other choices," Herman reminded him. "Please, Miss Brennan, won't you allow him to bathe, at least? Then he will be out of your life, I promise."

Jade crossed her arms while her stomach burned. She had a bad feeling about this. "I don't know. . . ."

"No more arguments about the past?" Herman put in, looking up at the towering Scotsman above him. "No threats or harsh words for the time being?"

Connor glared at him. "Ye ask too much, Mr. Fong."

"Miss Brennan is doing you a favor. Surely you can put aside the family differences for a few minutes."

"She'll likely try t' drown me, or shoot me when my back's turned."

"Oh, brother!" Jade rolled her eyes.

"Ye think th' Brennans wouldn't stoop so low?"

Connor glanced over his shoulder at her. "Ye must not know your own kin."

Jade held his fiery regard, and for the first time his words struck home. She'd never been able to understand or condone much of her father's behavior, or that of her brother, either. They'd criticized her choice of career and her propensity for frankness and candor, while they hid behind a facade of convention, saying all the right things but never communicating on a genuine level—not even with each other. Jade remembered the many times she had stomped away from the dinner table or out of her father's study, frustrated to tears by her father's aloofness and his glaringly obvious two-faced character—something the outside world seemed blind to and a character flaw that drove Jade to despair. She had never been able to get to the heart of her father, to really talk to him, and had decided his heart had been empty or made of stone.

She swallowed, shut off the memory, and allowed Connor's face to come back into focus. "Perhaps you shouldn't go lumping all the Brennans together," she warned. "A few bad apples don't mean the whole bushel's rotten."

"Unlikely." Connor's tense posture eased slightly, rustling the silk. "But then again, there's always a black sheep in a family—or white, as th' case may be."

She didn't know whether to take his comment as a compliment or an insult. Instead of answering, she inclined her head toward the hall, which led to the bathroom. "There are fresh towels in the bathroom. Everything you need."

Jade didn't look at Connor again and limped into the kitchen to make herself a cup of tea to steady her nerves.

She would need it to cope with the likes of Connor MacKenzie.

A few minutes later, Jade heard Herman taking his leave of Connor, and then he walked by the kitchen, left a small handgun in her possession, and promised to be back as soon as possible. After Herman left, Jade heard water running in the bathroom. She leaned against the counter, hoping Connor would spend most of his time in the bathroom so she wouldn't have to talk to him much before Herman got back.

Soon her teapot whistled, and she brewed a cup of chamomile, blowing away the steam as she carried her mug to the couch. Ever since she'd arrived in Seattle, she'd been upset and unsettled, and now with Connor MacKenzie in the picture, her unease had increased tremendously. She cradled the mug in her hands and tried to concentrate on the harbor scene below, with the green-and-white ferries plowing across the bay and the huge orange cranes, looking like angular tyrannosaurus rex dinosaurs, unloading container ships to the south; but her attention kept returning to the sounds issuing from the bathroom and the tall man with wild hair and fierce blue eyes.

To her dismay, she saw the bathroom door open ten minutes later, just as she rose to wash out her cup. Connor MacKenzie strode down the hall, bare-chested, with a dark green towel wrapped around his slender hips. His stomach was tight and ridged, more muscular than she'd been able to discern in the poor light of the cellar. He'd shaved off his long beard and appeared to be a great deal younger than she had expected. He couldn't be much older than she was. In the confines of the hall-way he seemed even taller, his shoulders wider, and the confident tread of his bare feet gave the impression of a powerful male lion padding toward her—all and all a bit dangerous looking and not the kind of guy she wanted to be alone with in her haunted condo. But even more startling was the strange glow that surrounded his figure—perhaps only a trick of light and darkness in the hall, but one Jade couldn't explain with any physics theories from her college years.

A chill passed over the surface of Jade's skin. Did Connor MacKenzie have some connection with the rumors about the strange occurrences in the condo? She decided to shut the thought off immediately. "Done already?" she asked.

"Aye. This modern age," he replied with a disarming smile. "Baths in every hotel room and all the hot water ye could want. A man could get used t' it."

"Something tells me you're going to be in plenty of hot water," she quipped, ignoring the odd sensation of breathlessness that had suddenly constricted her chest. "Come into the kitchen and I'll cut your hair."

"Ye know how?" he asked, ambling after her.

"I can do it." She dragged a chair from the breakfast nook to the center of the kitchen floor and motioned for Connor to sit down. "Let's get this over with."

He sank onto the chair and planted his feet in front of him, like a king sitting on his throne. Jade would have smiled at the picture he presented, had she not been acutely aware of an underlying current of danger emanating from him. The sides of the towel separated over his left thigh, which showed a good deal of muscle and sinew, even though his legs were long and lean. If it came to outrunning this man, she knew she wouldn't stand a chance.

"Look at this kitchen," he said, and waved his hand. "Look at that stove. It's about a third th' size of a stove from my time."

"That's because it uses electricity instead of wood or gas for heat."

"Ye dinna say!" He cocked his head. "I saw electric lamps once aboard the *Willamette*. . . ."

"The *Willamette*?"

"Aye, a steamer that had a regular run here. But I never expected everything t' become electric."

"Almost everything is."

"Were does th' electricity come from? Fong claims it flows out o' th' walls."

Jade couldn't help but smile. "Kind of. There are wires in the walls, Mr. MacKenzie. Much like gas lines were run in your day."

"But how can a wire carry fuel?"

"It isn't exactly fuel. It's energy—a charge that is sent along particle by particle in a little stream through the wire."

"A charge?"

"Yes. That's what makes our motors work in all our appliances."

"Ah." He frowned thoughtfully. "But where does the charge come from in th' first place?"

"From harnessing falling water, which turns turbines to create a charge, or through windmills. Also from nuclear reactors."

"Nuclear reactors?"

"Yes, but I'm not going to try to explain *them*. Let's get on with the haircut."

Deftly she picked up the comb she'd found for the job and positioned herself at the back of the chair, out of range of Connor's intense eyes. A moment of trepidation swept over her, but she quickly put her fear out of her mind and set herself to the task of untangling the ends of his shoulder-length hair.

"Didn't you use my conditioner?" she asked.

"What's that?"

"Stuff that takes the snarls out of your hair."

"Never heard of it." He shrugged, and she couldn't avoid looking down at his fine, wide shoulders. She bent closer.

"What's this on your skin?" she asked, studying the strange gold flecks that formed a glittering layer upon his flesh. His skin had a natural golden cast, but with the additional gold flecks, his body emitted an odd aura— which explained the glow she had seen in the hallway.

He raised his forearm. "It didna come off?"

She rubbed his left shoulder with the tip of her forefinger, trying to smudge away the gold particles. "No."

"Must be from the stuff in Fong's box."

"Do you suppose gold dust has become permanently embedded in your skin?"

"I hope not!" He chafed his forearm and frowned. "It'll come off in time, most likely."

"Until then, you'll glow in the dark."

"That's all I need!" He gave a snort of disgust. "It'll scare off the ladies."

"Ladies?" she countered. "How can you think of women at a time like this?"

"I always think o' women." He turned to look up at her, his mouth far too close for comfort. "Nothin' wrong wi' that!"

She straightened. "After spending a hundred years in a box, I would think you'd have more on your mind."

He gave a soft snort. "Aye, but you dinna have th' foggiest what it's like. . . ." He turned his back to her and sighed. "To dream o' women for a century, and never *have* one."

Jade paused. He'd dreamt during his deep sleep? Had

he traveled a similar path to the one she'd taken during her coma? She'd never spoken to another human being who had shared the same dark experience and thought it ironic that she might have something in common with Connor MacKenzie.

"You dreamed when you were in the box?" she asked, resting her right wrist on top of his shoulder.

"Aye. Terrible dark dreams." He shuddered. "I never want t' go back to 'em."

"It's awful to dream such dreams," she murmured, "without the ability to wake up and know they're only in your mind."

"Aye." He looked up again. "Ye seem t' know what 'twas like."

She nodded. "I had a similar experience."

"Ye did?"

"I was in a car accident, which left me in a coma for two months."

"Ah." His glance ran the length of her. "That accounts for your limp, then?"

"Yes." She regarded her leg and frowned. "I'm not what I used to be."

"Dinna despair. You're a fine-looking woman."

"Spoken like a truly desperate man." She chuckled wryly.

"Never desperate, lass." He winked. "Women have never been a problem for me and I dinna expect them t' be different now."

"Really?" She raised the comb. "I wouldn't be too sure. Women have changed over the years. You might be in for a surprise."

"I dinna think so," Connor replied. "People dinna change. They may put on different clothes and travel about faster, but they never change."

"I wouldn't be too sure about that, either."

"I would." He turned around again in his chair. Jade guessed that he was the type of man who couldn't sit still for long—a man of action, a man who cut a big swath and left the details for others. "Take you, for instance."

She remained rooted to the floor, even though she felt a pressing urge to step away from him. "What *about* me?" she asked in a cool tone.

"Ye live in this fancy place—all th' conveniences at your disposal. Ye've done well for yourself, workin' in the bawdy houses 'round town—"

"Bawdy houses?" she exclaimed.

"Aye. Ye must be a strumpet." His glance quickly traveled down her mohair sweater and short black skirt. "No real lady would be seen walkin' 'round in the duds ye wear."

"For your information . . ." Jade actually flushed. "I'm not a prostitute. And this outfit I'm wearing happens to be a Marini original!"

"Then I'd say ye were cheated." He gave a small snort again. "Ye didn't get much cloth for your coin!"

Jade's blush deepened. She could feel her cheeks flaming. "What would you know about fashion?" she countered. "You're a hundred years behind the times."

"Aye, but that's what I was gettin' at in th' first place." He nodded toward her outfit. "Ye take off the clothes, ye step away from th' electricity, and ye're like any other woman on the face o' th' earth from any other period o' time."

"I am *not*!" She frowned, resenting the way he'd lumped her with all the others. "And you're going to find that out real soon, buddy—as soon as you step foot in the real world."

"Then this isn't real? You're not part o' th' modern world?"

"You know what I mean." She brandished the comb, cutting off the current topic of conversation. "Now do you want your hair cut or don't you?"

"Aye."

"Then turn around and hold still."

"Ye're a hard one, ye are," he commented. But without further protest, he swiveled around in the chair, and she resumed her combing.

"Och!" he cried. "Be gentle, lass!"

"I'm not in the mood. And your hair is a mess."

"Then cut off those ends," he suggested. "I want it short anyway."

"Fine." She snipped off all the hair to collar length and worked from there, carefully sculpting the sides around his ears and gradually moving around his chair as she clipped away. They didn't speak any further, but she was highly conscious of her breathing and of his, especially when she stood between his feet and cut the hair at his forehead and temples. She knew it was silly, but she couldn't keep her breasts from reacting to the nearness of his head and shoulders. She could feel the arousing prick of her nipples tightening. She did her best to ignore them and hoped Connor hadn't noticed. Being this close to Martin, her old friend, had never produced such a powerful and immediate reaction.

By the time she finished, Connor's hair was damp only at the roots. She was surprised to discover his hair wasn't brown, as she had first thought, but an unusual blond color burnished in reds and golds, full of body and lights, and it slipped through her fingers in soft, silken waves. He had a lot of hair, too, with a full straight hairline in no danger of receding.

Jade gave a final part to his hair, smoothed the other side with her palm, and then stepped back.

"There," she announced, surprised that for a novice she had given him a fairly respectable haircut. But she was even more surprised by the man who had emerged from the beard and tangled hair. Connor MacKenzie might be a lying, cheating bastard, but he was one good-looking scoundrel—far too handsome to be trusted.

"Done?" he asked, brushing off the back of his neck.

"Yes."

"Thank ye." He rose and brushed most of the golden crescents of hair from the towel. "And thanks for the bath, too. I owe ye."

"Don't worry about it." She brushed off the chair and slid it back under the table. "Now all we have to do is wait for Mr. Fong to come back."

"D'ye mind if I sit on the sofa?"

She glanced at his towel. "Why don't you get a clean towel first, while I sweep up the mess here? I don't want hair all over the place."

"Done." He turned and headed for the bathroom, the muscles of his small rear rising and falling beneath the terry cloth. Jade watched him walk away, aware that she was ogling him but doing it just the same—and appreciating the view. He was the best-looking man she'd seen in a long time. If the circumstances were different, and he were not a MacKenzie and she a Brennan, and if he were not a strange traveler from another time, she might find him dangerously appealing.

When he didn't return from the bathroom in a reasonable amount of time, Jade decided to check on him. He was probably going through her belongings, looking for money or valuables. With the gun in her hand, she tiptoed down the hall. The bathroom door stood open, and the light was off. She stuck her head through the doorway. Connor wasn't there.

Jade continued her stealthy inspection of the bed-rooms. She peeked into the master bedroom. He wasn't in sight, and nothing seemed to have been disturbed. She crossed the hall and slowly opened the door to the second bedroom, praying the hinges wouldn't squeak. Her heart thumped beneath her blouse, and she gripped the gun more tightly, ready to fire at Connor should he try to take her by surprise. The door eased open, and she looked around the corner.

There was the Scotsman, sprawled facedown upon the bed, fast asleep, looking as innocent as a boy, with his eyes closed and his large left hand hanging limp over the side. She felt herself relax as her fear subsided. Perhaps Connor tired easily and had to build up his stamina, having been "suspended" for so long. She was surprised his muscles weren't completely atrophied, as would have happened to someone left unmoving for that length of time in a normal situation. During her coma, her limbs had been worked constantly by therapists so her body would retain its mobility. Perhaps the concoction of herbs and spices had preserved Connor's body enough to prevent muscle atrophy, and he had only to regain his strength to be as good as new.

For a few moments, Jade watched the rise and fall of his powerful rib cage as he slept and studied the peculiar glow around him—wondering what kind of creature she and Herman had raised from the dead. Then she shut the door quietly and let the Scotsman sleep, hoping Herman Fong would get back soon.

# 5

*Herman Fong didn't return* until late afternoon. He arrived at the door with two huge shopping bags, one filled with clothes and the other filled with groceries.

"Wait a minute," Jade protested when she caught sight of the food. "What's that for?"

"Excuse my presuming upon your good graces, Miss Brennan, but I must prepare a special meal for Mr. MacKenzie before he is set free. Otherwise he might suffer. His internal organs will not be prepared to digest normal food, unless certain precautions are taken."

"I told you I wanted nothing more to do with him!"

"Yes. But as I was buying his clothing, I remembered part of the ceremony I had forgotten—it has been such a long time since I read of it."

"Mr. Fong!" Jade sputtered.

"Was Mr. MacKenzie all right when I was gone?"

"Well, yes."

"No unusual lapses in behavior?"

"Not so far."

"Where is he?"

"In the guest room. He fell asleep."

"Ah." Herman nodded. "That is good. He will be very tired for the first few weeks."

"Mr. Fong, I don't have time for this."

He gave her a sheepish smile and picked up the bag of groceries. "I realize that you and Mr. MacKenzie do not get along, but grant me a few more hours. And after that, I promise you won't see either of us again."

"You keep making promises, but you're still here."

"I know, but please permit this one last request. In return, I will make you a most delicious Chinese dinner."

"You cook?"

"I am most accomplished."

Jade crossed her arms and considered his bargain. She couldn't cook and survived mostly on fresh fruit and vegetables, yogurt, and an occasional bowl of canned soup. A home-cooked Chinese dinner was a tempting offer. She could work out while he prepared the food. Besides that, she could use the company. Jade wasn't accustomed to spending so many hours alone, not even at the Swiss clinic, and hated to admit it, but she was lonely. And having people around would keep her from dwelling on the fact that she couldn't see Sabrina.

"You have yourself a deal, Mr. Fong."

"Thank you." He grinned and bowed.

"So what's on the menu?"

"For Mr. MacKenzie—ginseng tea and a special broth of ginger, herbs, and mushrooms. For you, a surprise!"

"Maybe I don't like surprises." She tried to peek in

the shopping bag, but he clutched it tighter. "And I eat mostly vegetarian."

"Then you will be pleased with my selections." He shuffled into the kitchen and turned when she followed him. "Now, leave me to my task, Miss Brennan. Go. Shoo!"

Jade frowned and tossed her hair, but only for effect, for her real anger had dissipated. She walked to her room and changed into her workout clothes. Keeping her music low so as not to disturb Connor, she went through her leg-strengthening routines, then did her aerobic workout. After about an hour, delicious smells began to waft into her bedroom. Her stomach growled and she kept an eye on the door, hoping Herman Fong would soon announce that dinner was ready.

Later at dinner, just as Jade put down her empty cup of green tea and was considering eating the last egg roll, she heard the intercom buzz. She pushed the button on the intercom and let the delivery people from American Music into the building. A few minutes later they arrived at the door with the equipment she had rented.

Without being asked, Connor carried the heavy keyboard and amplifier into the living room and deposited them along the far wall, out of the way, while Jade spoke with the deliverymen. Herman Fong cleaned up the dishes, contentedly puttering in the kitchen.

When the deliverymen left, Connor rose from inspecting the equipment and looked at her. "D'ye mind my askin' what this contraption is?" He pointed to the amplifier.

"That's an amp," she explained. "It amplifies the sound that comes out of the keyboard."

"Keyboard?"

"The keyboard is the instrument inside that case."

"Mind if I have a look?"

"Be my guest."

She stood behind him as he knelt and opened the latches on the case. He had put on the dark blue shirt Herman had bought for him and had folded up the sleeves onto his muscular forearms. Herman had guessed his shirt size accurately, as well as his jeans size. When she'd asked Herman how he could judge someone so well without measuring him, he had shrugged and said, "I know a tailor."

Whatever the explanation, Herman had chosen well, especially the hue of the shirt, which accentuated the navy blue of Connor's eyes and brought out the blond highlights of his hair. Jade had to admit that Connor looked almost as good dressed as he did naked. She also had to admit she liked the notion she'd seen him in the buff and was the owner of information no other present-day women possessed about him. But if Connor had his way, his social isolation would soon end. Jade crossed her arms over the tight feeling in her chest—a sensation that came over her whenever Connor was around. She tried to ignore her physical reaction to him and vowed to see him for what he really was: a scoundrel.

The Scotsman lifted up the lid. "'Tis like a piano," he declared.

"It *is* a piano." She looked at the black and white keys, once as familiar to her as part of her own body. Now the keys mocked her, eighty-eight slender enemies ready to prove she was still damaged, still unable to understand or speak the language of music. "It's an electric piano."

"More electricity, eh?" He grinned and stood,

unaware of the sheen of sweat that had broken out beneath her sweater. "What're ye plannin' t' do with it?"

"Work on a sound track." She slid her gaze off the keyboard and swept it up toward him.

"Sound track?"

"Music for a movie." She saw the blank look on his face. "A moving picture?"

He cocked one of his expressive brown eyebrows.

"Were there cameras in your day, Mr. MacKenzie?"

"O' course."

"Well, a movie is like a bunch of photographs running together to simulate real movement."

"Set to music?"

"Yes. In a way." She glanced back at the piano, sighed, and then turned away.

"But ye dinna care to make music anymore," he remarked behind her, his voice softening.

His insightful observation surprised her. She tried to smile but failed in the attempt, tried to think of something witty to say to hide her weakness from him but failed in that, too. Nothing came to mind but the truth. She pushed up the sleeves of her sweater and sighed once more. "It's not a question of wanting to. I haven't been able to."

"Why is that?"

Jade could hear dishes clattering and water running as Herman worked in the kitchen. She wished he would come out and interrupt the conversation. She wished anyone but Connor MacKenzie were standing behind her. He had a peculiar skill for drawing her out, and she wasn't sure how much she should tell him. Martin Griffith, her most trusted confidant and lyricist, had died in the accident. Since then she had kept her troubles to herself and had suffered considerable emotional privation over the last two years. She felt a deep need to talk about her troubles with another human being, yet no one had offered her the kindness of a listening ear, and she wasn't the type of person to blurt out her problems to just anyone. How odd that Connor MacKenzie's soft baritone could urge her to open up to him.

What could it hurt if she told him a few facts?

"The accident did something to my brain." She looked at the floor. "I can't make music any longer. I can't hear the melodies like I used to."

She blinked rapidly, refusing to let tears of frustration pool into her eyes, and went on. "But I have to find a way. I have to relearn the steps. Teach myself."

"Why?"

"It's my livelihood." She looked up at him. "I have a daughter, MacKenzie, a daughter I've never seen. My brother is trying to make me look incompetent by proving that I have no home, no means of support, and no husband. If I don't get something going with my work soon, I'll lose all possibility of being a parent to her."

He moved slightly so he could observe her face more fully. Jade didn't turn away to hide her pinched expression. Gently he touched her arm and she felt a slight shock before she eased just far enough away to break contact. He lowered his hand, apparently not offended by her reaction.

"You have a bairn ye've never seen? How old?"

"Two."

"Saints!" He swore. "Where is she?"

"She lives with my brother, Thomas, and his wife, Gail. They have a penthouse apartment on the top floor."

"Here in my hotel?"

"Yes."

"And they won't let ye see her?"

His incredulity struck her, for he was the first person to express sympathy for her situation, the first person to verify her own feelings of outrage. Jade shook her head, very close to tears, her throat too tight for a reply. She couldn't look at his face.

"I've never heard o' such nonsense," he declared. "Ye come with me, lass, and we'll have a chat with this Thomas Brennan—right now. We've both got a bone t' pick with the man!"

"It won't do any good. He's out campaigning. And I was informed they've sent Sabrina out of town."

"For how long?"

"Until Thursday."

"Then Thursday it is."

"Don't get your hopes up. You won't get anywhere with him. He'll take you to court before he'll give up this hotel. And if you tell your story to the authorities, they'll say you're crazy and will lock you away."

He studied her thoughtfully, and she knew he was gazing far beyond her face. "You have a point. I'll have to think of somethin' else t' get my place back." Then he snapped back to the present. "Ye say ye haven't seen your daughter. How did that come t' be?"

"It's a long story," she replied. "Maybe some other time."

He nodded, apparently content to let the personal subject drop. "Shall I set up the piano for ye, then?"

"Sure, if you want to." Jade marveled that they had temporarily forgotten their feud and had been carrying on a normal conversation for the last few minutes. "The stand for it is over there by the door." She pointed to the metal frame, which had to be unfolded, positioned, and screwed together. Setting up musical equipment had never been an activity of choice for her, so she was glad he had offered.

It didn't take Connor long to assemble the frame and carefully set the keyboard on top of it. Jade helped him with the cables and the pedals, and then she showed him how to plug in the equipment. As soon as he got the plug of the power cord within inches of the outlet, a spark flashed out of the wall and up his arm. He yelped in alarm and fell backward onto his rear, still clutching the keyboard plug in his hand.

"Connor!" Jade cried, dashing forward.

He looked up at her, momentarily dazed.

Herman scurried out of the kitchen. "What happened?" he asked.

"Connor just got shocked."

"Mr. MacKenzie!" Herman leaned over him and put his hands on the Scotsman's broad shoulders. "Are you hurt?"

Connor ran the fingers of his free hand through his newly cut hair. "Jolted a wee bit, but I'll live." He scrambled to his feet, with Herman lending an ineffectual hand. "What in blazes happened?"

"There must be a short in the plug," Jade put in.

"A short?" Connor repeated, not understanding.

"A break, so the electricity doesn't flow to the right place."

"Tha' was electricity I felt tearin' through me?"

She nodded.

Connor glanced down at the plug in his hand and then back at her, his eyes wide. "Powerful stuff, that," he declared.

"It is. It could have killed you." She reached for the plug. "I'll have to have the equipment checked before I use it."

"No music, then?"

"No music." Jade was grateful for a reason not to play, because to touch fingertip to key would force her to face the place in herself where she suffered the most painful and extensive loss. Notes on a page meant nothing to her injured brain but dots and sticks and perplexing words in Italian. She could play songs she had memorized before the accident, for that knowledge was lodged safely inside another part of her head. But she could no longer string chords and melodies together to tell a story or speak of an emotion—a talent that had given her a reason for living and a lucrative income.

But she hadn't given up hope. She had learned to speak again, learned to read. She was determined to regain her composing ability, too, no matter how many hours she had to sit in front of a piano. If success depended upon hard work and desire, she would slowly but surely rebuild the nerve pathways that connected her brain to her hands, and one day she would rediscover the mystery of a musical score. If, however, her brain was permanently injured and the pathways damaged beyond repair, as the doctors had warned it might be—

Jade shook off the possibility.

"Are you sure you're all right, Connor?"

"I'm fine. 'Twas but a fleetin' twinge."

"Well, thank you for setting the piano up for me."

"'Twas the least I could do." Connor actually smiled at her.

"And now it is time we leave Miss Brennan to her work," Herman put in. "Thank you for all your assistance." He bowed.

"Thank you for dinner, Mr. Fong."

"I have left the remaining food in your refrigerator."

"Great." She walked with them to the door. "Any time you want to come back and make dinner again, Mr. Fong, feel free."

He smiled knowingly and nodded.

Connor passed through the doorway and into the hall. Then he looked back at her. "Thursday," he said.

Not knowing what else to say, and fairly certain he wouldn't show up, she just nodded.

After the two men left, Jade realized how quiet the apartment was. Though she and Connor had exchanged uncivil words until their chat after dinner, his sudden absence left a stark and surprising void. Disturbed by the heaviness of the silence, Jade checked the kitchen to make sure Herman had left it tidy enough to suit her. He'd cleaned so thoroughly, she wouldn't have known he'd cooked dinner, except for the telltale leftovers in the refrigerator.

Jade walked to her bedroom, retrieved her CD player and headphones, and grabbed six of her blues albums, which she carried back to the living room. Then, putting her leg up to rest it, she leaned back and listened to the music, studying technique and interpretation, trying to retrain her brain by exposing it to as much music as possible.

That night, before Jade crawled into bed, she glanced at the three framed photographs standing on the bureau. One photograph showed her and her lyricist, Martin, laughing at the keyboard of a grand piano, their arms draped over one another's shoulders.

For a moment she gazed at him and smiled sadly. Black-haired, brown-eyed Martin had been her best friend, her writing partner of ten years. They'd done everything together, spent the holidays together, shared each other's triumphs and troubles, and had lived together at first when money was tight. Most people assumed they were longtime lovers, and Jade had often been asked why they weren't married. But the curious thing was, she and Martin had never even shared a simple kiss. Their friendship had never turned sexual, probably out of fear of losing a best friend and partner. Jade had never considered Martin as a romantic partner, because she had come to know him too well and was wary of his inconsolable depressions.

No one but Jade had known the depths of Martin's personal sorrow or had been aware that the poignant ballads he wrote were born of a wrenching blackness that sometimes boiled up and devoured him. Martin had always been out of step with the world, always puzzled by the way other people seemed to fall into relationships when he could never find the right kind of love to satisfy him. Jade had often thought he hadn't learned the tools for building a relationship and had grown up not knowing the master craft of loving another human being because his parents had substituted love and attention with belittling words and withering disinterest in his music. But then she wondered if perhaps she weren't overlaying her own childhood problems on him, and that he might have had some other reason for his depression that he had never shared.

She often suspected Martin might have been gay but couldn't admit it, even to himself. So he pursued love affairs that never gave him the sustenance he craved and suffered greatly for them. That he might not have shared this part of himself with her would have been entirely possible, for Martin had been a brooding enigma and, at times, a most difficult person to know.

But in her way, Jade had loved him and missed him acutely, now that he was gone. He'd been driving the day of the accident. Neither of them had seen the truck running the red light. If she'd only looked up in time. If she'd only left her purse alone and had shouted a warning, Martin might still be with her.

She gazed at his picture—smiling at the jaunty grin that hid his pain from the world—while a tear trickled down her cheek. She missed his sardonic jokes and wry view of the world. She missed sitting on a piano bench with him, working on a song for hours until the chords and words were just right, laboring until dawn on a task that was more an act of love than a job. She hadn't written a single note since the accident. The doctors called her problem aphasia, but Jade wasn't sure if her lost ability was due to head injury or to unutterable grief.

Jade lifted the second frame. That photo showed the pinched and squinting face of Sabrina as a newborn, her spidery fingers steepled below her pert little chin. Even as a newborn she'd had the long fingers of a pianist, and Jade wondered if Sabrina would share her love of music.

The third photograph was of her mother. Jade adjusted the ornate silver frame beside the others.

"I'm a mom, Mother," she said to the thoughtful face looking back at her. "But you wouldn't know it." She sniffed and rubbed her nose. "And I'm scared. I'm real scared I'll mess up, just like Thomas thinks I will."

She searched for reassurance in the large green eyes of her mother, so like her own. But the static features didn't speak to her, and deep inside, Jade felt the all-too-familiar empty hole of alone that no amount of worldly success had ever been able to fill.

Jade ambled to her bed and slipped under the covers, imagining as she usually did what Sabrina would look like when she saw her at last, how her little girl would act and talk. Yet beside the vision of Sabrina another image continually encroached—that of Connor MacKenzie's golden face and flashing eyes. He had a dominating personality, and she wondered if his strong spirit was the reason for his successful recovery from the Box of the Deepest Sleep. Such a spirit would refuse to fade away without a fight, just as his face would not fade from her thoughts.

It was at that moment, while she thought of Connor, that she heard the water turn on in the bathroom.

"What in the world?" she murmured, climbing out of bed. She stuffed her feet in her slippers and shuffled out to the hall. Light poured out of the bathroom doorway, and the sound of bathwater running was unmistakable. Jade froze. She was certain she'd turned off the light when she had finished taking her shower—she never forgot to turn off lights. And she would never fail to shut off the water.

Someone was in the bathroom. But who?

Then she remembered Phillip's comments about the ghost that supposedly haunted this condo and how water would run for no apparent reason. Jade rubbed the back of her neck in disbelief. A haunting was too preposterous. There had to be a reasonable explanation. It had been quite a leap for her to accept the appearance of Connor MacKenzie in the cellar, but that was as far as her imagination would stretch—it certainly would not carry her far enough to accept the presence of a resident ghost.

Perplexed, Jade looked at the bathroom door again and suddenly realized what was happening: that darn Herman Fong and his promises! He had promised to leave after dinner but obviously had found a reason to come back. He'd probably let himself in with his lock-picking tool and was fussing over Connor MacKenzie, doing who knew what. She actually wouldn't mind their company again, but not in the middle of the night.

Scowling, Jade stormed to the bathroom, harsh words ready to fire at them. When she got to the bathroom, however, she stopped short at the threshold and glanced around in alarm. No one was there.

"Mr. Fong!" she called sharply, expecting to see him step out of the linen closet on the right, grinning and bowing and asking for her continued indulgence. He wasn't going to win her over this time, no matter how good his cooking was. "Mr. Fong!" she repeated, more tersely. "I know you're there!" No one responded. She yanked open the door of the linen closet but found only dark and silent shelves, with no room to hide a full-grown man, even a small-boned man like Herman Fong.

More upset than frightened, Jade stomped into the bathroom and bent over to turn off the water. Much to her surprise, she found the taps were already shut. How could water flow past closed taps? She turned the knobs on and off again, but it had no effect on the flow. Hot water continued to thunder into the bathtub, steaming up the small window and mirror.

Jade hurried to the living room, where she'd left her phone. She dialed the number of the penthouse and was relieved to hear Phillip's voice on the other end of the line.

"Phil, you've got to come down here," she said.

"Miss Brennan, it is eleven o'clock."

"I know, but you've got to see this."

"See what?"

"What's going on in the bathroom. That story about water running? It's true!"

There was a long pause on the other end.

"Phil?"

"Yes, yes, I'm here."

"Would you please come down here? I'm not too crazy about being alone with this going on."

"Very well. I shall be there directly. Don't move."

"I don't intend to."

She unlocked her door and stood half in the hall, half in the foyer, her attention focused on the noise from the bathroom while she waited for the reassuring *ding* of the elevator arriving at the far end of the corridor. Minutes later Phillip appeared in navy blue pajamas and robe, hurrying toward her as fast as his sense of propriety would permit.

"Are you all right, Miss Brennan?" he asked.

"Yes. Come on." She led him to the bathroom and pointed at the tub. "See? The water started running all by itself, and now it won't shut off."

"Let me have a look at it." Phillip strode across the floor to the tub while Jade watched from the doorway. He leaned over the side of the porcelain tub and turned the knobs, just as she had done. But this time the water slowed and then stopped completely when he tightened the knobs.

"There!" he declared, brushing his palms together. "All fixed."

Jade's brows knitted in confusion. "I don't understand it. They had no effect when I turned them. The water wouldn't stop."

He gave her a reassuring smile. "You were probably still half-asleep. Perhaps confused?"

"No, I wasn't!"

"Well, as you can see, the water turned right off."

He cocked his head and gazed at her, as if searching

for signs of sleepiness or ineptitude—an inspection most people gave her these days and an inspection that humiliated her. Phillip probably assumed, as did most people, that her thoughts were as muddled as her speech. Put off by his attitude, she looked past his shoulder but froze once again when she caught sight of the mirror above the sink.

"Look!" She pointed at the steam-fogged mirror.

Phillip slowly turned.

The flowing lines of a Chinese character had been stroked through the steam, leaving a silver glyph behind.

"Hmmm," Phillip remarked, stepping closer.

"How do you suppose that got there?"

"Someone playing. Probably a child."

"Who? And when? When I was waiting for you to come down?"

"Why, no, Miss Brennan." Phillip leaned forward to study the glyph. "This writing could have been done any time. The body oil from a person's finger would remain on the glass and repel the steam."

"So you're saying anyone could have written this, any time."

"That's what I'm saying." Phillip straightened and gazed at her again. "You're not really considering a ghost is at work here, are you, Miss Brennan?" His tone was so full of condescending disbelief that she bristled immediately.

"Of course not!"

"I wouldn't think so. You, of all people!" He chuckled, as close to an outright laugh as she had ever heard. "The last of the hard-core skeptics."

"Yep," she retorted. "That's me. Doubting Thomasina."

Yet was it her? If she was so hard-core skeptical, why

had she accepted the possibility of Connor MacKenzie rising from the dead? Ever since she had returned to the old hotel, she had felt off center, not quite herself. And this latest development only shook her up more. She had to get control of herself and her imagination if she were to be a decent mother to Sabrina. Flustered, but not wanting to admit it—even to herself—Jade bent down to the cupboard under the sink to search for a sponge and cleaner to wipe off the mirror. She rose with a spray bottle and a sponge in her hands.

"I'll show myself out," Phillip remarked, glancing at the mirror again.

"Thanks. And thanks for coming down, Phil."

"You're welcome, Miss Brennan. And do get some sleep."

"I will. Good night."

"Good night."

The sponge squeaked on the mirror as she efficiently rubbed away all traces of the Chinese writing. Then to clear her mind of the past few minutes, she continued to clean until the tub and sink sparkled and the tile floor shone. By the time she'd finished, she had come to the conclusion that Herman Fong had written the glyph when he'd been in the bathroom with Connor, earlier that day.

She put away the cleaning equipment. Then, remembering the dirty towels left from Connor's bath, she scooped up the laundry and put a load in the washer. Finally she returned to bed. The comforting rumble and spray of the washing machine in the small laundry room across the hall was enough noise to distract her mind from the unsettling events in the bathroom. Jade closed her eyes and fell into a fitful sleep.

❖   ❖   ❖

Jade sat at the keyboard late Sunday evening, forcing herself to form chords with her hands, but she was unable to judge what sounded good and what didn't. Full of despair, she lapsed into playing songs that she'd written years ago and had played thousands of times. But those haunting melodies only reminded her of Martin, and how she missed his presence in her life. She had to get beyond her grief, had to concentrate on healing herself, if she were to ever write again.

Jade closed her eyes and repeated a phrase, listening to herself as she hit the high note. She couldn't tell if it was a C or a D, couldn't tell whether it made sense in scheme of the other notes, and her lack of ability crushed her.

Heartbroken, Jade switched off the keyboard and slumped in her chair. Two hours had passed and she'd made no progress at all. Jade rose, fixed herself a cup of herbal tea, and then retired for the evening, her senses still tuned toward noises in the bathroom, her nerves still on edge, even though nothing strange had occurred since Friday evening. She slipped into her bed and set her clock. She had to pick up her lawyer at the airport, take her to breakfast, brief her on the facts of the case, and then return for the home visit by ten o'clock. She sighed and pushed a hand under the cool mound of her pillow. Just four more days and she would see Sabrina.

# 6

"*This is a nice little place*," Laura Wettig commented the next morning, slowly rotating in the center of Jade's living room.

"It is, isn't it?" Jade replied, carrying a tray of teacups and cookies to the coffee table.

"Great view. I wouldn't mind living here myself."

Jade glanced at her lawyer, dressed as usual in a crisp navy suit and spike heels, a mix of business and femininity that she used to her advantage. She wore her blond hair in a simple page style, parted at the side and tucked behind her left ear, and accessorized her outfit with conservative but expensive gold earrings. Over the course of the years, Laura had become one of Jade's staunchest allies, because she knew what it was like to be a strong woman in a profession defined by male rules and how frequently strong women were judged and condemned—mostly by members of their own sex.

Laura was also one of Jade's best friends. She didn't

have many. Her career had taken precedence over long-term relationships. And since the accident, few friends had remained loyal. Laura Wettig, however, was one of the few people Jade still trusted and felt comfortable with, the kind of person she could call in the middle of the night—but never did. Laura had offered to drop everything and fly out to Seattle once she learned of Jade's reason for asking for her legal assistance.

Now, with Laura here, Jade felt confident that anything Dr. Nilsen threw at her could be deflected, explained, or supported. This interview would be nothing like the first one, with Gail smirking in the background.

Just as she set the tray on the coffee table, the doorbell rang. Jade straightened, and her glance met Laura's serious gray eyes. Laura gave her a thumbs-up sign.

Heartened, Jade swept forward to answer the door. Dr. Nilsen stood in the hallway, clutching the handle of her briefcase with both hands and smiling her usual professional smile that conveyed no friendliness whatsoever.

"Good morning," Dr. Nilsen greeted her.

"Hi, come in." Jade motioned toward the living room with a sweep of her hand as she closed the door.

Dr. Nilsen walked toward the couch, and her cloyingly sweet perfume lingered in her wake. She wore a short boxy red jacket with gold trim and metallic buttons and a pleated floral skirt that hung below her knees. Next to Laura's plain but smart attire, Dr. Nilsen looked overdone, like a house cluttered with too many knick-knacks and doilies.

Jade introduced the two women and offered Dr. Nilsen a seat.

"Thank you," she replied. "But why don't we take a

quick tour of your apartment first, so we can get that out of the way?"

"Bear in mind this isn't where Janine will be living with Sabrina," Laura put in.

Dr. Nilsen regarded the lawyer over the tops of her half-glasses. "I am aware of that, Ms. Wettig. But I need to evaluate it all the same, to see the conditions in which Miss Brennan ordinarily exists."

"I can assure you this apartment in no way typifies the home Janine owned," Laura continued. "I had the pleasure of visiting her house in Connecticut—which would have been an excellent place to raise a child. Janine keeps a spotless—"

"Yet Miss Brennan no longer owns that property, does she?"

Jade bit her lip, determined to keep her mouth shut. The way Dr. Nilsen had just spoken made it sound as if she were incapable of ever having a decent home again, of ever making anything of herself. Such an attitude infuriated her.

"This way," she declared tersely, leading the doctor into the kitchen. Laura followed, her high heels clicking on the floor tile. Dr. Nilsen didn't just look at the apartment, she snooped—sticking her head into the oven, refrigerator, most of the cupboards, and under the sink. She didn't say a word, but her expression was laced with disdain, and the longer the inspection stretched, the less confident Jade felt.

Laura remained silent, obviously aware that her supportive words on Jade's behalf had fallen on deaf ears. She would save her defense for court, if it came to that.

Dr. Nilsen stood in the center of the kitchen and scratched notes on a clipboard. Then she looked up. "And how many bedrooms does the apartment have?"

"Two."

"Shall we have a look?"

*Yes, let's!* Jade wanted to retort in a perky, sarcastic voice, but she knew such sarcasm would count against her. She would do nothing to jeopardize her chance to regain custody of Sabrina. Instead she showed the doctor to the hallway and opened the door to the spare room.

"Sabrina will have this room," Jade said, "until I get my own place."

Dr. Nilsen's head rotated on her thin neck, taking in the queen-size bed, the bureau, and the single nightstand. "It doesn't look like a child's room. And that bed would be unsafe for a two-year-old."

"She'll be buying a youth bed," Laura put in. "In fact, she showed me a set for Sabrina that she fell in love with and ordered. French provincial. Absolutely lovely."

Laura directed a quick warning glance toward Jade. Taking Laura's cue, Jade strolled into the room. "Yes, and as soon as the drapes I've ordered come in, this room will be a vision of pink and white. I found the cutest little sheep curtains and comforter set—you know, like Little Bo Peep."

Dr. Nilsen's penetrating stare bored through her, as if she saw through the fabrications being thrown at her. "All well and good, Miss Brennan. But the fact of the matter is, none of these things are in evidence to be evaluated."

"That's because I've been here less than a week," Jade retorted, losing her patience. "What do you expect?"

Laura stepped between them, smiling gently. "What Janine means to say is that she's made all the necessary arrangements, as much as is humanly possible. And by the time Sabrina gets back from Disneyland, Janine will have this bedroom completely prepared for her."

Dr. Nilsen studied Laura's grave face and then turned her attention to Jade. "You are aware, Miss Brennan, that Sabrina currently has everything a child could possibly need—every advantage, the best care, a beautiful home, two parents, and a sibling. What could you offer to compensate for the loss of such stability?"

"Love," Jade replied vehemently. "I will love her as no other can. I'm her mother!"

"Love may not make up for a lost lifestyle, a lost family."

"That depends upon what kind of family we're talking about," Jade shot back.

Laura held up a placating hand. "What Janine means is that she believes a mother's love is more important than material possessions."

"That's not what I meant at all!" Angry, Jade turned on Laura. "I don't want Gail and Thomas raising my child. *I* wouldn't want to be raised by them! Look at what they've done to their own boy! They're the ones who should be undergoing an evaluation—not me!"

"Jade," Laura admonished, touching her arm and squeezing it lightly in warning. Then she looked back at the psychologist. "She's overwrought. It's understandable for someone who's been through as much as Janine has."

Dr. Nilsen pursed her lips. "Is she taking some kind of medication?"

"I can answer for myself, thank you," Jade replied heatedly. "And no, I'm not taking any drugs. I'm just a little angry, that's all." She turned sharply and fumed out of the guest bedroom, into the hall.

Laura and Dr. Nilsen trailed after her. For a long moment Dr. Nilsen stood in the hallway, writing on her clipboard and shaking her head. Jade watched, her frustration mounting. She had expected this interview would go more smoothly than the first one, but she'd been wrong.

Finally Dr. Nilsen looked up from the form she'd been filling with her flamboyant handwriting, the kind that was illegible to everyone but the writer and a favorite secretary. "And your bedroom?"

"Right here." Jade reached for the door and pushed it open, allowing the other two women to walk in first.

"I beg your pardon!" a male voice thundered from inside her room. The moment Jade heard the familiar Scottish burr, she sprang forward, nearly colliding with Dr. Nilsen's hastily retreating form as she stumbled backward, blushing to the roots of her bouffant hairdo.

Jade choked back her surprise, flabbergasted to see Connor MacKenzie striding toward the door, shirt in hand, barefoot and bare-chested, his blue eyes snapping with displeasure.

"Haven't ye th' courtesy t' knock?" he demanded, zipping his jeans.

"Sir, we're dreadfully sorry," Dr. Nilsen sputtered, immediately losing her haughty poise with one threatening glare of the Scotsman's eyes. "We were just—"

"Didn't ye know I was home, love?" Connor asked, glancing at Jade and interrupting the doctor at the same time, effectively dismissing her blabbering.

"No," she answered, drawing on her considerable stage presence to get through this tense situation. Jade caught Laura staring at her. Only an instant passed before she collected her wits and recognized what Connor MacKenzie had just done for her. He'd destroyed Dr. Nilsen's equanimity. The woman had gone from imperious to apologetic in the space of a few seconds. However, he had also placed Jade in an awkward position. How would she explain the man and his sudden appearance in her life? Casual liaisons with men were prohibited to single mothers and were outside the parameters of Jade's personal values as well.

She sidled up to the Scotsman, hoping no one had noticed his strange golden aura. She had barely discerned it in the dim light of the hallway when she'd stood behind the other women. "When did you get here, Connor?"

"Just after nine." He bent and kissed her briefly on the mouth, a quick peck that should have had no effect upon her. But she felt his touch down to the soles of her feet in a warm, delightful shimmer. "I've missed ye, sweet." He pinched her bottom, and Jade yelped, not having to feign a reaction this time.

She smacked his hand out of the way, and he laughed. "Just stepped out o' th' bath and got caught half-dressed! Took me by surprise, ye did, lassies!"

Dr. Nilsen blushed crimson, whether from embarrassment or at being called a lassie, Jade couldn't guess. Before Dr. Nilsen could form one of her usual judgmental replies, Connor stuck out his hand.

"Connor MacKenzie," he declared.

Dr. Nilsen's hand raised toward his, as if of its own accord, while she stared at him, her lips still parted in shock. Jade watched them, worried that someone might notice the strange gold glow of Connor's skin. But the bright light of morning now streaming through the bedroom window behind him blotted out his unusual aura.

"This is Dr. Nilsen," Jade put in, seeing that the psychologist had gone mute in the presence of Connor's booming voice and dominating presence.

"A pleasure, madame." He raised the doctor's hand and dropped a light kiss on the back of it.

Jade watched the indignation drain from Dr. Nilsen's eyes as Connor gallantly lowered her hand.

"And my attorney, Laura Wettig."

"Ah!" Connor exclaimed. "We meet at last." He raised Laura's hand, apparently expecting to have the same subduing effect on the lawyer.

Laura, however, was her normal skeptical self and was especially suspicious of a man with Connor's charm. She narrowed her eyes. "You expected to meet me, Mr.—Mr.—"

"MacKenzie." He smiled, and his sunny face broke into a score of creases that heightened his charm. "And aye, I expected t' meet ye eventually. Jade's told me about ye many times."

"Has she?" Laura's discerning glance slid from Connor's smile to Jade's artfully bright one as Connor kissed her hand.

Jade nodded, not knowing what words would next tumble from the Scotsman's lips. She marveled at the man's gutsiness and his ability to manipulate a situation to his advantage.

"Aye," Connor continued. "Wanted ye at th' wedding, she did. But time was too short."

"Wedding?" Laura's head whipped around, and she stared at Jade.

"Wedding?" Dr. Nilsen repeated, fumbling with her paperwork and scanning the lines of information. "I thought you told me you were single."

"Well, I—"

"'Tis been a secret," Connor put in, pulling Jade up against the side of his torso and holding her tight with an arm around her shoulders. Something akin to an electric shock ran through her at his touch, but she had no time to think about it. "Jade wanted t' announce it later, when the time was right. But we couldn't wait 'til then. Personal reasons, ye understand."

"Jade?" Laura gasped. "You're not—"

"Pregnant?" Dr. Nilsen finished the sentence as she adjusted her glasses and busily inspected the lines of Jade's figure.

Jade bristled. What had Connor got her into? She'd never extricate herself from this mess, with all the lies he kept spouting, one after the other. She wanted to strangle him, but she couldn't move. His arm had locked around her in a viselike embrace the moment he'd felt her go stiff.

"It's a bit too early to know for sure, Dr. Nilsen, but a good Scotsman can see the signs of a woman breedin'." He patted Jade's tummy.

She wanted to grab his arm and bite through to the bone.

"This does change things," Dr. Nilsen commented, looking Connor up and down. "You say you and Miss Brennan are married?"

"Have been since April."

"Really?" Laura interjected, raising an eyebrow. "Where did you tie the knot?"

"Scotland. Edinburgh, t' be exact. My hometown."

Dr. Nilsen frowned and leveled her gaze on Jade. "Why didn't you tell me all this at our last meeting?"

"Because my sister-in-law was sitting there," Jade replied, having had time to recover from the shock and drawing on years of practice improvising through all kinds of surprises onstage—few of them pleasant. "I told you I wanted the information I relayed to you to be confidential."

"So you made up stories about being a single parent, about the artificial insemination?"

"That part was true. That was before I met Connor." She beamed up at him but all the while planned a painful, excruciating torture for him, to be applied the moment they were alone.

Dr. Nilsen frowned. "But that means we shall have to start over with the paperwork."

"Not all of it." Jade smiled reassuringly at the doctor, amazed that the psychologist seemed to believe Connor's tall tale. "Just a few things. I didn't stretch the truth all that far."

At that moment, the teakettle whistle pierced the air.

"Ah, fetch the ladies some tea, love," Connor suggested. "I'll finish dressin' and join ye in a moment. I'm sure we can help Dr. Nilsen with her forms and such. Does that suit ye, Dr. Nilsen?" He released his grip on Jade.

"Well, I suppose." Dr. Nilsen slipped her clipboard under her arm. "I must say, I don't know what to think. This is all such new information."

"It certainly is," Laura drawled.

"I'll be but a minute." Connor stepped back into the bedroom and closed the door.

Jade linked her arm through Laura's and hurried her toward the kitchen while the teakettle wailed. "I'm sorry, Laura. I wanted to tell you, but we decided it was best to keep it a secret—until Thomas and Gail got used to Connor. They would have been so shocked to know I married suddenly."

"Well, I expect to hear all," she replied. "Including how you two met."

"Of course," she promised.

Laura leaned close to her ear. "I don't know what's going on, Jade, but I'll tell you one thing—that man is a knockout!"

"Don't let his looks fool you," Jade retorted, and then slipped away from her friend to attend to the teakettle. By the time she carried the teapot to the awaiting tray in the living room, she saw Connor fully dressed and striding down the hall toward her. She shot him a meaningful glare that only he could see, but he merely held up his hands and winked. His cocky smile infuriated her. She could still feel the place on her fanny where he'd pinched her and the spot on her tummy where he'd patted her.

Dr. Nilsen sipped her tea and went through her forms again, asking her questions while Laura observed them silently, one slender leg crossed over the other and swinging her foot slowly, like a cat watching a flock of sparrows. Jade knew her friend was bursting with questions and was patiently biding her time until the psychologist left.

Through the doctor's questions, Jade learned that Connor was six feet tall, thirty-five years old, had been born in Scotland, and had lived in the Far East during his childhood. His father had been a Presbyterian missionary, his mother a housewife and poet. After the deaths of his parents from a virulent fever, Connor had emigrated to the United States when he was sixteen, first going to Alaska and then settling in Seattle.

Jade wondered how much of the facts were true and realized Connor let Dr. Nilsen fill in the dates of when these events took place.

"Any siblings?" Dr. Nilsen asked.

"None," Connor replied, and glanced out the window, as if struck by a painful memory. "No relatives a'tall."

"Have you been married before?"

"Nay. 'Tis my first."

"No dependent children?"

"None that I know of." Connor grinned in his winsome fashion and sank onto the arm of the couch next to Jade. "Not that I didn't sow a bit of wild oats in my day."

Dr. Nilsen lowered her chin enough to shoot a reproving glare at him over the tops of her half-glasses. "That seems like a cavalier attitude toward offspring, Mr. MacKenzie. Perhaps you have a problem accepting responsibility?"

"O' course not! I would have been glad t' give my name t' a son o' my loins."

"And had it been a girl?"

"Goes without sayin', madame. What're ye gettin' at?"

"Your comment seemed sexist, Mr. MacKenzie."

"Sexist?" Connor glanced down at Jade, and she could see the shadow of confusion in his eyes.

"He says things to shock people," Jade put in, guessing that Connor didn't recognize the modern word. "But in his heart he's a pussycat, and has a special way with children. He'll be a great father to Sabrina. Really."

Connor leaned toward the doctor and, in doing so, put his hand on Jade's shoulder. She stifled a yelp at his touch. Was it just her, or did others experience a zap when he made contact with them? Neither Dr. Nilsen nor Laura had reacted adversely to his touch when he'd taken their hands.

"I meant no harm, madame," Connor declared. "I made that comment because I'd like a son t' carry on my name. The Connor MacKenzie name could easily die out, ye see, as I'm the only MacKenzie left o' my family. And there's been some close calls, ye understand."

He squeezed Jade's shoulder, and Jade fought back a flush at his silent reference to the secret they shared about his death in the fire.

"I suppose I jumped to a conclusion." Dr. Nilsen

crossed through figures she had penned in a few days ago. "Now then. We need to know something of your employment history, Mr. MacKenzie. What do you do for a living?"

"Investments, mostly."

"You live off the interest?"

"Ye might say that."

"And what would your yearly income from that be, Mr. MacKenzie?"

Connor shifted and Jade glanced at him, worrying that he would never be able to support his facts. Once a judge discovered the lies on the forms, he would throw out her bid for custody without blinking an eye. "Two hundred thousand, give or take a bit."

Dr. Nilsen nodded and wrote down the figure.

"And references?"

"I can draw up a list, if need be, and send it by post."

"That would be fine." She reached into her briefcase and pulled out a business card. "My office address is on that card. I'll need at least three people who know you well, and who are not relatives."

Connor nodded. Sick at heart, Jade watched him slip the card into his chest pocket. Where would Connor MacKenzie, resurrected charlatan from the 1880s, find anyone who knew him, much less would vouch for his character? References would be the breaking point for them, and if not the references, his financial history would clinch a victory for Thomas and Gail. Surely Thomas's lawyers would run a credit report on Connor and learn the truth—that he had no money and no credit history. Jade doubted Connor even had a Social Security card.

To Jade's surprise, Dr. Nilsen seemed to accept him. Connor had charmed her from the very first moment, pulling his own brand of Gaelic wool over her eyes from which she'd never emerged. She'd even smiled once or twice at him as she'd recorded his comments.

"Well," Dr. Nilsen declared, lacing her fingers together on her clipboard and glancing up at them, "I have to say this interview has been encouraging. Very encouraging. After we verify the information on these forms, perhaps a visit with the child can be arranged."

Jade's hopes soared. "When?" she exclaimed.

"At the end of the week, if all goes well."

"Oh, that's wonderful!" Jade beamed, unable to contain her happiness.

"However, I must remind you, Miss Bren— uh, Mrs. MacKenzie, that your relationship to the child must be withheld at that time. It is imperative that the best interests of the child be upheld during this custody dispute."

"Of course!"

"Until it is decided who will be the custodial parents, we cannot inform the child of your biological connection to her. Such information would be very confusing to a two-year-old."

"I understand."

"I shall also be here during the visit to observe how the child interacts with you and Mr. MacKenzie, and to ensure proper procedure is followed."

Jade hadn't considered the fact that she might have to share her first moments with Sabrina with strangers. Disappointment leeched into her joy. "You'll be here?" she questioned, her voice catching.

"Of course. The child's welfare must be protected. That is my entire focus."

Connor rose. "And we're glad of it, Doctor." He extended his hand, and Dr. Nilsen got to her feet. "Thank you for comin'."

"My pleasure." Dr. Nilsen smiled when she shook his hand. "And my apologies for walking in on you, Mr. MacKenzie."

"'Tis forgiven and forgotten, madame."

"You may call the office Thursday morning to see how the paperwork is progressing."

Connor nodded while Jade stood up, amazed by Connor's easy manner with the psychologist. She stepped away from the couch, intending to show Dr. Nilsen to the door, but Connor assumed the courtesy himself. Feeling usurped, Jade trailed after him and stood at his side as they bade good-bye to the doctor. Once again, Connor made physical contact with her, this time laying his hand on her back, his thumb upon her collarbone and his long fingers following the curved column of her neck. His touch was heavy and foreign and sent a jolt up and down her spine. She steeled herself against the shock so she wouldn't jerk away and cause Dr. Nilsen to notice her strange reaction to her alleged husband.

But as soon as Connor shut the door, Jade jerked away from him and stormed to the window, each step plunging her deeper into anger.

Furious, she turned, crossed her arms over her chest, and leveled her eyes upon his.

"You've got some explaining to do, mister." Her words hissed through teeth gritted against barely suppressed rage. "I suggest you start. *Now*."

# 7

*Connor stared back* without a hint of chagrin or remorse in his expression, as though he felt fully justified in the false life he'd created for Jade.

"I heard what ye said about Thomas and Gail Brennan raisin' your child," he began. "I thought to help ye."

"Help me?" she echoed, seething. "Help me?" She took a step toward him. "You've ruined it for me, that's what you've done!"

"How's that?"

"All those lies you told." She waved a hand through the air. "It's not like the old days, when you could kill a man, leave town, and start over, and your past would never catch up with you."

"What're ye sayin'?"

"I'm saying that each piece of information you told Dr. Nilsen just now will be checked and verified. There are ways of doing that now—almost instantly. And when they find out that you lied about everything—Sabrina will be lost to me forever." She choked back the lump in her throat. "You thought you were helping me? Well, thanks for nothing!"

Connor blinked, taken aback.

"Wait a minute," Laura interjected, holding up her hands in an effort to keep the peace. "I'm not understanding all of this. In what way did Mr. MacKenzie lie?"

"In all ways," Jade retorted. "Everything he said was a big fib."

"'Twas not," Connor protested. "I'm a Scotsman through an' through."

"Yes, and that's about it!"

"I stretched th' truth in only one particular area."

"And forced me to go along with it in order not to lose all credibility. You never even asked if it was all right with me!"

"'Twas no time for askin'! I did what I thought best."

"Well, it wasn't your place! Your lying has ruined everything!"

"Enough, you two," Laura shouted, demanding their attention. They broke off their heated bickering and stared at her. She cocked her head and glanced at them in turn. "This would be amusing, watching you two fight like little kids, if there weren't so much at stake."

"I know," Jade said, fuming. "That's why I'm so angry!"

"I meant t' help ye!" Connor threw up a hand, exasperated. "That woman had ye on th' run, lass. I could hear it. I thought only t' help."

"I didn't need your help—especially when it included lying."

"I won ye th' chance t' see Sabrina, didn't I?"

"No, you didn't. When they find out we aren't even married, I'll never get to see her!"

"So you *aren't* married," Laura stated, pausing for confirmation.

"Of course not!" Jade glared at Connor. "Do you think I'd marry a guy who pinches women on the ass?"

"Ye liked it," he shot back, his blue eyes burning holes in her indignation. For a moment their gazes locked and held, and she experienced the same warm shimmer that his kiss had produced in her. Flustered and angry with herself at her reaction, as well as with Connor for getting her in this predicament, she turned her back to him and glared out the bay window.

"But why did you pretend to be Jade's husband?" Laura asked.

"I owed her a favor." Connor lowered his voice to a soft, velvety baritone. 'Tis only temporary, Jade— nothin' t' get in a tizzy about. Ye dinna have t' share a bed with me, for God's sake."

Jade raised her chin and clenched her teeth. She was beyond outrage, beyond logic. All she wanted was for Connor MacKenzie to clear out of her life, to start over with Dr. Nilsen, and to take a different tack with Thomas and Gail. But that was impossible now. She'd bumbled the first meeting, and now Connor had torpedoed this last one.

"Actually," Laura put in, "this marriage thing might not be such a bad idea."

Jade couldn't believe what she had just heard. "What do you mean?"

"Look at how Dr. Nilsen responded when she learned you were married."

"That's what burns me up!" Jade whirled to face her friend. "Why do I have to have a husband before I can be trusted to raise a child? And it doesn't matter what type of person he is, just as long as he's a damn man!"

Laura shook her head. "Jade, you've every right to be upset. But—"

"It's the principle of it!"

"I realize that, but—"

"Ye're dealing with the Brennans," Connor warned. "Remember, there's the long clean road and th' short dirty road. Th' Brennans always take th' shortcut."

"I'm a Brennan, too, MacKenzie," she retorted. "Or have you forgotten?"

Laura touched her arm. "I think what he's saying is that we're going to have to fight fire with fire. Thomas and Gail will do anything to retain custody. Anything, Jade."

"So you're advising me to go along with this ruse?" Jade pulled away her arm. "To lie? I can't believe you're saying this!"

"The principle you're struggling to uphold doesn't matter, Jade. Thomas and Gail don't really care if you're competent or not, or whether you're honest and fair. Character defamation is merely the method of choice to get rid of you. All they want is Sabrina. They want to win. One way or another."

"Without a care t' what's right or wrong," Connor put in. "In true Brennan style."

"You know, MacKenzie," Jade said through her teeth and without turning his way, "I don't need a constant critical review of my relatives!"

"But he's right, in a way." Laura nodded toward him. "You're going to have to bend the truth to get Sabrina."

"No." Jade crossed her arms over her chest, feeling betrayed by her friend and manipulated by Connor. "It isn't the way I do things."

"You're confusing two issues here, Jade. This isn't about proving your character. This is about getting your daughter back."

"It's the same thing, as far as I see it."

"No, it isn't." Laura sat upon the arm of the couch. "You know very well that you're able to raise your daughter. You don't have to prove it in court. You just have to get custody. That's our primary goal."

Jade stared at her friend, struggling with her innate sense of honesty and Laura's irrefutable logic but unable to admit to Laura that she *did* doubt her child-rearing abilities. She'd never raised a child and had never been around children. She trusted that once she was with Sabrina, her love for her daughter and her maternal instincts would carry her through, but she had yet to prove such a theory.

"I say this strictly off the record and only as a friend, Jade, but a marriage of convenience to this gentleman"—Laura motioned toward Connor, who stood near her side—"whoever he is, will help you win."

"But it's a lie!"

"It doesn't have to be."

"There is no legal document!"

"Herman Fong can get one," Connor interjected. "From what I can tell, he's got an amazin' network of acquaintances."

"That would involve forgery!"

Laura leaned forward. "If you marry Connor here in the States as soon as possible, a Scottish marriage certificate would only be a minor detail that no one will bother about. Thomas and Gail won't have a chance in hell of discrediting a genuine American document."

Jade stared at Connor and then glanced at Laura. "Are you suggesting that I actually marry this guy?"

"As your friend, yes. If he'll agree. He says he owes you a favor." Laura looked up at Connor. "What about it, Mr. MacKenzie?"

Connor narrowed his eyes and studied Jade for a long moment. "I never expected it t' go this far."

"Then you won't do this for her?"

"Marriage is a serious business, Laura darlin'."

"I can draw up prenups for you both, if that's what you're concerned about."

"What are prenups?"

Laura glanced at him in surprise, expecting him to know such a common term. "You know—prenuptial agreements. To protect individual property so it doesn't become community property through marriage."

"I'm not sure about this—" Connor rubbed his chin. "Actual vows and such with a Brennan—"

"I could write up explicit contracts between you two, stating the parameters of your marriage—no physical contact and that kind of thing. But if the Brennans' lawyers got their hands on the documents, you might have trouble convincing a judge that you are truly man and wife."

"I don't like it." Jade limped to the table and sank upon the couch. She poured a cup of tea, lifting it with hands she had to concentrate upon to keep from trembling.

"It's your only chance, Jade," Laura said. "After what you two told Dr. Nilsen today, I believe it's your only recourse."

Jade sat back, staring into the amber liquid in the porcelain cup, feeling forced into a corner with no way out—all because of Connor MacKenzie. She heard the rustle of the lining of Laura's navy suit.

"What do you say, Mr. MacKenzie?" Laura asked.

"Depends upon what's involved from here on out," he replied.

"You'll have to establish residence here at the apartment.

You'll have to make it appear that you sleep in the same room. You'll have to be demonstrative in public, and make sure people see you kissing and hugging."

Jade's heartbeat increased at the prospect of kissing Connor and at the mere thought of him in her bed. His effect upon her disturbed her. If he agreed to this idiotic plan, she'd have to make it clear that her body was off limits to him privately, no matter how they behaved toward each other in public.

"You'll have to acquire a marriage license immediately, and get married as soon as possible," Laura continued. "And when you meet Sabrina, Mr. MacKenzie, you must treat her as if she were your daughter, and really mean it."

"Not a problem." Connor smiled warmly. "Wee ones always had a special place in my heart."

"Oh?" Jade glared at him. "Then why didn't you ever have a family?"

"I liked variety too much to settle for just one lass," he replied, raking her with his eyes. "What about you? What's your excuse for bein' a spinster?"

Jade flushed at the old-fashioned term with its negative connotation. "I never met a man I could stand for very long."

"Or couldn't find a man t' abide your temper, more like."

"I don't have a temper, MacKenzie."

"And pigs fly!"

"You just have a knack for making me angry." Jade put down her cup with a clatter. "Deciding things for me, never asking how I feel about it, sticking your big nose into my affairs!"

"Well, ye know what they say about th' size of a man's nose. . . ." Connor winked at her.

"Jerk!" Jade jumped to her feet. "You chauvinistic, egotistical jerk! If you think I'd spend one minute married to you or allow you to live here with my daughter, you must have rocks in your head!" She fled from the living room, holding back tears of frustration, certain her life with Sabrina had ended before it had ever begun.

Stinging from Jade's words, Connor watched her run to her room.

"I've never seen Jade so distraught," Laura commented as she stepped up behind him. "If this continues, she'll make it hard for herself in court, should this get that far. Judges don't favor parents with anger-management problems."

Connor looked down at the slender woman near his elbow. "Wouldn't you be a bit frustrated if you were kept from seein' your only bairn?"

Laura sighed. "I suppose I would be."

"'Tis natural for a female to be angry when separated from her young."

"True, but this goes beyond Sabrina. You shouldn't have intervened, Mr. MacKenzie. You didn't do her any favors, you know."

Connor nodded and ambled toward the window, unsure what step to take next. He felt oddly disappointed in having been rejected by Jade and in being labeled egotistical and chauvinistic. He had no idea what the word "chauvinistic" meant, but the way Jade had spat it at him, he guessed it was a derogatory description of his character.

Ordinarily he didn't care what people thought of him and behaved accordingly, using his own sense of justice and decency as a yardstick. But with Jade—and a

Brennan, of all people—he suddenly cared how his character was perceived. Where did she get the idea that he was dishonest and immoral? From her great-grandfather Asahel Brennan? Now *there* was a fountain of truth and integrity!

He put his hand on the familiar woodwork of the bay window and gazed out at the unfamiliar cityscape, not really seeing the hustle and bustle below. For the most part, those people who had judged his qualities in the past—especially women—hadn't found him lacking. He'd been invited to countless social functions, had numerous debutantes and widows shoved in his path, and had never got the impression that others considered him a beast. In fact, most women considered him downright attractive. They'd told him so.

It bothered Connor that Jade thought he was unsavory, that she considered him too horrible to marry, and that she turned rigid at his touch. She even found his wink disgusting. He wasn't accustomed to such reactions. Had women changed so much over the course of a century that they found his type of charm passé—even off-putting?

It couldn't be true. Dr. Nilsen had nearly swooned when he'd kissed her hand. And reserved Laura Wettig had warmed up to him, once she'd had a chance to get over her initial surprise regarding the secret marriage. She had even taken his side. His charm hadn't failed him. Jade was just impervious to it. Unreceptive. She'd come round after a while, once she got past her preconceived notions regarding his character.

The trouble was, if Jade found out why he'd been in her apartment and why he'd offered to marry her, she would call him a conniving bastard, and she'd be right. He hadn't offered himself up to the altar of marriage because of a chivalrous desire to help a woman in distress. He'd been caught in Jade's bedroom, didn't want anyone to know why he'd been there, and had seen no other avenue of escape but to lie through his teeth— even if it involved claiming to be her husband.

He had assumed his lie would be innocent and short-lived. Now, he could see that the ruse might have more long-range ramifications than he ever intended.

"So, Mr. MacKenzie," Laura said behind him as she poured a cup of tea. He heard the rattle of a spoon on the saucer. "What's it going to be?"

"Ye mean with Jade?" Connor turned to face her.

"Yes. I'm not just her attorney, you know, I'm her friend. I care what happens to her. And what doesn't."

"Understandable."

"So what do you intend to do?" Laura took a sip of tea while Connor observed her. Both Jade and Laura were outspoken women, and he liked that in females. But while Jade was fiery and passionate, Laura was direct and businesslike, driven more by logic than emotion. Both were slender women with fine figures and attractive faces. But Jade's willowy body had a lithesome grace to it, where Laura's slight frame was an angular concoction of nerves and intensity. Laura was the type of woman who never stopped moving from dawn to dusk, never let herself relax and enjoy the pleasures of life, the kind of woman who drove herself even harder than she drove the people around her.

"About marryin' her?" Connor asked, knowing very well Laura Wettig would badger him until he gave her an answer.

"Exactly. I don't know what Jade did for you. That's none of my business. But I do know Jade's the kind of person who would give you the shirt off her back, no questions asked." She placed the teacup neatly in the saucer she held in front of her. "You said you owed her. And after the stuff you pulled with Dr. Nilsen, you'd better make good on it."

"Is that a threat I'm hearin', Laura love?"

"Let me put it this way, Connor my dear," Laura replied, looking directly at him over her primly held cup. "If what you told Dr. Nilsen imperils Jade's custody suit, I'll have her sue you for every penny you've got."

"Ye will, will ye?"

"And the facts you told Dr. Nilsen had better be the truth."

"'Twas. All except the part about Jade and me."

"You have investments?"

"Aye."

"Documents to prove it?"

Connor ran a hand through his hair. "I can get them."

"How about your U.S. citizenship? Are you a citizen?"

"Aye." He snatched a cookie from the tray and looked at the plain white biscuit, while he added under his breath, "And longer than ye think."

"Then do her the kindness to marry her, just until custody is decided."

"'Tisn't up t' me, Laura. Ye heard Jade just now. She'd rather crawl naked t' hell than become my bride."

"Leave it to me." Laura placed her cup and saucer on the tray and straightened. "After I talk to Jade, we'll all go down to the courthouse and get a marriage license."

"Aye-aye, Cap'n." He gave her a mock salute.

"And if all goes well, by the time Sabrina returns from Disneyland, she'll have a new father."

Connor nodded but felt his grin slipping. Tricking the authorities was one thing. Fooling with the trusting hearts of children was quite another kettle of fish.

Jade heard a soft rap on her door.

"It's me," Laura called. "May I come in?"

"Yes." Jade sat up and dropped her feet over the side of the bed while Laura pushed open the door and walked briskly toward her. She sank beside Jade and leaned back on the heels of her hands.

"He's quite a character," Laura commented, looking up at the ceiling.

"He's a jerk."

"He's your only chance." Laura's voice was quiet but adamant, the voice she used when she was convinced of a truth.

Jade looked over at her friend, and Laura's somber eyes met hers. "Are you serious, Laura?"

"I've never been more serious. You must marry him."

"But he doesn't want to."

"He's agreed to go through with it. We can get the license today."

"Don't we need birth certificates and stuff?"

Laura shook her head. "Not in the state of Washington. Not if you're over eighteen."

"What if he holds me to it—the marriage, I mean?"

"It doesn't appear either of you intends the marriage to be binding. And after you gain custody, you can file for a quiet little divorce."

"Speaking strictly as my friend," Jade remarked. "And not as my attorney, right?"

"Right." Laura patted her hand and rose. "Let's get the paperwork out of the way. And then you can buy me some lunch, okay?"

"With the fees you charge, you should be buying *me* lunch!"

Laura only laughed and waved her off as she walked out of the bedroom and shut the door.

Jade rose from her bed and trudged to her closet. What did a woman wear to the courthouse when she'd decided to marry a man she despised. Black?

# 8

*Early that evening,* Jade returned to her apartment, completely exhausted, her leg aching. For someone who had spent the last two years in a hospital and rehabilitation center, she'd had a long day: first undergoing Dr. Nilsen's inspection, then arguing with Connor, taking Laura to lunch and struggling to make up a credible story about Connor's past without telling the impossible truth about his time traveling, and then driving through rush-hour traffic to and from Sea-Tac Airport. Another such day and she'd lose all the progress she'd made in her recuperation process.

Laura planned to return early Thursday, and Jade couldn't wait until she came back. Having an ally like Laura had given her considerable hope for the future.

If she hadn't been so tired and preoccupied, Jade would have noticed the smell of yeast dough floating on the air, but not until she turned the key in the lock did she realize someone was cooking food in her apartment.

She pushed open the door, shocked to see Connor sitting on the couch, bent over documents piled on the coffee table. He glanced up just as Jade directed her gaze toward the kitchen, where she could see Herman Fong chopping mounds of fresh vegetables on a cutting board he'd put on the island between the kitchen and the dining room.

"Well, make yourselves at home, boys," she remarked, closing the door.

"Ah, good evening, Miss Brennan," Herman greeted her with a cheerful smile, stopping for a moment with his knife poised above a bunch of bok choy, the tip wavering in his trembling grip.

"Mr. Fong, what are you doing here?"

"Mr. MacKenzie needed some papers, which were in my possession."

"And the food?" She swept the air with her hand in the direction of the chopped vegetables.

"For you, Miss Brennan, I am preparing my special hum bao!"

"Laura told us to make it look like I live here," Connor remarked, coming up behind her. "So that's what I've set about doin'."

"Without telling me?"

"Hard to do, lass, when ye stay away th' entire day."

Jade sighed and slipped her purse strap off her shoulder. "We're going to have to talk about this, Connor."

"At dinner," Herman suggested. "Meanwhile, you drink something I made for you, Miss Brennan, and try to relax." He reached into the refrigerator and retrieved a glass filled with a frothy white mixture. He held it out to her.

"What is it?" Jade eyed the concoction with suspicion.

"Special drink. Cucumbers, milk, and ice. To refresh

you." He offered it again, insisting that she take it. "Such a busy day is bad for the nerves."

Jade regarded him carefully, unused to being taken care of like this and not entirely trusting such a gesture. "All right." She reached for the cold glass. "Thanks."

Then she turned to Connor and pointed the rim of the glass at his chest. "You've got some explaining to do still," she remarked. "And some ground rules to learn."

He crossed his arms and leveled his warm gaze at her. "Are ye always this hard, Jade?" His eyes swept over her face and into her hair. "Do ye never let up?"

"Not when people barge into my life and my house unannounced. You act like you own the place."

He raised an eyebrow. "I do, in a manner o' speakin'."

"That's up for debate."

"Everything's up for debate with you, Jade, or haven't ye noticed?"

Jade paused, suddenly struck by the fact that what he'd said might be true, but she'd never admit it to him. "Well, I don't need another debate right now," she declared, and headed for her room.

Once in the master bedroom, she took an agitated gulp of the drink and was amazed at the sensation created by the frothy liquid. Her heated words with Connor, which had lodged in her throat in a hot lump, melted away. She took another sip, and the tension in her shoulders eased. Jade held the glass up to the light of the window and for a moment contemplated the opaque white drink, wondering what secret ingredient Herman Fong had put in his cucumber cocktail. Whatever the drink was made of, it had indeed refreshed her, just as he had said it would.

She carried the glass into the bathroom and drew a tub of water. As she sank into the warm bath, she reached for the cucumber drink. Then she sat back, letting the cares of the day fade in the steam that rose above the tub. Jade closed her eyes and for a moment felt a sliver of peace.

Twenty minutes later, when Jade next approached the kitchen, she was in a much better mood. She set the table while Herman quickly stir-fried lettuce and garlic and then called Connor to eat. The Scotsman ambled toward the table, an annual report of the Seattle Light Company in his hand, and pulled out a chair without glancing up from the booklet. He paused until Jade sat down, then seated himself and turned a page, his brows knitted together in concentration.

"Seems the company has done well with all that electricity," he commented.

Herman Fong bobbed his head as he scooped stir-fried lettuce onto Connor's plate. "The other stocks have done well also. You could live comfortably."

Connor glanced up. "I'm not a man to settle for comfortable, Herman."

Herman grinned, his round cheeks turning into shining plums. "Of course not, Mr. MacKenzie."

Jade watched them, puzzled by the turn in the conversation. Herman paused at her elbow. "Salad?" he asked, tipping the small wok toward her plate.

"Why not?" she replied, uncertain if she'd like lightly cooked lettuce. He slipped a small pile onto her dish. "Thank you."

After he had served them, Herman returned to the table and sat down.

"What is all that stuff?" Jade asked, nodding toward the pile of papers on the coffee table.

"Stock reports, account balances, things o' that nature,"

Connor replied. Using chopsticks, he scooped a pile of kung pao chicken into his mouth.

"Do you mean to tell me you do have investments?"

"I said as much, didn't I?"

"But how is it possible?" She chewed the lettuce, which had a surprisingly succulent garlic flavor. "You've been out of commission for a hundred years."

"Oh, but Mr. MacKenzie had many friends in the Chinese community," Herman put in. "They have looked after his investments."

"For a hundred years?"

Herman nodded.

"Why—when he was supposedly dead?"

"There was no body to prove he was dead. And many believed that he would return, that he was special."

"What do you mean—special?" Jade glanced at Connor and then back at Herman, perplexed by information that conflicted with the stories told by her family. She reached for a hum bao.

"Mr. MacKenzie was called the Lion by the Chinese. My people considered him more than a man. Especially the Chin family, of which I am a member."

"The Chins were like my own family," Connor remarked. "I would have done anything for them." He glanced down at his food.

"Indeed, that is an understatement, Mr. MacKenzie," Herman commented. Then he turned back to Jade. "Mr. MacKenzie made it possible for many Chinese to come to America. He smuggled them over the Canadian border when the immigration laws discriminated against them, got them papers, gave them a start, and stood up for them. It would be impossible to count how many lives he saved in the old days. Overseeing his investments was but a small gesture of gratitude."

Jade glanced at Connor, amazed to hear positive things about a man whose character had been maligned by her family.

"You mean to tell me that Connor still owns stock in companies from the turn of the century?"

"And more." Herman nodded. "It was difficult to arrange at first, but the Chins managed to submit all the proper documents over the years. This Connor MacKenzie is the great-great-grandson of himself!"

"Aye." Connor winked. "A bonny name t' carry down through th' years, I'll have ye know."

Jade rolled her eyes and took a bite of her hum bao. The savory filling melted in her mouth.

"So dinna fret about Dr. Nilsen, Jade," Connor continued. "We'll give her a run for th' money."

"Unless she gets suspicious about so many Connor MacKenzies and finds out they exist only on paper."

"'Twill be enough." Connor finished his chicken dish and reached for another hum bao. He was amazingly facile with chopsticks.

"Still . . ." Jade's voice trailed off.

"Marryin' me willna be a complete disaster, Jade." He took a bite and continued to study her. "Ye dinna have to drag your feet so."

"I worry, that's all."

"Aye. And you'll be an old hag before your time if ye keep it up." He flicked her chin with his finger. "There now, a smile wouldn't hurt ye!"

She jerked away. "That brings us to another subject, Mr. MacKenzie." She dabbed her face with her napkin, blotting out the touch of his hand. "We are only pretending to be married. When we're alone, I don't want you touching me. Do you understand?"

"But I'm a demonstrative sort," he countered.

"I don't care what sort you are." Jade propped her wrist on the edge of the table. "When we're alone, it's hands off!"

"All right." He sighed. "But 'twill be damned unnatural."

"This whole situation is damned unnatural."

He sat back in his chair and studied her, his navy blue eyes glinting with humor. "Ye take the fun out o' things, Jade. Here we are, a fine specimen of manhood like myself, and you, a bonny lass, and ye're saying ye won't even kiss me—just for fun?"

"I don't kiss people just for fun."

"Ye dinna flirt, ye dinna laugh, and ye dinna smile." He shook his head. "How dreary life must be for a serious old woman like you."

"I'm not old."

"Ye act like my grandmother. A saint, t' be sure, but as straitlaced as they came."

"I'm not straitlaced. When I meet a man who interests me, I'm perfectly willing to be romantic."

He cocked his head. "An' when was th' last time ye were?"

"As if it's any of your business!"

"I should know about your past, Jade, should Dr. Nilsen inquire."

"If she wants a list of the men in my life, you just send her to me."

"A short list, I'll wager."

"So?" She jumped to her feet. "Better short than an endless string of half-remembered bawdy-house whores!"

"Bawdy house?" Connor leaped up, too, and glared at her.

"You're a womanizer!"

"Says who?"

"I do. And it's true, isn't it? I wouldn't let you touch me if you paid me!"

"Good," he countered. "Because I never had to buy a woman's affection, an' I dinna intend t' start paying with you!"

"Fine. You're never going to get my affection anyway!" Jade broke away from him and stormed to the keyboard. There, she pulled the headphones over her ears and plopped onto the stool, determined to blot out Connor MacKenzie by ignoring the sight and sound of him. She attacked the piano with a series of warm-up scales, ruthlessly running through the exercises she'd memorized as a child, until her mind was clear and Connor and Herman were long gone.

That night Jade tossed in her bed, dreaming of a waterfall. She stood at the base of the cascade and watched a little girl playing on the rocks high above. Suddenly the toddler slipped and plummeted over the cliff, screaming.

Jade jerked awake, her heart pounding furiously, aware of the sound of water still running, even though she'd left her nightmare behind. She ran a hand through her hair, which was damp with sweat, and lay back down, surmising that Connor must be using the bathroom at the end of the hall.

Then something cold and wet plopped on her cheek.

Jade lurched up to a sitting position again and stared at the ceiling, but she could see nothing in the gloom. While she stared, she felt another drop splatter upon her forehead. Alarmed, she dashed it away and scrambled out of bed. Someone in the condo above her must have left their water running so long that it had soaked through the floorboards and saturated the ceiling. She raced across the floor to the bureau where she'd left her cellular phone recharging and reached for it to call Phillip. He'd know what to do. But as she picked up her phone, she noticed a peculiar sheen on the wall behind the bureau.

The wall, which in the daylight was flat and painted off white, appeared to be dark and covered with a textured pattern of interlocking ovals, much like graceful fish scales. As she stood there, studying it, she realized a sheet of water was running over the dark textured shapes, glinting in the darkness. Disbelieving her own eyes, Jade stuck out her right hand and touched her index finger to the wall. A cold rivulet raced around her fingertip and over her nail.

With a gasp of astonishment, she retracted her hand and peered at the floor, where her bare feet sank into the plush beige carpeting. How could so much water run down the wall without pooling on the floor? She felt the carpeting at the baseboard near the dresser, expecting it to be soaked with water. The rug was bone dry.

Jade stumbled backward, knowing she wasn't dreaming but wishing she *were,* so she could explain what was happening. Surely her injured brain couldn't make up something as preposterous as this weeping wall. Yet what other explanation was there? She edged toward the door, her heart beating in fear, afraid to turn her back on the strange wall. She fumbled for the doorknob behind her, pulled open the door, and dashed into the hall. There in the darkness, she lifted the cellular phone, holding it in front of her face so she could see the numbers. Then she started to dial the penthouse, but her hands were shaking so much that she had to start over.

"Damn!" she exclaimed.

Before she could dial the number again, she heard Connor call out.

"Jade?"

Inordinately relieved to hear his voice, she glanced down the hall toward the living room, where he must have decided to spend the night on the couch. His burnished hair glowed in the darkness that surrounded the sofa. "Connor?"

"What're ye doin', lass?" he asked. "'Tis th' middle o' th' night!"

"Connor, come here!" She motioned with the phone. "There's something going on in my bedroom!"

She heard the jingle of his belt as he pulled on his jeans, and then he walked briskly toward her, shoeless and shirtless, with his eyes full of questions, his strange gold-flecked skin glowing in the darkness.

"What is it?" he asked.

"In there." Jade pointed toward her bedroom.

He grinned, his sleepy face still handsome and glowing, even in the dim light. "'Tis a novel way o' gettin' me in your bed, Jade. And a surprise, too."

"Keep dreaming, MacKenzie." She pushed open the door and flipped on the light.

"Och, lass," he sputtered, squinting. "Ye blinded me!"

"Sorry." She pointed the phone toward the weeping wall, which showed red in the light. "Look at the wall behind the bureau."

She remained in back of him, not ashamed to admit to herself that she was using his large frame as a shield, and ignored the way his energy made the hair rise on her scalp and torso. He walked to the bureau and paused for a moment.

"This wall—wasn't it white before?" He dipped for a closer look and then straightened.

"Yes, and now it's textured and running with water. See?" She glanced around his shoulder.

He reached out. "Saints!" he gasped, tentatively touching the veil of water. Then his finger passed through the cascade, and his right hand went through the wall up to his forearm, as if no physical barrier existed behind the stream.

"Connor!" Jade cried, grabbing his left elbow.

He pulled back and shook his arm while he stared at it, incredulous.

"I couldn't feel th' wall," he declared. "Just th' water, then nothin' but air!"

"Nothing?" She studied the glinting wall, trying to see through the water, but without success. Then she snatched a pen she'd left on the dresser and poked it through the water. It struck solid wall. Jade moved to the right, poking the pen at the exact place Connor had touched, but the pen hit a hard surface again.

"There's a wall behind here," she said. "Rock solid."

"Strange," Connor replied. "Let me try again." He reached out a second time and easily passed his hand through the wall, up to his wrist.

"Don't do that!" she screeched. "It scares me!"

He smiled down at her. "'Twas only testin' a theory, Jade."

"What theory? That you can do something I can't?"

"That this wall is related t' somethin' or someone a hundred years old, and doesn't work th' same for a modern person like yourself."

"What are you talking about?" She dropped the pen on the bureau and stepped farther away from the strange wall of water, reluctant to remain near it.

"See the pattern on th' wall, those interlockin' oval shapes?" he asked.

"Yes."

"That's th' pattern o' wallpaper hung here a hundred years ago. Flocked wallpaper, as a matter o' fact."

Then, as quickly as the water had begun to flow, it ceased, leaving the light, smooth, modern wall in view. Jade stared, unable to believe her own eyes. If Connor hadn't seen the wallpaper and the water, she would have blamed the vision on her head injury and left it at that. But Connor didn't suffer from brain damage, and he'd seen everything, too. So what was going on?

"It's gone," she whispered.

Connor shook his head and studied the wall. "'Twas like a door," he murmured. "Leadin' to another world. But what kind o' world?"

A shiver coursed through Jade, and she shuddered. "I hope we never find out."

"'Tis somethin' t' do with th' past, I'll wager."

"And something to do with you, maybe?" Jade stared at the wall as Connor ambled over to the window beside the bed and drew back the drape. She turned to watch him, wondering why he wasn't saying anything. Unease descended upon her.

"This was Qi An's room," Connor commented at last, his voice more hushed than usual.

Jade looked more closely at him. "Who?"

"Qi An Chin. Sam Lo's daughter."

"Oh." She noticed the serious expression on Connor's face and wondered how deep their connection had been. "She was the one who put you in the box downstairs."

"She was?"

"That's what Herman said."

Connor nodded thoughtfully. "Makes sense." Then he gazed at the wall again, his eyes looking past it. "Qi An had flocked paper on her walls," he continued. "Deep red. I had to special order it from Hong Kong."

Jade shuddered involuntarily again. "I was told this unit was haunted, but I never dreamed the rumor might be true." She hugged her arms and clenched her teeth together to keep them from chattering. "Not even when the incident in the bathroom happened."

He let the drape fall and turned to face her. "What happened in the bath?"

"A couple of nights ago, the tub in the bathroom down the hall started to fill all by itself."

Connor regarded her, his eyebrows pulled together in concern. "Water again," he murmured.

"And when I looked around, I found writing on the mirror."

"What kind o' writin'?"

"Chinese, I think."

"What did it say?"

"I don't know." She shrugged. "I don't know Mandarin or whatever."

"Could ye draw what ye saw?"

"I'm not sure I would remember it very well."

"It might be a clue t' what's goin' on here."

"I don't know . . ." Her voice trailed off.

"Well, I know one thing. You're as pale as a sheet." He reached for her elbow. "Let's get ye out o' here, lass."

She didn't protest as he guided her toward the door.

"Ye need a stiff drink." He led her to the living room, his hand lightly cupping her elbow. "Then ye can take a crack at drawin' what ye saw in Chinese."

"Okay."

He deposited her at the couch and headed for the kitchen. She was still shaking when he put a tumbler of amber-colored liquid in her stiff hands.

"Drink it up, Jade. Ye'll feel better."

"I should only drink a little. What is it?"

"Whiskey and soda."

She sniffed the mixture. "It smells horrible."

He took the glass from her and sampled the drink, to prove it was palatable. "'Tis fine. Go ahead." He sat beside her and pulled a piece of paper off one of the piles stacked on the coffee table.

She sipped the drink.

"No, lass. Drink it down. All of it."

"I hate the taste."

"It'll settle your nerves." He nodded at the glass. "Go on, now."

She glanced into his eyes, wondering why he showed such concern for her state of mind, and expected to find anything but the solicitous gleam that turned his intense gaze from blue to indigo. He continued to survey her, waiting for her to follow his instructions.

She tipped up the glass, held her breath, and swallowed the drink until the tumbler was empty.

"There!" She grimaced, hoping she could keep the whiskey down as she held out the glass.

"Good lass." He took the tumbler and set it aside. "That'll warm your cockles a wee bit."

"My cockles?" She smirked at him.

He grinned. "'Tis just an expression."

"I already feel it in my stomach. Like fire."

"'Twill be fine in a moment. You'll see."

She took a deep breath and nodded, then caught him smiling at her, his eyes twinkling in a genuinely friendly manner. Suddenly she became aware of the long length of his thigh inches from hers and the intimate row of their bare feet down below. Jade tore her gaze from the sight of his long slender feet and strong straight toes, while at the same time she became cognizant of her scanty attire. She was dressed in the oversize T-shirt she slept in with nothing on underneath. Being a modest person, she'd never pranced around in her nightclothes in front of a stranger before. Connor had probably gotten a great view of the contours of her breasts.

At the thought of him looking at her in that way, a sharp thrill coursed through her and her nipples hardened. Jade leaned forward.

"Where's a pen?" she asked, her breath coming more quickly than usual.

"Here." He reached for a ballpoint pen near a stack of reports. "Give it a try."

He leaned his right elbow on his thigh and watched over her arm as she put pen to paper. The width of his shoulders and his close proximity distracted her so thoroughly that at first she couldn't recall the slightest detail of the Chinese character. Forcing herself to ignore his disconcerting presence, she concentrated on the vision she'd discovered on the bathroom mirror.

"It went something like this." Jade drew a vertical line and capped it with a horizontal one, then paused, trying to recall what else she'd seen. Her memory was frustratingly blank.

"Did it have shapes down below?" Connor questioned. "Squares an' such?"

"I can't remember." She squinted, forcing her thoughts back to that night with Phillip in the bathroom. Then she drew a scribbled shape below the horizontal line and looked up. "I'm sorry, Connor. That's all I can recall."

He shook his head. "Could be a hundred things," he mused. "Not enough to go on, Jade. Can't ye recall anythin' else?"

She considered the past but saw only blackness in her memory. Finally she shook her head. "No. That's all I remember."

Connor sat back. "Ye may remember more later, lass. Dinna fret."

She sighed and put down the pen. For a moment she hesitated on the edge of her seat, thinking she should let Connor get back to sleep but reluctant, if not afraid, to return to her bedroom. Her nerves still felt frazzled, even though the whiskey had already mellowed the sharper edges. She turned slightly and threw a glance at Connor.

"Do you mind talking for a while?" she asked. "Or at least just sitting up with me for a few more minutes?"

"Still feelin' spooked?"

She nodded.

"Dinna mind a'tall." He adjusted the bed pillow he'd stuffed at the end of the couch. "I've been wantin' t' talk t' ye anyway."

"Oh, about what?"

"You." He turned his body toward her, crossed an ankle over his knee, and stretched his arm along the back of the couch, taking up most of the available space with his large frame.

# 9

*Connor's gaze swept* across her slight figure. "Did I bungle things for ye romantically, Jade, by pretendin' t' be your husband?"

"What do you mean, romantically?"

"Ye may already have a man in mind for the job, someone ye've set your cap for."

"I thought we covered that ground already."

"Well, that was in the heat of an argument, in front of th' others, not talkin' like this—nice and quiet like." He let his gaze drift over her face and into her hair. "'Tis a version of ye I've not seen before."

She fiddled with her watchband.

"Is it that hard to be friends wi' me, lass?" he continued.

"No." She glanced over at his face, more nervous than ever. "You're not so bad, MacKenzie."

"Why d'ye insist on ignorin' my Christian name?"

"Because I don't want to encourage familiarity."

"Why?"

Jade met his level gaze. "You're a charmer, MacKenzie. I don't trust charming men."

He nodded slowly, still regarding her thoughtfully. "So ye've lumped me with a bunch o' slippery characters, before ye even got to know me?"

"I don't see the point of getting to know you," she replied in a voice that sounded more tart than she intended. "Not when this is all temporary."

"Life's temporary, Jade. But ye can still enjoy it while ye're here."

"Meaning what?"

"Meaning that sometimes ye canna predict an ending t' whatever ye begin. Ye canna always control th' entire course o' things."

"I don't live my life without a certain amount of planning."

"But I get the sense that ye plan too much, and plan out all the surprises."

"I haven't been exactly ecstatic with the surprises life's shown me."

"Maybe your luck is due t' change, then, now that I'm part o' your life."

Jade had to admit that her life had taken a sudden detour since she'd come to Seattle and found Connor MacKenzie in the cellar. She just hadn't decided yet if the new route was good for her or not. "And why would your presence make a difference?"

"Because I'm a lucky sort." He grinned. "I've always been lucky, Jade. Things come t' me." He put his foot back on the floor, and his large hand slid up his thigh. "The Chinese have a saying that the more ye give, the more ye get back. And I've found 'tis true."

"Life's taught me something entirely different,

MacKenzie. And that's to expect the worst. Then sometimes—in rare cases—you just might not be disappointed."

"Ye haven't often got what ye wanted in life, Jade?"

"That's an understatement." She stared at the floor. "My mother died when I was just a girl. My father disowned me when I was eighteen. I finally get my career going, and my lyricist is killed in a car accident. Because of that I lose my child, my best friend, and most of my abilities. Yes . . ." She glanced at him. "I guess you could say my life has been a dream come true—a real peachy time."

"But ye're still here. Sabrina's not out of the picture. Ye still have friends and family, and that's what matters most." He leaned closer, both forearms on his knees. "Ye haven't lost all th' people ye love."

She studied him, knowing he alluded to his catastrophic loss of everyone he knew. "I don't mean to be insensitive about your own situation, MacKenzie, I'm simply trying to explain why I'm a bit skeptical that my luck will ever turn."

"Then explain somethin' else. Why did ye go about gettin' pregnant the way ye did?"

"You mean artificially?"

"Aye. I asked Herman what this 'artificial insemination' meant and couldn't believe my ears when he told me."

Jade drew up her legs and hugged her thighs to her chest. "It's the modern way of bearing children. No strings attached."

"Why'd ye do it, though? A beautiful woman like yourself—" He waved a hand toward her. "Surely ye could have had your pick o' husbands."

She slanted a look toward him, deciding that the

warmth in his words was evidence of enough sincerity to warrant a sincere answer. "I wanted a child. I wanted someone to love and make a home for. And time was running out for me. I'm thirty-eight, you know."

"I wouldn't have guessed. Ye look much younger."

"Thanks." She remained gazing at the side of his face and realized that in all the years she'd spent dating, she'd never met a man who possessed all the qualities she desired in a mate—kindness, intelligence, humor, ambition, and physical beauty—not until Connor MacKenzie had burst into her life. He had all those qualities and more, and he made her pulse race, something no other man had ever done. He also had the ability to infuriate her, a trait she shouldn't disregard. "But in all the years, I never found a man I wanted to marry."

" 'Tis true?" Connor asked softly. "Ye never met a man ye loved?"

She shrugged and set her chin on her knees. "It's a confusing time to live. Men and women are changing. You say people never change, but I think there's something going on these days. Something subtle and hard to define."

"Like what?"

"It has to do with rules and roles. A shift in power."

"From men to women?"

Jade nodded and clutched her legs more tightly. "Women don't need men anymore to survive. So much in life in the past was based on need. On interdependence. Some people are still trying to live with the old rules, and it just isn't working any longer."

"Ye dinna think women need men anymore?" Connor's expressive eyebrows raised. "What about for companionship? For lovemaking?"

"Those things aren't necessary for survival."

"Nay, now. Dinna say that." He reached out and tucked her hair behind her right ear, to better see her face. His touch sent a crackle through her, made her hair stand on end. "A life without love wouldn't be worth livin', Jade."

She didn't pull away, didn't move.

"Ye want t' go through th' years without knowin' a man's love?" he asked incredulously.

"No," she replied. "But I want the love of a strong man. And to tell you the truth, I haven't met all that many."

"What do you consider a strong man?"

"Someone who knows who he is, is confident enough to go after his dreams. Someone who isn't looking for a mother, a maid, or a trophy to hang on his arm."

"Ye've met only such shortsighted men so far?"

Jade nodded and turned just enough to look into his eyes again. "I want a man to want me, not need me. There's a big difference."

"Aye." His blue eyes seem to shift to a darker shade of navy, until they appeared almost black. "You want to be wanted for yourself—truthfully, elementally—not for what ye can do for a man."

"Exactly." She smiled quietly, amazed that a man from a century known for its lack of suffrage could understand what she had just said.

"'Tis th' only way, lass," he finally replied. "'Tis the reason I never took a wife myself. I was always busy with my hotel and business investments at first. And then when I made a bit of a success o' myself, it seemed th' women wanted me for th' new Connor MacKenzie. Not th' lad who'd arrived in town with no more'n a nickel in his pocket and a stout heart. Nay, they wanted me for th' pretty baubles I could buy for 'em, th' travelin' an' th' parties." He shook his head at the memory. "Not that I didna have my fun with th' ladies. I did. But I kept my heart out o' such a mercenary playin' field."

Jade chuckled. "You sound like me. Once I penned a few hits and made a name for myself, you wouldn't believe the guys who found me attractive."

"For what it's worth, Jade, I've never heard o' your songs, and I still find ye damned attractive."

She blushed and shot him a quick glance.

"I mean that in a strong sort o' way," he added, winking.

She grinned and realized how much she was enjoying this frank talk with him. She hadn't really talked like this for years, not even to Martin.

"Upon my word, sir," she declared, feigning a Southern accent, "how you do turn my head!"

"I'd like t' turn it a bit more." He reached out again, cupping her cheek with his hand and leaning toward her in a fluid movement that caught her off guard. He urged her to tip her head toward him, which compelled her to let go of her knees and reach out for balance. Her hand slipped into the crook of his arm, which flexed as he drew her closer for a kiss.

Then his lips opened upon hers as his fingers eased around her ear and jaw, holding her mouth to his, his strange energy buzzing through her at every contact point. For a moment, Jade closed her eyes and surrendered to the kiss and the strange humming field of electricity she felt surrounding her. His lips were surprisingly gentle—as if he were tasting her, not trying to consume her. His tongue found the perimeter of her lips and pushed lightly against them, while the kiss deepened, feeling as natural to Jade as her own breathing.

Something inside her burst to life at his touch—the

sharp flicker of desire—while a fuller sensation fanned outward near her heart. Then she felt his other hand encircling her and pulling her toward his body. She wasn't ready for full body contact yet—especially with a man she'd literally raised from the dead. Jade stopped him with a palm on his bare chest and pushed away from him, her hands and lips tingling and her heart thumping. A peculiar sensation of elation and well-being surged through her.

"Connor!" she gasped.

"Just practicin' for Thursday," he replied, smiling at her.

"I don't need any practice!"

He cocked his head. "Sure about that, are ye?"

She jumped to her feet, too flustered to tell him the truth—that his kiss had felt far too arousing and far too unusual for her peace of mind.

"Don't toy with me, MacKenzie."

"Who said I was toyin'?" He stood up, towering above her. "You're th' one doin' the pretendin', Jade. Ye liked it. Ye like me, too. Why keep lying t' yourself?"

"Oh, you're something!" She hated to be told how she felt, especially when it was true. "Do you think every woman is attracted to you?"

"We're not talkin' about every woman. We're talkin' about you, lass. I've seen ye look at me."

"Just because I look—"

"An' I've seen th' look in your eyes."

"You wish!" She took a step toward the hallway, too upset to remain in the living room with him; but he detained her by clutching her arm. Something close to an electric shock zipped up her arm and into her shoulder.

"Why do ye fight it so, Jade?" His gaze bored into hers. "Canna ye just let it go—see what happens?"

Jade stared back at him. "I don't have that luxury any longer. I have a child to consider. A future to protect. It would be idiocy to consider you. You're not even real!"

"I'm as real as they come, and ye know it."

"You're real? Then why do I get an electric shock when I touch you?"

"Maybe you're mistakin' passion for electricity."

"I don't think so."

"Maybe your body knows somethin' your mind refuses t' register." His eyes smoldered down at her. "Why don't ye give it a try an' see?"

"Because you might not be around for the long haul. Herman says—"

"Dinna limit me to the things others canna promise either," he retorted. "Nothin' in life is forever, lass. Ye know that, don't ye?"

"Better than anyone."

"Then why not take joy in what ye can, while ye can?"

"Because I know what it's like to lose it. It hurts."

She yanked away and stepped backward, moving toward the hallway.

"Ye'll go th' rest o' your life, then, doin' without, for fear o' feelin' a loss?"

"No. But I know a chancy situation when I see one."

"So I'm chancy, am I?"

"This entire setup is shaky. And far too convenient for an opportunist like you."

She saw a shadow of protest pass through his eyes, and before he could make a reply, she turned and hurried away, too upset to be frightened of her bedroom. Jade shut the door behind her, left on the light, and fell into bed, her mind whirling with thoughts of Connor MacKenzie and memories of the sensations she'd felt in his arms.

*  *  *

Late the next afternoon, when Connor heard the front door open, he paused, frustrated, still holding the crowbar in his hand, while he listened for Herman's voice in the living room. Then he sighed and climbed down the ladder he'd set up in Jade's bedroom. Jade had returned and he still hadn't located his hidden cache of gold. Could it be that someone had found it years ago during the remodeling? Or was he looking in the wrong spot? His room had been directly above Qi An's, and his gold should have been hidden somewhere between her ceiling and his floor. Without the gold, he'd never be able to buy back his hotel, regardless of his many investments.

He still had half of the ceiling to dismantle and intended to continue the task whatever Jade said in protest. He wasn't about to leave his hard-earned money in the hands of the Brennans, especially after having been cheated out of his hotel by them a hundred years ago.

He heard the front door close, heard Herman say, "Good afternoon, Miss Brennan."

"Mr. Fong," she replied in her wry voice. "Why am I not surprised to see you?"

Connor smiled to himself and shook his head. Regardless of Jade's rejection of him, he still appreciated her dry sense of humor. He picked his way through the ragged clumps of drywall he'd pried off the ceiling, then laid the crowbar on the floor beside the dresser. He brushed the white dust off his shoulders and the sleeves of his shirt, all the while considering how his next conversation would play with Jade, when he explained the reason for demolishing her bedroom.

He straightened and glanced at the framed photographs

that lay beneath the plastic sheet he'd draped over her furniture. His gaze caught and held on one of the pictures—that of a dark-haired man and Jade sitting on a piano bench, their shoulders touching, her head tilted toward his. A shaft of jealousy streaked through Connor, as strong as the one he'd felt when he'd first seen the shot that morning. He was sure he'd found the reason Jade shied from his touch. She'd loved the man at the piano. She'd lost him. Perhaps she still loved him. Though he saw no point in grieving over the past, he'd have to respect her sentiments and keep his hands to himself.

Connor scowled. Not touching Jade would be difficult, for more and more he wanted to draw her into his arms and simply hold her, to give her the comfort and care he knew she needed—something he needed himself, were the truth told.

Awakening to a different world, without any familiar anchors, had left him more shaken and more lonely than he cared to admit. This world spun at a different pace. He would swear the earth rotated faster, that the days and nights whizzed by more quickly, than in his day. And the noise level and crowds of people boggled his mind—just going out on the street was an affront to the senses. It wouldn't have been half as bad, had he been "normal." But he seemed to have a queer effect on machines. Clocks ran backward, automobiles stalled when he walked by, people with those tiny radios and headphones scowled and fiddled with their dials if he was close at hand. Many times when he entered a building, he'd see the lights flicker off and on. It was damned unnerving. He worried that one day he'd be found out as the cause of the trouble, and then his secret would be spread all over the city by the papers. He'd be labeled a freak.

He wasn't real. Jade had hit the nail on the head when she'd said that. He'd never shied from the public eye and in his other life had enjoyed a high-profile existence as a leading citizen of Seattle. But he would rather die than be labeled a freak and have people discover where he'd come from and what had happened to him. That was nobody's business but his and Jade's.

*Jade.* Connor sighed when he thought of her. He longed to wrap his arms around her, to feel her naked body against him, to lose himself in her arms—not just because she was a woman and he needed comfort and understanding, but because she was Jade. He admired her spirit, her frankness, her curiosity, and her vulnerability. And he loved her lithe figure and dark red hair. Her lips had been as soft as he'd imagined and deliciously yielding to him, until she had checked herself and pushed him away. He'd never met a woman who set so many barriers around herself—which was both a challenge and a damned nuisance.

He glanced at his dulled reflection in the plastic-shrouded mirror and ran his fingers though his hair. What had the dark-haired man possessed that Jade found more attractive than his attributes? He knew his looks easily surpassed those of the man at the piano, and of most other men as well. But then beauty had always been in the eye of the beholder, and Jade might not consider him handsome because of some blasted personal preference.

Connor saw a white smudge on his nose. Hastily he brushed off the powder and then ducked out of the bedroom, where he nearly collided with Jade coming the other way.

"Afternoon," he greeted her.

"MacKenzie." She glanced at him and then at the

door behind him. "What were you doing in my bedroom?"

"Well now." He held up his hands. "Dinna get your hackles up."

"Don't worry about my hackles." She took a step closer and tried to see around him into the room beyond. "Or my cockles, either. Just tell me what you're up to."

"Investigatin'." He'd thought of the lie the night before, when he'd been roused by Jade's cry. Though he hated to lie to her, he had gone too far to go back and explain why he'd been caught twice in her bedroom. If she discovered he'd lied once, she'd never believe him. He didn't want to take the chance of losing her trust forever.

"Investigating what?" She shot a dark look at the mysterious wall near the bureau, her face pinched with concern.

"Not the wall, Jade, th' ceilin'." He motioned toward the room behind him. "T' make sure it wouldn't come crashin' down on ye in the middle o' th' night."

"What?"

She pushed past him and walked into the center of her bedroom, where she rotated slowly, her face tilted upward. He trailed after her, hoping she would believe his tale.

"What in the world have you done?" she gasped, leveling a stare of incredulity at him. "You've torn out half the ceiling!"

"I know it looks terrible," he put in, "but 'tis only temporary."

"Connor, Dr. Nilsen's coming back in two days! I can't have a mess like this in here!"

" 'Twill be fine. Dinna worry."

"You never even asked if I wanted it done!"

"'Twasn't a matter o' askin', lass. I couldna see worryin' about ye when ye slept."

Jade heaved an exasperated sigh and crossed her arms, mute with anger.

"Come Thursday, ye won't know anythin' happened in here," he put in.

"I'd better not." She clenched her jaw and glared his way, her beautiful green eyes narrowed to slits of emerald fire.

"Dinna worry. 'Tis a simple task to put up a ceiling." He stepped toward her.

"Don't come any closer, MacKenzie." For a moment they regarded each other, and he couldn't read the guarded expression in her eyes. Then she heaved another sigh and her shoulders slumped as she dropped her purse on the bureau.

"Somethin' else is eatin' ye, lass," he commented, anxious to change the subject as quickly as possible. "What is it?"

"Oh, the whole visitation thing." She shook her head. "I just spent all day hunting for bedroom furniture for Sabrina—the kind Laura described to Dr. Nilsen. Plus drapes with sheep on them. It took me all day! And now I have one day to assemble furniture, hang drapes, and buy linens, towels, and everything else for Sabrina." She stuffed her hands in her pockets. "And I wanted to make her visit special, you know, with a cake and stuff for her birthday. But I just can't do it all in one day."

"I'll help ye."

Jade's head rose in surprise. "You?"

"Ye cut me to the quick, lass!"

"I meant no offense, MacKenzie. I just don't expect you to pitch in on such things."

"I've done my share o' putterin'."

"But what about the ceiling?"

"I'll hire some of Herman's friends t' replace it. 'Twill be easy enough. I'll just tear the rest down after dinner."

"Herman's making dinner again?"

"Aye. Steak and potatoes—t' keep my strength up." He winked at her, doing his best to coax a smile. Jade was much too grim for a woman as beautiful as she was, and he was determined to change her outlook.

"I don't know about this," she commented. "I should be paying him wages."

"Ach, no. He loves it. Gives him a sense o' direction. Besides, he's well taken care of through my estate, believe me."

"He's your employee?"

"Ye might say so."

"Then I owe you."

Connor grinned. "Now that has some interestin' possibilities, lass. Especially if you'd consider a trade."

She gave him a spirited smirk and brushed past him. "I'll make a trade, MacKenzie."

"Ye will?"

"Yes. I won't get my hackles up if you won't get your hopes up."

"Ah, lass!"

She actually smiled as she left the room, a smile that was bereft of her usual sarcasm. Connor counted the genuine expression as a small reward and grinned as he picked up the crowbar to resume his task.


That night, before retiring, Jade wandered out to the kitchen for a cup of herbal tea and found Connor standing at the bay window, leaning against the woodwork, a drink in his hand. He hadn't heard her step in the hall, and for a moment she stood quietly watching him. For the first time since she'd met him, she saw a grave expression on his face, his trademark smile nowhere to be seen, as he stared out at the city below. His golden glow, which usually surrounded him like a full body halo, seemed off center, as if it were detaching from him and drifting to the left.

A ripple of apprehension passed through her. Could his slipping aura have something to do with his soul detaching from this world? Herman had mentioned the possibility that Connor's soul might not have recovered entirely from its long hiatus, that he might still be connected to Qi An in some way. Could this new manifestation have something to do with finding the "door" in her room? Jade hadn't entirely believed Connor's explanation about fixing her ceiling earlier in the day; she wondered if he'd been investigating the flocked wallpaper wall instead but didn't want to confide in her.

Worried, she brushed a few strands of hair off her forehead, and at the movement Connor turned and spotted her.

"There ye are, Jade."

She gave him a weak smile and pointed to the kitchen behind her. "Thought I'd get some tea."

"Join me in a whiskey instead?" he asked.

"Thanks, no. I don't drink much—because of my— since the accident."

He nodded and looked back at the lights of the city below. "'Tis quiet tonight," he remarked. "Sometimes if I close my eyes, I can almost think myself back to my other life."

"Do you miss it?" She strolled toward him, trying to look and sound casual to conceal her concern.

"Aye." He sighed. "'Twas a simpler time. A quieter time. Much quieter. That's the real difference."

"We have so many machines now. They're all noisy."

"True. But I miss some sounds. Like hooves clattering on brick streets. Paperboys callin' out th' news. Homemade music driftin' off a porch after supper. That was th' sound of home t' me."

"Like lawn mowers on summer mornings." Jade stopped beside him and gazed at the twinkling city three stories below. "Or the sound of windshield wipers and jazz on a rainy night."

"Jazz?"

"A type of music. I like listening to jazz and driving at night."

Connor looked down at her. "You're a romantic at heart, Jade. Ye know that?"

She smiled softly. "I've got you fooled."

"You're bonny when you let your guard down."

She blushed. "I don't generally let my guard down."

"I gathered that."

She shot a glance up to his face and found him regarding her, a warm expression glinting in his eyes. She knew if she made the slightest move toward him, he would gather her into his arms, bend down to kiss her lips, and hold her against his tall, lean body—a prospect that made something twist deep in her belly and her breath catch in her chest.

"I should make the tea," she commented, turning from the window.

He touched her elbow to detain her, and the familiar shock buzzed through her. "Runnin' away?"

"Of course not."

"Ye dinna like t' talk t' me?"

"I wouldn't say that." She lifted her chin. "In fact, you get me to say too much."

"What's wrong wi' that?"

"Because with you, MacKenzie, I think it's best t' keep my guard up."

"Ye dinna trust me."

"It isn't that. I just don't need any more complications in my life."

"Ah, there you're wrong, lass. Ye need a man like me t' show ye what life's all about."

"I know what life's all about," she retorted. "And getting distracted by someone like you would only derail me."

"From what?" he asked softly. "What's so grand about th' path you're on?"

"It's the path to Sabrina," she replied. "The only road I can take right now."

# 10

*Thursday arrived swiftly,* and before Jade knew it, she was opening the door to Dr. Nilsen and showing the psychologist into the living room. Jade could hardly speak, she was so apprehensive about the time to come when Sabrina would arrive at her door. Her heart pounded in her ears, and she actually wished that Connor would show up soon to stand beside her and take some of the socializing responsibility off her shoulders. The thought surprised her and irritated her at the same time, for she had never craved the company of a man and had always felt capable of doing things on her own.

"Shall we do a walk-through before the child arrives?" Dr. Nilsen suggested.

"All right." Jade led the way to the second bedroom, which had miraculously come together last night at ten P.M. She opened the door to Sabrina's room, proud to show off her and Connor's handiwork. Sabrina's room was an attractive combination—not too feminine, not too cute, but still inviting—from the Little Bo Peep curtains to the pale mauve throw rug they'd found. Her white-and-gold bed, as described by Laura, was covered with a Little Bo Peep comforter, in the center of which was an irresistible stuffed animal of a sheep, with big brown eyes and a ribbon tied around its tail.

Dr. Nilsen marched into the center of the room, pivoted, and then leveled her stare at Jade. "It's small. But attractive."

"Thank you." Jade clasped her hands in front of her, knowing she would never have been able to complete her tasks had Connor not pitched in wholeheartedly. In fact, she'd just finished decorating the cake at nine-thirty that morning, without much of a chance to dress for the home visit. "I hope Sabrina will like it."

"She has everything at home, I hope you understand. Her own television, aquarium, and stereo system."

Jade flushed. "But she's only two!"

"Thomas and Gail believe in giving their children everything," Dr. Nilsen replied. "Surely you are aware of that."

"I don't think it's necessary—at least not so many material things."

"She's used to it, though. I just want to make you aware of the fact."

Jade nodded. "Shall I show you the bathroom?" She motioned toward the hall. "We equipped it with a stool, potty chair, and things like that."

"Very well." Dr. Nilsen marched back to the hall and inspected the bathroom. As they were finishing the inspection, Jade heard Connor come in the front door. He spotted them and smiled.

"Good mornin', Dr. Nilsen," he called.

"Good morning." Dr. Nilsen's frosty tone melted at the sight of the Scotsman. "How are you, Mr. MacKenzie?"

Jade felt a wave of relief at seeing him, felt her body relax a bit.

"Fine." Connor held up a small paper bag. "Had t' make a candle run."

"We're having cake and ice cream for Sabrina's birthday," Jade put in as they strolled down the hall.

"How nice."

"Better late than never," Connor commented. "Shall I put the candles on the cake, Jade, or do you want to?"

"I'll do it." She took the box from him, glad to have an activity to occupy her, and walked to the dining room table, where the cake, dishes, and utensils were lined up in neat rows. Jade was nearly crazy with anticipation and knew better than to attempt to make small talk. She'd stutter and say all the wrong things. Better to let Connor jabber away, since he seemed to have a gift for making people feel at ease.

Carefully she placed two purple candles in the icing rosettes just above Sabrina's name. Then she stepped back and cocked her head while she studied her handiwork. Her mother had always baked her birthday cakes and decorated them herself—everything from castles with chocolate bar drawbridges to ranch houses with pretzel fences. Jade had decided to carry on the tradition, even though her culinary skills were woefully lacking in comparison with her mother's skill. Still, her creation—a carousel with animal cracker cookies stuck to colorful straws holding up a fancy paper roof—wasn't too bad. Connor had claimed it was the best cake he'd ever seen—an exaggeration, probably, but one she had decided not to examine closely. His praise had warmed her more than she let on.

Just as Jade put the box of remaining candles away in a drawer, she heard the doorbell ring. She straightened, her spine rigid, and saw Connor turn toward her, his eyes meeting hers, fully aware how much this moment meant to her. Jade's mouth went dry, and for a second she couldn't get her feet to move.

"She's here," Connor declared, holding out a hand toward Jade.

The gesture brought Jade to her senses. Grateful for his presence, she hurried toward him and slipped her hand in his and didn't move away when their shoulders pressed into each other. Connor squeezed her fingers and smiled at her, his eyes alight with anticipation, and she looked up at him and wrapped her fingers around his upper arm, drawing support from his calm strength.

Together they crossed the short distance to the door, and he reached out to open it.

Gail stood in the hall, holding Sabrina's hand, while Robbie jumped up and down in the corridor behind them. His movement became just a blur, however, as Jade took in the vision of her little girl through a sheen of joyful tears. All else faded into the background.

Sabrina was gorgeous—from her red gold curls that fell in waves to her shoulders, to her round baby face and huge blue eyes, which stared up at her in a mixture of curiosity and innocence. She was dressed in a pink frock with short puffed sleeves, which displayed her cute pale arms and chubby wrists. Her legs were straight and well formed, and she wore black Mary Janes and frilly anklets. But what Jade noticed above all was Gail's thin hand clutched around Sabrina's wrist—a gesture of possession, not affection. Jade wanted the connection to be broken, wanted all cloying reminders of Gail's floral perfume washed off her daughter, wanted to throw her arms around Sabrina and never let her go.

"Come in, come in," Connor greeted them, picking up the slack for Jade, who was more tongue-tied than she'd ever been in her life.

"You must be Connor," Gail remarked, pulling Sabrina across the threshold.

"Aye," he answered, but Gail had already turned to look over her shoulder.

"Robbie," she called, "come in and say hello to your aunt Janine and uncle Connor."

"No!" Robbie retorted. "Don't want to!"

Jade's heart squeezed together. Was she not going to get to hug Sabrina? Not even touch her? She had dreamed of the day that she would drop to her knees and hold out her arms and Sabrina would run to her and fling her arms around her neck. That dream had brought her out of the coma and had been the reason she had opened her eyes during those first weeks when it would have been much easier to fade away. The prospect of seeing her baby had taken her through two years of brutal physical therapy, had given her the will to learn to walk again, to learn to read and speak again. And now she was here, ready to kneel down, throw out her arms, and hug her baby for the very first time—and the moment was being stolen from her by Robbie's disruptive behavior.

"Looks like there will be cake and ice cream," Gail put in. Her grip around Sabrina's wrist went slack, as if she were all but forgetting the little girl.

"Cool!" Robbie tore through the doorway and pushed past Sabrina, nearly knocking her off her feet. If Connor hadn't reacted immediately and caught Sabrina, she would have fallen on her face.

"There now," he said, swinging Sabrina up into his arms. "You're a bonny wee one, Sabrina!"

Sabrina stared at him, momentarily dazed by the sudden change in altitude, or perhaps surprised by the same electric zap Jade experienced whenever Connor touched her. Then the child stared at Jade, one blond eyebrow dipping in concern.

"Why is that lady crying?" she asked, pointing a delicate finger at Jade.

"Oh, she's just happy t' see ye, Sabrina." Connor glanced at Jade, and his warm, understanding smile helped melt the lump in her throat. "Here, give Jade a hug, why don't ye. She'll feel better then."

He thrust Sabrina toward Jade before she had a chance to react, before she could worry about the stares of Dr. Nilsen and Gail. And then Sabrina was in her arms, all cotton and petticoats, all chubby arms and legs, smelling like baby shampoo and powder and a sweet scent all her own that was oddly familiar to Jade. Sabrina's little-girl arms wrapped around Jade's neck, squeezing her breath away, and at the touch Jade felt her heart breaking with happiness and wonder. She put her nose in Sabrina's burnished curls and hugged her tender little body as years of pain and loneliness fell away.

After a moment, Sabrina pulled back slightly and inspected Jade's face. "All better?" she asked, her little red mouth puckering in concern.

Jade choked back more tears. "Much," she replied, drinking in the sight of her child's open face. She wanted never to let Sabrina out of her arms or out of her sight.

In the periphery of her vision, she saw Gail's hands reaching up as if to take Sabrina away, but Connor stepped into the other woman's path.

"Why don't ye show Sabrina her cake, Jade?" he suggested, protecting them from interruption with his large frame.

Jade settled the girl on her hip. "Would you like that, Sabrina?" she asked.

Sabrina nodded and smiled, proudly holding up two fingers. "I'm two now!"

"I know, Sabrina. But I missed your birthday, so I thought we'd celebrate all over again. If that's okay with you."

"Another birthday?" she asked. "With toys?"

Jade nodded and grinned.

"Goody!" Sabrina squealed. Then she caught sight of the cake. "Dizzyland!" she cried, clapping her hands.

Jade's heart burst with joy. She had thought having a child would be rewarding, but she'd never dreamed it would feel like this.

"Look, Sabrina," Connor said, placing his hand on Jade's shoulder. "See the animals?"

"Merry-go-round!" she cried.

"And there's your name," Jade put in, pointing to the icing letters that spelled "Happy Birthday, Sabrina."

"Sabrina starts with S," she said. "That's an S."

"What a smart cookie," Connor commented.

"I'm a girl." She glanced at him, giggling. "Not a cookie!"

"Are you sure?" He raised her arm to his mouth and pretended to take a bite. "Hmmm. You taste like a cookie t' me. Chocolate chip."

"I'm not choc'late chip!" She beamed at him, and Jade suddenly noticed that Connor's hair coloring was identical to Sabrina's, as was the shade of their eyes. They could easily be mistaken for father and daughter. The thought made her heart do a queer little flip-flop in her chest. She had a sudden urge to reach up and kiss him with all her heart and soul, for being so wonderful with Sabrina and for all he had just done for her in providing the chance to hold Sabrina in her arms.

Robbie ran through the apartment, arms out, making noises like a plane and coming dangerously close to hitting the cake.

"Have a care, lad," Connor admonished as the boy streaked by.

Jade watched Robbie sneer and run away while Gail sat on the couch, chatting with Dr. Nilsen, seemingly oblivious to her son.

"Let's light the candles and sing 'Happy birthday'," Jade said. "Would you light them, Connor?"

"Sure." He lifted the matchbook and turned it over and over before he realized what to do with the modern form of matches. Jade stood by, wishing the others would magically disappear—especially Robbie, with his incessant mouth noise—and leave the three of them alone.

Sabrina clapped when the flames flared brightly, and then Jade started the song, which everyone joined in on except for Robbie, who had buzzed down the hall toward the bathroom. Jade lowered Sabrina toward the cake, urged her to make a wish, and then told her she could blow out the candles.

The girl took a deep breath, much more than she needed for the two small candles, and then blew out the flames.

"Good job!" Jade exclaimed. She turned to the other women. "Gail, Dr. Nilsen, would you like some cake and ice cream?"

"Just a little piece," Gail answered, rising.

"None for me, thank you," Dr. Nilsen replied.

"How about Robbie?" Jade didn't think the boy needed any more sugar but didn't wish to deprive him during the celebration.

"Of course." Gail glanced at the boy, who ran past the keyboard, slapping the keys as he went by. Jade expected Gail to reprimand Robbie for abusing a musical instrument, but his mother didn't say anything to him.

Jade turned her attention back to the child in her arms. She hated to put Sabrina down, but since she was the hostess, she was compelled to serve her guests. "There you go, Sabrina," she said, depositing her gently on the floor. "Go find a seat at that little table over there and I'll get you some cake."

"Okay!" Sabrina toddled off toward the child's activity table and chairs that Connor had set up in a corner of the living room.

"She's bonny," Connor commented as they turned toward the table. "She's got your eyes and chin."

"She is wonderful, isn't she?" Jade felt tears surging to the surface again.

"Ye going t' be all right, Jade?"

She nodded and reached for the cake, determined to keep her hands busy so she wouldn't break down. Carefully she removed the paper top and set it aside.

"Jade!" Connor exclaimed under his breath as he grabbed her wrist. "Look!" She glanced at him and then down at the cake, where a Chinese character had been drawn in the icing.

"That's it!" She pointed at the top of the cake in the center of the animal ring. "That's what I saw on the mirror. But how could it have got there?"

Connor's grip tightened. "I didna touch the cake, that's for sure," he said. "I've been out."

"And I just put the roof on a few minutes ago. The icing was fine then."

Connor stared at the symbol scratched on the top of the cake.

"What is it?" Jade asked. "What does it mean?"

" 'Tis a symbol for someone's name."

"Whose?"

Connor blinked and then looked down at her, his usual merry eyes unusually somber. "Qi An's."

"But what—"

Gail stepped up behind them and poked her head around Connor's shoulder. "Is something wrong?" she inquired. "Anything I can help you with?"

"N-n-no," Jade stammered, not wanting Gail or Dr. Nilsen to think anything was amiss. "We're just cutting the—um—the—um—cake."

She grabbed the knife and sliced through the double layer cake before Gail could catch sight of the Chinese writing. Connor dished up ice cream on the side, and then Jade served everyone, giving Sabrina the first piece.

"For the birthday girl," she said, smiling, as she slid the plate in front of her.

"Thank you, Auntie 'Nine."

The name broke Jade's heart. She wanted to be called Mom or Mother, not Auntie. But that would have to wait. As long as she got to see Sabrina she could wait a little while longer.

"You're welcome, sweetie."

Before Sabrina could take a bite, Robbie ran past and struck her dish, sending it sliding across the small table. It flew over the side and crashed on the living room carpet.

"Robbie!" Jade cried.

Sabrina's face crumpled, but she didn't say a word.

Robbie smirked at Sabrina and then buzzed away, running headlong into an immovable wall that had suddenly materialized in front of him.

"Lad!" Connor thundered. "No more flyin' for you!"

Robbie tried to dart away, but Connor caught him by the back of his shirt.

"Let me go!" he yelled.

"You're not goin' anywhere, Robbie boy!"

"Mommy, Mommy!" Robbie shouted, flailing his arms. Connor leaned forward just enough so the boy's fists struck open air.

"Let him go!" Gail demanded, jumping to her feet. "Do you hear me?"

"Not until he apologizes t' Sabrina."

"Can't you see it was an accident?" Gail hissed, mincing toward him with short angry steps.

"Madame, 'twas no accident. 'Twas intentional—plain as day."

"Mommy, Mommy!" Robbie wailed.

Jade glanced at Connor, worried that Dr. Nilsen might think he was being too harsh but certain that Robbie's behavior merited discipline—something he never got from his parents.

"Let him go!" Gail exclaimed. "This instant!"

Connor regarded her calmly. "Madame, this is my house. I expect my guests t' behave accordin' t' my rules."

"He's just a boy!"

"He's entirely capable of learnin' his manners." Connor tightened his grip. "Now, Robbie lad, say you're sorry to sweet little Sabrina there."

"I don't have to!" He kicked, trying to hit Connor's shin, but Connor stepped nimbly out of the way.

"Keep it up, lad. I can use th' dancin' practice."

Robbie scowled and stuck out his lower lip.

"Look at her," Connor said, nodding toward Sabrina. "You've made her cry. 'Twas what ye wanted, hmm?"

Robbie glared at Sabrina.

"Now go over there like a man and say you're sorry."

"I don't have to." Robbie squirmed but couldn't tear free. "Mommy!"

"Mr. MacKenzie," Gail seethed, "I'm warning you—"

Connor ignored her. "Show us what you're made of, lad."

He propelled Robbie toward the chair where Sabrina sat, staring up at him, her eyes huge and troubled. Jade had a feeling that this wasn't the first time Robbie had been cruel to her. Her heart squeezed together painfully at the thought of Sabrina growing up with a mean older sibling and no champion to come to her defense.

"Tell her, Robbie." Connor pushed him closer, his hand still clutching the boy's shirt.

"Sorry," Robbie mumbled.

"What?" Connor leaned down. "I couldn't hear ye."

"Sorry."

Connor nodded toward the girl. "Sorry, *Sabrina*."

"Sorry, *Sabrina*."

"That's better." Connor released him. "Now clean up th' mess."

Robbie turned to face him, incredulous. "What?"

"Clean up th' cake. In my house, if ye make a mess, ye take care of it."

"Really!" Gail cried. "This is just too much!" She turned toward the psychologist for support. "Dr. Nilsen—"

"Let him continue," the doctor said, nodding at Connor.

Connor crossed his arms. "Hie to it, Robbie."

"No way! I don't have to!" Robbie stomped his foot. "I'm calling my dad!"

"So you'll have another man fight your battles for ye, will ye? What kind of a man are ye?"

"I'm not a man!" Robbie retorted. "I'm a boy!"

"And how do ye think ye'll get t' be a man, if ye call your daddy to fight for ye? Time t' grow up, Robbie. Ye got it in ye. I can see it like nobody's business."

Robbie stared at him.

"A man takes responsibility for his actions. Now go on. Jade'll show ye where the paper towels are, won't ye, Jade?"

"Sure." She beckoned for Robbie to follow her. He grimaced but reluctantly trailed after her into the kitchen.

While Robbie halfheartedly cleaned up the mess, Jade looked across the bar to Connor, marveling at the man's effect on the boy. Connor gave her a quick wink and then leaned closer to Sabrina to say something in her ear. The little girl smiled up at him. Jade watched them, and in that moment she knew she was falling in love with Connor MacKenzie.

# 11

Late that afternoon Jade and Connor stood before a judge, one couple out of four who had come to be married at the courthouse. Jade wore a camel-colored silk dress and had swept her hair up into a French roll. Connor wore a dark brown suit, crisp white shirt, and braces. Sometime that afternoon he'd gotten his hair professionally trimmed. Jade glanced at him from the side as he repeated the vow to honor and cherish her and watched his square jaw moving just below his ear, saw his Adam's apple bob in his corded neck, just above the knot of his tie. He'd never looked more handsome.

Then it was her turn to repeat the vows to him. She could barely look him in the eye, afraid of what he might detect in her expression, because with Connor she wanted the words to carry their full meaning and knew that wasn't why they had come to the courthouse. This was all a ruse, and she had to keep that fact foremost in her mind.

"Have you a ring?" the judge inquired.

"Aye." Connor reached for Jade's hand and raised it slowly. Then he slipped his hand into the pocket of his trousers and produced a small ring topped by a generous emerald. Jade's lips parted in surprise as he slid the valuable piece onto her slender finger. Why had he gone to such expense for a mock marriage?

Jade glanced up at him, but he only smiled and raised her hand to his mouth. He kissed her fingertips, something she'd never seen a groom do at a wedding, and the romantic gesture melted the strength in her legs. Her eyes locked and held with his, and she felt herself swimming in a warm pool of delight, lost to Connor's gaze.

The judge droned on about the significance of rings as a symbol of respect and loyalty, but Jade didn't hear a word he said. She was fighting an internal battle, trying to make sense of this ceremony with Connor and wishing the vows they'd exchanged might bind them together for more than just a few weeks.

"I now pronounce you man and wife," the judge announced, folding his hands in front of him. "You may kiss the bride, Mr. MacKenzie."

Connor turned to her and slipped his arms around her as he bent to her mouth. She laid her forearms against his chest and curved her hands upon his shoulders on either side of his neck. Then his tender kiss swept her away, and all other sensation vanished. She breathed in his clean scent and opened her mouth to him, wishing they were anywhere but in a public place. For the first time she felt his strong length against her, felt the firmness of his torso and the lean hardness of his legs, and her body responded with a rush of desire. She wanted to press against him forever and wrap her arms around him in a true heartfelt embrace. All too soon, Connor eased back.

"Ye look lovely," he whispered in her ear.

She blushed and glanced at the judge, who observed them with a bland expression. Jade guessed the man saw giddy newlyweds every day.

"Congratulations," the judge said, offering a hand to Connor.

They shook. "Thank you," Connor replied.

"Best wishes to you both." He shook Jade's hand as well and then smiled at them.

"Thank you." Jade slipped her arm through Connor's and strolled toward the courtroom doors.

"'Twas nice," Connor commented.

"Not as bad as I expected." She flashed a jaunty grin. How could she tell Connor that she wished they had truly meant what they'd said to each other a minute ago? How could she tell him that her feelings for him had begun to change since the birthday party, when he'd been there for her in many important ways? How could she tell him that his handsome face and warm smile dominated her thoughts?

"Ye kiss me like ye mean it."

"Oh?" She gave a small, nervous laugh. "I kiss everyone like that."

"Sure ye do." His eyes smoldered down at her. "Vixen."

She took a deep breath to steady her nerves and headed toward the door.

"May I interest you in dinner, Jade? A night on th' town?"

"You mean, with you?" Jade stopped in her tracks. "How will you pay?"

"Dinna worry, love. Herman cashed in a few stocks." He smiled and his eyes twinkled kindly. "Here we are, all dressed up. 'Twould be a pity not to go kick up our heels a bit."

Jade considered the idea, wondering what kicking up heels meant to Connor and what type of place he would find to his liking. He was probably the hard-drinking, hard-playing type of guy, who liked a rough crowd. She wasn't keen on spending her wedding night in a dingy tavern on the waterfront. Yet if they returned to the condo, what would Connor expect of his new wife? Would he try to coerce her into spending the wedding night in bed with him? She wasn't sure how she would handle such a confrontation and if she'd keep her head on straight enough to tell him no.

Dinner, away from the condo and her bedroom, would be a good time to lay down some rules and come to an understanding about their new relationship.

"Well, Jade, what d'ye say?"

"Dinner sounds great." She squeezed his arm. "We have some things to discuss anyway."

"And some champagne t' drink. A bit o' dancin', too, if the music's right."

"Where do you have in mind to go?"

"The Olympic, o' course." He flicked her chin. "'Tis not every day a man gets married to a beautiful woman. Let's make it special, even if we are just pretendin'."

"All right." Mustering a smile, she passed through the courthouse door to the sidewalk and waited for Connor to join her. He'd chosen one of the finest hotels in town, and she was pleasantly surprised at his selection. Maybe he wasn't as earthy as she supposed. Connor took her hand and placed it back on his forearm.

"Mrs. MacKenzie." He gazed down at her, his eyes dancing. "Has a certain ring to it, doesn't it?"

"Don't go getting any stationery printed," she warned, cocking a brow at him. Her best defense was to keep things light with Connor.

"Ha! Always the romantic!" He set off toward the Olympic.

"I didn't think romance was part of the plan."

"Let's just pretend for tonight," he replied, pulling her closer. "Who knows, ye just might like my brand o' wooin'."

"I believe wooing ends at the altar, Mr. MacKenzie."

"Not in my book." He leaned over for a quick kiss and then straightened, grinning down at her.

Looking away, Jade walked on and found people glancing at them and smiling, as if they recognized two people in love. Was that the image she and Connor projected? Or were passersby simply responding to Connor's undeniable good looks? She couldn't help smiling as she walked beside him, because regardless of their relationship to each other, she was proud to be seen on this man's arm.

She smiled and looked up at the skyscrapers above their heads, and suddenly a bit of melody popped into her head, a joyful phrase evoked by the wonderful day she'd had with Sabrina and now was finishing with Connor. Jade tried to place the melody, to attach it to a familiar song that she'd learned before the accident. But she couldn't recall any song that contained that particular light-hearted melody. Could her injured brain be healing at last, allowing her to compose music again? Jade tried to bring back the phrase, to repeat it in her thoughts, but it was gone—as quickly as it had appeared.

"What're ye thinkin'?" Connor said, looking down at her.

"How lovely the evening is," she replied, dashing away her fleeting hope of recovery. She squeezed his arm. "Let's go celebrate."

*   *   *

Midnight had come and gone when Jade and Connor returned to the condo. She felt a bit tipsy, having shared a bottle of champagne with Connor, and also a bit giddy, having enjoyed the dancing and the chatting of the last few hours. In the elevator he'd sneaked a quick kiss, and she had allowed it, then pulled away breathlessly when the elevator doors opened.

While Connor used the bathroom, Jade sat at the keyboard in the living room. She turned on the switch. The melody she'd heard that afternoon popped into her thoughts again. She concentrated and managed to pick out the first few notes, appalled at the amount of effort it took to think of the sound and then force her fingers to find the corresponding notes. The process had once been seamlessly automatic. Yet this was farther than she had ever come with her music, and new hope flared in her chest. She repeated the string of notes, hesitantly searching for each one like a child learning his first song at the piano, while tears streamed down her face.

Connor came up behind her. She felt the buzz of his presence before he reached out and cupped her shoulders. When he bent down and kissed the nape of her neck, she felt a strong electric shock in her fingertips and jerked back, afraid of being electrocuted by the keyboard.

"Sorry," Connor exclaimed. "I didn't mean t' startle ye."

"I felt a shock," she replied, staring down at the piano. "Maybe there *is* something wrong with this keyboard."

"Only when I'm close t' it, I'll wager." He stepped to the side. "What was that ye were playin'? It sounded sweet."

"It's something new." She swiped at her wet cheeks with her fingertips.

"Ye've been cryin', lass." He tipped up her chin and regarded her face. "Why?"

"It's just been so long," she whispered. "I thought my music was gone forever."

"Nay," he murmured. "'Tis been but asleep."

"It's so far away, though. And it will take so much work to get it back. And what if it doesn't? What then?"

For a moment neither of them said anything while they looked into each other's eyes.

"And do ye miss your piano-playin' friend?" Connor inquired.

"Martin?" Jade swallowed and eased away from Connor's hand. "I miss him every day."

Connor nodded silently. He stepped away from her and walked into the kitchen. "Care for a nightcap?" he called, his voice brusque.

"No thanks." She swiveled on the piano seat to face him, wondering at his sudden change in tone. "I've had far too much already."

He poured a small glass of whiskey. "My plan was t' get ye roarin' drunk, ye know, and then have my way wi' ye."

"Sorry to disappoint you." Jade laughed softly and rose.

He looked up at her. "Ye never disappoint me, lass."

A warm feeling washed over her. "I could say the same of you, Connor. You don't know how much it meant to me when you told Sabrina to hug me this morning. If it hadn't been for you—"

"'Twas nothin'." He waved her off.

"And what you did with Robbie." She strolled toward the bar. "That boy has never been disciplined in his life."

"'Tis obvious."

"But you got him to do your bidding."

Connor took a sip of his drink. "I'd have it no other way."

"Do you always get your way?" she asked, tilting her head.

"Always. Except with you." He winked at her over his glass. "That's what I like about ye, Jade. Ye're a challenge. A real challenge."

"Well, I'm certainly not a short dirty road," she added, remembering his Scottish proverb about the differences between short dirty roads and long clean ones.

"Nay. That you're not." He studied her. "And how ye ever showed up on th' Brennan family tree is a real conundrum."

"I'm not sure if I should take that as a compliment or not."

"Well, th' Brennans in my day were not t' be trusted. And from what I can see of your brother's brood—no reflection on you, Jade—th' family hasn't changed all tha' much."

"I never felt accepted by them," she remarked, running her fingernail along the edge of the counter. "Ever since I was a kid."

"'Twas probably a good thing. Ye've got fine qualities, Jade."

She glanced up at his face again. "Thanks."

"I mean that as a friend. I'm not just bletherin' away t' get ye in bed."

"I know." Her heart swelled and she turned away from him, so he couldn't see her eyes. She'd never felt as close to a human being as she did right at this moment with Connor. A few more minutes in his presence, talking so intimately and frankly like this, and she'd run into his arms and beg him to make love to her.

Flushing at the thought, Jade changed the subject.

"I wanted to thank you for the ring," she said, twisting it around on her finger. "It's lovely. But you didn't have to go to such expense."

"I wanted t' get ye an emerald, so I did." He took another drink. "A lass with eyes like yours needs an emerald."

"When this is all over"—she glanced up at him—"I'll be happy to return it to you."

"Ye think that's what I want?"

Their eyes locked for a long moment. Jade could feel a current of energy flowing across the counter between them, drawing her toward him, but she stood firm. His words were heavy with meaning, but she wasn't sure how to interpret them and wasn't certain what she *wanted* his words to mean.

"I don't know what you want," she replied finally. "I don't usually read people's minds."

"Well, I dinna want the bauble back. It's yours t' keep, regardless o' what happens between us."

"All right. Thanks." She looked at the ring for a moment and then decided to change the subject again, not sure what they could talk about safely. Each topic of conversation seemed to lead them back to the personal difficulties that existed between them.

"And what about that Chinese character in the cake this morning? How do you think it got there?"

"Curious, that." Connor frowned. "Dinna know."

"Do you think this condo is haunted by Qi An? That she is still here in her old living quarters?"

"Sounds preposterous."

"But what other explanation could there be?" Jade sat on a stool beside the counter. "Herman said that Qi An had been interrupted when conducting that ceremony with you. She would never have left the ceremony unfinished, unless someone had kept her from it. And they never found her body after the fire."

"Qi An was killed?" He stared at her, his voice cracking.

Jade felt a pang of jealousy at the sound of shock and pain in his voice. "Herman thinks so. And because of the ceremony being interrupted, he believes her soul might be in limbo, perhaps in danger."

Connor downed his whiskey and set his glass on the counter beside the sink. His expression had sobered and his eyes had grown dark by the time he looked aside to her. "The Brennans." His eyes smoldered. "The damn Brennans!" He looked up at the ceiling, more distraught than she'd ever seen him. "The bastards!"

"I'm sorry, Connor."

He didn't seem to hear her and instead paced the floor, from the refrigerator to the end of the counter. "Why?" he exclaimed. "Why her?"

Jade didn't know what to say. Any apologies made in her family's name wouldn't bring Qi An back to life. Yet she had to say something, if only to encourage Connor to vent his grief. "What was she like?"

He stopped short and glanced at Jade. "Qi An?" His eyes went out of focus. "She was beautiful. Innocent. A voice so soft and quiet, 'twas like th' brush o' angel wings."

Something twisted in Jade's chest at his words.

"Were you in love with her?"

Connor ran a hand over his hair. "Aye, in th' way a young man loves a sweet young woman. But her father asked me t' honor his family by keeping my feelin's t' myself."

"Why?"

"Qi An was special. Very special. She had been

trained from an early age by a secret society Sam Lo could never tell me about."

"Was she some kind of priestess?"

Connor nodded. "She was destined t' marry a member o' that society, not a raw Scot like myself."

Jade shook her head. She would never consider Connor "raw."

"I kissed her only once." He gazed down at the floor and smiled sadly. "When we were alone and she was selectin' th' paper for her room."

"You mean the red wallpaper?"

"Aye. 'Twas a chaste kiss, there by that wall in your bedroom. I wanted more, but she ducked away and didn't speak t' me for days afterward."

Jade studied him, wishing he would keep such information to himself. She didn't care to visualize Connor with other women.

"T' tell ye th' truth, Jade," Connor continued, "had she become my wife, I would have split her in two. And if not me, then th' bairns we might have had. She was tiny. Like a child. Not even five feet tall. And ye see what I am—not exactly what you'd call a short man."

"Hardly." Jade thought back to the moment she'd spent pressed against him during the marriage ceremony. She had felt the firm muscles of his six-foot frame under his well-tailored suit, felt his undeniable strength and virility.

"Then, as the years went by, I accepted the fact that she would never be mine. 'Twas hard. But I knew 'twas th' right thing t' do."

"Did she—did she love you?"

"She never said. She wouldn't have said anything t' dishonor herself or her family."

"Couldn't you tell, though?"

"Sometimes I would see a certain light in her eyes. Aye, 'twas love, as much as there could be between us."

"That's why she put you in the Box of the Deepest Sleep. She wanted to save your life, no matter what danger it put her in."

He sighed heavily. "And died, herself, doin' it."

"You can't hold yourself responsible for that."

"But I can find out what happened to her." He shrugged out of his suit jacket. "She needs t' be found. Laid t' rest properly. That's why she's been makin' all th' fuss."

He strode past her, loosening his tie. Jade turned on her stool, curious as to why he had suddenly swung into motion.

"What are you going to do?" she asked.

"Take off these fancy trappin's and go down t' th' cellar."

"Now?"

"Aye. Maybe I'll find some clues."

She slid to the floor. "Want some company?"

He turned and regarded her for a moment. "Thank ye, Jade, but ye need your sleep. Sabrina's comin' for breakfast tomorrow, remember?"

"That's right."

"Ye want t' enjoy th' time with her, and not be fallin' asleep in your porridge."

Jade mustered a smile and nodded, but she couldn't help feeling excluded from Connor's life. Perhaps he had loved Qi An more than he let on, needed time alone to deal with her loss, and didn't want another woman infringing on that memory. The possibility sliced through her, cutting to the bone.

"I'll see you in the morning, then," she said.

"Aye."

"Will you have breakfast with us?"

"Wouldn't miss it. Wake me, so I'm off th' couch before they arrive, will ye?"

"Sure." She stood near the line of stools, suddenly unsure of what to do next. "Be careful, Connor."

He raised a brow. "Wifely concern, Jade?"

"Just concern." She wanted to reach out and touch his face, but the new information about Qi An had put a damper on her burgeoning feelings for Connor. She remained standing with her arms at her sides. "Good night."

"Night, lass." He unbuttoned the cuffs of his sleeves and gazed down at her.

She turned and hurried to her room, more perplexed than ever about the twists her life path was taking now that Connor MacKenzie had entered the picture.

For the longest time she lay awake as visions of the day swirled in her head. She smiled as she remembered Sabrina's embrace, the way she'd squealed in delight at the sight of her birthday cake, the happy way she'd put her toys in her new bedroom—the guest bedroom, it had been termed to eliminate confusion—and kissed the nose of the sheep on her bed. Then the vision of Connor's sunny face rose up. Jade squeezed the pillow beneath her head and closed her eyes, wishing he were lying beside her, wishing she had waited for Connor to have a baby—wishing that Sabrina were their child.

# 12

*At the sound of her alarm ringing,* Jade woke up the next morning, startled out of a dream. She pushed off the alarm and sat up and eased her legs out of bed. As she moved, she realized that her leg didn't ache nearly as much as it had a few days ago, and she marveled at the sudden leaps in her recovery since she'd come to Seattle. She had to attribute a major portion of it to her emotional happiness, both with Sabrina and Connor. What would happen if either one of them dropped out of her life? Would she suffer a relapse? Jade frowned, refusing to entertain the possibility.

She put her feet to the floor and stood up. It was then she saw the glow near the wall by the bureau.

She gasped and staggered back, falling into a sitting position on her bed. A golden cloud hovered near the dresser, the same type of cloud she'd seen surrounding Connor. She stared at it, frightened witless, but it didn't move toward her.

After a moment of frantic indecision, she bolted for the door and ran down the hall to the living room, where Connor was sleeping on the couch. She skidded to a stop beside him, her chest heaving and her knees trembling.

"Connor!" she gasped. He didn't respond. His eyes remained closed, his dark brown lashes sweeping his cheek. A slight growth of beard accentuated the contours of his strong face, making him appear more masculine than ever. But something about him didn't look right.

She suddenly realized that Connor's usual glow was absent. In fact, his skin looked unnaturally pale in the morning light.

"Connor!" Jade repeated. She reached out and touched his bare shoulder. His skin was cool. He didn't seem to hear her or feel her light touch.

Frightened, Jade shook his shoulder roughly. "Connor!" she cried. "Wake up!"

His eyelids fluttered and then opened. "What in blazes?" he exclaimed, glancing up at her, his vision not yet focusing.

"Are you all right?" she asked, raking him with a quick but intense inspection. To her relief she saw a slight glimmer begin to appear just above the surface of his skin.

He squinted. "Shouldn't I be?"

"There was a glowing thing in my room," she said. "Just like your aura. Floating by that wall. I ran. And then when I got out here, yours was missing!"

"Whoa, lass. . . ." He struggled to sit up against his pillows. "Slow down. What are ye sayin'?"

"You know that weird glow around you most of the time? That golden light? I saw something just like it in my bedroom, and when I came out here, your glow was gone. And then when I tried to wake you, you wouldn't respond!"

"'Tis no wonder. I got only a few hours o' sleep."

"I don't think it was that." She swallowed and glanced back down the hall, not sure what she expected to see. "I think part of you was missing. I think part of you was being dragged back to that red wall—that doorway to the past, as you called it."

He ran a hand through his red gold waves and scowled. "Sounds peculiar, dinna ye think?"

"No. Not if you could have seen yourself—all white and cold like you were a few minutes ago."

"I feel th' same as ever. Just a might tired. But that's t' be expected."

Regardless of Connor's assurances, Jade shuddered. She surveyed his lean physique, which once again glowed with an unearthly vibrancy, and worried that she might come upon Connor one day and not be able to wake him. The thought struck her mute.

She appraised his condition, from his rippling bare abdomen, past his strong corded neck, and up to his face. There she found him regarding her, a warm light in his eyes, obviously relishing her newfound concern. But he didn't make his usual teasing comments or reach out for her. Jade stepped back, suddenly unsure of where they stood with each other.

"So did you find anything last night?" she asked. "In the cellar?"

"Nay." Connor rose slowly to his feet. He had worn his jeans to bed. "Not a single clue. Even the box was gone."

She nodded and watched him stretch. "A hundred-year-old trail has to be a bit cold."

"Still, I thought I'd find somethin'. I just had th' feelin'."

Jade crossed her arms. "If you could, would you choose to go back?" She swallowed. "I mean, to that other time?"

"I've never been one to speculate on what ifs," he replied. "Seems like a waste of time t' me. I deal best with th' here and now. That's what I've been tryin' t' tell ye."

"But what if you could go back in time and prevent Qi An's death? Would you?"

"Of course I would." He frowned and shot a sidelong glance at her. "What're ye gettin' at, Jade?"

"Nothing really." She brushed back her bangs, feeling jealous of a poor dead woman and despising herself for it. "I should take a shower, before Sabrina shows up. But I wanted to make sure you were up first."

"Thanks. I am." He studied her and shook his head slowly. "Are ye sure you're all right, Jade?"

"I'm fine." She flashed him a jaunty smile she didn't feel inside and turned to go back to her room. There she found the glow by the dresser had dissipated, just as she expected. But how long would it be until Connor's aura detached from him forever?


Later that morning at a nearby park, Jade watched Connor letting out the string of a kite for Sabrina, who stood by his leg and didn't reach much past his knee. The two-year-old clapped merrily when the kite sailed up into the sky, borne on a strong breeze off Elliott Bay at the bottom of the bluff. Phillip Lake, her brother's butler, ran up a second kite a few feet away, efficiently completing his task before he handed the string over to Robbie. As soon as the boy took command, he let out so much string that the kite luffed and fell.

Immediately Robbie turned on the older man, shouting a string of recriminations at Phillip, blaming the old
man for failing to do his job correctly. Connor looked
over his shoulder at the butler and the boy as Robbie
continued to berate Phillip.

Jade slipped her hands in the pockets of her slacks
and looked skyward, slightly disgruntled by the morning's arrangement. Though no one had come out and
said it, the reason for Phillip's presence in the park
was to make sure she didn't run off with Sabrina. The
idea that Thomas and Gail didn't trust her angered her
and hurt her, which put a damper on the morning's
activity.

She watched Phillip trot across the grass, the kite flut-
tering close behind him. After a minute he launched the
kite successfully, only to have Robbie bring it down
again. The kite, colored to look like a manta ray, hit the
ground nose first and stuck in the damp earth.

"Stupid kite!" Robbie shouted at long-suffering
Phillip. "You got a stupid kite, Phillip! This one doesn't
work!"

"I assure you, Master Robbie, the kite—"

"I want a different one!" Robbie glanced around, and
his attention landed on Sabrina's kite, which soared
gracefully above their heads, a hundred feet up, its vio-
let tail streaming across a bank of fluffy white clouds.
"That one!"

He dashed across the grass and lunged for Sabrina.
She cried out, dropping the plastic spool that held her
string, and ran for Jade, who swept her up in her arms.

"It's okay, Sabrina," Jade cooed, holding her close.

"Bad boy," Sabrina commented, glaring at Robbie
from the safe haven of Jade's arms.

Robbie swooped down for the bouncing spool but

stopped short when a large foot stepped on the plastic spindle.

"Hey!" the boy exclaimed, looking up to find Connor glowering at him.

"Hands off," Connor warned.

"I want it!" Robbie shouted. "Mine's busted!"

"That doesn't mean ye can grab Sabrina's."

"Why not? Babies can't fly kites!"

"She was flyin' one just fine until ye butted in." Connor reached down and picked up the spool. "Now go over and apologize to Sabrina."

Robbie screwed up his features into a contorted scowl, just as Phillip arrived on the scene.

"My apologies, Mr. MacKenzie," Phillip said, looking out of place in his gray suit as he held the kite before him. The black tail dragged over his well-polished shoes. He'd been with their family for as long as Jade could remember, and in all those years she couldn't recall ever seeing Phillip Lake outside the house.

"No need for you to apologize," Connor replied. "'Tis Robbie's responsibility. Go on, lad."

"I don't have to!"

"Ye do if ye want t' stay in th' park."

"Phillip," Robbie demanded, pointing at Connor, "make him leave me alone!"

"I'm afraid he's got a point, Master Robbie. Your behavior was out of line."

"But it's not fair! Sabrina got the good kite! I should have got the good kite!"

"You selected the kite yourself, Master Robbie, if you recall," Phillip replied in an overly patient tone. "You insisted upon the manta ray."

"Well, it's not the one I really wanted. That's the one I

want!" He pointed at the kite flying high above their heads. "Right now!"

"Sorry, lad," Connor said. He turned his back on the boy. Jade watched Robbie flush red, not accustomed to adults who failed to cater to his demands.

Robbie flung himself on the ground and pounded the sod with his fists and feet, yelling at the top of his lungs that he wanted the kite and they'd better give it to him.

"D'ye hear that bird?" Connor asked Jade over his shoulder, affecting a casual tone, even though people in the park had stopped to stare at the child throwing a tantrum.

Jade dragged her stare off Robbie and glanced at Connor. "What bird?"

"That mourning dove. Listen, sounds sweet, doesn't it?" He cocked his head and cupped a hand behind his ear, while Phillip bent down to reason with the boy.

"I don't hear it," Jade declared, playing along, even though she didn't know what Connor was up to.

"Let's go see if we can find it." He took Jade's arm and guided her away from Robbie, who increased the volume of his tirade when he realized the adults were walking away from him.

They got only a few yards away before Robbie ran up behind them, screaming at them for ignoring him. Phillip brought up the rear, fussing with the kite and looking helpless and embarrassed.

"Do settle down, Master Robbie," he pleaded. "I beg you. People are staring."

Snarling and crying, his face red and his eyes wild, Robbie lunged for Connor's legs. Connor stepped aside nimbly. The boy caught open air and tumbled headlong into the grass. He scrambled to his feet, his jeans stained and his face streaked and blotchy. Jade's heart went out to him, for she could see past the bad behavior to a boy who was frustrated beyond all reason.

"Had enough?" Connor asked, giving over the spool of string to Jade. She felt the tug of the kite and helped Sabrina take command of it, happy to hold her daughter as long as she could.

Connor turned to face Robbie. "You'll get nowhere throwin' such fits, Robbie."

Robbie swiped his blotchy face with the back of his hand and said nothing.

"There's a trick t' flyin' a kite, lad. I'd be happy t' show ye, as soon as you apologize to Sabrina."

"I don't have to!" Robbie retorted. "My parents never make me!"

"Well now, you're not with your parents, are ye?"

Robbie glared at him.

"This is the real world, Robbie boy. Th' way your parents do things isn't necessarily th' way th' rest of us get on."

"That's stupid!" Robbie retorted. "I'm glad you're not my father!"

Jade studied Robbie's troubled eyes, which were focused intently upon Connor, and realized the boy was saying the exact opposite of what he felt inside.

"I spend my time with friends," Connor continued, undaunted by Robbie's venom. "And friends treat each other with respect."

Robbie rolled his eyes and crossed his arms.

"If ye think that's blether," Connor said, "then hie out o' here. I dinna care t' look at ye." He turned toward Phillip. "Take th' lad home, Phillip."

Robbie stepped forward. "Wait—"

Connor gazed down at him, patiently silent.

"Okay." Robbie's nostrils flared and his mouth trembled at the corners.

"Ready t' apologize, then?"

Robbie hesitated and threw a sharp look at the kite in Phillip's hand and then back up to Connor. "Okay."

Connor nodded toward Sabrina, who still sat in the link of Jade's arms. Jade set her upon the ground and adjusted her little sweater.

Robbie trudged up to his cousin and stopped in front of her. "Sorry, Sabrina," he stated.

"Bad boy," Sabrina said, pushing out her lower lip.

Jade knelt down beside her. "No, Sabrina. Tell Robbie that you forgive him." She glanced at her daughter's profile, her little-girl nose and round forehead, knowing how difficult it was to learn to forgive and knowing the importance of starting such an education early in life. "Robbie's sorry. He means it."

Robbie stood without moving, his stare riveted on Sabrina. Jade looked into his eyes and saw for the first time the sadness that was usually hidden behind an impish smirk.

"I 'give you," Sabrina repeated.

"Good. Now shake hands."

The children shook hands solemnly while Connor ambled up behind the boy.

"Okay, lad," he said, laying a hand on the boy's shoulder. "Let's fly that kite."

Robbie looked up at the tall man behind him. "If you get it up in the air, I'll do the rest."

"Ach, no." Connor smiled. "A kite needs t' be wooed into th' sky with a gentle hand. 'Tis an art. I'll show ye."

He guided the boy off to the side and bent down to instruct him. Jade watched as he showed Robbie how to hold the kite, how to run with it on a short lead until it caught the wind, how to slowly let out the line, patiently feeding the string as the kite climbed upward. Then he gave the kite to the boy, and with much laughing and joking, and a fall or two, Robbie got the manta ray into the sky. After a moment, when Robbie was sure that he had control of the kite, he looked over his shoulder at Connor and beamed—the first true smile that Jade had ever seen on his face. Connor gave him a thumbs-up signal and then stood next to him, watching the kite and pointing at the sky—at planes, birds, and clouds—and granting Robbie some sorely needed and willingly given attention.

Jade's heart went out to Connor once more, loving him for his special way with people and his admirable zest for life. Martin had viewed life through a dark filter, battling the world at every step. But Connor had a knack for sailing through, making others smile and laugh and becoming better people just from being around him. No wonder the Chinese had expected his spirit to return and had guarded his investments for a hundred years.

Phillip strolled across the grass to Jade and stood next to her, watching Robbie chattering away to Connor. He shook his head. "I've never seen the boy like this," Phillip remarked. "Your husband has a way with children, doesn't he?"

"He likes them. They must sense it."

Phillip nodded.

Jade reached down to help Sabrina with her kite, but her mind kept repeating the phrase *your husband, your husband*. Her heart surged at the thought of Connor being her husband for real and all that it entailed. Had she been alone with him on the grassy knoll, she would have run to him, flung her arms around him, and pressed kisses all over his face and neck.

Instead she steadied Sabrina's kite and turned her thoughts away from the soaring feeling for Connor that she could no longer deny. At that moment she realized Connor had the power to either make her deliriously happy or shatter her heart forever.

An hour later they returned to the condo, where Herman had volunteered to make a special lunch for Sabrina. Gail had been slated to attend but called to beg off and asked Phillip to stay in her place. Phillip was more than happy to extend his time with Jade and to talk with Herman in the kitchen. Though Robbie was supposed to go back to the penthouse for lunch, he shocked everyone by calling his mother to ask if he could stay and eat Chinese food with Sabrina and his aunt and uncle.

Jade watched him talking on the phone, his posture stiffer than it had been for the last hour. She saw his little shoulders droop and knew his mother had refused his request. Robbie pushed the phone off and set it down on the counter, his expression clouded.

"What did she say?" Jade asked.

"No." He frowned. "I have to go to soccer practice."

"Oh. Well, maybe next time we can arrange it beforehand."

"Yeah." He sighed. "Sure."

Robbie trudged toward the door, with Jade trailing behind him.

"I'll walk ye back, lad," Connor offered, opening the door. "You can show me that autographed baseball collection you were talkin' about."

"You want to see it?" he asked.

"Sure. I said so, didn't I?"

Robbie glanced at him in surprise, as if amazed an adult would carry through with what he said.

Connor looked at Jade and smiled. "Be back momentarily, love."

"All right." Her eyes locked with his for a heart-thudding

moment. Then she leaned toward him, just a fraction closer, and he bent down to her mouth to kiss her soundly.

"Mmm," he said, pulling away all too soon.

Jade flushed with pleasure and noticed Robbie was staring at them, blushing as well.

"Hurry back, sweetheart," she said softly, playing the role of doting wife and liking the way it felt. "Bye, Robbie."

"Bye, Aunt Jade."

She grinned at his use of her nickname, the first time he'd ever called her something other than Janine.

Jade watched them walk down the hall to the elevators and then closed the door quietly. After lunch, when Sabrina went back to the penthouse with Phillip, she'd corner Herman and ask him some questions about the glow she'd seen in her bedroom, the old red wallpaper, and Qi An's name in the cake icing—and if they posed a threat to Connor's well-being, as she worried they might.

# 13

That evening Connor sat on the couch reading the paper while Herman made cinnamon rolls and cookies for the next day. As Connor perused the technology page—trying his best to grasp the concept of hard drives, the information superhighway, and some unfathomable thing called a Web page—he breathed in the smell of rising bread dough and cinnamon, a fragrance that would never change, no matter what year showed on the calendar. Across the room, Jade sat at the keyboard, playing from memory. She'd left the headphones unplugged at his request so they could all enjoy the scales and songs she played. Her music flowed softly through the apartment, curiously soothing. Connor smiled, almost content, as the day wound quietly down around him.

He didn't look forward to another long night on a short couch, but there was no way he'd leave Jade alone during the evening hours, now that Qi An had made her mysterious presence known. Though Qi An had always been gentle and kind to him, he wasn't certain she would act similarly to someone she might perceive as a rival. And no one could guess what had happened to Qi An's soul during the ceremony and the ensuing hundred-year hiatus.

Jade had asked Herman a bunch of questions that afternoon, and he had warned them that nothing could be predicted regarding Qi An or even Connor, for that matter. Connor tightened his grip on the paper as a cold shaft of fear spiked through him. The thought that he might someday cause harm to Jade shook him to his core. He'd rather put a gun to his head than hurt her.

Connor looked up from the paper and let his gaze wander over Jade's profile. She had an oval face with a pert nose and brows that tipped downward toward the bridge, a clue to her fiery nature, along with her deep red hair. Her eyes were the color of jade, a smoky gray green in the dim light of the living room. He'd never met a woman with such eyes. They could flash as clear as emeralds or glint like polished onyx—always changing to reflect her moods, her intelligence, and her heart.

Something sharp sliced through him when he thought of Jade gazing at her piano partner with those eyes. He wanted her heart to shine through her eyes for him, not for some long-gone man from the past. Connor sighed and dropped his glance to her mouth.

From the side, the fullness of Jade's upper lip was as seductive as the slight cleft in her chin and the feminine flare of her jaw below her ear. He knew, though, from gazing at her face full on, that Jade's mouth was set slightly off center to the tip of her nose, a nearly unnoticeable facial flaw that lent her a distinctive beauty that continually drew his eye. Whenever he looked at those lips, he longed to kiss them back into place—gently, fiercely, and every manner of kiss in between.

Jade tipped her head backward and closed her eyes during a mournful part of her ballad, and Connor noticed a small mole on the tendon of her neck. It rose and fell as she sang the chorus to the song, sailing on the tide of her pulse. Connor could barely keep his seat, so strong was the urge to slip up behind her, kiss that small brown dot, and seek the warmth he knew burned just under the surface of this woman. He longed to wrap his arms around her, to lay his cheek on her sleek, glossy hair to convince her to let go and reach for the same passion in life that she chased in her music—and to have faith that everything would turn out well.

But he couldn't make such a promise. When it was all told, he might be the very reason her world would crumble.

Just as Connor returned to the paper, he heard the doorbell chime. Herman padded across the room to answer the bell while Jade broke off playing and swiveled on her stool. Connor folded the paper together as Herman opened the door to a copper-haired man, with wire-framed glasses and gray at his temples. He looked somewhat familiar, and Connor rose to his feet, trying to place the man's face.

In the periphery of his vision, he saw Jade slowly rising as well, her expression setting into an unreadable frosty mask.

"Janine!" the man greeted her, holding out both hands to grasp hers in something more than a handshake and something far short of an embrace.

Jade stood at the piano and ignored his gesture.

"Thomas." Her voice was flat and brusque. "I'd like you to meet Herman Fong. Herman, this is my brother, Thomas."

"Herman . . ." Thomas pumped his hand. "Nice to meet you!"

Herman bowed to Thomas and then shut the door behind him.

Jade glanced at Connor. "And this is my husband, Connor MacKenzie."

"Ah, Connor!" Thomas stepped forward and shook Connor's hand heartily. "I've heard some good things about you."

"Have ye now?" Connor purred, sizing up Jade's brother. He could see the family resemblance between Jade and Thomas, in the red hair, fair skin, and slight stature. But he quickly decided he liked the female version much better. Jade might be volatile and harsh, but she was frank and open. Connor could tell at a glance that Thomas was her complete opposite: amiable, glib, and dishonest to the bone. Thomas was far too polished—from his wide, white smile, most likely practiced before a mirror, to his neatly pressed slacks and polo shirt. Every article of clothing he wore appeared brand-new, as did the expensive watch glinting on his left wrist. When he moved, he gave off a subtle scent that smelled like money dipped in musk.

Connor smiled grimly to himself. Thomas Brennan might smell like money, but he probably didn't have any, just like his ancestor Asahel Brennan, who had burned the Elliott Hotel a hundred years ago. The Brennans were famous for putting on a show of wealth and then not having the capital to back up the display.

Thomas shifted under Connor's close inspection. "Gail tells me Robbie's been talking about you all day."

"He's a fine boy," Connor remarked. "He just needs a firm hand."

Thomas nodded and smiled. "We do our best. But the boy's got a lot of energy. A *lot* of energy."

Connor saw Jade frown and glare out the window as she discounted her bother's comment, obviously recognizing a bucket of blether when she heard it.

"Why are you here, Thomas?" she inquired without looking at him.

"Well, to tell you the truth, I came to ask a favor."

"You? Tell the truth?" Jade glared at him, her eyes like ice. "Why the sudden change?"

"Jesus, Janine!" Thomas rolled his eyes. "I do everything I can to cooperate with you on this Sabrina thing, and this is what I get from you?"

"Cooperate?" Jade turned on him, suddenly livid. "You think what you're doing is cooperating?"

"You're damned right!" He shot a glance at Connor, as if to make sure the Scotsman was going to stay out of the family argument, and then quickly turned back to his sister. "You don't know what I've had to put up with. Gail's on the warpath with this one!"

"Don't blame it on Gail. She does everything you tell her to do."

"Oh, yeah?" Thomas laughed nervously. "You don't know her that well, do you?"

Connor studied Thomas's quick nervous gestures, his fleeting unfriendly smiles, the tic at the corner of his left eye, the way he moved his chin, as if tugging away from an annoying barb in his shirt collar. This nervous little man had control of Connor's beloved hotel and legal possession of Jade's precious daughter. The fact galled Connor, sending the bile of long-suppressed hatred up his throat. He watched Thomas, taking stock of his strengths and weaknesses, learning what made him tick, so he would know when and how to strike. He aimed to topple Thomas Brennan from the throne of his little empire and once and for all make the Brennans pay for their decades of murder and theft. The only problem was the fact that this man was Jade's brother.

"I've been jumping through hoops since I came to Seattle," Jade finally replied. "I'm not about to bend over backward for you, Thomas."

"Hey, I never said a thing about you moving in here without asking. I could have raised a stink about that. But I didn't, did I?"

"Maybe because you felt a small twinge of guilt." Jade crossed her arms. "For the loan you never made good on."

Thomas smiled and shot another quick glance at Connor, his eyes betraying the unease he tried so hard to conceal. Just to pressure him, Connor stepped closer.

"Ye owe Jade money?" he asked.

Thomas stepped back. "A small sum. I'm good for it."

"Are ye?"

"Sure!" Thomas jerked his chin up again. "Once the election's in the bag, I'll have it made. I've got some deals going that will set us up for life."

"Deals, eh?"

"Another condo project downtown and two hotels in Portland. Great potential. Excellent sites."

"Speculation," Connor commented.

"Hey, life is a gamble!" Thomas slapped Connor on his upper arm and laughed. "That's what makes it so interesting!"

Jade shook her head, her dour expression cutting off Thomas's outburst. "So what's the favor this time?"

"Okay." Thomas sobered and shoved his hands in the pockets of his slacks. "It's like this, Janine." He looked at Connor and then back to his sister. "I'm running for mayor. I've got an image to project. You know, a certain family image."

"Get to the point."

"Let's put it this way, Janine. Do you know how many times the Brennan family has been photographed?"

"What does that have t' do with th' price o' eggs?" Connor inquired.

"Plenty. I'm Thomas Brennan, mayor-to-be. I've got my lovely wife, Gail, by my side. And America's most popular number of children. Two. Well-scrubbed, fledgling athlete Robbie, and darling little Sabrina, looking like an angel in my arms."

Connor felt bile burning a path up his throat.

"I hate to sound like a typical politician, but projecting the right image can make or break a campaign, you know. John Q. Voter responds to the family man, especially a guy with cute little kids like the ones I have. That Sabrina's a real asset, let me tell you."

Bile spread into Connor's gut and ate into his heart as well, though he knew it was anatomically impossible. He sucked in a deep breath, aware that if he spoke, he would bellow a torrent of swear words, yank Thomas off his feet, and throw him out the bay window.

"You want to use Sabrina for your campaign?" Jade asked, her voice frozen into a monotone.

"You don't have to make it sound so bald, Janine." He let out a dry, nervous laugh. "But, in a way, that's what I'm asking for." He sank to the couch and propped his elbows on his knees. "Gail's talked to the psychologist. Apparently, you aren't as incapable as we thought. Especially now that you're married and everything."

"Gee, thanks," Jade murmured tersely.

Her sarcasm didn't register with Thomas. "Well, we

were worried," he replied. "Your lifestyle wasn't exactly *Sunset* magazine, if you know what I mean."

"My lifestyle was fine." She stared down at him. "And I don't think that was ever the issue, anyway."

"Gail's become very attached to Sabrina. And Sabrina to her."

"That may be true. But I'm her real mother. I have rights, too."

"Sure, but why can't they wait until this fall?" He looked up at her. "That's only a few months, Janine."

"You mean until the election?"

"Yes. If you get custody of Sabrina, I'll have a hard time explaining the loss of a daughter to my constituents."

"You could always tell the truth."

"And give the press a field day? No way! The family will look like a bunch of wackos—you getting pregnant, living with that weird guy for all those years, brain damage, sudden marriages. I can't have that, Janine. It will destroy the image we've tried to create. And if I don't win the election, my deals might not go through. I could be ruined."

Jade turned her back on him, apparently struck mute with anger.

Connor tilted his head. "So you're sayin' ye want th' use o' Sabrina until November?"

"Yes." Thomas's expression brightened, obviously blind to the effect his callous words were having. "Exactly."

"Just a wee steppin'-stone t' your financial success?"

"Yes. A matter of months, we're talking here. Not even a year!"

"Ye sicken me," Connor declared. He jerked his thumb toward the door. "Out with ye!"

"What?" Thomas jumped to his feet, his expression incredulous.

"Ye heard me! Get out!"

"What!" Thomas held up his hands and glanced from Connor to Jade, perplexed. "What did I say?"

Jade turned, her face white as marble, her eyes hard as ice. "Sabrina is not a campaign gimmick," she declared, so angry that her voice came out just above a whisper. "She's a child. She's my daughter."

"Janine, this will kill my campaign. Have a heart!"

"I have one!" she shouted, and whirled around to face the bay window, her spine stiff and her shoulders rigid.

The anguish in her voice cracked something deep inside Connor. Anger and frustration boiled through the fissure, and he could feel rage pouring out of his eyes. He turned on Thomas, his cheeks blazing, and saw the smaller man blanch.

"Get out," Connor growled.

"Just a—"

"Get out or I'll thrash ye!"

Connor jabbed his thumb in the direction of the front door. Thomas gaped at him but apparently thought better of replying and ducked away. Herman opened the door for Thomas, who strode across the room and then paused on the threshold, a safe distance from the Scotsman. He turned.

"Was that a threat, MacKenzie?"

"Take it however ye like," Connor replied.

"The chief of police is a personal friend of mine, you know."

"I dinna care if ye know th' pope."

"This won't look good for you, MacKenzie."

Connor snorted his derision.

Thomas jerked up his chin, glared at Herman as if to

demand what he was staring at, and then turned on his heel and left.

For a moment Connor stood by the end of the couch and studied Jade, whose back was turned to the room. He couldn't read her and didn't know if she was burning with anger or weeping in frustration. He only knew how angry he felt and guessed that Jade's reaction to her brother's visit must be ten times stronger than his.

Quietly he walked up behind her and laid a hand on her shoulder, aching to pull her into his arms but not about to foist himself on her should his attentions be unwanted. She'd had enough trauma in the last few minutes.

"Are ye all right?" he inquired softly, gazing down at the side of her face. He couldn't see evidence of tears, which was a good sign.

"What a bastard," she declared under her breath. She glared out the window at the twinkling lights below, her eyes hard, her arms stiff at her sides. "I'm ashamed to call him my brother."

"His priorities need polishin'," Connor commented, raising his other hand and then cupping both her shoulders.

"Oh, he keeps his priorities spit shined to a high gloss." Jade made no move to pull away. "They're just a whole lot different from yours and mine."

"So I gather."

"I appreciate you sticking up for me like that." She chuckled sadly. "I think you scared him."

"'Twas my intention." He leaned closer, his nose just above her ear. "But I dinna want t' worry ye, Jade. D'ye think he'll make it worse for ye now?"

She looked down. "Probably. Thomas will do anything to win. And he doesn't care who he steps on along the way."

"Not even a two-year-old girl?"

"Not even." Her voice cracked, and she took a deep, ragged breath.

"Jade," Connor murmured into her hair. He closed the slight gap between them and slid his arms down her torso to her waist, pulling her into a comforting embrace. To his surprise, she leaned her head back to his chest. The top of her head came to rest below his chin, just as he imagined it would. He tipped his head to the side and gently pressed his cheek to the crown of her auburn hair while his arms drew her more tightly against him. He closed his eyes and let the intoxicating closeness of her slender body infuse him with a smoldering fire he had to fight to keep from igniting into a full-fledged blaze.

He wanted to protect this woman, to help her triumph over her problems, to show her how exquisite love could be between a man and a woman when their hearts recognized each other. He was beginning to realize that deep inside, in many ways that mattered, he and Jade thought and felt alike. Her demons were his. Her joys paralleled his. He'd never felt as strong an urge to nurture a woman, to cherish and protect her, or simply to spend time in her company, because he'd never felt such a bone-deep love for anyone, not even Qi An.

In the few short days since he'd met Jade, she had become part of his every day, part of his worries, part of his happiness. It felt natural and right to hold her like this, to feel the rise and fall of her torso in the link of his arms, to drink in the warmth of her body.

Then she turned in his arms and slipped her long

hands up the front of his chest. "Thank you for being here," she said softly. "You don't know what it means to me."

"Maybe I do, Jade." He drew her closer again and hugged her tightly. "Maybe I do."

"Cookies are done," Herman called, walking out from the kitchen with a plate of fragrant samples.

Jade pulled away from Connor and flushed, obviously embarrassed by a public display of their growing affection for one another, and stepped to one side. Connor let her go, slightly hurt by her reaction. What did she care if Herman saw them standing together, holding each other? Was there something about him that she was ashamed of? If she respected him, wouldn't she be proud to be seen in his company, even if she'd been caught kissing him?

"Thanks," she said, reaching for a molasses cookie, her cheeks ruddy.

"Fresh from the oven," Herman said, holding the plate out to Connor.

"Ye shouldn't have," Connor said. And he meant it.

# 14

*A half hour later,* Jade held open the door as Connor and Herman left the condominium. Herman was going home for the night, and Connor had decided to accompany him and retrieve some books on Seattle history from Herman's vast library. Connor was determined to catch up on all the events he'd missed over the course of a century.

"After I read a few books, lass, you'd best beware," he warned with a wink. "I'll understand all about modern females then. And electricity."

"Those are two distinct topics, you know," she retorted, doing an ineffective job of hiding a smile. "Don't go mixing them up."

"Have no fear. I won't."

Jade looked up at Connor, her cheek near the edge of the door, waiting for something, but not sure what. Then she realized she expected a good-bye kiss, which she was growing accustomed to sharing with Connor during their moments of pretense before others. Yet there was no need for pretense now, no reason to act a part. Herman knew their marriage was a sham. There was no need for a kiss good-bye.

Slightly disappointed, Jade straightened and slid her hand down to the doorknob. The line between pretense and truth was no longer as distinct as before. For her, the task of pretending she had no feelings for Connor was proving more difficult than acting like a newlywed in the presence of the others.

As if he'd read her thoughts and meant to confuse her more, Connor leaned down for a kiss. His lips brushed hers, warmly and intimately, and she glanced up at his dark blue eyes, which danced with their own peculiar brand of midnight fire.

"I'll be back, lass," he said softly. "Dinna work too hard now."

"I won't." She tried to keep her chest from heaving with suppressed emotion. He had made her heart thud furiously from the moment they'd met, and her reaction to him only grew more intense with time. Ignoring her elevated pulse rate, she glanced at Connor's short companion. "Good night, Herman."

"Good night, Miss Brennan." He bowed.

"You are coming back for breakfast tomorrow, aren't you?"

"Of course." He bowed again. "Eight-thirty, Miss Brennan."

"See you then."

For a moment Jade lingered on the threshold and watched them walk down the hall. Then she closed the door and returned to the keyboard. She picked up a sheet of paper and studied the English words next to the Italian words written on the left. *Andante con moto, alla ingharese, quasi un capriccio, piano, allegretto.* Jade sighed and shook her head. The only item in the string that was vaguely recognizable was piano—a word that had become part of the English language and one she had learned as a baby. How long would it take until the Italian phrases meant more to her than italicized musical terms, until the black ribbons of notes meant more to her than a maddeningly secret code?

Disheartened, Jade turned on the keyboard and played a simple chord. She sang each component of the chord and then tried another, naming the notes as she sang them, trying to brand them into her muddy memory. Some notes and tones would hold and remain with her forever. Some would simply fade away, until she played them thousands of times. Some might never stick. Despair crept in with its whining little voice, telling her that she was a broken human being, that she should quit wasting her time, that she should give up—but she took a deep breath and forced herself to keep working.

Sometime around ten, Connor returned to the apartment with a load of books that he stacked on the coffee table. While Jade continued to practice, Connor poured himself a shot of whiskey and sank onto the couch to read. She didn't quit playing, and she knew they were both absorbed in their own work, with no need to converse with each other. But she appreciated the company nonetheless.

Jade worked far into the night, just as she had done before the accident, and by the time she was ready to quit, she'd made progress—a minute amount, but enough to measure. Feeling a bit better about her condition than she had when she'd sat down earlier, she turned off the keyboard, stood up, and stretched, twisting slightly to check on Connor.

Jade smiled at the sight. He lay on the couch, fully dressed but fast asleep, with an open book facedown on his chest. He still held the empty whiskey glass in his hand, which was propped on his thigh, while the other hand hung out in space, his upper arm moving with the rise and fall of his breathing. His chin rode on his shoulder, and his wide masculine mouth was squished into an M against his biceps.

A soft feeling stole over Jade as she gazed at him. She could have stood there an hour and watched him sleep, but he looked uncomfortable, and she knew she should do something. Quietly she moved to his side, carefully lifting the book off his chest and then slipping the glass from his grasp. He shifted and mumbled something under his breath, but he didn't wake up. Jade set the book and glass on the table and then walked to the hall closet to get his pillow and blanket. Though the bed in the second bedroom would have been much more comfortable than the couch, he refused to sleep in Sabrina's room, not wishing to mess it up in case she stayed overnight soon.

Carefully Jade spread the blanket over Connor's long lean frame, making certain she covered him from his feet to his shoulders. Then she placed the pillow on the table near his head, should he awaken in the night and want to use it.

Just as she straightened to leave, he turned on his side and his eyelids fluttered open.

"Thanks," he murmured, gazing up at her, his eyes surprisingly clear.

"You're welcome." She lingered beside him, not particularly anxious to leave.

Her pause allowed him time to regain full consciousness. He reached for her wrist.

"Come here for a minute," he said, tugging at her arm enough to urge her down next to him. He scooted back to provide her room, wedging himself to a sitting position against the arm of the couch.

"Connor, I—"

"Dinna ye know how t' tuck in a person properly?"

"I haven't tucked many people in."

"Well, maybe you need some practice." He smiled and his eyes crinkled at the corners. "For when ye tuck in Sabrina, that is."

She grinned slowly. "You're incorrigible, Mr. MacKenzie."

"And you're lovely when ye smile," he answered, then added in a softer tone, "Mrs. MacKenzie."

For a long moment their gazes locked and held. Then Jade realized that Connor's quiet smile had turned into a wide, mischievous grin.

"So what do you suggest I do to improve my technique?" she asked.

"A good-night kiss, for starters."

"Okay." She leaned forward and pressed a light kiss on his forehead, knowing she was being a tease. She straightened and ignored his wry smirk. "What else?"

"A song."

"A song?"

"Aye. A bedtime song."

"Like what?"

"You're the musician, Jade."

She pursed her lips, thought a moment, and then sang "Comin' Through the Rye," doing her best to mimic his Scottish burr and changing the gender to suit her purposes.

*If a body meet a body,*
*Comin' through th' Rye.*

She smoothed back a stray lock of hair that tumbled over his forehead, as a mother would do to her child, and continued the song.

> *If a body kiss a body, need a body cry?*
> *Every lassie has her laddie,*
> *Nane they say hae I.*
> *Yet all th' boys, they smile on me,*
> *When comin' through th' Rye.*

Connor's eyes shone and he was grinning from ear to ear when she finished. Jade had never felt a greater thrill from an audience than she did at that moment.

"Anything else?" she asked, glad her voice didn't betray the catch in her throat.

"Another kiss, lass," he answered. "But a real one this time. Full on the mouth."

"I wouldn't kiss Sabrina that way."

"I dinna want ye kissin' me like you'd kiss Sabrina." He reached for her, his large hand easily encompassing the back of her neck. The down at the nape of her neck rose at the electricity in his touch. "Or anyone else, for that matter."

His mouth found hers and he surrounded her with his strong arms, pressing her hard against him. He must not have been asleep long, because he still tasted of whiskey, and he had come fully awake in a matter of seconds.

Jade closed her eyes and surrendered to his kiss, collapsing onto his chest, soaking up his delicious warmth and the infusion of energy she always experienced in his embrace. She hadn't realized until now that she was freezing from her hours spent sitting at the piano and that melting into the furnace of Connor's embrace was more satisfying than she'd expected. She snuggled against him while his hands swept down her back and over her rump. He pulled her all the way onto the couch with him, until she lay against his full length, thigh to thigh, her breasts crushed into his chest.

Jade's body flared into full arousal at his touch, and all she could think about was what it would feel like to lie naked in this man's arms, to feel him inside her and around her, surrounding her with his heat and affection. He seemed to have an overabundance of both.

"Ah, lass," he murmured near her ear, sending a flood of shivers down her neck and back. "Ye dinna know what ye do t' me!"

"I think I do," she replied, letting her head loll back so he could kiss her throat. "Because you're doing the same thing to me."

"Am I now?"

"Yes."

Heat poured from his eyes, melting her inside as well as out.

"And what exactly am I doing to ye, lass?"

"Driving me crazy," she breathed, dipping to his mouth again.

He moaned against her lips and then opened his mouth upon hers. Their tongues found each other and intertwined as Connor caressed her derriere in both of his hands and pinned her against his hard length, which was easily felt beneath the light blanket between them.

Her breath caught in her throat as he moved his hips up and down in rhythm to the gentle thrusts of his tongue. Gradually Jade pulled away from his mouth, but he continued to move against her, lost to sensation. She looked down at him to find his eyes closed and his lips slightly parted, while his breath came hard and fast between his teeth. As she gazed at him, his golden aura seemed to sink back down around him, as if it had been enveloping the both of them as they kissed.

Jade paused, suddenly alarmed. What kind of man was Connor MacKenzie? Though she was falling in love with him, she didn't know enough about him to be comfortable with his physical condition. He wasn't a normal human being. How could she consider making love with someone who was supernatural? She had enough problems in her life without taking on an otherworldly relationship that might endanger herself and her daughter as well. What was she thinking?

She wasn't certain of his intentions, either. After all, a mere handful of days had passed since they'd first been introduced, and he'd admitted to being hungry for the company of a woman. Was Connor even aware that it was she on top of him, or was he imagining Qi An's fragile body in his hands, giving him such pleasure? The thought that she might be no more than a convenient respite made Jade flush and brought her plummeting to her senses.

She pulled away and sat up, pushing back her bangs with a faltering hand.

Connor blinked, confused. "What's wrong?" he asked.

"I should go."

"Go?" His voice cracked.

"Yes." Jade eased off him and slipped backward until her feet found the floor. She stood up. "What we're doing isn't part of the agreement."

"T' hell with th' agreement."

"It's too soon—for me."

He stared at her, his cheeks crimson and his eyes searching her face. "Hie out o' here, then. I'll not force ye t' do anythin' ye dinna care to."

"Connor, it's not that I—"

"Ye want t' go, then go."

Connor broke off the stare with a scowl of disappointment and dismissal and reached for the pillow. With the
effort, the skin pulled taut at his sharp jaw, and for a
moment all she wanted to do was to kiss him there—to
kiss him and forget about her concerns, and in doing so
give of herself and her love in all ways. She wanted him to
look at her once more, to see past her misgivings and read
what was in her heart. But it was clear that Connor was
not about to make eye contact again, at least not tonight.

"Good night, then," she murmured.

"Night." He didn't look at her.

With a sigh, Jade walked out of the living room, concerned that she might have pushed Connor away one
too many times, but certain she had taken the most logical path given their circumstances.

Late the next morning, Jade went up to her brother's
penthouse unit to take Sabrina and Gail to lunch, an
outing they had arranged the day before. Jade suspected
that Gail wanted to play "rival mothers" and impress
upon Sabrina that she was the best mother of the two.
Jade's objective was to observe Sabrina's true relationship with Gail, in order to decide whether or not it was
in her daughter's best interests for Jade to insert herself
as a mother figure right from the start or ease into it
over a period of years. However much she longed to
become Sabrina's mother in every sense of the word,
she would try not to immediately sever Sabrina's attachment to Gail if a true loving bond existed. What Jade
had seen so far and knew of Gail from previous experience made her suspect that such a bond was thin at best.
But she had to be sure.

She rang the buzzer and waited for Phillip to open the door while her thoughts turned back to Connor. By the time she had gotten out of bed that morning, Connor had already slipped out of the apartment, leaving no indication of where he'd gone or when he'd return. His silence and absence left a big hole inside her, which she found hard to ignore. She'd never allowed another human being to affect her thoughts and actions as much as Connor did, and she was wary of his influence. Better that he stay away for now, when she was more vulnerable than usual.

Phillip opened the door. His jaw went slack and his face grew ashen at the sight of her. Jade knew immediately that something was amiss.

"Phil," she said, her brows drawing together, "what's wrong?"

"We didn't expect you here."

"Why not?" She swept into the foyer, her ears tuned for the sound of children but hearing nothing. "Gail told me to meet her here at eleven-thirty."

"Did you not encounter the police on your way up?"

Jade glanced at him over her shoulder. "Pardon me?"

"Two policemen were sent to your apartment."

"Why?" Jade faced him squarely, her heart in her throat. "What's going on?"

Before Phillip could answer, Jade caught sight of Gail marching down the hallway toward her, her expression livid and her cheeks pink with rage.

"I thought I heard your voice," Gail declared. "You have some nerve coming here!"

"What do you mean?" Jade was completely taken aback by the vicious tone in Gail's voice. "We had a lunch date." She glanced at Phillip and then back at her sister-in-law. "Will somebody please tell me what's going on?"

Gail's dark eyes narrowed to slits, and her thin lips compressed until they made a single red line. "Don't play innocent with me, Janine. You might fool that psychologist, but you don't fool me!"

"What are you talking about?"

"We know you have her."

"Have who?"

"Sabrina! You've kidnapped her, haven't you!"

Jade's mouth fell open as the rest of her limbs froze in place. "What?" she whispered.

"You won't get away with it. Thomas's policeman friends are already here. So you might as well give her up."

"But I don't *have* Sabrina." Jade glanced around, desperate to dash away to search for her daughter but unable to break out of the shock that immobilized her.

"Liar," Gail retorted. "Where is she?"

"I don't know!"

"I'll bet your supposed husband has her, doesn't he?"

Jade paused. She had no idea where Connor had gone. Or with whom. She recalled Herman's warning that Connor's nature might suddenly twist, that his soul might turn dark. She thought of his affinity for children and how easily he could entice a little girl to go with him, should he so desire. Her heart shouted at her to disregard such a possibility, but her mind reeled out of control, grabbing at any explanation for Sabrina's absence.

Gail took Jade's pause as an admission of guilt.

"I knew it!" she shouted. "You two have taken her and think you can fool us with this charade."

"I don't have her, Gail," Jade replied firmly, commanding herself to get control of her fear and to think clearly. Mental clarity was imperative—for all of them—if they were to find Sabrina. "I swear I don't."

"Liar!"

"When was the last time you saw her?"

"Oh, spare me," Gail retorted, rubbing her temples with her fingertips. "I'm not stupid."

Just then a jingling sound caught Jade's attention, and she turned to see two policemen walking through the still open doorway, their neatly pressed blue uniforms in keeping with Gail's spotless home. One of them was tall and dark, well built and attractive in a cold sort of way. The other was short and stocky, with bad skin, a broken nose, and thick, pudgy hands. Jade guessed the tall officer was the brains of the pair and the smaller man was the brawn, accustomed to backing up his partner with a very real threat of violence.

"Bill, Danny," Gail called, obviously on a first-name basis with the officers, "here she is!"

Both men raked Jade with their dispassionate eyes, and their stares—quite similiar to the stare she'd received from Dr. Nilsen—chilled her in their cool concern.

Jade paled.

"We need to ask you some questions, ma'am," the taller officer stated. His black hair was cut in a short buzz, and she noticed a hole in his ear where he probably wore an earring during his off-duty hours. He pulled out a tablet and took a pen from his shirt pocket.

"Why waste the time?" Jade inquired. "Sabrina could be in danger!"

"Janine's quite an actress, Officer Stevens," Gail put in. "She can be very convincing."

Bill Stevens lifted his eyes to Gail's pinched face. "Thank you, Mrs. Brennan. I'll keep that in mind. Is there a place we can ask Miss Brennan a few questions?"

"It's MacKenzie," Jade corrected him. "Mrs. MacKenzie."

The policeman glanced at her and then at Gail. "I thought you said her name was Brennan."

"It is. I mean, it was!" Gail snapped, rubbing her forehead, in obvious physical distress. "Until her supposed marriage!"

"My marriage is just as legal as yours, Gail," Jade remarked, surprised to find herself defending her marital state.

"Ladies, please!" Stevens held up his hand. "We have to get this investigation under way."

"Where's Thomas?" Jade asked, glancing at her sister-in-law.

"He's out of town. And I'd like to get this cleared up before he gets back."

"You mean you haven't told him?" Jade asked, incredulous.

"I didn't want a fuss raised. And I assumed *you* had her."

"Well, I don't!"

"Ladies!" Bill Stevens injected again. "We will separate you two if necessary."

"It isn't necessary," Gail answered with a sniff. "You can question her in the library. Follow me."

She led them down the hall. Flanked by the policemen, Jade trudged toward the dark little room where she'd first met Dr. Nilsen. The library still reeked of bad vibrations from her last visit, and she was reluctant to cross the threshold, especially when she knew she should be searching for Sabrina, not spending precious time on useless interrogation.

Just as Jade turned to enter the library, her attention was caught by a sudden movement at the end of the hall. Someone had apparently been watching them and had ducked out of sight—someone not quite four feet tall with short brown hair. Robbie.

Jade passed into the library and stopped in the center of the room. "Has anyone questioned Robbie yet?" she inquired. "He might know something."

"Robbie has nothing to do with this," Gail declared. "Don't try to blame Sabrina's disappearance on an innocent child."

"I was merely suggesting—"

"We'll handle the investigation, ma'am," Officer Stevens put in, cutting off Jade's remark. "All you have to do is answer some questions."

His stocky partner motioned toward the chair by the desk, the same chair where she'd been grilled by Dr. Nilsen. "Why don't you have a seat, Mrs. MacKenzie?"

"No thanks," she replied. "I'd rather stand."

Danny seemed to take her refusal personally and glared at her while he folded his arms across his wide chest. His silver watch glinted in the dim light. "Suit yourself," he drawled, never releasing her from his dour regard. His unfriendly scrutiny caused guilt to flare up inside Jade, making her tense, even though she'd done nothing wrong. Gail paced in the background, her glare burning a hole in Jade's back.

"Really, gentlemen, this is unnecessary." Jade glanced from one face to the other. "I am not a kidnapper."

"We'll let the courts decide that," Stevens replied, his voice exasperatingly calm. He flipped open his tablet and looked up at her expectantly. "We're just here to get the facts. Now, just where *were* you this morning?"

"At the apartment downstairs."

"And what apartment would that be?"

"You've been there. You know which one."

"Just answer the question, Mrs. MacKenzie."

She scowled at the senselessness of his question. "Unit three fifteen."

Stevens wrote something in the tablet. "Were you there all morning?"

"Yes."

"Can you verify that?"

"What do you mean—with witnesses?"

"Yes."

"No." Jade shook her head. "I was there alone."

"Make any calls?"

"No. I was working."

"What kind of work?"

"Composing." She watched him write, her frustration mounting. "What does all this have to do with Sabrina?" she asked.

"We're asking the questions," the short officer put in. "And if you don't cooperate, we're going to be here longer. Is that what you want, lady?"

"No." Jade sighed and shoved her hands in her pockets.

"Ask her where Connor is," Gail said, pointing at Jade. "Ask her where her alleged husband is."

Officer Stevens surveyed Jade's face. "Where is your husband, Mrs. MacKenzie?"

"Probably at Herman Fong's house."

"Who is Herman Fong?"

"A friend."

"Where does he live?" Officer Stevens paused and looked up, ready to write down the address.

Jade raised her chin. "I'm not sure."

"And he's a friend." Dubious, the officer stared at her, waiting for an explanation.

"We haven't known each other that long. I'm sure he's in the phone book."

"But your husband might not be with Mr. Fong? Is that right?"

"That's a possibility."

"Doesn't Mr. MacKenzie keep you informed as to his whereabouts?"

"Most of the time." She thought back to the previous evening, how she'd left him on the couch, silent and hurt. "But we had an argument last night—well, not really an argument. Just a misunderstanding."

"A fight," the stocky policeman put in.

Jade glanced at his face, surprised at the sudden flicker of interest in the man's expression. "No, not a fight. Just some unpleasant words. He left before I got up this morning."

"As you can see," Gail interjected archly, "not the most stable relationship."

Officer Stevens ignored Gail's outburst. "What is Mr. MacKenzie's relationship to Sabrina? Is he the natural father?"

Jade looked down. "No."

"And it's a good thing, too," Gail commented. "The man's horrible with children. A tyrant."

"Mrs. Brennan . . ." Officer Stevens sighed and rolled his eyes. "Would you please not interrupt?"

"But he's got Sabrina," Gail cried. "And you need to be aware of what kind of people we're dealing with. He's got Sabrina, and Janine put him up to it. It's obvious!"

"We'll put out an APB for him, but there is no proof of wrongdoing, Mrs. Brennan."

"Then where is Sabrina?" Gail clenched her fists at her sides. "Somebody's got to have her!"

"Where was she this morning?" Jade asked sharply. "Who was looking after her when she disappeared, Gail?"

Everyone turned their attention to Gail, who drew herself up, haughty in her umbrage.

"Don't you dare accuse me of shirking my duty, Janine! I have taken care of that child for two long years—two long years!"

Jade stared at her sister-in-law, knowing for certain now how little love was lost between Gail and Sabrina. Gail saw her role as caretaker of Sabrina, a duty she had to perform, perhaps for Thomas's benefit. A loving mother would not expect thanks from anyone. A hard feeling surrounded Jade's heart when she thought of how little love Sabrina must be receiving from Gail and how much she herself disliked the woman. But concentrating on their enmity would do nothing to help find Sabrina. And time was ticking away.

"Gail . . ." She forced herself to be calm. "This isn't the time to air our differences. This is a time to work together. To find Sabrina. Let's concentrate on that, all right?"

"Of course," Gail replied coldly. "That's what I've been trying to do all along." She glanced at the desk, where a fancy brass phone with an old-fashioned rotary dial gleamed up at them. "Thomas will have to be called." She pinched her lips together and rubbed her temple. "I just pray the press doesn't get hold of this."

Jade clutched her arms to her chest and looked toward the window, blocking Gail and the policemen from her thoughts. Where was Sabrina? And who was with her little girl?

# 15

"*How is she?*" Herman asked, peering around the doorway into Jade's bedroom.

Connor glanced at Jade, who sat on her bed, numb and exhausted, staring at nothing. His heart went out to her, but there was nothing he could do but encourage her to sleep. He had returned to the apartment near dinnertime to find Jade missing. When he'd gone up to the Brennan penthouse to see if she was there, he'd learned from Phillip that Sabrina had been kidnapped or lost, and the police were looking for him as a possible suspect.

Connor had been searching the city ever since, stopping cars and clocks and dimming lights wherever he went, but uncaring of his effect on the modern mechanical world in his quest to find Jade's little girl. He'd found nothing, and the police hadn't caught him, either.

Worried and tired, Connor had dragged himself back to the condominium around one o'clock in the morning to find Jade just letting herself in the door.

She'd hugged him then, clinging to him wordlessly, until he'd urged her into the apartment and helped her out of her jacket. He'd never seen her so distraught, her lips so pale, her eyes so haunted. She hadn't improved much since then, but at least he'd convinced her to go to bed.

"Jade'll be fine," Connor replied to Herman's question, sounding more confidant than he felt. What would happen to Jade's mental state should Sabrina never be found—or not be found alive? Jade had told him once that fate hadn't smiled on her much, that many things had been taken from her during the course of her life. Could she sustain another wallop and not have it break her spirit forever?

"I brought her a cup of tea," Herman said, offering it to Connor. The fine china rattled in the old man's trembling hands. Connor took the delicate cup and saucer, holding it carefully so it wouldn't spill.

"Thanks. I'll see she gets it."

Herman bowed slightly. "Please tell her that I have alerted all my acquaintances regarding Sabrina's disappearance."

"I will, Herman. Thank you." Connor smiled and patted the old man's shoulder in gratitude, well aware of the extent of the list of Herman's acquaintances. The more people contacted, the higher the odds were of finding Sabrina.

"I will say good night then, Mr. MacKenzie."

"Good night." He smiled, distracted and distant.

While Herman let himself out of the apartment, Connor ambled across the bedroom carpet, carrying the tea. "Herman made you a cup of tea," he ventured, holding it in front of Jade. She gave no indication that she saw it.

"I'll put it on th' nightstand, lass," he added, setting the saucer down with a clatter. For a long moment he stood beside the bed, studying her and wondering what he should do. She looked so lost, so grief-stricken, that he felt compelled to do something. But what? What would give her support? An embrace? Would she reject him as she had last night, find him too aggressive? One thing he knew for certain: he had to act. He couldn't stand there and see her pain without trying to alleviate it.

"Jade?" he asked.

She didn't respond.

He sat beside her. "Jade?"

Her mouth trembled.

Connor reached out and traced the hollow of her cheek with his fingertip. At his touch, she closed her eyes. Tears squeezed out between her lashes, rolling like moonstones down her face. The sight of her weeping turned something inside him, like a knife blade to the gut.

Gently he urged her to sink against him, drawing her head to his chest with one hand while he pressed her back with the other. She reached around his torso and clung to him, shaking and crying, and gradually twisted until she was halfway in his lap. Connor leaned against the headboard of the bed and held her tightly, certain that Jade found comfort in his arms and glad he was the one to offer solace to her.

For a long, long while she remained in his arms, her face pressed into his shirt and her palms flat on his back. But he was sure she touched him more to reassure herself of his solid presence than to cherish him. Perhaps she found him more a rock than a romantic interest. He wanted to be far more to her someday, but for now he was willing to be her rock.

Connor closed his eyes and fought the urge to roll her onto her back and cover her with his body, to help her push away the darkness in the only way he knew how. Yet here she was, weeping in his arms, her embrace as chaste as that of a child, while his male body burned for her.

"Jade," he whispered hoarsely, "I should go. Ye need t' rest."

"Please," she murmured. "Stay just a while longer. Please."

Her arms tightened around him.

"Only if ye lie down and try t' sleep."

"I'll never sleep, not when Sabrina is out there somewhere, lost."

"Ye must try. In the mornin' we'll find her." He smoothed her hair. "I'm sure of it."

"But I should be out there, looking for her—"

"Ye have been. Ye're beat. Ye canna go on without rest." He touched her cheek. "They've got dogs out there, Jade, and Herman's friends will search all night, too. Somethin' will turn up. Ye just wait an' see."

"Oh, Connor," she exclaimed. "I can't bear to think she's out there in the rain somewhere, out in the dark, crying and scared. I can't bear it!"

He held her again and kept stroking her hair, knowing he should stand up and go but aching to remain. For a long while they were silent, and all he could hear was her breathing. Then Jade slipped her hands around to the front of his shirt, her palms on the flat planes of his chest.

"Connor, don't leave me alone tonight."

"I'll stay as long as ye like. Just scoot yourself down, Jade." He glanced at her clothes and saw she was still wearing her slippers. Once she settled down, he'd make her more comfortable.

Jade stretched out upon the bed and immediately turned toward him, reaching out for him. The gesture touched him and made him feel needed and necessary. He lay prone on the mattress and then gathered her in his arms, holding her close to his body and hoping she wouldn't notice the way his male member instantly responded to the nearness of her lithe figure. Connor stroked her, careful not to linger overlong at her firm breasts or her seductively trim waist. Her hips, lean but wondrously womanly, were far too close for comfort. His erection stretched even fuller, painfully tight.

"It's strange," she commented, her voice muted by despair. "When you're here, I'm not so worried."

"Why is that strange?"

"I can't explain it," she added. "I think it's your aura. That golden glow you have."

"Ye dinna think it could be me, Jade, and the fact that I care about ye and Sabrina?"

"Perhaps." She gazed at him, her cheek propped on the edge of her pillow, as she looked at him through a red curtain of her unruly hair, like lengths of beads hanging in the doorway of a bawdy house. He gazed back at her, wondering what he could say, what he could do, to ease the pain in her eyes. The best approach was to keep her talking until she grew drowsy.

"What are ye thinkin'?" he asked, gently sweeping the strands of hair from her eyes.

"Just how strange it is to be talking like this to you."

"Why?"

"You're one man I never dreamed I'd have in my bed."

"Life takes peculiar turns." Connor smiled slowly. "I never thought I'd be one hundred and forty-five years old."

"You don't look a hundred and forty-five."

"I don't feel it, either." He eased one hand down the side of her torso and into the feminine dip of her waist. Jade closed her eyes, as if savoring his touch, and Connor decided to take the chance and kiss her. He leaned forward and kissed the small mole on her neck, the one he'd dreamed of kissing. Jade sighed and turned slightly in his arms, enough to present her cheek to him. While her hands framed his shoulders, Connor pressed a kiss on the swell of her cheekbone, the line of her jaw, and then at the corner of her mouth. He could sense her hesitation as she considered the next move and weighed the consequences. His heartbeat thrummed in his throat as he waited for her to decide.

Then she turned a fraction more, until their lips were nearly touching, as if she wanted him to continue his chaste exploration of her body. But he had to be sure this time just how far she planned to go. Last night she had taken him to a certain height and then left him hanging. He didn't want to repeat that frustrating experience.

He looked down at her, drinking in her serious regard. "Shall I stop?" he whispered.

"No," she replied. "I need you tonight. To hold me."

Without saying more, Connor slanted his mouth upon hers and their lips came together in a searing kiss, full of tenderness and sadness, a bond made poignant by their worry for Sabrina. Her hands slid to his chest and grabbed handfuls of his chambray shirt as the kiss deepened and grew hotter. Connor felt his nipples growing hard beneath the slight pressure of her small hands.

He rolled toward her, just enough to ease one leg across hers and urge her onto her back. She complied and sank back into the pillows without taking her hands off his chest. He bent to kiss her again, and this time Jade slid her hands up his chest, past the column of his neck, until her palms lay flat upon the sides of his face and her fingertips reached into his hair. He eased back slightly, to look at her face, to make sure she wasn't weeping. A spike of compassion coursed through him as he gazed down at her and saw the sorrow and desolation in her green eyes.

She needed him to sweep her away from her shadows, to provide a space where she was only Jade and he was only Connor, and there was nothing else, no past or present to haunt them—if only for a little while.

He needed to travel to such a space as much as Jade did. Sabrina's disappearance had affected him more than he would have believed possible. He slipped a hand down to her torso and cupped one of her full, rounded breasts, rolling her nipple between his fingers until she moaned in his mouth and writhed beneath him. He pressed himself against her hip, wanting more than anything to tear off her clothes and plow into her, to lose himself inside of her warmth; but he forced himself to remain in control.

Carefully he unfastened her silk blouse, holding himself back as each button slipped free. Then he let the fabric fall away to reveal her beautiful breasts, concealed by a cream-colored satin bra, so dainty in comparison with the clumsy foundation garments made of cotton and whalebone that he'd laboriously unhooked on women in the past. By the looks of this scant garment, he'd have only to pop one snap and Jade would be released to view. Connor spotted the fastener in the front of her brassiere and undid it gently. Her breasts tumbled free, all pale ivory and pink, her nipples standing up like rose-colored shoe buttons.

"St. Andrew," Connor murmured in awe. He'd never seen such perfect breasts, never expected such pale white skin, flawlessly clear and achingly smooth. Not one freckle or mole marked Jade's skin below her shoulders. Her flesh was like a snowfield, virginal and pristine.

He sank to her breasts, burrowing his nose between them and then taking their tips into his mouth, one after the other. She tasted musky, womanly, heavenly, and her sighs of delight sent him soaring. Jade arched beneath him as he kissed her breasts, and she stopped breathing altogether as he lightly pulled a nipple between his teeth. For a moment she paused, rigid and still, her back like a rod of steel. Then all the air seemed to rush out of her and she collapsed onto the bed.

"Connor!" she gasped, incredulous.

"Ye like that, then?" he asked, finding it difficult to speak.

"Oh, yes!" She sighed and drew his head back down to her, obviously asking him to continue.

He wanted nothing more than to give pleasure to this woman, and by the looks of it, her response to his touch was all that he could hope for, all that he could ever desire. He loved the lean silhouette of her body, so different from the plump women of his century. He could feel the outline of her ribs, the curved crests of her hipbones, and the wonderfully taut stretch of her abdomen where her navel dipped in just above her seductively flat stomach. He didn't know how much longer he could wait to see her completely naked, to feel that pale lithe body, those slender limbs, beneath his own.

Connor took her other breast in his mouth and kissed it, sucked it, laved it, and bit it until Jade's nails dug into his back. She tipped her hips upward, and he took the opportunity to slide his hand between her legs.

She was on fire for him.

"Ah, God!" Connor sank his nose into the small of her neck, no longer entirely in control, and surged against her leg.

"Connor!" Jade whispered hoarsely.

Her hands came around him, first across his shoulders and then down his back to his rear. She pressed him against her and moved her hips beneath his, making it clear that she wanted from him exactly what he burned to share with her.

Connor slipped a hand between their hips and unfastened her jeans. Then, as he kissed her, he pushed his hand into her pants, past the soft hair behind the zipper, and into the warmth between her legs. She was ready for him, and he couldn't wait another moment.

Deftly he yanked down her jeans as she reached for the buttons of his shirt. He didn't get her pants and underthings all the way off before she urged him back down and curved her arms around his bare torso beneath his open shirt. Connor's skin burst into bloom at her touch, and his breath came hard and fast as he dipped to her mouth again. Her nipples pressed into his bare chest, and he could feel her quick, shallow breaths rising and falling against his abdomen, her skin so close to his, it was as if her flesh had become part of his own. He thought he'd explode. Did she want him or not? Why did she pull him down before he'd fully undressed her?

"Connor!" she gasped again, sliding her fingertips into the top of his jeans, laying his concerns to rest.

Trembling, he lifted himself upward a few inches, enough to unfasten his pants and free himself. Then, with his mouth dry and his pulse thundering in his ears, he bent forward to kiss her. Their lips came together and held for a long, incredible kiss. Then he slipped forward, his mouth on her throat, his shaft poised just above her warm moist flesh.

"You're so beautiful," he murmured, barely able to hold back.

She smiled faintly and closed her eyes. "You make me feel beautiful," she replied, her voice breathless with desire.

Connor's heart swelled until he felt as if his chest would burst. He slid his hands down the inside of her long slender thighs and around the curve of her trim hips, pinning her beneath him. Then, holding his breath and closing his eyes, he pushed into her, savoring the moment, because he was certain this night of lovemaking with Jade would be unlike anything he'd ever known.

Jade cried out and locked her arms around his back, arching up to meet him, and he sank into her, driven by love for the first time in his life.


Fitful with worry, Jade tossed and turned that night and woke up in the wee hours of the morning, surprised to find Connor's side of the bed empty. After just a few hours of lovemaking, it already felt natural to have him sleep at her side with his hand on her flank. She yawned and turned over, expecting to see him in the bathroom. The light wasn't on in the bath, but she didn't think he would have turned it on anyway, accustomed as he was to living without electric lights.

A strange feeling of well-being still hummed inside her as well as out, a result of the time spent in Connor's arms. During their passionate joining, she'd felt more connected with him than with any other human being in her entire life. But looking back on those precious hours, she couldn't be sure if the sense of well-being was due to the fact that she loved him, that he'd given her so much comfort in the face of Sabrina's disappearance, or that he emitted an energy for which her body had an unquenchable thirst. Certainly no other man had affected her in this way. But she had never loved a man as she loved Connor. Was a transfer of energy a sign of true love? She'd never heard of such a thing.

For a moment she listened for the sound of Connor puttering around in the apartment, but she heard nothing. Then she decided to snuggle back down and pull the covers around her shoulders while she waited for him to come back to bed. When she reached for the comforter, she was surprised to see a faint glow surrounding her left hand. Jade raised it up against the darkness in the room. There was a definite yellow light following the silhouette of her slender fingers. Jade turned her hand, palm up, and inspected it again. Lemon-colored light filtered into the night. Had she acquired some of Connor's special energy field during lovemaking? A chill passed through her.

Then a movement across the room caught her eye. A gleam on the wall by the bureau flashed in the darkness, and then a series of ripples glinted silver and white. She gaped at it, alarmed even further. The flocked wallpaper phenomenon, running with water, had returned.

Jade jerked to a sitting position, suddenly and thoroughly awake.

It was then she saw Connor, standing at the corner of the wall, his golden glow so faint that she could barely see it.

"Connor!" she exclaimed, scrambling out of bed.

He turned, his face unreadable in the gloom, but his eyes glowing in the darkness like those of a nocturnal creature. Jade flushed cold at the sight of him and stepped back, her thighs bumping into the bed frame behind her. Who or what had she just made love with a few hours ago? Whose seed had she taken deep inside her? Jade swore under her breath at her lack of fore-thought. In the heat of passion she had forgotten Connor's otherworldly roots and had seen only the man. What if there were consequences to their lovemaking? What kind of life sprang from century-old seed? Still, she would never regret spending the last few hours in his arms.

"Do you hear it?" Connor asked, tilting his head and staring intently at the wall.

She listened, straining to discern the slightest noise, for Connor's sake, but heard nothing other than her own blood racing in her ears. "Hear what?"

"Th' voice."

"What voice?"

"Someone is calling me."

"Who?"

Connor paused, as if listening again. Then he ran his hand over his hair. "I'm not certain."

"What are they saying?"

"I canna make it out. 'Tis too faint."

He stepped closer to the wall, his hand on the dresser, as he strained forward to hear better. His head slipped through the facade of wallpaper and water and disap-peared from view.

"Connor, don't!" Jade shouted, suddenly terrified for his safety. She dashed forward and grabbed his arm to yank him away from the wall. His free arm flailed out-ward, knocking aside the picture frames perched on the dresser and sending them sailing. The photograph of Sabrina hit the solid wall behind the bureau and bounced to the floor. The photo of Martin, however, sailed right through the wallpaper into nothingness and vanished.

Stunned, Jade watched it disappear, mute with incredulity.

Connor pulled out of her grip. "The voice—it's getting louder," he declared, turning back to the wall.

"Don't!" She peered at the watery wallpaper, frightened of its power, and saw that Connor's aura had partially detached, as if it were being sucked into the nothingness behind the wallpaper. The aura looked streaked and distorted, pulled by an unseen force. "Keep away from there, Connor. Please!"

"But someone's callin' t' me," he retorted, never once taking his stare off the wall. "I can hear it plainly now."

"No, it's too dangerous!"

"Why do you say that?"

"Because." She staggered backward as a realization struck her like a blow. "I think it's a place of the dead." Her heart hammered in her chest as fear gripped her heart. "Qi An is there. Martin is there." She reached for his elbow and her hand shook so hard, she could barely make contact. "They're dead, Connor! I think only the dead pass through."

"Then how can I?" He turned to her, his eyes blazing. "I'm not dead, am I?"

She gaped at him, not certain of the answer.

Almost immediately he turned to the wall again and held up his hand for silence. Jade watched as more of his aura streaked toward the wall and disappeared. For an instant neither of them moved or breathed, as Connor listened and Jade struggled to catch the slightest sound.

"Ah, no!" he gasped, his expression white with shock.

"What?" Jade glanced at him and then at the glistening wall. "What, Connor?"

"It can't be," he continued, his voice drifting off in confusion.

"What?" she demanded.

Connor turned his gaze to Jade and then took both her shoulders in her hands. "Jade, I'm hearin' "—he swallowed, and his eyes rapidly searched her face—"I'm hearin' Sabrina in there."

The bottom fell out of Jade's stomach. For an instant she tried not to comprehend what Connor had just said, as if ignoring his words would keep the truth at bay. But an instant later reality rushed over her, burning her hopes, like a forest fire raging through a beautiful valley, destroying everything in its path.

"Sabrina?" Her hands covered her mouth in horror. "In there?"

"Aye. I can hear her wee voice."

"What's she saying?" Jade stared at the wallpaper, trying to see through the thick wet wall but failing. "Connor, what's she saying?"

"She's callin' for me, Jade. Callin' my name."

"But she can't be in there!" Jade pointed to the flocked wall, refusing to believe her baby was in another dimension, a place where only the dead belonged. "Not unless she's—"

"Maybe she's lost in th' old part of th' hotel."

"Old part?" Jade protested. "That's not an old part! That's a gate to the past. To the dead! Oh, God, Connor!"

"Now, Jade, ye canna be certain." He squeezed her shoulders. "Dinna think she's lost!"

"But if she's there—"

"Then I'll find her!" He released Jade's shoulders and faced the red wallpaper.

"Wait, it could be a trick! What if Qi An is tricking you by impersonating Sabrina?"

"She wouldn't trick me, Jade. She wasn't like that."

"She could be now. Herman said her spirit may be evil now." Jade flung her arms around him from behind. "Don't go, Connor. Please don't go in there—I beg you!"

"I have to. If Sabrina's in there, I have to!"

"But this is where you kissed Qi An, remember? This is the place she has the strongest hold on you—on your soul!"

"Let me go, Jade."

"She wants you. Don't you see?"

Connor glared at her and then pulled out of her grip and ran to the side of the bed, where his jeans lay on the floor in a heap. He yanked them on and zipped them while Jade watched, trying to think of a way to keep him from leaving. Once Connor passed through the wallpaper, she might never see him again.

Yet what if he *was* hearing Sabrina?

A huge ball of desperation clogged in her throat at the thought. What would she do without his sunny warmth? How would she go on without Connor in her life, in her bed? Yet how could she keep him from trying to find Sabrina? What if her little girl were lost in that other place, with no one to help her? As she watched Connor pull on his shirt and walk toward her, tears welled in her eyes, blurring her vision too much to allow her to see his expression.

"Jade, I have to go. Ye know I do." He caressed the side of her face. "If Sabrina's in there, I must find her."

"It's a trick. Qi An will get you. I know it!"

"Ah, love . . ." He clutched her to his chest and held her tightly.

She wound her arms around his powerful torso, hugging him with all her strength. "Don't go, Connor. I'll never see you again!"

"Aye, ye will. Have faith, lass!" He pulled back and gazed down at her, a sad smile tugging up the left corner of his mouth. "What, with all th' tears, I'd think ye harbored feelin's for me, Jade."

She clenched her teeth, unable to speak, her heart breaking in painful jagged pieces, as her hands slid from his wondrously warm body. She wanted to tell him how much she loved him, how much she wanted him in her life, but the words wouldn't form on her lips, made wooden by despair. He was going to Qi An, to be in his rightful time, to be with the woman who had loved him enough to die for him. How could Jade match such sacrifice with her simple affection, however sincere it was?

"I'll be back," Connor promised, touching her arm. "Dinna worry, love." He pressed a quick kiss on her mouth and stepped away. Slowly he put a hand through the wall and then a foot, testing the unknown world on the other side.

"There's stairs," he said over his shoulder, his voice full of hope.

"Connor! I—"

Then he took another step and was gone.

# 16

*Waiting for a sign* of Connor's return or word about Sabrina, Jade spent the rest of the night sitting on the bed, her chin resting on her knees, while she watched the dripping red wall where Connor had disappeared. Gradually dawn blossomed outside her bedroom window and birds sang to the rising sun, but still Connor made no appearance, and Jade grew desperate. Yet there was nothing she could do. She couldn't pass through the wall and follow him. All she could do was wait.

With the morning light, the old flocked wallpaper and water faded, leaving the modern wall in its place. Heartbroken, Jade watched the transition occur, saw the glint of water disappear and the texture of the flocked paper recede. Without the old wall in evidence, she doubted Connor would have a portal through which he could return. A single tear slipped down her cheek and dripped onto her hand.

She had known he would vanish from the moment he'd announced he was going in for Sabrina. She only hoped Connor hadn't plunged into more danger and that wherever he was now, he was safe and sound—and that Sabrina had no connection with the death behind the ancient wallpapered wall.

"You'd better be good to him, Qi An," Jade muttered, brushing tears off her cheeks. "Damn good to him!"

Disconsolate, she slid off the bed, her limbs stiff with cold, her joints cramped from sitting in the same position for hours. She had to force herself to move, to step beyond the sadness that welled up like a black cloud around her. Tears rolled down her cheeks as she dragged herself out to the living room, found her phone, and called the penthouse. Phillip answered the ring, his voice sounding older and more tired than she'd ever heard it.

"Any news?" Jade asked, wiping the dampness off her cheek.

"I'm afraid not," he replied.

"Nothing from the police? Nothing at all?"

"No, Mrs. MacKenzie. Not a word."

Jade sighed and tried to hold back more tears. "Okay. I'm going to go out for a few hours to have another look around. If anything comes up, would you please leave a note on my door?"

"Of course, Mrs. MacKenzie."

"Thanks."

Jade bit her lip and hung up the phone, feeling hopeless and desperate. She glanced at her hand and found that the last vestiges of Connor's glow had dissipated, which left her more disconsolate than ever. Even the emerald wedding ring seemed dark and cloudy. She took a shower, pulled on a pair of jeans and a sweatshirt, left her valuable ring on the bathroom sink where it wouldn't get lost or scratched, and slipped out of the hotel.

The May morning was chilly and windy, with the sharp smell of rain on the way and a stiff breeze off the bay that pierced through her sweatshirt. Jade hunched over against the wind and continued walking, barely aware of the cold. Few motorists or pedestrians were on the streets yet, and all the shops were dark, except for a twenty-four-hour market on the corner. Jade shoved her hands in her pockets and hurried down the sidewalk, wondering if it was safe to walk around Pioneer Square at this time of day. Transients huddled in doorways, still asleep in their dirty blankets, while some had already got up for the day and were poking through the trash in the alleys. A few lone taxis cruised by, their drivers wondering if she wanted a lift, and a delivery truck idled outside a Starbucks coffeehouse. Regardless of personal danger, Jade continued her search, looking down every alley, every stairwell, and every side street for a sign of her little girl.

After an hour, the wind had frozen her hands and feet and she knew she had to turn back. The clouds above finally burst, and rain slashed at her face and hands, driving her back to the old hotel. Caught in the downpour, she ran the last block and then cut through the vacant lot. Normally she didn't go through the lot, since the brambles and refuse piles were too dangerous to pass through. But this time she didn't care if the brambles caught at her jeans. She dashed across the rough terrain, watching for dips and hidden obstacles.

Halfway across the lot, she caught sight of a familiar purple color and her heart lurched in her chest. She ducked down, peering into the bank of brambles, while the wind caught the strip of color and fluttered it in the air again. Frantic, she plowed through the briars, uncaring that the thorns snagged her hands and sweatshirt. She grabbed the purple strip, yanked it out of the bushes, and held it up in the rain, her heart pounding furiously. She'd found the tail of Sabrina's kite.

"Sabrina!" she shouted into the storm.

Yesterday the police had looked through the vacant lot in search of clues and found nothing. She could only suppose the strong wind had blown the tail into view.

"Sabrina, where are you?" Jade glanced around wildly, the kite tail clutched to her breast and rain streaming down her face. "Sabrina!"

No one answered her call. She scrambled out to a clearing and called again. No response. Jade glanced at the kite tail in her hand. Had Sabrina decided to go outside and fly her kite yesterday? All by herself? Surely she wasn't capable of finding her way out of the condominium complex alone. Had someone gone with her?

Jade instantly thought of Robbie. A vision of him ducking out of sight at the end of the hall flashed into her thoughts. In that moment, she guessed what had transpired yesterday. Robbie and Sabrina had left together to fly kites, perhaps to repeat the enjoyable time they'd spent in the park with her and Connor and Phillip. They'd come to this vacant lot, thinking it was a good place to fly their kites, and something had happened—something Robbie was afraid to divulge.

Jade swore under her breath. She dashed across the vacant lot toward the hotel, turning her ankle and almost falling flat on her face before she reached the sidewalk. A man and woman waiting for a bus looked at her in fright and stepped out of her path as she streaked past them and ran up the street. Drenched and shivering, she

punched the buttons at the entry door of the old hotel
and let herself in.

Not even the doorman was on duty yet. Jade hurried
up the stairs, oblivious of the polished maple staircase
and woodwork, reminders of the master craftsmanship
of another age and the flawless taste of the man who had
built the hotel, and turned toward the bank of elevators
on the right. She slipped into a car and punched the button for the penthouse. A lifetime elapsed as she waited
for the elevator to travel to the top floor. Before the
doors slid completely open, she dashed through them
and ran to the penthouse door. She rang the bell and
then pounded on the door, dancing in impatience on her
numb feet.

Phillip, dressed in a navy robe and maroon pajamas,
answered her summons and stared in horror at her sod-
den hair and clothes.

"Miss Brennan!" he gasped, forgetting her new name
in his shock.

"Phil, where's Thomas?"

"Out. Do come in at once. You're drenched." He held
open the door, as formal as ever, even in his nightclothes, and urged her to step into the foyer.

Jade hurried into the house and then turned, too
focused to be concerned about her wet condition.
"Where exactly is my brother?"

"Mr. Brennan's doing an interview for the morning
news with a local television station."

"Why?"

"Someone found out about Miss Sabrina. It's all over
the papers that she's been kidnapped."

"Oh, great." Jade hoped Thomas wasn't using Sabrina's
disappearance as a photo opportunity, but she couldn't be
sure. The thought repulsed her.

Phillip glanced at her hand where the end of the kite tail fluttered from her fist. "Dear God, is that what I think it is?"

"Yes." Jade raised her hand. "I just found it."

"Where?"

"In the vacant lot."

"Vacant lot? My word!"

"Where's Gail?"

"Still in bed."

"Wake her up."

Phillip glanced down the hall and then back at Jade. "Are you aware that Mrs. Brennan suffered a debilitating migraine yesterday?"

"Perhaps she's better now."

"It was one of her worst. Her doctor had to be summoned."

"Still, please wake her up, Phil. And Robbie, too."

"Master Robbie?"

"Yes. I have to talk with them."

"I shall do my best. Please wait here." He bowed slightly and walked away. Jade waited impatiently and began to shiver, holding her arms and clenching her teeth to keep from shaking. Her jeans were so wet, they clung to her thighs and knees, and her shoes sloshed and squeaked whenever she took a step. She paced the tile floor of the foyer, wondering if Phillip would ever return.

After a good five minutes, Gail appeared at the end of the hall, tying the belt of her white satin robe, her face pale and haggard. Jade watched her approach, feeling sorry that her sister-in-law suffered acute migraines but wondering if Gail's illness was her body's way of defending itself from a stressful situation.

"Why in the world are *you* here?" Gail demanded

before she'd even made it all the way down the carpeted hall. "It isn't even seven!"

"I know it's early," Jade replied. "But I found something important." She held up the purple fabric. "Look!"

"What is it?"

"The tail of Sabrina's kite."

Gail shrugged, her eyes clouded and dull. "How do you know? Looks like any old piece of purple cloth to me."

"It's the right color, the right shape."

Gail cursorily inspected it with dull, disinterested eyes.

"Even Phillip recognized it," Jade put in.

"So?" Gail retorted, her words slurred, as she looked back at Jade. "What are you getting at?"

"I'm getting at the fact that Sabrina must have been in the vacant lot yesterday."

"Perhaps she was, but what of it?" Gail waved her off. "That lot has been searched. Thoroughly." She turned to Phillip, one hand to her temple. "Get us some coffee, Phillip. And two of my pills, the blue ones."

"At once, madame."

She looked back at Janine. "I must sit. I had a wretched migraine yesterday and it feels like I'm getting another one." Gail staggered to the living room, done in three shades of melon, with a collection of tiny cacti on the coffee table. She collapsed on the sofa while Jade walked in after her, amazed that the news of the discovery hadn't affected Gail as much as she had thought it would. Perhaps her sister-in-law's distressed physical condition overrode all other concerns—even Sabrina's safety.

"I can't believe you would come to the house at six o'clock in the morning and wake me up."

"I thought the situation merited it," Jade declared, standing by an overstuffed chair. "And I need to talk to Robbie."

"Why?"

"He might know something." Jade perched on the arm of the chair, too agitated to sink to the cushion of the chair itself. "Sabrina wouldn't have gone out there alone. She's far too little to work the elevator and doors."

"Who's saying she did?"

"If she didn't"—Jade shook the kite tail in the air— "where did this come from?"

"Who knows?" Gail dropped her head back on the couch. "You're grasping at straws, Janine. One shred of fabric and you think you've solved the mystery of Sabrina's disappearance."

"Gail, I know this belongs to her kite. I saw it. I held it."

"You're going over the edge. . . ." Gail sighed and lifted her head wearily. "Don't make this harder for yourself. If something has happened to Sabrina, you're going to have to face it head-on. No false hopes."

"What do mean?" Jade couldn't believe Gail could accept Sabrina's disappearance so easily. "You think I should give up?"

"Children disappear these days. It's a horrible fact of life, but it's part of our world."

"How can you sit there and say that?"

Gail shrugged again. "Thomas is highly visible these days. There's bound to be a disturbed person who wants to make a point."

"By kidnapping a child?"

"It's been done before. It's something we may just have to accept. The police have searched everywhere."

"B-b-bullshit!" Jade jumped to her feet. "I want to see that kite of hers."

"Really, Janine. You're taking this too far."

"The tail will be missing. I'll bet on it!"

Gail heaved a heavy sigh and looked up at the ceiling.

"You want to prove me wrong, Gail. That's what you want, isn't it? To prove me wrong. Well, let's see that kite!"

Before Gail could act, Jade heard Phillip's discreet cough behind her. He walked calmly into the living room and placed a tray on the table.

"Thank you, Phillip," Gail said. She popped the blue pills in her mouth and took a dainty sip of water from the glass Phillip gave to her. Then she leaned forward to pour from a carafe that had been fashioned to look like a piece of terra-cotta. "Janine?" She looked up, the carafe poised above a second cup.

"No thanks." Jade looked up at Phillip. "Did you wake up Robbie yet?"

"I'm afraid that—"

"My son has nothing to do with this," Gail snapped. "And Phillip will not be waking him."

"But he might know—"

"Robbie had a trying day," Gail countered, raising the coffee cup to her thin lips. "We all did. And we don't need you barging in on us, waking us at dawn with your crazy ideas."

Jade jumped to her feet. "They're not crazy!"

Gail ignored her outburst. She sipped her coffee. "I suggest you go home and get some sleep. You look awful."

"Sleep? How can anyone sleep with Sabrina missing?"

"Janine . . ." Gail set her cup on its saucer. "The police have done all they could. They're professionals. Let them do their job."

"I don't think they're—"

"All this frantic behavior isn't good for you. You've had a brain injury, Janine. You could have another seizure if you're not careful."

"Seizure?" Jade threw back her shoulders, frustrated beyond measure by Gail's callous attitude. "I've never had a seizure, and I'm not about to."

"Our doctors say you could have one at any time," Gail said, rising. "I insist that you let the authorities handle this matter. For your own sake." She rubbed both temples with her fingertips and swayed a little. "Phillip, Mrs. MacKenzie is distraught. Please escort her to her apartment."

"Distraught!" Jade cried, seething. She threw off Phillip's touch when he reached for her arm. "I'm not distraught! I'm mad. Mad as hell!"

"Janine, I can't deal with this any longer," Gail declared. "I simply can't."

Phillip leaned closer. "Please, Mrs. MacKenzie. Come with me."

"If this is one of your tricks—" Jade broke off, because the idea was too heinous that Gail and Thomas would try to fool her into thinking Sabrina was missing.

Gail paled. "How can you say such a thing!"

"You sent her off to Disneyland so I couldn't see her, didn't you?"

"It was her birthday, Janine."

"But you knew I was coming. What if this is just another one of your ploys?"

"You twist things," Gail retorted. "You're not well!"

Gail's comment cut Janine to the core, but she gave no sign that the remark had stung her. Instead she regarded Gail with a steady, cool stare.

At Jade's impassive silence, Gail seemed to crack. She pointed to the doorway behind Jade. "Get out this minute," she demanded. "Get out, or I'll call the police! I'll have you put away! I can do it, too!"

Jade glared at Gail, furious and heartbroken, power-less in her efforts to talk to Robbie or get through to Gail.

"I mean it, Janine!"

"Please, Mrs. MacKenzie," Phillip urged. "It would be best if you get into some warm clothes before you catch a chill. Come. I'll see you to your apartment."

Jade clenched her jaw and pivoted. "You don't need to come with me, Phil," she said between gritted teeth. "I'm not that mentally impaired."

Phillip nodded grimly and followed her to the foyer. Without a backward glance at Gail, Jade trudged to the front door of the penthouse. Phillip paused before he opened it for her.

"I should be happy to call the police," he said, his voice kinder than she'd ever heard it, "and inform them of this latest development."

Jade glanced at him in surprise. "You don't think I'm grasping at straws?"

"No, I do not." Phillip pulled open the heavy wooden door. "And when it comes to Miss Sabrina, we should leave no stone unturned."

"Good. Tell the police I'll be in the vacant lot, will you? I can show them where I found the ribbon."

"Very good, Mrs. MacKenzie. I will call Mr. Brennan as well."

Back at the apartment, Jade changed into a pair of khakis, a shirt and wool sweater, warm socks, and her black ankle-high boots. Then she pulled on her jacket and slipped out of the building again, ran down to the corner market, bought an umbrella, and then hurried back to the vacant lot. The wind nearly blew the umbrella inside-out, and she had to grip the handle in both fists to keep it from sailing away.

Jade returned to the spot where she'd found the tail of the kite. The kite reminded her of Connor, and she felt a hard lump form in her throat. Forcing herself to put him out of her mind, she concentrated on searching for Sabrina. With water running off the points of the umbrella, she inspected the ground carefully, looking for the slightest sign that Sabrina had been there. Most of that section of the lot was covered with blackberry brambles. She picked her way through the thorny vines, creeping along and checking every square inch of land. She found an old property line stake and used it to push aside the blackberry canes.

After a few minutes, even her boots were soaked through. Her hands were blocks of ice, and water dripped off the tip of her nose. Sighing, Jade decided she'd have to give up for the time being. It was then she saw an old moss-covered plank in the brambles. She leaned down and pushed away the vines with the end of her stick. The plank was so green with moss that it blended in with the surrounding foliage, enough to allow it to go unseen by the casual observer. Jade set aside the umbrella and stepped closer, holding the brambles away with her hand and bending down for a better look. A second plank lay alongside the first, but it had been broken in two, its rotted ends hanging with moss. Beside the second board, deep in the brambles, gaped a dark hole, bordered by a series of rotted, broken wood. By the looks of the boards, someone had broken through them and fallen into the hole.

"Sabrina!" Jade called, her voice strangled with fear

for her little girl. She tried to lean over to get a better view down the hole, but the light was too poor, and she was afraid of falling into what might be a deep abyss.

Jade sniffed, her cold nose dripping with rain, and wiped her wet bangs out of her eyes. Then she pushed aside the blackberry canes and knelt at the edge of the hole, squinting to allow her eyes to adjust to the darkness.

Below her, she could see the rough edges of a cylindrical hole that dropped six feet or so into the earth. At the bottom of the hole was a layer of small stones, like those in a creek bed. Jade could just barely make out the black edges of the periphery of the shaft, where a second horizontal tunnel branched off toward the railroad tracks that ran along the base of the hill on which the old hotel had been built.

"Sabrina!" Jade shouted into the hole. She waited, her breath coming in fast puffs, leaving a cloud of moisture hanging in the air near her mouth.

Jade thought she heard a faint sound in the distance.

"Sabrina!" She leaned down as far as she dared and yelled louder.

The sound repeated.

"Oh, God," Jade whispered, closing her eyes. Was she hearing Sabrina or just the echo of her own voice? And if it was Sabrina she was hearing, was the child hurt? Stuck? Why wasn't she coming back to the place where she'd fallen in?

"Hang on, Sabrina!" Jade shouted into the hole. "We're going to get you out of there."

Behind her, she heard the clunk of car doors slamming shut in the rain. She rose, the thorns scraping through her hair to her scalp, clawing at her sweater, scratching her hands and wrists. She pulled free, feeling like a fly caught in a monstrous spiderweb, and staggered backward into the clearing.

Two officers loped across the hilly lot toward her while a fire truck pulled up behind their squad car. Jade motioned frantically for the policemen to join her at the bank of brambles.

"I think I found her!" Jade cried. "I think I found Sabrina!"

"Where, ma'am?"

Jade turned and pointed to the shaft she'd found in the bushes. "There's a hole in there. It looks like someone fell into it."

The young officer stepped closer to the brambles and then slipped a flashlight out of his utility belt. He aimed the beam through the splintered mossy boards.

"Looks like an old well," he observed.

Jade stepped up behind him. "I think I heard her down there. When I called to her, I swear I heard something. It was really faint. But I heard something. I know I did."

"We'll get a ladder down this hole and find out." He rose and pivoted to give his instructions to his partner, who trotted back to the fire truck.

Within seconds two firemen hurried up, carrying a ladder, rope, and a powerful flashlight, while the police cordoned off the area with yellow plastic tape. Already a group of onlookers had drifted onto the lot to see what was going on, and cars slowed in the commuter traffic of early morning to get a glimpse of the rescue operation.

Jade retrieved her umbrella and held it with a frozen hand as she watched, anxious to do more but knowing the situation was being handled by professionals. Ruthlessly, the firemen cut back the briars and threw them to the side, revealing the shaft and its ancient wooden covering. Jade stared at the gaping black hole, sick with worry that her baby might be down in that dank place, possibly injured and thinking no one cared about her.

"Don't worry," one of the officers remarked to her. "If she's in there, we'll find her."

"Please hurry. Please!"

With admirable efficiency, the firemen positioned the ladder in the hole, snapped on their helmets, which looked like miners' hats, and disappeared into the shaft, one after the other. At first she could hear the hollow echo of their boots on the rocks at the bottom of the shaft and the clinking sounds of their equipment as they bent to pass through the tunnel she'd seen. Then there was nothing but the hiss of rain on the grass, the spattering of drops on the umbrella above her head, and the hum of traffic behind her.

Then she heard a familiar voice demanding to be let through, that he was the father of the girl. Jade turned to see Thomas striding purposefully across the vacant lot toward her, reporters and cameras jostling for position behind him, the bunch of them looking like a Chinese dragon in a parade.

"Janine!" he called, coming to stand quite close to her. She raised the umbrella to allow him room while he nodded to the policemen. "I just got called. You think Sabrina's down there?"

Jade glanced at the rotting boards surrounded by the stumps of blackberry canes. "Yes. I heard something down there. I definitely heard something."

"God, I hope it's her."

In minutes the reporters had set up their equipment just beyond the police barrier. One blond woman already stood to the side, delivering her version of the story. Jade watched her, deaf to the reporter's words and immune to the bustle around her. She'd never felt more alone, more removed from the world, for all she could think about was Sabrina in that dark, musty hole. Sabrina all alone.

Thomas leaned closer and his voice dropped to a level saved for private jokes and confidences. "So where's Gail?"

"She got another migraine this morning." Jade fumbled for a tissue in the pocket of her jacket.

"Jesus." Thomas shook his head. "I can't tell you how this has upset her. Gail is so sensitive, you know. She's been crazy with worry."

Jade nodded, too preoccupied to argue the point.

"How long has the rescue crew been here?"

"Just a few minutes."

"Someone mentioned that you found her."

"I saw the tail of her kite stuck in the bushes."

Thomas peered at her, seemingly puzzled by her explanation, but before he could say anything more, he was cut off by the harsh crackle of the radio held by the young officer standing next to Jade.

"Say again?" the officer said. "I didn't copy that, Darrell."

"We found her," a scratchy voice announced.

Jade's heart leapt in her chest, and she exchanged a quick glance with her brother. "Is she all right?" she demanded of the officer. She stared at the radio, as if the answer to her question lay in the small handset. "Ask him if Sabrina's okay!"

"Darrell, what's the condition of the girl?" the policeman asked. The radio crackled again, allowing only a portion of the reply to transmit.

"—down another hole."

"She's in a hole?" Jade cried.

"—old well," added Darrell's crackling voice.

The police officer looked at Jade, his brown eyes full of compassion. "Looks like she fell into an old well, an even deeper hole."

"But she's all right? She isn't hurt?"

The officer questioned the fireman and then turned to Jade. "She doesn't seem to be hurt. They'll know more when they get her out."

"How long will that take?" Thomas inquired, jerking up his chin nervously. "Can't you people work any faster?"

The officer's eyes shifted to a cooler color. "In cases like these, Mr. Brennan, we have to be extremely careful. We don't know how deep the second shaft is. Or where the girl is positioned. She could have broken bones."

"Dear God!" Jade gasped. "Please, don't let her be hurt!"

A microphone poked through the air beside her cheek. Jade turned in surprise to stare at the reporter, a tall rangy fellow with black hair and a mustache.

"You're the kid's aunt?" he asked.

Jade paused, not certain what she wanted to say. An entire nation of people might hear her reply on the news later that day, and it was likely that Sabrina would be able to view the clip years from now and see her mother lying about their relationship. Before she could decide upon a response, she saw Thomas closing his hand around the shaft of the microphone and pulling it toward him.

"I'd just like to say that my sister, Janine, and I are grateful for the quick response of the city to this rescue operation. It is at a time like this when I'm proud to live in Seattle—a big city with a small-town heart."

Jade said nothing, too disgusted at hearing Thomas slip in his campaign slogan at a time like this and too worried to make the effort to speak.

"Mr. Brennan"—another microphone was thrust in his face—"what do you think happened here? Was it an accident, or something much more?"

"Who do you think would kidnap your child?" someone else asked.

"Could this be an act of terrorism, Mr. Brennan, as a result of your work with the—"

Janine drowned out the questions with silent prayers for Sabrina and the men who were working to free her. She looked down at the hole, relieved that her brother was handling the press but wishing everyone else would just go away. There was only one person she wanted at her side at this moment: Connor. And she had no idea where he was or if she would ever see the handsome Scotsman again.

# 17

Minutes ticked by as everyone waited at the top of the old well. Even the reporters fell silent and stood in a ring, pressed against the police barrier. Jade's stare was riveted on the round hole, and her ears strained for the slightest noise that would tell of the firemen's return.

Then, in a flurry of trampling and clinking and the flash of a bright light, Jade saw the top of a fireman's hat and then the glint of the red gold hair of the child he carried in his arms up the ladder.

"Sabrina!" Jade cried, tears of joy flooding her eyes.

"Thank God!" Thomas exclaimed. "Thank God!"

The fireman paused on the ladder and handed Sabrina to the waiting policeman above. The child wrapped her arms around the policeman's neck as he rose and turned to the crowd. Everyone clapped and cheered as Darrell and his fellow firefighter climbed out of the hole. The crowd went wild, but their jubilation was no more than superfluous cacophony to Jade as she rushed forward and held out her arms for Sabrina.

Reacting to Jade's gesture, the policeman surrendered the child to her. Jade gathered Sabrina to her breast and hugged her tightly, crying for joy, while her heart soared with love for her baby. Flashes went off like fireworks behind her as the reporters shot the reunion from every possible angle.

"Sabrina!" Jade squeezed her. "Sabrina! Are you all right?"

"I heard you up here, Auntie Jade!" Sabrina cried. "I called and called!"

"Oh, Sabrina!" Jade kissed her pudgy cold cheek. "I heard you, too!"

"I'm hungry!"

Thomas bent closer. "Of course you are, pumpkin. Of course you are."

Jade held tightly to Sabrina, worried that Thomas might insist upon holding her. "We'll get you home right away," she said, loving the sound of the phrase and hoping she could take her to the condo, not the penthouse.

"First we have to make sure she's all right," the policeman put in. "In fact, let's head for the aid car to see how she's holding up."

"Okay." Jade shifted Sabrina onto her hip and began to walk toward the truck, while everyone trailed slowly behind.

Sabrina screwed up her features and looked closely at Jade's face. "Can I have noodles?"

The crowd laughed at Sabrina's question.

"You can have as much as you like."

"Mr. Thong's?"

Jade smiled at Sabrina's childish mangling of Herman Fong's name.

"You can have anything you want, sweetheart," Thomas cooed, stroking her hair, but awkward in his movements, as if he weren't accustomed to touching her.

While they waited for the paramedics to lift Sabrina into the back of the truck and settle her onto a stretcher, Thomas turned his attention to the firefighters. "Which one of you is Darrell?" he asked.

"I am." The fireman swept off his helmet, revealing black hair cut close to his head, which matched his neatly trimmed black mustache.

"I want to thank you for all you've done." Thomas shook Darrell's hand, in much more familiar territory than while touching his own child. "Your chief will hear about this, you can count on it."

"It was a team effort, Mr. Brennan." Darrell glanced at Sabrina, whose blood pressure was being taken. "And I was glad to help."

"Sabrina had a close call there," his partner added. "That second shaft was pretty deep. Probably fifty feet or so. Something kept her from falling farther. We don't know what, but she's one lucky little girl."

"Uncle Connor did it," Sabrina said, rising up on an elbow.

Jade froze. "What?"

"Uncle Connor. He grabbed me."

"Now wait just a minute," Thomas put in, ducking closer to the back door of the aid vehicle. "Connor took you down there?"

Chastened by the harsh tone in her supposed father's voice, Sabrina stiffened and stared at him. She put a finger in her mouth and made no reply.

"Sabrina, did Uncle Connor put you in that hole?" Thomas repeated.

"No, Daddy, he helped me."

"What do you mean?" the policeman asked, much more gently than Thomas.

Jade reached into the van and patted Sabrina's leg in a gesture of support. "Was Uncle Connor with you?" she asked softly.

"His hand was."

"What do you mean, his hand?" Thomas sputtered. "What kind of nonsense is that?"

"Thomas!" Jade admonished. "Just give her a chance to talk, would you?"

Sabrina stared at her father with big eyes. Thomas obviously had little skill in questioning children.

The policeman smiled at Sabrina. "Would you tell us, Sabrina, what happened when you fell in the hole?"

"I was scared. I couldn't get out. I called and called. But nobody heard me."

"Poor Sabrina." Jade's heart ached for her, for the time she had spent all alone and frightened. "But you were a brave girl."

"Then what happened?" the policeman asked, encouraging her to continue.

"I heard a lady talking. She was in another place, so I went there. She told me stories and I wasn't so scared."

"What other place, Sabrina?" Jade asked.

"More back. Where it was dark. She told me not to be scared. I wasn't then, Auntie Jade."

"A lady?" Thomas frowned. "Who was this lady?"

Sabrina shrugged her tiny shoulders. "I don't know. She was nice."

"What did she look like?" Thomas continued.

"I couldn't see her. But she talked funny."

Jade studied her daughter's face. "What do you mean?"

"She talked funny. Like Mr. Thong."

A chill swept through Jade. Whom had Sabrina heard down in the well? What did she mean by a "funny" way of talking—had the woman spoken with an accent, as Herman did?

"So when did Uncle Connor show up?" Thomas asked, his voice still heavy with suspicion.

"When I tripped and fell. I fell into another hole."

"Did he push you?"

"No, Daddy!" Her brows came together in a scowl. "He helped me, I said."

Jade watched the medic take Sabrina's pulse. "How did Connor help you?"

"He grabbed my pants."

Jade looked at the dirt-smudged overalls Sabrina wore over a long-sleeved sweater. At least the child had been dressed warmly enough to survive a night in the cold earth. "When you fell in the other hole, he caught you?"

Sabrina nodded.

"Why didn't he pull you out?" Darrell asked.

"He couldn't."

The fireman cocked his head, confused. "Why not, Sabrina?"

"'Cause he couldn't come all the way through the door."

"What door?"

"I don't know. It was dark!" Sabrina sniffed and shifted on the stretcher. "I'm hungry. I want to go home!"

"Sir, we have to take Sabrina up to Harborview Hospital for observation," the other medic said to Thomas. "Just for a few hours. It's standard procedure in a case like this."

Thomas nodded and frowned, glancing back at the hole still ringed by the police barrier.

"I'll go with Sabrina if you'd like," Jade offered.

Thomas looked at her and his frown eased. "Okay. Then I can stay here and see what they find out about MacKenzie." He reached into his wallet and drew out his insurance card. "Here, you'll need this."

Jade slipped the card into the pocket of her jacket.

The female paramedic came to the back of the truck. "Come on, ma'am. You can ride with us."

"All right." Still, Jade hesitated and glanced at the hole, worrying that Connor was down there somewhere, trapped, and she was leaving him.

"Did you see a door in the tunnel, Darrell?" she asked.

"No. I didn't look around much, though. We were concerned with getting Sabrina out."

"Would you mind taking another look?"

"Not at all." Darrell plopped his hat back on his head. "Matter of fact, I'm kind of curious myself."

"If you find the man," Thomas said, "don't let him get away. He's wanted for questioning by the police." He threw a dark glance at Jade and then instantly looked away.

Jade's joy at finding Sabrina fluttered and fell, like an old rag tossed to the ground.

"Please call me if you find anything," Jade said.

"Sure will, ma'am." He stuck his head into the back of the truck and wiggled Sabrina's foot. "You take care, Sabrina."

She raised her head and grinned brightly. "I'm going to have noodles!"

"Good for you."

"Thank you all for rescuing Sabrina."

The firemen nodded and the policeman gave her a smart salute as Jade climbed into the aid vehicle.

"Say 'Thank you' to the nice men," Jade instructed her.

"Thank you," Sabrina exclaimed, and waved. "Bye-bye!"

The cameras whirred and clicked as another excellent photo opportunity presented itself. Jade sat at Sabrina's side and took her hand while the door slammed shut. She smiled down at Sabrina. Her baby was safe and sound. The moment might have been triumphant, might have been the happiest day of Jade's life, except for one thing. Where was Connor? Was he trapped between the well and the wall, stuck in a netherworld again, half-alive and half-dead? She wouldn't be able to rest until she knew where he was and whether or not he was safe.

A few hours later Sabrina was released from Harborview, with only a scrape on one arm to bear witness to her ordeal. Jade took her home in a taxi and decided to take her up to her own apartment before she returned her to Thomas and Gail. Sabrina was still adamant about eating Herman's noodles, and Jade hoped Herman could be located by phone once they got home.

She carried Sabrina across the sidewalk to the beautiful old hotel, its lines still more elegant than the most expensive building in the city. She walked up the steps, chattering away to her daughter, knowing she should be gloriously happy now that the child of her heart had been found. But part of her heart was still missing since Connor had disappeared, and she knew she would never be quite whole without him. Jade took a resolute breath and climbed the stairs to the front door of the building. For Sabrina's sake, she'd put Connor out of her mind for now. There'd be time to worry about him when Sabrina was back with Gail.

Troubled, Jade glanced up at the front door, surprised to see Mr. "Thong" waiting for them at the top of the stairs.

"Ah, Miss Sabrina!" he exclaimed, bowing. "A happy good morning to you!"

"Hi, Mr. Thong!"

He smiled and patted her shoulder as Jade punched buttons on the keypad near the door.

"Are you here to make me noodles?" Sabrina asked.

"Of course, small one." He grinned at Jade. "Mrs. MacKenzie, I am so happy to see your Sabrina safe and sound."

"How did you know to come?" Jade asked, always perplexed by Herman Fong's uncanny abilities.

He shrugged and his moth-wing eyebrows raised. "I have a friend at the television station where Mr. Brennan was being filmed this morning."

"Oh, one of your friends." Jade shook her head and pushed open the door. "I forget about your army of acquaintances."

"One can never have too many," Herman declared, and then passed into the lobby.

Jade followed, shaking her head in wonder at the frail, mysterious man who had come into her world and altered her life in so many ways.

A few hours later Jade sank onto the couch, exhausted, while Herman placed a tea tray on the coffee table and sat on the couch opposite her.

"Tea?" he asked.

"Thanks," she answered, raising her head and smiling

at him. Herman had made lunch for Sabrina, and then Jade had given her a long bath, washing all traces of her ordeal from her hair and skin. She hadn't realized the tenderness she'd feel in shampooing her child's hair and looking down on Sabrina's trusting face, her eyes closed and her mouth curved into a cherubic smile. She hadn't realized the silly happiness she'd derive from piling bubbles onto Sabrina's head and pretending they were flamboyant hats or animal ears and hearing Sabrina's infectious giggle. And she hadn't been prepared for the wonderful feeling of gratitude for having been blessed with a healthy, well-formed child, as she toweled off Sabrina's sturdy limbs. This child had come from her body, had been born of her heart and spirit, and she was a beautiful being.

Sabrina seemed completely at ease with her, too—even happy—as if she sensed there was a blood connection between them, a link far deeper than aunt to niece. Not once had she asked for Gail, and it was plain to see the child wanted to spend time with Jade, which made her heart burst with love.

After the bath Phillip had dropped by, bringing a change of clothes for Sabrina and news of Gail's latest horrific migraine. He had stayed for tea and listened to the story of Sabrina's rescue while the child sat on Jade's lap, a biscuit in her hand. While they'd talked, Sabrina had gradually drifted off to sleep, sagging against Jade, until her head lolled onto her upper arm and the biscuit dropped to the carpet.

Jade had carried Sabrina to her Little Bo Peep bedroom and there had experienced the most wonderful feeling of all—that of tucking her child into bed and kissing her warm cheek while she slept, smelling her fragrant little-girl scent of clean hair and sweet breath, and then drawing the covers snugly around her and looking down at her dear little angel, safe and sound and contented. Jade sat beside Sabrina, gazing at her, tears rolling down her cheeks. To know this moment with her baby and to have it taken away forever would break her heart. Absolutely break her heart. But to know this moment at all—even just one time—was enough to fill her to the brim with joy.

As long as she didn't think of Connor.

"It's ginseng," Herman commented, breaking into Jade's thoughts by handing her a delicate porcelain cup from a set he'd brought over a few days before. "You need the strength."

"Thank you, Herman. It's been a rough few days."

"But all over now, perhaps?"

She shook her head and looked down at the tea. "There's still Connor."

"And where is he?"

Jade relayed the events of the last twenty-four hours—how Connor had walked through the wall and disappeared. How he'd heard Sabrina and apparently had been responsible for saving her in the well.

"In a well?" Herman inquired.

"Yes. Sabrina fell into an old well, it seems, but how she got out of the building is still a mystery."

"I have heard of a well." Herman sipped his tea. "Stories in my family told of a well used by the Chinese as an escape route."

"Escape route?"

"Yes. Sometimes they had need of fleeing from the authorities. They had a way to get from the city to the railroad tracks. To the water. Through an old well."

Jade leaned forward. "The tunnel Sabrina was in headed toward the railroad tracks."

He nodded. "Very likely the same well."

"And the weird thing is, Sabrina mentioned a lady down there."

"A lady?"

"Yes. Someone who told her stories during the night and kept her from being afraid. Sabrina said the lady talked like you."

"Like me?" His eyebrows raised.

"I'm not sure what she meant. Maybe your accent?"

"What did the lady look like?"

Jade shrugged. "Sabrina couldn't see her. It was too dark."

"Curious." Herman sipped his tea again. "And you are telling me that Mr. MacKenzie passed through a special time portal after hearing Sabrina. But he couldn't get all the way to her."

"Something prevented him from doing so." Jade fell silent and stared at the surface of her tea, where silver reflections of the window behind her rippled in the cup. The reflections reminded her of a mirror, which made her think of the mirror in her bathroom where Qi An had left her mark, and Jade was certain now who had been in the well with Sabrina.

"Qi An!" she declared.

"What?" Herman asked, lowering his cup.

"Qi An! It had to have been Qi An down there with Sabrina."

"Not possible, Mrs. MacKenzie. Qi An has been dead for over a hundred years."

"What about her spirit, though?" Jade leaned forward eagerly. "You said her spirit might still be alive because she never completed the ceremony."

"Yes, that may be true."

"Well, what if she's down there—her spirit, I mean?

That may be why Sabrina heard her but couldn't see her."

"Quite possible . . ." Herman nodded and slowly put his cup in its saucer, taking time to carefully consider the implications of her words.

"Qi An comforted Sabrina last night and opened the door for Connor so that he could help her, too." Jade rose to her feet. "Her soul must be good, Herman. Qi An is obviously still a loving spirit."

"So it seems, Mrs. MacKenzie."

Jade paced the floor to the window, more upset than ever. She could despise an evil Qi An for capturing Connor's heart and pulling him out of the present and back to the past—or wherever it was that Connor had gone. But she could not be angry with a woman who had done so much for Sabrina. There was no room for hate in her heart for a person so selflessly giving as Qi An had proved to be a second time. Still, Qi An had a connection with Connor that Jade wanted for herself. She leaned against the woodwork as Connor had done two nights before—an eternity ago, it seemed now—and sighed a deep sigh of loss and grief. Connor was gone from her. She knew she had to accept that fact and go on with her life, but it would be one of the most difficult things she'd ever have to do.

She was still standing at the window when her intercom buzzed. Jade padded across the carpet and pushed the button.

"Yes?" she inquired.

"It's Sergeant Baldwin," a man's voice said. "From this morning?"

"Oh, yes, Sergeant. Would you like to come up?"

"Yes."

She buzzed him in and turned to Herman. "It's the

policeman who helped with Sabrina this morning. He might have some new information."

"I will make more tea," Herman offered, rising.

"There are more cookies in the cupboard, too." Jade glanced at her reflection in the mirror above the mantel of the fireplace, grimaced at the pale face she barely recognized as her own, and then decided not to worry about her appearance. Moments later, Jade heard the doorbell ring.

"Good afternoon," Sergeant Baldwin greeted her, clasping his hands in front of his lean body.

"Hi, please come in." She motioned toward the living room. "This is a friend of mine, Herman Fong."

"Mr. Fong," Sergeant Baldwin said, nodding. "How do you do?"

"Fine, thank you." Herman bowed as the shrill whistle of the teakettle sounded in the kitchen. "If you will excuse me, I will attend to the tea."

"Won't you sit down?" Jade suggested to the officer.

"Thanks." He walked to the chair beside the couch and lowered himself to the seat, his severe uniform incongruous against the floral print. He didn't lean back, but sat with his forearms on his knees and his feet far apart. While he sat, he absently rotated his wedding band around his ring finger. "You've probably guessed why I'm here," he began, his brown eyes locked on her face.

"Did you find something in the well shaft?"

"Yes." He looked around. "Where's Sabrina?"

"She's taking a nap."

"Good." He scooted even farther to the edge of his seat. "Mrs. MacKenzie, did Sabrina tell you about anything she saw in the well?"

"Just what she told us after her rescue. Why?"

"She didn't mention anything that scared her?"

"No. Just the darkness. Why?" Jade searched his face. "What did you find?"

Sergeant Baldwin glanced to the side and then back to Jade. His hesitation only made her curiosity burn brighter.

# 18

*Jade leaned forward,* as edgy as the young police-man beside her. "What *did* you find down there, Sergeant?"

"The remains of a human female."

Jade stared at him in shock as Herman skirted the couch with the refilled teapot.

"R-remains?" she stammered. "You mean a dead body?"

"No, skeletal remains. Whoever the woman was, she'd been dead quite some time."

Herman sat beside Jade and said nothing. His outward disinterest intrigued her, but she kept her curiosity to herself.

"You know it's a woman for sure?" she asked, hoping the policeman would provide more information.

Sergeant Baldwin nodded. "Yes, you can tell by the bone structure. The investigator working on the case is pretty sure she was of Asian descent, fairly young, and had been murdered."

"How does he know that?"

"Marks on her rib cage and sternum. Likely, the woman was stabbed."

Jade shared a swift but meaningful glance with Herman.

"So what will happen next?"

"With the remains?" Baldwin shrugged one shoulder, which made his badge glint in the sunlight streaming through the window. "They go to forensics. Then they'll probably keep them around for a while. But the murder took place long ago. Chances are the person or persons who killed the woman are long dead themselves."

Jade nodded and reached for a second cup of tea.

"That's not the reason we're concerned, though. We're more worried that Sabrina might have seen the bones."

"She didn't say anything about them."

"She didn't mention them at all?"

"No."

"Good. She might not have seen them. They were strewn against one wall, kind of out of the way."

"Not that close to the second shaft?"

"No. And we're hoping Sabrina didn't notice them, especially the skull. She had enough of a scare without adding a dead body to it."

"I'll say."

"If she says anything, Mrs. MacKenzie—and I'll mention this to her parents as well—please make sure she sees a child psychologist. She might have some stuff to work through if she spent an entire night sitting next to a skeleton."

"I will," Jade promised.

"It might not come up for weeks. Even months."

Jade nodded. "I can assure you, Sergeant, that Sabrina will be closely watched."

"She is well loved," Herman put in. At the single remark from the old•man, the policeman studied Herman briefly and then turned back to Jade.

"What about the door Sabrina mentioned?" Jade asked. "Did the firemen find anything?"

"Nothing. I don't know what she was talking about. There was nothing in the tunnel but rocks and dirt and the skeletal remains. Nothing."

"What about in the well shaft itself? What kept Sabrina from falling?"

Sergeant Baldwin scratched his head. "That's the strange part," he mused. "We couldn't see anything that would have broken her fall. She should have plunged to her death. It was straight down for sixty feet."

"Oh, my God!" A chill shot through her at the thought of Sabrina falling down a dark shaft. She forced the image out of her mind.

"It's a miracle your niece is alive, Mrs. MacKenzie."

"So it seems." Jade stared at the floor, baffled by the facts of Sabrina's rescue, but knew there was much more to the miracle than the police or firemen would ever guess.

"She mentioned your husband being with her, Mrs. MacKenzie, and that he saved her." Baldwin glanced around the room. "Can you tell me where Mr. MacKenzie is?"

Jade's mouth went dry. "N-no." She swallowed. "As I told the police yesterday, Connor and I had an argument and that's the last I've seen of him."

"Is it like your husband to run off like this and not come back?"

"No." Jade crossed her arms, unwilling to divulge much more about Connor's relationship with her or anything about his past.

"Biscuit?" Herman asked, offering the plate of cookies.

"Thanks." Officer Baldwin reached for a cookie, took a big bite, and chewed thoughtfully.

Jade watched him, not sure what else to ask. Obviously the men had found no sign of Connor in the well. His safety and well-being were paramount to her now, but she didn't know how to proceed in her search for information about the Scotsman. Should she explore the well on her own? Would she have to wait for the wall to change in her bedroom until she could find a clue as to his whereabouts? Perhaps there was some way of contacting Qi An. If Qi An had talked to Sabrina, why couldn't she talk to Jade?

"Once we find your husband, ma'am," Baldwin put in, "this whole thing won't be so much of a mystery."

"I hope he shows up soon." Jade's heart flipped painfully. "I'm worried about him."

"Will you be filing a missing persons report?"

Jade glanced at him, worried that he would pursue the topic, because she was sure it would be best to keep the police out of Connor's affairs. "I think I'll let it go for another day, Sergeant, just in case he shows up."

"We'll let you know if anything happens on our end." Baldwin rose and brushed cookie crumbs off the front of his uniform. "Well, I'd better get up to the Brennans, tell them what we've found."

Jade thanked him for his help and showed him to the door.

As soon as the policeman left, Herman shuffled out of the kitchen, buttoning his quilted jacket with shaking hands as he headed for the door.

Jade looked up from her seat at the couch. "Herman, are you leaving?"

He glanced at her and bowed. "I must attend to something, Mrs. MacKenzie." He bowed again.

"Will you be back soon? I must talk to you about Qi An."

"I will be back as quickly as possible. Rest while I am gone, for we will have things to do upon my return."

"What kinds of things?" she asked suspiciously, knowing of Herman's network of connections and his incredible cache of arcane knowledge.

"When I come back, you will see." He bowed and slipped out the door.

Jade stared after him, more perplexed than ever.

With everyone gone and Sabrina asleep, Jade had a moment to think about the future. One aspect bothered her more than anything: the possibility that Sabrina might slip away from the penthouse again and come to even greater harm. Jade didn't trust Robbie, and she didn't trust Gail's love for Sabrina, either. More than ever, Jade was reluctant to return Sabrina to her brother's house and knew she had to do something about it or worry herself to death.

She picked up the phone and dialed the number for Dr. Nilsen. Though she had never liked the psychologist, she had no recourse but to work with the woman to ensure Sabrina's safety. Dr. Nilsen had heard about Sabrina on the news but was surprised to hear Jade's version of the story, especially when she learned of the lack of parental involvement on the part of Gail and Thomas. Dr. Nilsen agreed to a meeting between the couples as soon as possible and scheduled a tentative evaluation for the next day at three. She promised to call the Brennans to make certain they would be available.

Jade hung up the phone, wondering what she would tell Dr. Nilsen about Connor's absence. His disappearance would only make Jade's situation look worse in the eyes of the doctor. And no doubt Thomas and Gail would use Connor's absence to denigrate his character and his relationship with Jade. The meeting might do more harm than good. What if, at the end of the evaluation, Dr. Nilsen found both couples lacking and recommended that Sabrina be placed in a foster home? Jade flushed with apprehension but knew she had to go through with the meeting, for Sabrina's sake.

She made a second call to Laura Wettig, asking for advice, and was happy to hear Laura offering to fly out again. Jade thanked her and hung up the phone, feeling more confident now that Laura was on the way.

She rose and ambled down the hall to Sabrina's room. For a few minutes she watched her daughter sleeping, and then she walked on to the bathroom a few yards away.

The bathroom surrounded her in silence, and the porcelain and mirror gleamed in the dim light that pushed against the frosted glass of the window. Jade turned and faced the mirror where she had first seen the Chinese symbol for Qi An's name. She breathed in and concentrated her thoughts on the silver plane before her.

"Qi An," Jade called softly, feeling as if she were praying at a pagan altar. "Thank you for helping my daughter. I know that it was you at her side last night." She paused for a moment and choked back a thick feeling in her throat. "I also know that you love Connor, Qi An, and want him with you. You gave your life for him. But he is a man made for life. His is a spirit meant to live on in the world, where he can bring light into the lives of the living." Jade paused and closed her eyes, wondering if her plea would be heard. Then she looked up at the mirror again. "But if you are determined to keep him with you, please let me know if he is all right. Please, give me a sign that he is safe. That is all I ask. Some kind of sign."

She waited for a response, hardly daring to breathe. Silence hung in the bathroom. Not even a drip plopped out of the faucet. After a few minutes Jade sighed and looked around, not knowing what she expected to see. Nothing unusual caught her eye—only her emerald ring, the beautiful piece of jewelry Connor had slipped upon her finger the day she'd become his wife. She picked up the ring and pushed it onto her finger, remembering how happy she'd been that day to walk beside Connor and how lovely their evening had been together.

No ordinary mortal man would ever measure up to Connor MacKenzie. She'd wear the ring always, as a symbol of her undying love for him. Her heart heavier than ever, Jade left the bathroom and returned to Sabrina's side.

She lowered herself into the soft chair she'd bought as a place to read stories to Sabrina and laid both arms along the cushioned supports. Her gaze drifted to the emerald ring, so green against her fair skin. For a moment she thought she saw a pale glow around the stone, the same kind of nimbus that had surrounded Connor when he had been in her world. Jade jerked to attention and raised her hand closer to her face. All she could see was the square-cut emerald and its band of gold. The glow must have been a trick of the light, and in her desperation she'd made it into something far more meaningful than it actually was. Disheartened, Jade sank back against the chair and sighed.

For a long while she sat there, listening to her child's breathing—which was curiously comforting—until a sudden realization moved over her. Because of Qi An, Sabrina had survived her ordeal. Because of Qi An, Connor had managed to be at the right place at the right time, to grab Sabrina's overalls and save her from death. Had Sabrina been Qi An's gift to Jade, in return for Connor? In gaining Sabrina, had Jade lost Connor forever, as part of a bargain with a spirit woman?

Hot tears rolled down Jade's cheeks and into the corners of her mouth. She was happy to have Sabrina back safe and sound, but her heart grieved for her lost Scotsman.

As the day drew to a close, Jade watched the sun melt behind the Olympic Mountains, which jutted out of the sound like blue humps. A little while later, she said good-bye to Sabrina and hugged her close while Phillip looked on, waiting to escort his tiny charge back to the penthouse for dinner. Gail had finally revived and had requested the return of the girl, much to Jade's disappointment. Until the evaluation the next afternoon, she had no choice but to give Sabrina back to her legal parents.

Jade closed the door after them and sank against the wood panels, awash in loneliness now that everyone had left the apartment. She hadn't always been aware of such loneliness—not until Connor and Sabrina had come into her life and marked it forever.

Sighing, she pulled away from the door and fixed herself a light dinner of soup and crackers; she had just finished eating when Herman rang the bell. She made no effort to hide her relief at seeing him. Herman, however, barely took time to bow.

"Hurry, Miss Brennan, and get a warm jacket." He

didn't even venture all the way into the living room. "We have something to do."

"What are you talking about?" Jade inquired, her hand still on the doorknob.

"You will see. Just get a coat and come with me."

She obeyed without asking any more questions, simply because of the urgency in his voice. She followed him down the hallway, pulling on her jacket, which was still a little damp at the hem from her search early that morning.

"Where are you taking me?" she asked as they rode the elevator down to the lobby.

"You will see." He waited for her to exit the car first and then hobbled across the lobby and out the front door of the condominium building. At the curb a taxi idled in the indigo veil of early evening. Herman opened the door and motioned her inside. She slid across the vinyl seat and crossed her legs.

She turned to him. "What's the mystery?"

"You will know all soon." He leaned forward and gave directions in a foreign language to the driver, who Jade realized was Chinese as well.

As the taxi pulled into traffic, Herman glanced out the rear window of the cab and then settled back, fiddling with the crease of his pants, his hands trembling.

Jade realized it was futile to ask him any more questions. Instead she stared out the window, watching the brick buildings of Pioneer Square giving way to less imposing buildings of wood and cement, scores of sidewalk vendors, and corner groceries of the International District. In her years growing up in Seattle, she'd rarely ventured into this area and didn't remember seeing so many signs in so many different languages, from Thai to Korean.

The taxi crawled up a hill near the freeway and then turned to the right, into a dark street lined by houses built with their rooftops nearly touching each other. Every few minutes Herman looked behind the cab, as if worried about being followed. Finally, the taxi pulled into the driveway of a dark building situated at the terminus of the dead-end street. Tall laurel shrubs shrouded the house from the road and cast it in darkness.

Jade shivered as she climbed out of the taxi and waited for Herman to retrieve a cardboard box from the trunk of the vehicle. The driver left his cab idling as he took the box from Herman and carried it to the front door of the house, where a single light threw out a feeble glow. Jade stood to one side while Herman let the knocker fall upon its brass plate.

The driver put down the box, bowed, and didn't take Herman's money.

"I will return to the Elliott," the driver said, "as you have requested."

"Good. Be observant."

"I will." The driver bowed again. "I await your call."

"A thousand thanks." Herman returned his bow.

The taxi driver vanished into the dusk while Herman and Jade waited on the stoop of the house. Moments later the door opened to reveal a small, elderly woman dressed in a black silk outfit comprising a boxy jacket and loose pants.

"You have brought her, then?" the woman asked, glancing at Jade and then ushering them into the house, which was lit only with sputtering candles.

"Yes."

A second chill passed through Jade. Was her safety in jeopardy? Surely Herman wouldn't lure her into danger.

She looked around, seeing only a bare lacquered table upon which sat a bonsai arrangement and a stack of cushions against the far wall. This was obviously not a typical house. But if not a residence, then what?

"Herman, what's going on?" Jade asked in a whisper.

He ignored the question. "Bring the box, Miss Brennan." He motioned with his hand. "And follow me."

Jade bent and picked up the cardboard carton, which had been taped shut. Whatever it contained was fairly heavy, and she grunted as she hoisted it against her torso. Herman couldn't have carried the box very far, as frail as he was.

"Where to?" she asked.

"Out back."

He and the older woman led her through the hushed halls of the building, which appeared to be a temple or place of learning, not a home at all. They exited the house and walked down a flagstone path lit by lawn lamps to a smaller outbuilding. Somewhere off to the right a fountain gurgled, the only reassuring element in the entire place.

Herman held open the door for Jade, and she passed into a room hung with red silk and rich gold brocade. In the center of the room, backed by a wall of windows, was a waist-high raised dais. A red dragon, hand-painted on paper screens, stretched around the remaining three walls of the room, his head fierce and terrible. Incense burned in the four corners of the room, and the air hung heavy with the scent of sandalwood mingled with the sharp tang of the hot paraffin of burning candles.

"Please put the box here," Herman said, patting the silk-covered dais. Jade moved forward, still wondering what was going to transpire. Carefully she deposited the box on the dais and then stepped back to allow Herman to pull off the tape. He opened the flaps and leaned forward for a better look.

She heard him sigh. The old woman shuffled forward.

"It is in order, then?" she inquired.

"Yes."

More than anything, Jade wanted to step forward and have a look in the mysterious box. But she sensed that she should allow events to unfold without her intervention, so she hung back, practicing a patience she didn't know she possessed. She remembered Herman's admonitions the day they'd resurrected Connor, about how a flippant attitude could ruin a ceremony. She had no intention of interfering with this proceeding in any way.

Then Herman launched into a prayer, like the prayer he had chanted in the bowels of the Elliott. As his voice droned in a singsong tone, he reached down and slowly raised a human bone from the box, then deposited it lovingly upon a circle of snow white silk. Jade watched him, aghast but fascinated, knowing without being told that these were the remains of Qi An, the lost priestess who'd been murdered a hundred years ago. This was Qi An being laid to rest at last, her earthly spirit finally being reunited with her celestial one. She would become whole, at peace. What, then, would happen to her ceremonial counterpart, Connor, wherever he was?

A full twenty minutes passed before Herman removed every bone from the box. Then he carefully wrapped the ends of the silk around the bones, all the while praying. Once the bundle was secured, he carried it to another box, which sat near the windows, surrounded by a forest of blazing candles. Jade recognized the shiny decorated box, just like the one Connor had stepped from days ago. It could have even been the same one, since she wasn't sure what had happened with Connor's box.

Slowly Herman lowered the bundle of bones into the chest, chanted another prayer, and then closed the lid carefully. The box seemed to float amid all the flickering lights of the candles. He turned.

"It is over," he declared, his voice hoarse. "She can rest now."

The old woman nodded. "The others have been contacted and will come to pay their respects."

"The chest must be removed as soon as possible," Herman advised. "To ensure that the police will not find it."

"It will be done immediately."

They bowed to one another, and then Herman gave a slight motion for Jade to follow him. Quietly she trailed after him, out of the building, down the path, and into the house, where they waited for the taxi to take them home. They stood in the dimly lit foyer while off in the distance a sonorous bell began to sound, a bass tone of velvet black sadness.

"Herman," Jade ventured in a hushed voice, certain now of the nature of his task, "those bones were Qi An's, weren't they?"

He nodded.

"How did you get them?"

"The police had no business taking them."

"So you stole them?"

"Not exactly. An acquaintance of mine helped me locate them and get them out of the building."

"You and your acquaintances." She couldn't help a small smile from pulling at the corners of her mouth.

"The police might have kept Qi An's remains for weeks, perhaps months. I couldn't allow it."

"Connor suspected that she was not at peace, that her body needed to be found and properly buried."

"He was right." Herman clasped one gnarled hand over the other. "And there she was, in the well all those years."

"What do you suppose happened?"

"I believe she was interrupted during the ceremony where she lost the jade necklace that you found. She must have gotten away, though, and ran to draw her assailant away from Connor. Perhaps she fled out of doors, down the bank."

"And she was stabbed there?"

"Quite possibly. And then thrown in the well, where her body might never have been found."

Horrified, Jade drew a closed fist to her lips. "But she lived long enough to drag herself partly through the tunnel."

"With a thought to get to the railroad and help."

"Poor Qi An! She probably bled to death down there. All alone."

Herman nodded grimly.

Jade paused for a moment as she considered such an awful demise, that of dying alone and in such a dark, dank place. Then a thought occurred to her. "Do you suppose that's why water was always involved?"

"Water?" Herman looked up at her. "What do you mean?"

"Whenever Qi An tried to contact us, it was usually through water—the faucets in the bathtub, the steam on the mirror, the watery wall in my bedroom. She was trying to tell us where she was, in the only way she knew how."

"Hmmm," Herman mused. "I hadn't thought of that."

"They were water clues. Only I didn't know about the old well, so I couldn't make the connection."

"I knew about the well. But it did not occur to me to connect it with Qi An."

"And now that we have, her spirit will be at rest?"

Herman nodded.

"And Connor? What about him?"

Herman frowned and pursed his lips. "I am baffled."

"Why?"

"Unless it takes more time than one would think." He crossed his arms, apparently lost in thought.

Jade leaned toward him. "What are you talking about? What time?"

Herman drummed the fingers of his right hand on the sleeve of his quilted jacket and then turned to her. "Does it not make sense, Mrs. MacKenzie, that if Qi An's soul is finally at peace, and she is a whole spirit at last, then Mr. MacKenzie is also whole?"

Jade's heart began to thud inside her. "What are we talking here, Herman—whole as in spirit or whole as in flesh?"

"I would assume flesh. That would be logical."

"Are you saying that after the ceremony with Qi An back there, Connor should be a real person, a normal human being again?"

"That was my belief." Herman's frown grew deeper. "I had thought he would have appeared at the closing of the ceremony."

"Where is he, then?" Jade asked, her voice full of anguished hope. "Is Connor alive somewhere? He must be!"

"But in what condition?" Herman put in. "As healthy as you and I? Or as a man who has been lying in a box for a hundred years?"

"You're saying he might not be the same?"

"I am cautioning you, Mrs. MacKenzie, so that if and

when we locate Mr. MacKenzie, you will be prepared for the worst."

Jade saw the lights of a cab sweep the shrubbery near the drive as her blood seemed to stop pulsing in her veins. She felt light-headed and nauseated as a wave of shock and despair slammed against her, a wave of such magnitude, she thought the force of it would knock her to her knees.

Herman didn't have to say anything more, for she had comprehended the horrible underlying message in his words. They might find Connor. But he could very well be a corpse.

"Ah, our cab has arrived," Herman declared. "Come."

# 19

*Jade felt Herman's hand* at her elbow. "Are you all right, Mrs. MacKenzie?" he asked, craning his neck to see up into her face.

She nodded. "I'll be fine. It's just the thought of Connor being—"

She broke off, unable to put the macabre concept into words.

"But you understand what we might discover."

Jade nodded again.

"Many things might have gone awry in a hundred years."

"I realize that," she whispered.

"The taxi is waiting." He urged her out the door and into the chill of the May evening.

Mist hung in the air, making it hard to breathe, or perhaps it was the painful pressure in her chest that made every breath an agony. Jade stumbled toward the taxi, only half-aware of her surroundings and worried that her injured brain, struck once again—this time by soul-wrenching grief—would cease to operate altogether. She'd be a living hull of a person, unfit to cope with life or with her daughter. Yet without Connor, she didn't know if her life would be worth living anyway.

Then one of the rear doors of the taxi opened. A figure got out and straightened, a tall figure with broad shoulders and long, lean legs. Instantly she recognized those powerful shoulders, those straight, muscular legs. Jade's breath caught in her throat as she gaped at the familiar form and struggled to make out his features in the darkness. The only thing missing was his peculiar golden glow. But then, his translucent aura could have been swallowed up by the mist.

"Connor?" she gasped.

"Jade?" A familiar baritone voice reverberated in the fog.

Without thinking more—without caring one way or the other whether he was a whole human being or the walking dead—Jade ran down the walk, skittered across the drive, and flung herself against Connor's chest.

His arms came around her in a solid embrace, as warm and strong as ever. His chest rose and fell beneath her cheek as she hugged him fiercely, and his voice rumbled in her ear as he murmured her name. He held her tightly, his arms around her shoulders and waist, his nose in her hair.

"Ah, love," he breathed near her ear. "I thought I'd never see you again!"

"I was so frightened!"

"Sabrina—she's all right?"

"She's fine. Oh, Connor!"

Unable to speak another word, Jade tipped up her

chin and his mouth sank upon hers in an ecstatic kiss of homecoming. She curved her arms around his torso and pressed into him, not caring who watched or how long the kiss went on. Connor was here with her in her world, holding her and speaking to her. He was whole and safe, and that was all that mattered.

His hands swept up her back and one pushed into her hair as he kissed her fully and deeply. Then he finally drew away, his lips lingering upon hers as if he were loath to break the connection.

She looked up at him. "Connor, where have you been?"

"Trapped. In a tunnel that ran from the hotel basement t' th' sea."

"Why couldn't you get out?"

"First I had t' attend t' Sabrina. Once I grabbed on to her, I couldna let go. She would have dropped."

"You saved her life."

"Aye. Just in th' nick o' time. But I hadn't th' power t' get all th' way to her."

"That's what she said. No one believed her."

" 'Tis a tale hard t' swallow by anyone who wasna there." He squeezed her. "Apparently, Qi An had th' power t' draw me close, but not all th' way."

"But why couldn't you come back through the wall the same way you left?"

"I dinna know, lass. After th' men came for Sabrina and took her away, somethin' happened. 'Twas as if th' wind dropped out o' my sails. I couldn't move."

"Most likely when the authorities found Qi An's bones," Herman put in. "And removed them."

Jade glanced at Herman, surprised to see him standing near her elbow. She hadn't heard his approach. But then, her senses had been occupied solely with Connor for the last few minutes, and she'd been aware of nothing but the man in her arms.

"They found Qi An's body?" he asked.

"Yes, Mr. MacKenzie. She died in the tunnel, as far as we can tell."

"Ach!"

"Didn't you have an opportunity to speak with her, Connor?" Jade stepped back so she could better see his face. "Sabrina claimed to have heard a woman talking to her. I assumed it was Qi An."

"Aye. She told Sabrina tales th' whole night through, t' keep her from bein' frightened." Connor glanced down. "But we had no time t' speak privately. Such talk would have terrified th' wee one. I thought to talk t' Qi An once Sabrina was rescued. But then I lost my strength. All my abilities. I couldna even see, lass."

Jade shuddered. What Connor had just described sounded like a textbook definition of death. What would have happened if Herman had not retrieved Qi An's bones and completed the ceremony? Connor might have lain in the tunnel, unable to move or call out, and died there, just like Qi An. She thought of her own time spent in a coma and what would have happened had she not been cared for, fed, and stimulated.

"We shouldn't stand out here in the cold," Herman suggested.

"Yes, let's go home." Jade reached for Connor's hand, glad to have something to occupy her mind other than the prospect of Connor's death.

He guided her into the cab, and she snuggled against him as Herman slipped into the front seat. It would be a long time until she let go of Connor, until she had enough faith in the world and fate to trust that he wouldn't disappear. Connor draped an arm around her shoulders and kissed the top of her head.

"Ye had a rough few days," he murmured. "Haven't ye, sweet?"

She nodded, suddenly on the verge of tears. She buried her face in the small of his neck and breathed in his male scent, laced with the musty smell of damp earth. His embrace tightened around her, giving her the sustenance she'd craved for the last twenty-four hours, a special sustenance only Connor could provide.

"Just hold me," she whispered. "And I'll be all right."

They rode in silence down the hill and rolled quietly through the streets of the International District, back to the Elliott, whose towers and turrets were ablaze with light. Jade's heart swelled with joy at the sight. She'd never seen anything more welcoming and never looked forward more to a night than the one she planned to spend with Connor in her bed. A delicious thrill coursed through her, spreading out in a surge through her womb and her breasts and all the places Connor had kissed when he'd made love to her.

"What're ye thinkin' about?" Connor asked, tipping up her chin with the crook of his finger.

She raised her eyes to his, knowing her love for him poured out of her in a hot torrent. "You."

A slow smile blossomed on his wide masculine mouth. "Good thoughts, then?"

"Excellent ones."

He grinned, and his eyes danced with merriment as he gazed down upon her. "I'm thinkin' th' same."

"Are you? How can you be sure?"

"'Tis enough t' see your eyes, lass, t' know what's goin' on in your head."

"I'm that obvious?"

"Only t' me." He gave her a quick kiss as the taxi pulled up in front of the Elliott. "But then I have—what d'ye call it—an inside track."

He winked at her and opened the door. Flushed with desire, Jade slid across the seat to let him help her out of the cab. Herman's voice stopped her progress, however, and she held up a hand to caution Connor.

"I am going home for the evening," Herman declared.

"You don't want to come up?" she countered.

"It is late for an old man such as myself." He smiled. "Besides, I believe I would be a hindrance for both of you tonight."

She smiled at him. "Good night, then, Herman. And thank you for all your help."

"And yours. Without you, we should never have found Qi An."

He settled back in his seat, and Jade rose up from the cab. Connor placed her hand in the crook of his arm and led her up the short flight of stairs to the lobby of the condominium building.

In the elevator they stepped into each other's arms, unable to contain their wonder at being together again. Jade pressed kisses upon his face while he pressed her against the wall, trapping her with his large frame. Blatantly, he pushed against her and gently bit the lobe of her ear until she gasped with pleasure. The door slid open and she moaned in disappointment.

"Ye dinna want t' stay in the lift all night, do ye, Jade?"

"I wouldn't mind," she answered. "If you keep kissing me."

"There's more than kisses in store for ye, I'll have ye know."

"Is there?"

"Aye." Connor held out his hand. "Gi' me your key."

Jade located her ring of keys in a pocket of her purse and gave them to him. As soon as the keys were in his fist, he swept her into his arms.

"Connor!" Jade laughed softly.

"Ye're cold as ice and ye've had no sleep since God knows when." He adjusted her with a little toss and then carried her toward her apartment. "Ye must be tuckered out."

"I'm not *that* tired." She wrapped her arms around his strong neck and laughed gaily as he nuzzled her.

"I want ye t' conserve th' strength ye do have," he said, grinning, "for later."

At her door he adjusted her again, put the key in the lock, and then kissed her thoroughly before he turned the knob.

"You feel so wonderful," she murmured against his lips. "I've been cold all day."

"I've plenty o' heat for th' both of us." He kissed her again, along her jawline and up to her ear. Chills shimmered through her, melting away her memories of the freezing rain and her soggy shoes and replacing them with the sensations of the warmth of his hands and the reverberation of his deep baritone voice. By the time they stumbled into the dark apartment, she was ready to toss off her clothes and ravish Connor where he stood. Instead she let herself be carried into her bedroom, where he deposited her gently on the bed and then straightened.

"I smell like a turnip patch," Connor declared. "I must have a bath first, Jade."

"On one condition."

He gazed down at her and raised a brow. "That bein'?"

"That I may join you."

He grinned. "Wouldna have it any other way." He held out his hand and clasped hers, tugging her to her feet. She embraced him again, pushing one hand into his soft burnished hair and urging him to bend down for a long kiss. She'd never have enough of his kisses, never tire of his touch, and having thought she'd lost him made his presence in her life all the more precious. He had become everything to her—confidant, lover, best friend, and father to her fatherless child—and she wanted never to lose him again.

Connor gradually pulled away, chuckling as he gazed down at her. His mouth tilted up at one corner. "Keep it up, lass, and we'll never make it t' th' bath."

"So?" She cocked an eyebrow.

Connor smiled and started to unbutton his shirt, but she gently pushed aside his hands and unfastened the garment, her heart pounding at the thought of disrobing him. While she unbuttoned his cuffs, he reached down and unsnapped her jeans and pulled out the hem of her sweater. She tossed his shirt on a nearby chair and then turned back to kiss his nipples. She could feel each one harden beneath her tongue, which sent a shaft of desire spiking through her. Jade ran her palms over the well-developed muscles of his chest and down the hard contours of his upper arms, then laid her cheek against his breastbone and closed her eyes, transported into a world of pure sensation while she listened to his breathing.

"You're different," she commented softly.

"In what way?"

"I'm not getting that zap when you first touch me." She snuggled closer. "That crackle of electricity."

"Am I losin' my touch, then?"

"Perhaps you're just more real now. Perhaps the effect of your gold bath is wearing off."

Connor paused and went quiet for a moment as he considered her words. "Or maybe you drew it out of me th' last time."

"What do you mean?"

"Well, from my readin' on th' subject of electricity, I learned a few things—such as energy flows downhill."

"And I'm downhill?"

"In a manner o' speakin'. You've been injured, Jade, in your brain. And what is a brain but a vast network of electrical connections?"

She drew back and looked up at his face. "How do you know about neurology?"

"I read about brain injuries, too."

Jade gazed at Connor, struck anew by the interest and care he showed for her. "So you're saying," she remarked at last, "that my injured electrical system might have drained off your extra helping of energy, so to speak?"

"'Tis a theory." His hands slid slowly down her back. "But I'm no scientist."

"Interesting thought, though." She tilted her head. "Didn't you also read some books about women?"

"Aye." He grinned. "Modern women."

"And what did you learn about them?"

"Why, that"—he pulled her hips to his, and she felt the mark of his full arousal—"is something I plan to show ye, not tell."

Connor drew her sweater over her head and dropped it upon his own, then covered her breasts with his hands. Gently he massaged them, his long fingers easily encompassing her. Jade let out a sigh that mingled with his own low moan.

"So far, so good," she murmured breathlessly.

"There's more," he answered. "Much more."

Connor slipped off her brassiere and gathered her in his arms to bring her bare skin to his. Nothing compared to the coming together of their naked bodies, his tanned strength like polished birch pressed against her pale surrender like young bamboo. He was hard where she was soft, blazing where she slowly melted, and he consumed her with his insistent mouth as she yielded to him willingly and completely, her body bowing backward over his arm.

"Ah, Jade," he whispered, crushing her to him, "how did I live before you?"

His words sent a shiver of pleasure down her spine. "The same way I lived before you came into my life, Connor. Innocent of the full scope of things. The richness. The rightness."

"'Twas just existin' before."

"I'll never be satisfied with anything else."

"Or anyone else." He pulled back to look down at her, his eyes serious. "I seem t' keep comin' back t' ye, Jade, like it was meant t' be."

"Don't you think it was?"

"I never put much stock in fate, until now." He kissed her mouth. "Come."

Without another word he pulled Jade to the master bath, turned on the water in the tub, and then pivoted, backing her against the sink.

At the sound of the water thundering into the porcelain bathtub, Jade thought of Qi An.

"She wanted us to know she was in the well." Jade put her hands on Connor's chest. "That's why she kept giving us water clues."

"Qi An?"

Jade nodded.

"She's at rest now." Connor traced the line of Jade's

lip. "And I owe my life t' her. But I canna think o' her at a time like this. And I dinna intend t' try."

"Good." Jade smiled up at him and reached for the buttons of his jeans. "Because I want you to think only of making love to me."

"Done," he growled near her ear. "And wi' pleasure."

In a few moments Jade had freed him of his pants and he had pulled hers off as well. Then, before she had time to think of what to do next, she felt Connor stripping away her panties and urging her back against the cool edge of the marble counter.

They stood entirely naked in the dim light of the bathroom, with the water running behind them, filling up the tub as the sound filled her senses. Steam swirled around them, fogging the mirror. She felt herself being lifted upon the counter and Connor stepping between her knees.

"Wrap your legs around me," he said, his voice hoarse with desire.

She complied and felt his shaft come up against her womanly flesh. Jade gasped as he pushed into her.

"Are ye comfortable, love?" he asked.

"Yes. Very." She let her head loll back as he pulled away and then entered her again, deeper this time. The contrast of the heat of him inside her and the cool marble beneath her put a new and sharper edge on their lovemaking.

"Oh—" Her mouth suddenly went dry with desire. "Connor, that's—"

"Yes?"

"That's so—" She broke off, lost for words, and not because of her brain injury this time, but because of the way he was making her feel.

"That's so what, lass?"

"Hmmm." She smiled but couldn't open her eyes. The position they were in opened an entirely different world to her. She felt something urgent and glorious building in her, like a delicate prelude that began with the soft tones of flutes and violins, increased with the deeper strains of cellos and woodwinds, and then broke into a powerful fugue of brass and timpani, sweeping her along on a torrent of drums. She braced herself on the counter and let her body soar where only her soul had taken her before.

"Connor!" she gasped as something inside her burst into profusion, like a huge choir singing at the tops of their lungs, filling her with an ecstasy so glorious, so celestial, she forgot where she was or that she'd ever known anything but Connor like this inside her. Delicious spasms surged within her depths, more encompassing and overwhelming than any orgasm she'd ever experienced.

He didn't seem to hear her. His eyes were closed and he plunged into her with deep, hard strokes, his lips pressed together, his hands clamped around her waist. Then he let out a hoarse cry as his seed spilled into her, filling her with a fire all his own. She felt the release deep within her, and her body answered with more incredible spasms that embraced him as fiercely as her arms locked around his neck. For a moment he lifted her onto him as they fused together completely, and he held her like that until he caught his breath, until she'd stopped trembling. Then, still holding her, he leaned backward, shut off the faucet, and stepped into the tub with her. Slowly they disengaged, and then he lowered her to the hot water. She sighed with delight as her body sank below the surface.

"That feels heavenly," she murmured.

"The water or the lovemakin'?"

She opened her eyes and gazed up at him. He knelt above her, straddling her thighs. "Both," she replied, smiling slowly. She felt utterly relaxed, entirely loved, and thoroughly content. "Whatever you read in those books, Connor, I heartily approve of your course of study."

"Do ye now?" he replied, kissing her forehead and trailing more kisses down the side of her face. "Well, 'twasn't hard, since you're my favorite subject."

"And you're mine." She reached up and embraced him, her heart suddenly and fully exposed, making her more vulnerable than she had ever been. But with this man she had no fear of vulnerability. It was a gift she offered willingly in return for his uncommon understanding of her. She knew he would never violate her trust or throw her vulnerability back at her as a sign of weakness. "I'm so glad you've come back, Connor! I was so worried about you!"

"Ah, Jade." He drew her up against him, until they knelt thigh to thigh in the water. He held her close, showing her with his reverent hands and tender kisses how he felt about her. Jade's heart surged, burning a hot trail up her throat.

"Connor," she whispered near his ear. "I love you. I love you so much!"

His arms tightened around her, but he said nothing.

"I don't care who you are or what you are anymore. I just want you with me, in my life. No one else."

"Ah, lass." He smoothed back the hair from the side of her face and gazed down at her, his blue eyes dark as indigo. "It may not last. I may not be here long. Ye must remember that."

"What do you mean?"

"I'm fine now. A real man." The word *real* rolled off his tongue in his deep Scottish burr. "But none o' us can predict how long I am for this world or what I might become."

"I don't care!"

"It matters t' me. I'll not see ye hurt, Jade."

"What are you saying?" She pulled back. "What happened to your 'live now, for tomorrow we may die' attitude?"

" 'Twas before Sabrina," he replied. Then his expression softened, and the line of his mouth grew more serious. "And before ye came t' mean so much t' me. 'Twas a flirtation before. An undeniable attraction. But it's grown, this feelin' between us, and now there's much more than my manly appetite at stake."

"I'm a grown woman," Jade countered. "I'll take the chance."

"I canna make promises," Connor continued, "or vows that my condition would force me t' break one day. 'Twould break your heart, Jade. Ye've had enough o' that."

She gazed up at him, drinking in the golden cast of his handsome face and his strong Celtic features. "I'm not asking for any promises." She caressed his cheek with the palm of her hand. "I'm just asking for today and tonight, for as long as we can have them."

"I can give ye today," Connor murmured. "And tonight."

Connor kissed her and Jade closed her eyes, wishing he would tell her that he loved her and wanted to be her husband in all ways . . . and hoping she could be as brave as she claimed to be, should Connor ever disappear again.

❋   ❋   ❋

Late the next morning they ate a leisurely breakfast of eggs, toast, and grapefruit and read through the paper as they sat on stools at the bar. Connor was dressed in jeans and a forest green corduroy shirt that brought out the coppery highlights of his blond hair. Jade kept glancing at him as she ate her omelet, certain that he'd never looked more attractive but still afraid that each time she looked at him might be the last.

"What're ye starin' at?" he asked, glancing up from the front page.

"You." She smiled, still holding the fork to her lips.

"Keep it up and we'll have t' go back t' bed."

"You think that's a threat?"

He grinned and leaned closer, crackling the paper against the countertop. "There are things t' be done today besides makin' love."

"Besides the evaluation with Dr. Nilsen?" She'd told him of the afternoon meeting and of her relief that he'd come back in time.

"Aye. Speakin' t' your brother, for instance. This building is mine, and I intend t' reclaim it, one way or another."

"Good luck." Jade returned her attention to the paper just as someone pounded on the door. She and Connor exchanged worried glances. No one had buzzed her intercom, asking permission to enter the building, and the knock sounded demanding and unfriendly. Jade rose, dropping the paper, which floated to the floor.

"Shall I answer it?" she asked in a low tone.

"Of course. Why not?"

"The police might still be looking for you—Thomas's cronies."

"I've nothin' t' hide."

"I think you do," she whispered.

"Not where Sabrina's concerned." He stood up and ambled around the edge of the counter as she walked to the front door and opened it.

Two policemen stood in the doorway.

"Mr. MacKenzie?" one of them asked, his voice terse.

Connor walked up beside Jade, taller than all three of the people around him. "Aye?"

"We'd like you to come down to the station this morning."

"What for?"

"To answer a few questions." The officer glanced at Jade and then back at Connor.

Jade slipped her hand around Connor's elbow. She had no doubt that Thomas had instigated this new inquiry. "Are you arresting him?"

"No, ma'am. We just need him to clarify some points in our investigation, that's all."

"Points?" Connor boomed. "Concernin' what?"

"Concerning Sabrina Brennan."

"I've nothin' t' tell ye."

"It will only take a few minutes. And it'll be strictly off the record, Mr. MacKenzie."

Connor looked down at Jade, his eyes full of questions.

"Shall I go with you?" she asked.

"Nay. Ye got Laura comin', things t' arrange. I'll be back as soon as I can."

"I'll call Herman. Have him meet you there with a lawyer."

"Good." He stooped and kissed her quickly. "Dinna worry, lass."

"I'll try not to." She gave him a smile to hide her darkening sense of concern and watched him walk away with the police.

# 20

*As soon as the police left,* Jade stormed up to the penthouse and pounded on the door.

"Mrs. MacKenzie!" Phillip exclaimed when he saw her flushed face.

"I want to see Thomas," she demanded. "And I want to see him now!"

"I'm afraid Mr. Brennan is at his office."

"Then I want to see Gail."

"Mrs. Brennan is occupied with a brunch at the moment."

"Here?"

"In the solarium. But she gave explicit—"

Jade brushed past him and rushed down the hall toward the solarium, which was on the southern side of the building. She heard Phillip behind her, requesting that she come back, but refused to listen to his protestations.

Gay feminine laughter and the clink of crystal wafted out

of the doorway ahead of her. Jade burst across the threshold into a room full of sunlight and plants and a table ringed by well-dressed, well-coiffed women. The noise level dropped instantly, and ten flawlessly made-up faces turned toward her, ten pairs of eyes surveyed her.

Gail rose to her feet. "Janine!" She couldn't hide her irritation at the surprise appearance of her sister-in-law.

"I want to talk to you, Gail," Jade said.

Gail glanced at Phillip, her eyes narrowed in vexation.

"I'm sorry, madame. She insisted upon seeing you."

"Very well." Gail dropped her linen napkin to the table and swept the ring of ladies with her eyes, smiling graciously to cloak her anger. "Excuse me for a moment."

Deftly Gail skirted the table and marched past Jade without looking at her. Jade followed her sister-in-law out to the hall, down the corridor, and into the living room, which was close to the front door—conveniently located for a boot out of the house. Gail minced to the cactus-covered coffee table and turned, her dark eyes as hard as pieces of coal.

"This had better be good," she snapped. "I'm getting tired of being interrupted by you."

"Gail, Connor has just been taken to the police station."

"And?"

Jade stared at her, amazed by her sister-in-law's coldness. "They've taken him in for questioning!"

"An appropriate thing to do with men who kidnap innocent children, I would say."

"Connor didn't kidnap Sabrina!"

"So he tells you."

"I know him. He wouldn't harm a hair on a child's head."

"Oh? You must have forgotten how he treated Robbie, then."

Jade crossed her arms and glanced at the cold fireplace across the room. Gail would never see Robbie in a realistic light, and it was useless to try to reason with her.

"I know Thomas is behind this latest fiasco. Tell him to quit harassing Connor, or I'll sue him."

"It isn't harassment." Gail tossed her head. "It's pursuing justice. MacKenzie kidnapped our daughter, and he will be brought to task for it."

"That's a bunch of crap, and you know it."

They glared at one another until a movement at the edge of the room caught Jade's eye. She stepped to the right to get a better look. "Robbie?" she called, peering around the corner of the wall that housed the fireplace.

He stood in the shadows, holding a plastic superhero figure, which he propelled through the air while he pretended not to take notice of his aunt.

"Robbie, what are you doing over there?" Gail's voice sounded unnaturally shrill.

"Robbie, did you know your uncle Connor has been taken to the police station?"

The superhero paused in flight for a moment and then zoomed downward with a hiss. Robbie dipped, flying the figure close to the carpet, and then rose up and threw a glance at Jade, a glance full of dark surprise.

Jade ignored Gail, who marched toward her, anxious to insert herself between her son and her meddling sister-in-law. But Jade would not be stopped from talking to Robbie this time. She moved closer to the boy.

"The police think Connor tried to kidnap Sabrina. He could get in a lot of trouble, Robbie. He needs your help."

The plastic toy hovered in the air. "My help?" Robbie asked.

"Yes."

Before Jade could say anything more, she was elbowed aside by Gail, who grabbed Robbie's wrist.

"That's enough, Janine!" she hissed. "Let's go, Robbie." She pulled him toward the other entrance to the living room.

"Don't come here again without calling first," Gail threw over her shoulder. "Or I'll be the one filing harassment charges."

"I'll see you this afternoon," Jade retorted. "And Connor had better be finished with the police by that time, or I'm going to the commissioner."

"About what?"

"Questionable on-duty activities of some city employees."

Gail turned, livid. "Is that a threat?" she barked.

"Just a warning." Jade turned and stormed out of the living room, past Phillip's shocked face, and barged out of the penthouse.


The rest of the morning flew by, and just after noon Jade's intercom buzzed. She jumped to her feet and sprinted across the room to let Laura into the lobby. A few minutes later, her doorbell rang. Jade flung open the door.

"Laura!" she cried, opening her arms wide.

Laura gave her a funny look and then stepped across the threshold for a hug.

"Thank you for coming!" Jade squeezed her and realized with a start that she had never embraced her friend, not in all the years she had known Laura. She'd never reached out before, which she now saw as a sad lack on her part. Since her accident, and since coming to know

Connor, Jade had learned the importance of overcoming her own cool reserve, of breaking through the invisible wall she'd stood behind all her life. There was nothing more important than showing the people she loved how she felt about them. Connor had helped her come to such a realization.

"I had to come, Jade," Laura answered, patting her back. "Sabrina has been on the national news, you know."

Jade drew away. "She has?"

"Yes." Laura walked into the apartment. "And so has your darling hubby."

A sickening feeling fanned out in Jade's stomach. "I've been too busy to watch TV lately. What're they saying about Connor?"

"That he's a man with a mysterious—and I might add suspicious—past. They're raising questions about his involvement with Sabrina's disappearance."

"Oh, dear." Jade closed the door and stood in front of it, too worried to move. She glanced up. "We can keep him out of jail, can't we?"

"I hope so, for his sake. Kidnappers of children don't fare well in prison." Laura studied Jade closely. "There isn't a possibility that he's involved, is there?"

"Are you serious?"

"I'm your attorney." Laura shrugged. "I had to ask."

"He would never do such a thing!"

Satisfied with Jade's response, Laura nodded. "All the arrangements have been made?"

"Yes. We're due to meet at three at the Brennans'. With any luck, Connor will be back before then."

"Where is he?"

"Down at the police station answering some questions."

"With a lawyer, I hope."

"Yes. Herman Fong found an attorney for him."

"Good." Laura sat upon the back of the couch and swung one of her shapely legs. "Then we have a minute to talk."

"Would you like some tea? Instant coffee?"

"No thanks. I'd like you to level with me, Jade."

Jade felt the color drain from her face. "What do you mean?"

"I want you to tell me what's really going on."

Jade swallowed and gazed at her friend, wishing she had confided in Laura from the very first. Laura would be offended that Jade hadn't been completely honest with her when they'd last spoken of Connor. But getting by on half-truths was no longer possible. Laura had to know everything about Connor in order to defend him. All Jade could do now was count on Laura's understanding and long-term friendship to see her through the next few impossible-to-believe minutes.

Sighing, Jade walked to the chair near the couch and collapsed in it. "If I tell you, you won't believe me."

Laura pivoted to look down at her. "Try me. I've heard everything."

"Not something like this." Jade clasped her hands together and stared at her emerald ring, which blurred in her vision. "The things I told you before about Connor were only partly true."

"I had a feeling you were withholding something."

"I didn't know what else to do."

Laura took a seat on the couch and leaned toward Jade to squeeze her arm gently. "You've been under a lot of strain, Jade. I've been worried about you, and hoped you'd talk to me. That's what friends are for—to talk to each other. You know you can always call me, don't you?"

"Yes." Jade glanced up at Laura. "And you don't know what it means to me that you've flown out here twice at the drop of a hat. I appreciate that more than—"

"It's all right. I just want to know the truth. Who *is* this MacKenzie character?"

For a moment Jade stared at Laura's solemn face, her clear gray eyes and firm mouth. Then she started from the beginning—the moment she found the jade necklace in the cellar—and told her everything up until the moment the police had arrested Connor that morning. Laura listened, rapt, and sometimes shook her head in disbelief. But never once did she interrupt, which surprised Jade.

When she had finished, Laura sat back and regarded her thoughtfully, a little crease between her dark blond eyebrows. "That's some story," she finally remarked. "And if anyone else had told me such a tale, I'd call them crazy."

Jade blushed, still sensitive about remarks made about brains, especially hers.

"But knowing you," Laura continued, "I have to know it's true."

"It is!"

Just as she finished, she heard the door opening behind her and the buzz of familiar voices as Herman and Connor bustled into the apartment, talking animatedly. Jade jumped up.

"Connor!" she exclaimed. She ran to him and embraced him. He smelled like cigarette smoke, but she barely took notice of it.

"Lass!" he greeted her.

"Are you all right?" She pulled back and searched his face, then raked him with her eyes.

"I'm fine." He squeezed her. "And glad t' be home."

Laura ambled up to the happy group. Connor turned to look down at her.

"Good t' see ye, Laura," he said, sticking out his hand. "How are ye?"

"Never better." She smiled and shook his hand. "Did you get thoroughly grilled by the police?"

"They did their best, but I mostly held my tongue."

"Good."

She glanced at her watch. "Well, is everyone ready for the OK Corral? We have ten minutes."

Jade turned to Connor. "You'd better take a quick shower, Connor, and change. Herman brought over a suit for you to wear."

"He needn't bother." Laura put her hand on Jade's arm.

"Why not?"

"He's not going."

"I'm not?" Connor thundered. "Why in blazes not?"

"Because, Mr. MacKenzie," Laura replied, "it will be best if you're not there to be questioned. The Brennans' attorney is one of the best in the business. He could make George Washington look like a liar."

"But what about Sabrina and Jade?"

"I'm Jade's attorney. I say you cool your jets here at the condo while we handle the meeting."

"Cool my jets?"

"An expression," Herman explained. "She means you should take it easy."

"Take it easy while they're deciding whether or not t' leave Sabrina with those reprobates?"

"Better than letting Ben Goldstein rip into you about your past, present, and future and everything in between. Spend the afternoon with Goldstein, and you might end up in jail."

Connor glared at her. "I'll not go back there. Not alive."

Jade slipped her arm around Connor's torso and gave him a hug. She felt for him. He'd spent enough time in a prison of his own, more time than humanly conceivable. His spirit would not endure another dark stretch like that, and she knew it.

"This is do or die here tonight," Laura said grimly. "We want to win custody of Sabrina and make sure Connor is not charged with kidnapping. If Gail and Thomas decide to press charges, we could be in deep trouble."

"Why?" Connor asked.

"Because your documentation would never stand up under questioning."

"What's wrong with his documentation?" Herman inquired.

Laura glanced at him kindly. "It's far too perfect, Mr. Fong. Someone would smell a rat right away." She looked up at Connor. "Besides, I know your story. I made Jade tell me everything."

"Ye did?" Connor exclaimed.

"I had to." Jade squeezed him again. "Laura will do her best. You can count on it."

"But will it be enough?" Connor asked, and then glanced at Laura. "No offense, love."

"None taken, dear." She gave him a wry smile. "But that's why I can't have you at the meeting. You can't tell your story. It's too farfetched. And if you can't tell the truth, you'll look like a liar in everyone's eyes but ours. Ben will eat you alive and make sure you end up in prison, or wherever the Brennans want you to go." She touched his arm. "Now, if you will excuse me for a minute, I'll go freshen up."

She walked down the hall toward the bathroom, while Jade gave Connor a quick kiss. "That's for luck," she whispered.

He held her, his hands locked around her waist. "I'm serious, Jade. If th' meetin' goes poorly, I'll run. I'll have to."

"I know."

"Ye willna be able t' come along, not with Sabrina."

"I know."

Their eyes caught and held, and Jade felt hers grow hot with tears. "We won't lose, Connor," she said. "We can't."

"Ah, t' have your faith," he murmured against her hair.

"I thought you were the one with boundless faith."

"Not always. I'm only human." He hugged her tightly for a few moments without speaking. Then he reached up to stroke her hair. "Remember that time I called ye a bad apple? Said the Brennan family tree was blighted?"

"Yes." She closed her eyes and listened to the rumble of his voice, which had become as dear to her as his touch.

"Well, my grandmother used t' say that th' best apple will always be on th' highest bough." He kept stroking her hair. "It took a while t' reach ye, Jade, but I did. And it was worth th' trouble. Ye're th' sweetest and best of th' whole Brennan lot."

His words sent a glow through her, which caused the tears to spill out of her eyes. "Thank you, Connor," she whispered.

"Th' Brennan name has taken on a whole new meanin' with you on th' tree."

"But I'm not a Brennan anymore," she teased.

"True. And 'tis proud I am that ye've taken my name."

"Really?" she looked up at him, tears glistening on her lashes.

"Aye. Ye do credit t' the MacKenzie clan."

At that moment, Laura breezed back into the living room. "Everyone ready?" she asked, her eyes bright as she surveyed each of the people in turn.

"Get rid of the tears, Jade," she said. "Paste on a smile."

Jade grinned tremulously and wiped away the moisture on her cheeks.

"Herman, grab the briefcase."

"Shall I accompany you?" Herman inquired.

"Of course. You're our character witness, Mr. Fong."

Laura herded everyone toward the door. Connor and Jade brought up the rear.

"Get Thomas Brennan talking," Connor advised. "That's all ye have t' do. A man like that—well, his mouth often breaks his own nose, if you get my drift."

"I get it." Laura held out her hand to him. "Try to relax now."

Connor shook hers warmly. "Thank ye for your trouble, Laura."

Jade was the last to leave. She held the door for everyone while Connor stood behind her. As she reached for the knob to close the door, Connor bent over and kissed her neck at the shoulder.

"Hurry back," he murmured. "I'll miss ye."

Jade drank in the sight of him standing there—circles under his eyes and his hair tousled, but still the most attractive man she'd ever met. Just looking at him made something twist deep inside her, made her flush with desire and heat—the same reaction she'd had from the moment she'd first laid eyes on him. Close to tears again, Jade kissed Connor soundly and hurried after the others.

She waited at the elevator, too worried to join in the nervous banter around her. This was it. Connor would either be part of her life, accepted as her husband and father of Sabrina, or he would disappear into the night, never to be seen again.

# 21

*At three o'clock sharp,* Jade found herself being shown into the dreaded library of the penthouse. Nothing good had ever come of the time she had spent in the dark little room, and she worried that she might sustain another loss in this dreary place.

"Thank you for coming," she said to Dr. Nilsen, who stood just inside the doorway of the library, dressed in a red suit with navy blue piping and big square buttons.

Dr. Nilsen nodded to her and then glanced past her down the hall, as if expecting someone else. "Where is Mr. MacKenzie?" she inquired.

"He's being questioned by the police."

"The police?"

Laura leaned closer. "A ploy, Dr. Nilsen, to keep him away from the proceedings."

"Whose ploy?"

"I would assume the Brennans."

"Oh?" Dr. Nilsen directed her attention to the couple sitting on the edge of the couch.

Phillip appeared at Jade's elbow. "Would you ladies care to take a seat?" He motioned to chairs facing the small couch. Two coffee carafes sat on a low table in between, along with an assortment of cookies.

Jade took a seat next to Laura and glanced across the table at her adversaries: Thomas, Gail sitting on the sofa, and their lawyer, Ben Goldstein, who sat in a chair near Thomas. An older man, a retired judge named Clarence Dinsmore, had agreed to serve as a mediator and sat at the end of the table nearest the door. Oddly enough, Dr. Nilsen pulled out a chair at the opposite end, as if to establish her independence from either camp, and sat down in a cloud of primary colors and perfume.

"Would anyone care for coffee?" Gail asked, playing the perfect hostess as usual.

"None for me, thank you," Laura replied crisply. "Anyone else?"

Jade would have liked a warm beverage to hold in her hands, but no tea was available, so she declined. No one else took refreshments, either.

Laura clasped her hands together in front of her on top of the highly polished table. "Let's make this quick, shall we? I'm sure we all have better things to do than quibble over this matter."

"I don't consider Sabrina's welfare quibbling," Thomas retorted.

"My point, Mr. Brennan," Laura replied, staring him down, "is that this is no quibbling matter. Sabrina's safety is of prime importance. And we don't have to spend hours debating that fact."

"I don't expect to," Thomas replied hotly. "There's little doubt in my mind whom Sabrina should live with. Us!" He grabbed Gail's hand.

Gail raised her chin. "The inference that we lack the ability to care for a child is simply ludicrous! Outrageous."

Laura observed the display without a hint of emotion crossing her features. Jade wondered how her friend retained her composure so well. She herself wanted to leap across the table and choke the words out of Gail, to put a stop to her incessant posturing.

"The facts compel us to believe otherwise." Laura opened her briefcase. "We have come to the conclusion that Sabrina is not safe in your custody."

Gail and Thomas exchanged shocked glances, and then Thomas leaned forward. "And she's safe with that child molester my sister's supposedly married to?"

"We're not here to discuss Connor MacKenzie."

"We damned well are!" Thomas jerked his chin up, as if his tie were too tight. "He's part of it!"

Ben Goldstein leaned close to Thomas and whispered something in his ear, and Thomas sat back, frowning but silent.

Ben cleared his throat. "The facts speak for themselves," he declared, glancing down at a folder in front of him. He picked up a paper. "Sabrina disappeared at the same time as Mr. MacKenzie. She claimed he was in the well with her, along with a woman she never saw—perhaps you, *Miss* Brennan?" He stressed the word *Miss*, as if to cast aspersions on her married state as well as her claim not to have had knowledge of Sabrina's whereabouts at the time of her disappearance.

Jade felt her cheeks grow red with indignation. "Why would I have kept my daughter in a cold well for an entire night?"

"Maybe to make everyone believe she'd been kidnapped," Gail snapped, "so you could run off with her."

"Why would I run off with her? My chances of gaining custody of Sabrina were good. Thomas told me that himself. In fact, he tried to get me to agree to delay the process until after the election because he wanted to use Sabrina to get more votes."

Dr. Nilsen turned to study Thomas, and for once Jade approved of the dour regard of the psychologist's eyes.

"Still, Miss Brennan," Ben continued, "isn't it a little strange that you were the one to find the well?"

"Not really. I just searched more thoroughly."

"More thoroughly than the police canine unit?"

"It must have rained too hard for the dogs to get a good scent."

Ben tilted his head and said nothing, and his silence was more mocking than any remark he might have made.

"I got lucky," Jade added, her anger rising.

Ben looked back down at his folder. "Perhaps you can answer some of my other questions." He picked up another paper. "My firm has discovered plenty of interesting information about your supposed husband, Miss Brennan."

"Such as?" Jade asked coldly.

"Such as your marriage in Scotland. You've never been to Scotland, Miss Brennan, have you?"

"I object to this line of questioning," Laura protested, turning to Clarence Dinsmore. "Janine isn't on trial here."

"She may not be." Dinsmore held up a beefy hand. "But her relationship to Mr. MacKenzie should be made clear."

"They're married. That's all that needs to be established."

Laura reached into a folder and produced their marriage certificate. "Janine and Connor were married at the King County Courthouse last week." She handed the document to Dinsmore and waited as he adjusted his glasses and perused the certificate.

"This seems to be in order," he commented, gazing over the top of his reading glasses at Ben Goldstein. "What's the problem, Ben?"

"The problem is they lied about their marriage, both to Dr. Nilsen and to my clients."

Laura slipped the marriage certificate into the folder. "Come now, Mr. Goldstein. People fudge a little about their marriage dates all the time when it's necessary."

"What do you mean?" Ben glanced at Jade, and his gaze traveled down her figure. "She's pregnant?"

Laura raised an eyebrow, letting him draw his own conclusions.

"They love each other," Herman put in quietly.

"What's that, old man?" Thomas inquired, leaning his cheek on the palm of his hand.

"Mr. and Mrs. MacKenzie. They love each other. A very important fact that has not been mentioned."

Everyone at the table paused and stared at Herman for a confused moment, as if love had no bearing on the subject at hand. Then Ben cleared his throat again.

"Be that as it may, Connor MacKenzie has shown himself to be a liar. He claims he didn't kidnap Sabrina. But can he prove where he was the morning she disappeared?"

"He was with my brother," Herman said, adding a curt nod to his statement.

Ben and Thomas exchanged a quick glance. "Doing what?" Ben asked.

"Fishing. All morning."

"Where?"

"Gig Harbor."

"That's the first time I've heard that story," Thomas drawled.

"No one asked my brother."

"No one knew you had a brother, Mr. Fong."

Herman shrugged. "No one asked me if I had a brother."

Jade looked down at the table to hide a smile. Herman might play the part of a simple old man, but she would bet he was more cunning and resourceful than anyone in the room.

"An alibi," Ben declared. "But a flimsy one. Anyone can see there is something going on here—some kind of conspiracy."

"Nothing more than this." Laura put her hands flat on the folder in her lap. "We want to ensure that Sabrina is safe in the future. And we want the Brennans to stop harassing Mr. MacKenzie because of their idiotic notion that he kidnapped Sabrina."

"Idiotic?" Ben leaned forward. "Explain to us how Mr. MacKenzie saved Sabrina from falling. Explain to us why, if he could grab her overalls, he didn't just pull her out and get her out of the tunnel?"

"Explain to us how Sabrina got into the tunnel in the first place," Laura countered. "How did a two-year-old girl unlock all those doors, manage to get down the elevator, and sneak past the attendant in the lobby, without anyone seeing her? And who was supposed to be watching Sabrina that morning?"

All eyes turned to Gail, who blushed a deep crimson. "One cannot watch a child twenty-four hours a day," she exclaimed. "It isn't humanly possible."

"And where was Robbie at the time?" Jade put in.

"Why does that matter?" Thomas retorted. "He's just an innocent boy, Janine. He has nothing to do with this."

Jade forced herself to hold her tongue regarding Robbie's innocence.

"So." Clarence Dinsmore flipped through the pile of documents in his hand, studying them quickly. "What I've gathered so far is that you claim Connor MacKenzie did not kidnap your niece—er, daughter?" He regarded Jade with bloodshot eyes.

"That's right."

"You believe in his innocence."

"Yes. I do."

"Yet you haven't known him all that long."

"No, sir, I haven't."

"How long have you known him, Mrs. MacKenzie?"

"Objection," Laura put in. "Janine isn't on trial."

"I'll answer him, Laura," Jade said. She glanced at Dinsmore, deciding to tell the truth, to get it out in the open, hoping the truth would save the man she loved, even though it might impact on her custody proceedings. "I've known Connor less than two weeks."

"There!" Gail cried, almost jumping out of her seat. "See? I told you!"

"I married him because I needed a husband to satisfy Dr. Nilsen's requirements."

"I knew it!" Gail exclaimed. She reached out and clutched Thomas's hand.

Jade ignored her sister-in-law's outbursts. "But he's a good man, Judge Dinsmore. The best. And I have fallen in love with him, just as Mr. Fong has told you. He will make a wonderful father. I know it in my heart."

"You would vouch for his character?"

"Absolutely."

Clarence studied her thoughtfully and then flipped through more papers.

Thomas watched the judge read and grew increasingly agitated. After a few minutes, he couldn't contain himself. "This is crazy!" he interjected. "What's the point of debating all this? MacKenzie could be anybody! And any*thing*. An ax murderer, for chrissake. You can't tell what a person's like after just two weeks!"

"I'm more sure of Connor than I've ever been about anyone in my entire life," Jade answered.

"Well, that's fine and dandy for you, Janine, if you want to wear rose-colored glasses. But we're talking about the welfare of Sabrina here. The man's a jerk. It's as plain as the nose on my face!"

Dinsmore held up his hand and looked across the low table at Dr. Nilsen. "What were your observations, Doctor, in regard to Mr. MacKenzie?"

Dr. Nilsen folded her hands in her lap, and the metallic buttons on her cuffs glinted in the soft light. "I found him to be a very personable, well-grounded man. Strict with the children. But fair."

"In your professional opinion, did he act peculiarly in any way with Sabrina?"

"Not at all. He seemed at ease with her. Natural. However, I must add that it is sometimes difficult to spot deviancy in adults, especially those who prey upon small children."

"Thank you, Dr. Nilsen."

She inclined her head toward the judge.

"But the fact is, Mr. MacKenzie was in the tunnel with the girl," Dinsmore said, his brows knitted together above the bridge of his nose.

"Yes." Ben leaned toward the judge. "The child claimed he was there. Even Miss Brennan seemed to think he was down there, by the comments she made to the police."

"It's obvious he couldn't have been fishing in Gig Harbor and in the tunnel at the same time." Dinsmore looked over the tops of his glasses at Jade.

"I made those comments to the police because I didn't know where Connor really was at the time!" Jade sputtered. "I didn't know he was fishing."

"Oh, give me a break." Thomas rolled his eyes. "He wasn't fishing. We all know that! He was down there in the tunnel with your daughter, doing God knows what. Admit it, Janine, you blew it. You picked some yo-yo to bring into your life, and you know if anyone finds out what kind of scumbag he is, you'll never get custody."

Jade jumped to her feet. "He's not a scumbag!" she cried. "He's not the one using Sabrina for his campaign. He wasn't the one on national television, using Sabrina's disappearance to make a bid for his election. You're the scumbag, Thomas! You are!"

"Miss Brennan!" Dinsmore pounded the table with his fist. "Miss Brennan, you must get hold of yourself!"

She stared at him, completely blank for a moment.

"Please, take your seat, Miss Brennan. We won't get anywhere with such outbursts."

"Sorry," she muttered, and sank to her chair. Laura slipped her hand over her wrist and leaned closer.

"Don't do that again," she advised. "It makes you look like a wacko."

Jade flushed. She suddenly felt like a wacko. Wacko and desperate—the way she had felt during her interviews with Dr. Nilsen, when she knew she was losing ground with the doctor and failing to meet unrealistic and dispassionate expectations. A sickening sense of dread uncoiled in Jade's stomach. She slumped in her chair, knowing that slowly but surely she was losing Connor and probably losing Sabrina as well.

Laura and Ben continued to drone on about the facts of the situation, providing document after document of proof, statements by the police, the firemen, character references for Connor, comments of the neighbors about what they'd heard going on in Jade's apartment. An hour dragged by, and Jade grew more and more disconsolate. Laura had been confident that Connor would be cleared of all blame, but each of her statements was twisted and shot full of holes by Ben Goldstein.

Just after four o'clock, Clarence Dinsmore shuffled through his papers one last time, took off his glasses, and rubbed the bridge of his nose with his stubby fingers. Then he gradually raised his head and gazed at the group before him. All eyes were riveted upon him.

"One major point dominates this case," he began solemnly. "And that is the whereabouts of Mr. MacKenzie at the time of the child's disappearance. If we can't trust Mr. MacKenzie, we can't consider him a fit father."

Ben Goldstein nodded smugly.

"Your Honor . . ." Indignant, Laura turned to the judge, her back as straight as a board. "Just because a man has an argument with his wife and is gone for the day doesn't make him a criminal."

"If that were the only issue in this case, I would have to agree with you, Miss Wettig. But there are other considerations."

"All manipulated by the Brennans." Laura's pale eyes glowed in her grave face. "The fact of the matter is, Your Honor, these two people were remiss in their duty as parents, imperiled the life of their adopted child, and are trying to place the blame for their own mistakes on an innocent man, whose reputation, not to mention his life, will be permanently altered by their lies."

"Objection!" Ben retorted. "That is purely conjecture."

"Miss Wettig . . ." Dinsmore held up his hand. "Your points are well taken, but there are too many unanswered questions and a lack of hard evidence to make a determination of innocence or guilt at this time." He paused and laced his fingers together. "It is my decision, and I'm sure Dr. Nilsen will agree with me, that Sabrina be placed in foster care until this matter is settled in a court of law."

Dr. Nilsen nodded solemnly.

Thomas's face went slack and Gail sucked in her breath. Jade's heart plummeted. That Sabrina would end up in foster care had been her greatest fear. She felt Laura's hand slide over hers and give her a squeeze of support. The meeting was over, along with Jade's future happiness with Connor. Shaking, Jade rose, wondering how she would sleep at night knowing her baby was living with complete strangers. And how would she tell Connor that he was still implicated in Sabrina's kidnapping? How would she be able to kiss him and then watch him walk off into the night? She would never see him again, never make a life with him, as she longed to do. Her heart ached like a raw wound as she stumbled toward the door.

At the door Ben shook Laura's hand, his eyes glinting with the light of invigorating competition. Laura had the grace to comment she would see him in court. Thomas and Gail chatted in low insistent tones with Dinsmore and Dr. Nilsen as they walked toward the front of the house, while Herman brought up the rear. Jade trailed behind them, hoping no one would turn around, for she had begun to sob and couldn't hold back the tears streaming down her face.

Phillip hovered in the foyer, offering wraps, as Jade's party prepared to leave. Jade stood in the hall at the entry to the foyer, her vision swimming but still clear enough to make out a small figure dressed in a large blue space helmet standing behind Phillip. It was Robbie, hovering in the background again, watching. Jade swallowed and pressed her lips together, forcing her tears back before anyone caught her weeping.

"Aunt Jade is crying," Robbie commented, his high-pitched voice rising easily above the hum of the lower adult tones. "Why is she crying?"

All eyes focused on Jade, who stared blankly at the door, her shoulders thrust back, deciding she didn't care what they thought of her after all. She was proud of her love for Connor. She might have known him for only a short while, but she loved him with all her heart. With this evening's work, she would lose him once more and forever, and that loss was worth all the tears she could cry.

"Robbie!" Gail admonished him. "What are you doing out of your room?" She turned to Phillip. "Phillip, take him back to his room at once."

Phillip swept the boy up in his arms. Robbie squirmed around and pointed a toy gun at Jade. "Zzzt, Aunt Jade. You're dead!"

Thomas laughed nervously and took Robbie from Phillip. "Come on, sport. You're supposed to be watching your movie."

"But I want to talk to Uncle Connor."

"He's not here." Thomas took a step, but Robbie struggled so much that he slipped out of his father's grip

and dropped to the floor. Thomas reached for him, but
Robbie darted out of his path.

"Is Uncle Connor in jail?" Robbie asked, sticking out
his lip. "Aunt Jade said the policemen took him."

"They did, that bad man," Gail declared. "Don't you
worry."

"But why?"

"He was mean to our little Sabrina," Gail explained,
using baby talk, which infuriated Jade. Her tears subsided as she listened to Gail talk down to her son. "Mean
people go to prison."

"Uncle Connor isn't mean!"

"He took Sabrina and put her in a bad place, Robbie.
In a terrible hole under the ground."

Robbie scowled at his mother. "He did not! She fell in
there all by herself, the stupid girl!"

Jade stepped closer to the boy, as did everyone else.
Thomas was aware of the sudden shift in the foyer and
snatched Robbie off his feet. "What movie put that idea
in your head, cowboy?" He laughed nervously and
glanced at the judge. "Kids!" He grinned his false smile
and started to carry Robbie down the hall, but the
judge's voice stopped him.

"Just a moment, Mr. Brennan," Dinsmore said.

Thomas pivoted slowly, his face a shade paler in the
faint light of the hall.

"I'd like to hear what the boy has to say."

Robbie smirked at his father. He pointed the gun at
his dad's head. "Zzzt!" he buzzed. "You're toast!"

Chagrined, Thomas deposited his son on the floor and
then stood behind him, a hand on his shoulder. The
judge approached Robbie slowly, and his bulk threw the
boy into complete shadow. Robbie stared up at him
fearlessly.

"Don't come any closer, mister," he said. "I've got a laser pointed at you, right at your brain."

The judge displayed no amusement but managed to lower himself to his knee, so that he was on Robbie's level.

"You can put that away, Robbie," he suggested, glancing at the gun. "I'm not taking prisoners this evening."

"You'd never get me anyway," Robbie retorted. "I can run like that." He snapped his fingers.

"I'll bet you can." The judge leaned his forearm on his knee. "Now then, you just mentioned something I'd like to know more about. You said your uncle Connor wasn't mean?"

"No. He's cool. He taught me how to fly a kite."

"And you mentioned that Sabrina fell into a hole?"

"She sure did." Robbie shook his head in disgust and rolled his eyes.

"Where did she fall, exactly?"

"Out back of the hotel. In some bushes."

Thomas leaned down. "The boy can make up stories, Your Honor. You've got to understand that about him."

"I'm not making up a story!" Robbie retorted. "That's what Mother told the policemen, but it isn't true!"

Gail went stiff and glanced nervously at Dr. Nilsen.

"How did Sabrina get outside?"

"The dumb girl followed me, that's how. She didn't want me to use her kite."

"So you got out of the hotel by yourself?"

"Yeah." Robbie curled his lip. "I've got a secret way. Nobody knows about it."

"So Sabrina followed you and fell into the hole?"

"Yeah."

"Why didn't you tell anyone?"

"Because." Robbie scowled, and his eyes suddenly

rose to Jade's. She gazed at him, sending him a mental message to be truthful and real, the way he'd been after a day spent with Connor, the way people always were after time spent with Connor—a state of being a person recognized as the finest path to take once they'd experienced genuine personal integrity. "Because I—"

"For goodness' sake!" Gail sputtered, pulling Robbie against her legs. "He's just a child and you're interrogating him! I won't stand for it!"

"Mother, don't!" Robbie squirmed out of her hands.

"Do you want to tell us more, Robbie?" Dinsmore asked patiently.

"Yeah." Robbie shook off his mother's hands. "Because that stupid Sabrina is getting Uncle Connor in trouble, and it just isn't fair!"

"Why do you say it's her fault?"

"Because she fell in the hole. She deserved to be in there!"

"Why didn't you tell anyone, though, Robbie?"

"Because I hate her, that's why! And I wanted her to stay in there for a while." Robbie crossed his arms. "She gets all the toys. She gets everything. Ever since she came here, they've forgotten all about me! It's always Sabrina. Sabrina, Sabrina, Sabrina! Even Aunt Jade likes that big baby better than me!"

Jade's heart broke at his words. If he only knew the truth, he wouldn't be hurting so much. She wished she could gather his rigid little body into her arms and give him a much needed hug. As if he felt her kind regard, Robbie glanced up at her again. Jade gave him a small smile of gratitude and love and saw the hard light in his eyes soften.

Slowly, Judge Dinsmore rose to his feet. "Well, now, this puts a whole new light on things, everyone."

"Shall we go back and discuss this new development?" Laura suggested. "Reconvene?"

"What's the point?" Ben shook his head in disgust. "Out of the mouths of babes—"

"My sentiments exactly, Ben," the judge declared. He turned to face Thomas and Gail. "It still isn't clear why Sabrina claimed Mr. MacKenzie was in the tunnel with her. I suspect it was her child's imagination kicking in as a form of self-preservation. She only pretended to see him and hear the woman's voice. Both children apparently respect and like Connor and Janine, and perhaps look to them for support. We may never know what really went on in that tunnel. But we do know that Mr. MacKenzie did not nor did he ever intend to kidnap Sabrina. Therefore, I see no reason to charge the man with any crime."

"Of course." Thomas scrambled to make the best of this clumsy situation, while joy blossomed throughout Jade's entire being. "I had no idea, Your Honor. This was all news to me."

"I expect it wasn't news to your wife."

Gail raised her chin but didn't say a word. She rubbed her temple with a trembling hand, and her huge diamond wedding ring glinted in the evening light. Jade guessed a migraine was on the way for Gail, brought on by the worst kind of punishment Gail could suffer—that of public humiliation.

"We'll deal with our son," Thomas promised, his smile less than confident as he clumsily put his arm around Gail's shoulders. "You can count on that, Your Honor."

"I suggest you do so as soon as possible. I don't want to see this lad in juvenile court in the future." Dinsmore's gaze dropped to Robbie's gun. "I also suggest you procure a different sort of toy for Robbie."

"Of course," Thomas agreed. "We will."

"Cool!" Robbie chirped, not aware of the judge's underlying meaning.

Phillip met Jade's eyes and gave her a small nod of congratulation. Her joy spread, fanning out in glorious, wonderful waves.

Laura turned to Jade and hugged her with an arm around her shoulders. Jade felt very close to tears again.

"But what about Sabrina?" Laura asked.

Dr. Nilsen stepped forward. "This latest development has forced me to make a decision regarding the child."

Jade waited for her to speak, her heart thundering in her ears.

# 22

"*Please, go ahead.*" Judge Dinsmore motioned Dr. Nilsen to the forefront with a sweep of his hand. "I am most interested to hear what you have to say."

"Before I continue, perhaps we should let Robbie get back to his movie," Dr. Nilsen suggested meaningfully.

"I'll take him to his room," Phillip offered, reaching for the boy's hand. "Come along, Robbie."

The boy yawned and complied, apparently too bored to be interested any longer, now that Connor was cleared of wrongdoing. He padded off to his bedroom as Dr. Nilsen strolled forward, her perfume trailing behind her. She stopped and regarded Thomas and Gail for a long moment, until she was certain Robbie was out of hearing distance. Jade waited in nearly unbearable anticipation.

Finally Dr. Nilsen spoke. "I've been evaluating both the Brennans and the MacKenzies for the last two weeks," she began. "It is true that Janine and Connor have some items to be resolved, such as her employ-ment prospects and Connor's as well, in addition to a less than stable home environment. It is true that Thomas and Gail have provided a stable home for Sabrina over the last two years, but not until this evening did it become apparent that Sabrina's welfare was in jeopardy due to Robbie's behavior, which is obviously not under control."

"But it will be," Thomas put in.

"I'm afraid, Mr. Brennan, that we cannot operate on promises. Sabrina could have died in that tunnel."

"Accidents do happen," Ben Goldstein stated in an attempt to support his client.

"There is more here than an accidental fall. I think we all know that." Dr. Nilsen glanced at Gail. "I am concerned about Robbie's psychological state. I also have seen problems with certain interactions here tonight." She paused and gestured toward Jade. "On the other hand, Connor and Janine are a team. I've seen them work together. It is obvious to anyone who sees them that they care for each other, and they possess the parenting skills that are so important in raising children these days."

"What are you saying?" Gail gasped, a hand to her throat.

"Easy, Gail," Thomas crooned.

"I'm saying, Mrs. Brennan," Dr. Nilsen replied, her voice softening, "that it is in the best interests of Sabrina that she be placed with her birth mother. Immediately."

Jade's heart leapt. She wanted to jump for joy, shout out loud, throw up her hands, and yell at the top of her lungs. But the stricken look on Gail's face tempered her thrill of victory, took the glory out of her own happiness. After all, she knew how it felt to be a mother and lose a child. She gazed at Gail and felt a sudden and deep empathy for her.

Numbly, Gail stared at Dr. Nilsen as her hand slowly pushed up her jaw, past her cheek, and stopped at her temple. Her fingertips massaged the skin at her hairline. "Thomas," she gasped.

"Her migraines," Thomas said, apologizing to the psychologist. "Please excuse us. She needs to lie down immediately. Take her medication."

"Of course," Dr. Nilsen replied with a knowing nod.

Gail leveled her bleary eyes at Jade. "Well, what are you waiting for, Janine?" she asked. "Go. Take her. Wake her up from her nap and drag her out of bed. She's yours."

"Why don't you talk to her first, Gail, so she won't be alarmed?"

"Talk to her? I can't cope with anyone when I'm getting a migraine—especially her!"

"Gail, take it easy," Thomas urged, throwing a smile at Dr. Nilsen. "I'll take care of everything. And I'll get Sabrina. It'll be just a few minutes."

Phillip walked down the hall just as Thomas turned with Gail to head for the bedroom.

"Phillip, get her pills, will you?"

"At once." Phillip glanced at Gail. "But first, I would like to inform you that I am tendering my resignation as of this evening."

Jade gaped at Phillip, shocked by his announcement. He'd been with the Brennan family for at least forty years.

"Great. Fine. Whatever." Thomas sighed wearily and urged his wife to continue her stagger toward the master bedroom.

Jade watched them go, happy but suddenly exhausted

and wishing she had Connor's strong arms to cling to. She couldn't wait to tell him everything that had transpired in the last few minutes, couldn't wait to hold Sabrina and tuck her into her own bed at the apartment with Connor at her side, the three of them together as they were meant to be.

Herman sidled closer to her. "Do you think Mr. Lake intends to seek employment with you?" he asked.

"Does that worry you, Herman?" Jade asked, glancing down at him in surprise.

"Of course not, Mrs. MacKenzie." Herman bowed slightly but kept his stare trained on Phillip's retreating figure. "But I would like to remind you of my special talents, especially in the area of cooking for children."

Jade grinned. "I don't think Phillip cooks at all."

"Too bad for him," Herman purred smugly.

Laura joined them. "What do you say Herman and I go back to the apartment, order something for a party, and send Connor down here to help you with Sabrina's things—if he's home by now?"

"That sounds great!" Jade exclaimed.

"I could use a drink," Bob Goldstein remarked. "How about you, Dinsmore?"

"Wouldn't mind. Dr. Nilsen?" The judge raised an eyebrow and looked expectantly at the psychologist.

"Oh, what the heck," she said, displaying her large rack of teeth in a wide smile.

"I think Connor has some Scotch downstairs," Jade said. "You're welcome to it."

"I will procure more," Herman said. "Leave all to me." He ducked out before Jade could thank him. Then everyone drifted away from the penthouse, chattering and laughing, leaving her in the foyer, standing all alone.

She waited, her ears tuned toward the *ding* of the

elevator down the hall, a sound that would signal
Connor's arrival. After a few minutes she became too
anxious to stand still and wandered out of the penthouse to stand at the elevator door. She watched the
indicator light blink on and waited, her heart pounding,
as the silver doors slid open.

Connor stood there in the bright light, his face glowing with happiness.

"Comin' in, lass?" He winked. "I know ye love t' kiss
me in lifts."

"I love kissing you anywhere," she replied. "And
everywhere!"

"Then have at it, because I love it when ye do."
Connor stepped from the car and held out his hands.
She rushed into his arms, hugging him with every fiber
of her being, happier than she'd been in years.

"Oh, darling," she exclaimed, "it's over! It's finally
over!"

"I beg t' differ," he replied, bending to her mouth.
"'Tis only just begun."

"You mean for you and me?" she asked softly.

"Aye."

"Then you like me a little?" she teased.

"I love ye, Jade. Ye know I do."

"I just wanted to hear you say it."

"I'll be tellin' ye every day. You'll soon be sick of it."

"I dinna think so," she said, poking fun at his Scottish
burr. "Say it again."

"I love ye, lass." He smiled down at her, his eyes a
dark navy blue. Then his smile gradually softened to a
tender, serious expression, and he cupped her cheek
in his hand. "Will ye be my wife, Jade, for real this
time?"

"It's *been* real for me," she replied, tipping her head

to kiss his palm, her heart bursting with happiness. "It has been since the moment I said 'I do.'"

"Ah, lass, it's been like tha' for me, too."

"Then we can quit pretending?" She gazed up at him, and he brushed his thumb over her lower lip.

"Aye. No more playacting." His voice dropped to a gravelly intimacy. "Want t' know how I really feel about ye?"

"Yes."

Without saying anything more, Connor gathered her into his arms and kissed her, and by the time he rose from her mouth, Jade had no doubts whatsoever.

# Epilogue

## The Elliott—One Year Later

*Connor paced the floor* in his office and glanced at his pocket watch. Another few minutes and Jade would walk into the Elliott for dinner, never expecting the surprise that awaited her. He put away his watch and slipped his hand between the lapels of his black suit. He felt for the slender velvet box that held an emerald necklace to match the ring she never took off her finger. Her sentimental attachment to the ring touched him deeply, since he had been the one to slip it on her hand in the first place a year ago. He'd wanted to impress her then by giving her something out of the ordinary, in hopes that she might fall in love with him. Never in his wildest dreams had he imagined what that emerald would buy for him.

Connor lit a cigar and raised it to his lips as he gazed out the window toward Elliott Bay. He took a thoughtful puff and savored the fragrant smoke before letting it out in a succession of little rings. Jade never allowed him to smoke in the Elliott, but sometimes he cheated when she wasn't around. He smiled at the thought of his fiery-haired, passionate wife taking him to task for stinking up his office with cigar smoke. He was a lucky man to have found Jade, and he knew it. After a year their love for each other was as strong as ever, if not stronger than the day they'd married. He'd never regretted offering himself as a husband to her and knew he never would.

A soft knock on the door broke his musings. Connor tamped out his cigar. "Yes?" he called.

Herman Fong poked his head around the edge of the door. "She's here," he said.

"Thanks, Herman."

Herman smiled impishly and bobbed out of sight. Connor followed his retreating form down the hall to the foot of the stairs, where the lobby opened upon the doorway to Sabrina's, one of the most lavish and popular restaurants in town. The concept had been Jade's, and she'd based the decor of the dining room on the salons of Paris in the late 1800s—deep green velvet, dark wood, and stained glass, with lush ferns and lights that looked like gas lamps. To Connor, stepping into Sabrina's was like stepping into a piece of home, and he thanked Jade every day for giving him a familiar haven to retreat to when the modern world threatened to overwhelm him.

The bar was equally as intimate and dark and a favorite haunt of some of Seattle's most prestigious people, who came to hear the finest music in town. Jade saw to it that every act booked was the best in the business. Sometimes she even sat at the piano and played. Connor liked those nights best of all, and would lounge in the corner, nursing a Scotch, thankful that he'd had a small part in restoring her ability. Crazy as it seemed, his theory had proved correct in that his special aura and energy transfer had somehow healed her. After Sabrina's kidnapping, and their nights of lovemaking, Jade had sat at her piano and found that her composing ability had magically resurfaced. She'd cried that day and then had come to him in such sweet rapture that he still flushed at the thought of what she'd done with him in bed that night.

They made a good team, he and Jade. Using the gold he'd found in the ceiling of Jade's apartment, they'd bought the building from Thomas, who had been more than happy to get out from under his debt and as far away from Connor as possible. Thomas had ridiculed their idea to restore the Elliott, which had made Connor all the more determined to pursue such a dream. Now he could say with complete satisfaction that he'd bested the Brennans once and for all. The Elliott was absolutely stunning.

Together he and Jade had transformed the hotel into the showplace it was meant to be a hundred years ago. The condominiums had been retained above, but the lower two floors had been restored to the original design: restaurant, coffee shop, ballroom, conference rooms, and a score of boutiques, all done completely in period furnishings. The result had exceeded all expectations—even his own memory. Overnight, the Elliott became *the* address in town in which to reside, and Connor was proud to own "the castle" once again, especially the penthouse, where he lived with Jade and Sabrina. He felt like a king once more, but this time around he was blessed with a queen, a true partner and friend, which made all the difference in the world.

"All ready, sir?" Phillip Lake inquired with a reserved smile. He stood near the front desk, dressed in his usual black and white, the most proper and efficient maître d' in the city.

"Aye," Connor replied. "Ye got th' cake an' such?"

"Yes. Mr. Fong outdid himself, to put it mildly."

Connor grinned and caught a glimpse of Jade coming up the stairs to the front door. "Make sure she comes t' th' bar," he said, and ducked out of sight.

The bar was filled with their friends and acquaintances: the new mayor and his wife, Herman's family, Dr. Nilsen, Laura Wettig, Jade's agent, her musician friends, some local actors, parents from Sabrina's preschool, and a score of Connor's new business associates. They all sat in the dark, stifling giggles and whispering until they heard Jade talking to Phillip in the lobby.

She breezed into the restaurant, chattering with Sabrina, and walked into the bar.

"Surprise!" Everyone jumped to their feet and blew noisemakers, while Connor flicked on the lights to display a room hung with crepe-paper garlands and flowers. Sabrina squealed with delight and clapped her hands.

"Happy anniversary!" Herman exclaimed, handing Jade a champagne glass. She accepted the drink but stood there in shock, a priceless expression of surprise on her beautiful face. Connor gazed at her and found himself falling in love with her all over again. His heart beat against the velvet box at his breast while Herman gave him a glass as well, and sparkling cider to Sabrina. Connor felt the cool stem of the fluted glass in his hand and moved forward, his eyes focused entirely on his breathtakingly attractive wife.

"Happy anniversary, love," he said, raising his glass.

Jade beamed at him, her eyes brimming with love.

"A toast!" exclaimed Jade's agent. "To the happiest, hippest couple in town!"

"Here here!" someone answered.

"Was that hippest or hippiest?" Jade asked with a crooked smile.

The crowd roared with laughter.

"To you, lass," Connor said, his eyes locking with hers and making the connection that still took his breath away. "Happy first anniversary, love. Ye've made me th' luckiest man alive."

She touched the rim of her glass to his. "And to you, Mr. MacKenzie," she said, her eyes twinkling. "You damnable Scot."

He grinned. "Brennan swine."

"Chauvinist pig."

"Bawdy house babe."

"Ouch, that hurts!" she cried, her shoulders shaking with laughter.

"I'll make it better, then," he murmured, and bent down for a long kiss, his hand cradling the back of her head. Her lips were warm and soft, and he found himself growing embarrassingly hard as the kiss continued. When at last he pulled away, he saw that her eyes were still closed as she savored his touch, and his heart burst with satisfaction that he could still deeply affect this talented, intelligent woman.

Slowly her lids fluttered open and she gazed up at him. "You're wonderful," she said.

"So are you." He smiled down at her. "Let's go upstairs."

She grinned at his choice of words, which was their secret code for making love. "We've been stair stepping a lot," she commented.

" 'Tis good exercise."

"Hmm. Then why am I getting so fat?" She looked away and made a big deal out of placing her untouched champagne glass on a nearby table.

It took only a moment for her words to sink in. Connor grabbed her hand. "You're not—" He broke off, too hopeful to put his thoughts into words as his eyes passed over her deceptively slender figure.

"I am," she answered, and gave him a quiet, sweet smile that soared straight to his heart. "I just found out."

"Ach, that's great news!" Connor swept her into his arms and twirled around, kissing her joyfully. "Think of it, lass. A new Connor MacKenzie on the family tree!" he cried. "Th' real thing this time!"

She wrapped her arms around his neck. "You *are* the real thing. And there will never be another Connor MacKenzie," she said, laying her head upon his shoulder. "Not like you, my darling. Never in a million years."